Nothing Out There

Mae Harcourt

Library of Congress Control Number: 2026928316

Ebook ISBN: 979-8-9944364-0-0
Paperback ISBN: 979-8-9944364-2-4
Hardcover ISBN: 979-8-9944364-1-7

Second Edition, 2026

Published by Mae Harcourt www.maeharcourt.com

Cover design: SeventhStarArt www.seventhstarart.com

Editing: Marilyn Haynes www.mheditorialservices.com

Interior formatting: Rowan Hart www.maeharcourt.com

Interior art: Ivy DeWitt, Hawthorn & Aster
www.hawthornandaster.com

Printed in the United States of America

*To middle school me.
You would love this one, queen.*

1

POISE. OBEDIENCE. PURPOSE.

The organization saved me.

That's what they said, and I believe them. I have no reason not to. They said I was lucky. Special. Chosen. That I had been given a second chance.

I don't remember the first.

They say I should be grateful. That my past is irrelevant. That whatever came before this place wasn't worth keeping.

So I don't ask about it. Not out loud, at least.

It's easier when everything is clean and simple. The girl I was before was…complicated, or so I'm told.

I wake before the lights most days—if I even sleep at all. I dress before the enforcers can tell me to. It's safer that way. I smooth my uniform again and again, fingers tracing each pleat of my skirt. It's white today. That means something is happening.

I've only been alive for 183 days. Before that, I was someone else. Brielle thinks she was a dancer. June says she's ridden a horse. I'd like to think that I used to swim in the ocean, losing myself in the endless expanse of cerulean waves.

We don't know, of course. But sometimes it's fun to imagine something beyond drills and classrooms and perfect manners.

I'd never tell my mentor that.

I walk to the mirror like they taught us. Back straight,

eyes calm, smile passive but never soft. The small plaque above the mirror is engraved in gold. On it lies the mantra I've repeated every morning for the last 183 days.

Poise. Obedience. Purpose.

I recite the words softly, studying the way they feel on my lips.

Poise. Obedience. Purpose.

Twice for good measure. Then, I add my own.

I am becoming exactly who they want me to be.

The girl in the mirror says them too. She smiles back at me, but something in her tone is off. Her hands fidget with the hem of her dress, and this morning—just for a second—I think I see a bruise on her throat.

When I blink, it's gone. The words still linger on my tongue, now metallic and wrong.

I am becoming...

Something I don't remember choosing.

2

EVALUATION PENDING

A swift elbow to my ribs ends my moment of self-reflection, followed by the overly warm fluorescents that signal we have to get moving.

"Maysie!" Juniper groans, bumping me out of the way with her hip. "Other people have to get ready." She's fumbling with a pin in her hair, fighting a losing battle against the auburn curl mountain. I stumble back, giving her space to work as I run through my mental checklist again. There's no clock in here, which certainly doesn't help the panicked chaos that has become my morning routine.

"Sorry," I mumble. "That hurt, y'know." She giggles in response, motioning for more pins. I slide a few off our shared dresser and pass them to her.

Brielle's hovering in the bathroom doorway, toothbrush half in her mouth, wiping her hands on her skirt. "Is this really happening?" She garbles through the brush, already drifting back to the sink.

"What do you mean?" I ask, half-listening, half-panicking. Socks. I need my socks.

She flutters into the room, hands gripping her hem tight enough to leave wrinkles. "Like what if he's just toying with us?"

"Avery said it's real," I offer, sifting through my sheets to find the pink hair ribbon I forgot to remove last night.

June flashes a wicked grin, the fluorescents glancing off

her skin with a warm sheen as she side-eyes Avery. "Well, Avery's always—"

"It's real," Avery interrupts, throwing a glare June's way. She's the only one of us actually ready. Skirt perfectly pressed, lavender headband framing her golden hair, hands folded nicely in her lap like she's in the running to be voted world's cockiest statue. "Mister M told me last week."

That tracks. Mister M would hand over his ID badge if she asked nicely.

"I'm not awake," Ivy informs us from inside her blanket. It's more of a muffled decree than a statement. "Therefore, it's not real."

"Profound," June mutters, dragging a comb through her curls. "Maysie, do I look like I tumbled out of a ventilation shaft?"

"You look like you fought the ventilation shaft and won," I say, not looking up as I dig in my drawer for my other flat, coming up with nothing but a single sock and a crumpled paper June scribbled faces on and left under my pillow last week. "Has anyone seen—"

"Your shoe?" Bri pauses mid-pace, looking me over. She turns in a small circle that somehow checks all four corners at once. "I saw it last night. Maybe under Ivy's bunk?"

I nod a thank you to her. Sleek black hair halos out from the blanket where Ivy's splayed out, still half-asleep. I nudge her leg out of the way so I can peer under the frame, which makes her hiss, "Five more minutes." I roll my eyes, craning my neck to get a better view. Not there, *of course*. My head conks against the ladder to June's bunk when I try to stand.

"Ow!" I wince. "I will be so grateful when I never have to see a stupid bunk bed ever again."

"I second that!" June calls from the bathroom.

If Avery's right, this will be our last morning in this room. The training wing is on a different floor of the facility. Different ballgame. Hopefully, similar rules.

We'll still be together, thankfully. I've grown quite close to my four pod-mates. Sharing a tiny bunkroom and spending twenty-four-seven with the same people will do that to you.

The door swings open, hinges groaning as all four of our pod enforcers file in. Lance at the front, armed and dangerous with a clipboard, ready to bark commands. Ralston's trailing him, clutching a silver velvet box like his life depends on it. Colt lags behind, practically dragging a reluctant Ryder by the arm. Ryder, naturally, is about as awake as Ivy. He's fumbling with the zipper of his black uniform jacket, one boot still untied.

Four men who aren't men so much as boys. Older than us by only a year or two, if I had to guess. They provide round-the-clock surveillance, though we're rarely graced with the presence of all four of them at once.

"Line up," Lance orders, pushing up his glasses.

We shuffle into a crooked line. I tug on Bri's sleeve as she slips beside me. She squeezes my fingers once—our comfort signal. My right foot drags, heavier with only one shoe; the other gone to some void that swallows things when you need them most.

The enforcers jump straight to work, not bothering to wait for Ivy, who's just now rubbing the sleep from her eyes and sulking toward the bathroom.

Lance takes our right arms one by one, noting our wrist-cuffs' vital readouts before powering them down. Colt collects the cuffs, stepping away to put them on their chargers.

I rub the raw skin on my wrist, ignoring the sting and the discoloration blooming in a cuff-shaped ring.

The relief is short-lived as Colt returns with five daytime cuffs, passing two to Ryder, who peels himself off the wall and follows. Colt stops in front of Juniper, motioning for the wrist she has pinned behind her back. She sticks her tongue out. He rolls his eyes and puts his hand out, expectant.

"June—" he starts.

She groans, extending her arm at a snail's pace. "Y'know, maybe we wouldn't get so many blisters if we swapped which wrists they're on every once in a while."

Lance clears his throat. "As I've said a thousand times, the cuff's readouts are more accurate on the dominant arm."

June huffs, then smirks. "I'm suddenly feeling like a lefty," she announces with a flourish of her other arm.

Colt laughs, rubbing the back of his neck with his free hand. "I'm pretty sure that's not how it works—"

"No, no," I interrupt, crinkling my nose in amusement. "You should let her try. I'd love to see miss lefty attempt her workbook reflections."

June turns to me, slapping a hand over her mouth with a fake gasp. "Maysie! You're supposed to be on my side."

"June," Colt repeats, hand still outstretched.

"Fine," she concedes. He snaps the cuff on as soon as she's close enough. It blinks once, then settles into a solid green that says she's synced and steady. Colt nods at me as he strides past to Brielle, who's already waiting, palm up. Ivy stumbles out of the bathroom just in time for Ryder to place hers.

My cuff always has the most issues syncing, so I have the daily privilege of going last. The doctors say it's nothing. They say my pulse is fainter, so the system takes longer to detect it. Which is all well and good until I'm stuck waiting in the medical wing for a manual sync.

When it's finally my turn, I bite my lip hard to distract from the shock that hits me as it boots up. The cuff will send pulse waves until it connects—which could take seconds...or minutes. Worst case, it may not sync at all. Colt offers me a sympathetic smile, shaking my wrist to help the system deduce I'm alive. When it finally hits green, I exhale a pent-up breath.

Ralston approaches next, withdrawing the enamel pin that bears my designation, 214, from the velvet box. He nods wordlessly, and I pull my brown hair back so he can affix it. To my relief, he manages to do so without poking me. Once it's straight, he moves down the line.

Two minutes later, the morning ritual is complete. Five cuffs swapped. Five vitals taken. Five pins placed. Five girls ready to tackle whatever's coming next. Well...more like four. Ivy is still nodding off in my periphery.

Just as the enforcers step back, the door opens again. The air goes taut the way it always does when he appears.

Our omnipotent mentor, Mister M, doesn't enter so much as glide, as if the room hangs on his every word. In a way, it does. Mister M has overseen every part of our training since we were brought into the advancement program. From meals to drills, he's there, typically barking orders. Always eager to call out even the slightest misstep.

Despite his attitude, it's hard to deny his charm. Mister M is polished in every sense of the word. Golden brown hair styled to the nines, with matching gold-flecked hazel eyes that catch on every light, granting them a permanent perverse glint.

His attire matches the other mentors: dress pants, collared shirt, and a tailored jacket that frames his form perfectly in hues of crimson and black. Every mentor seems to have their own color palette; Mister M clearly favors red.

Which is convenient, because I just so happen to hate the color red with every fiber of my frail being. Always have. To the point where Mister M claims it was one of the first things I said to him when I woke up from my reset. He always tells the story in the same playful lilt, yet he offers no explanation for why I got to start my new life stripped down to nothing but a number and a meaningless hatred for a primary color.

"Good morning, girls," he announces, words dipped in sugar that doesn't hide the edge beneath. Mister M strides down the line, hands clasped behind his back, humming a low tune. His gaze lingers on Bri's trembling hands.

He smirks.

"Try not to faint, Brielle. The floor is hard. It won't catch you." Bri flushes pink. Mister M reaches down, tugging the ribbon out of her hair and dropping it into her hand. "Try again," he says, waving her off. Tears well in her baby blue eyes as she flees to the bathroom. His attention cuts to June. "Wipe that grin off your face. You look like you're waiting to be punished."

"Maybe I am," June mutters under her breath.

Mister M's face contorts into a sneer. "Believe me, you're not half as interesting as you think." He moves to Ivy, still half-slouched and in yesterday's uniform. He tilts his head in what could only be described as annoyed amusement. "Did they wake you too early, darling? You look half-dead."

Ivy narrows her eyes. "I'm awake."

"Could've fooled me," he retorts, already turning.

Avery earns a nod of satisfaction; he tips her chin up with one finger, and she smiles. "Perfect. As expected," he says.

I force my breath steady as he turns to me.

"And you—" His gaze travels down and catches on my left foot. "Try not to lose half your wardrobe before the door even opens."

My face burns. "Yes, sir."

"Yes, what?"

"Yes, Mister M." The words are chalk on my tongue. I make myself stand taller, forcing a smile like I can take a joke. Only it's never a joke when it's from him. At least, not one anyone else finds funny.

"Beyond your lack of footwear, you look…passable." His attention has already flicked past me. *Passable.* That's better than usual. I'm used to "boring," "uninspired," even "average" if he's feeling generous. He doesn't care much for me, but I do my best to appease him whenever possible.

Lance clears his throat in what, for him, is a gesture of announcement. "Pins placed. Vitals recorded. Cuffs synced."

"Good," Mister M says. He steps back to take us all in with one sweep of approval that never quite reaches me. "As you may have heard, today is an important day. You'll be advancing to the training wing." His gaze snaps to June. "Should you pass today's tests, of course."

"I look forward to it," June quips, chin tipped up in defiance. Mister M hums, unimpressed.

For 183 days, we've been in a phase they like to call intake. A messy in-between where the board members and doctors decide if we're truly worth the time and effort. While it's true that we were saved, our spots in the program aren't guaranteed, and they don't let us forget it. Ever.

Though, no one ever tells us what happens to girls who fail.

He pivots to me, leaning in a bit too close for comfort. "You have thirty seconds to find your shoe before I make you hop to breakfast." The spark in his eyes tells me he's not joking. I gulp hard. Nod. And turn, scanning the room for the thousandth time. Mister M herds the other girls into the hall, sparing me a sidelong glance. "Better hurry."

Ralston clears his throat from behind me. I turn to see him plucking my shoe from where it was apparently wedged behind the dresser. Relief floods my chest. I whisper my thanks and grab it from his hand, stumbling into step behind Ivy.

Shoe found, day saved. Catastrophic mistakes avoided: four. Five if you include covering for Brielle's broken paintbrush last week…but we still got reprimanded, so "avoided" might be a stretch.

I tug the flat on in an incredibly ungraceful half-hop, half-step combo, and spare one final glance back at the bunkroom I've called home for six months. No matter how today goes, I have a sinking feeling that I'll never see it again.

Mister M halts just short of the dining hall, turning to face us.

"Remember," he starts, smirk spreading wide across his lips. The gold in his eyes dances like tiny flames.

"You'll be perfect today. That's what you've been training for. That's what's expected of you." His gaze slides down the line, catching on each of us. "Perfection." His eyes sharpen, landing squarely on me. "Or nothing at all."

3

RUMORS AND OATMEAL

My oatmeal is gray again. Thick, gluey, impossible to swallow without water. I prod it with my spoon and glance around the breakfast table. Avery's pin catches the light as she whispers to Mister M. He's watching her closely, eyes focused on her glossy lips. Beside her, Ivy slouches, staring at the abstract artwork of the sky that frames the otherwise barren back wall.

The tier one dining hall is loud, no matter the time. Mentors barking orders, girls crying when attendants make their rounds with injections, enforcers calling out diagnostic orders like they aren't the same every week. Each table is a pod: six girls, one mentor, four pod enforcers who act like they're not listening even when we all know they are.

Our table has an empty chair. They all do, eventually. But ours has been that way for 183 days.

No one asks about the girls who used to occupy them.

June nudges me, jade eyes sparkling. "All right. If you *had* to kiss one of the enforcers, who would it be?"

Brielle's spoon clatters to her bowl in an ungraceful fashion. "June!"

"That's what you want to talk about?" I ask, shaking my head.

"What?" June teases. "You'd rather talk about oatmeal?"

Of all the things she could bring up right now, she's thinking about romancing the pod enforcers? Meanwhile, nerves are tugging my attention in all directions. Today is a huge day, a huge step forward in what has so far proven to be a very stagnant six months of existence. We'll be one step closer to the finish line, graduation.

Graduation means I did it right, that I earned my place. That's all I need to focus on today.

Although, it's not a terrible question now that I think about it. The pod enforcers aren't hideous. I'd even venture to say they're attractive, in their own ways.

Ryder's look is effortless. Purposefully effortless. He keeps his sandy blonde hair short, and I doubt it's ever been touched by a comb. His skin is sun-kissed and lightly freckled. Impressive, considering we never go outside.

Lance is the opposite, pale enough to make ivory look deep. He keeps his jacket zipped to the throat, every line of him permanently rigid. What gets me, though, are his eyes. Startlingly gray and unyielding. He never smiles; I'm not even sure he knows how.

Ralston isn't like either of them. For one, he's massive. Easily over six foot, built broad enough to block a doorway. Deep umber skin, close-cropped black hair, onyx eyes that should be intimidating, but aren't. He isn't kind, exactly, but his presence is solid. Even June behaves better when he's on duty.

And Colt...well, Colt may just *be* attractive. Broad shoulders, rich brown hair that's always a little too mussed, soft caramel eyes to match. He's not sharp like Lance or polished like Mister M. He's charming in a boyish sort of way, all toothy grins and a mouth he can't seem to keep shut.

"It's an honest question!" June throws her hands up in surrender.

"I guess if I had to pick..." Bri taps a finger to her lips, eyes drifting to where the four of them are posted along the wall, hopefully out of earshot. "Ralston's not so bad."

Ivy finally looks up, unimpressed. "Gross. We see them every day. Watching us eat, sleep, escorting us to the bathroom. You really think that's romantic?"

Brielle huffs, cheeks pink. "Well—"

"She's right," I say. "They're not exactly handsome strangers we can swoon over. It's hard to be starry-eyed when they're the ones dragging us to drills at dawn."

Juniper feigns a swoon, pressing a hand to her head. "Still. Colt's shoulders—"

"I beg you," Ivy groans.

Mister M clears his throat. "Girls," he says, flicking his wrist in warning. "Meals are a quiet activity. If you wish to chatter, do us all a favor and keep it hushed." He turns his attention back to Avery with unmistakable approval.

"Sorry, Mister M!" Bri and I chant in unison, then giggle not-so-quietly at our perfect sync. He shoots us a sharp glare.

"Anyways," June says. "I heard a rumor." She looks a little too eager as she leans in, a loose curl slipping from her poorly-pinned bun and into her bowl. I cringe, but she doesn't seem to notice.

"Spill," I say, reaching to tuck the strand behind her ear.

"Apparently, the graduates with the highest performance scores get to travel around the country to perform!" My eyes widen, as do Brielle's. *Traveling.* I don't know how much of the world I'd seen before I was saved, but I would assume it doesn't count if I can't remember it.

I try not to mind. I'm better now, and soon I'll be someone worthy of all the effort the organization has invested in me.

"Do you think it's true?" Brielle whispers, eyes flicking to me.

"I'm sure it is," I tell her, placing my hand closer so our pinkies touch. "Who would make up something that wonderful?"

The conversation spirals until we're arguing over whether Bri looks better in green or red, or how many mentors Mister M could take in a fight. Silly? Maybe. But terribly entertaining. It's cut off far too soon by the chime that signals our transitions.

Typically, we'd be herded to morning drills, then lectures, then review block. Instead, Mister M veers right, down a hall I've never traveled. It's long, lined with navy carpet runners beneath metal sconces. Music pours from a set of open French doors ahead.

Inside, a girl with tanned skin and perfectly styled midnight curls is poised at the piano. Her spine is ramrod straight, red uniform dress smoothed over her lap in precise pleats. I can't help but notice she isn't really looking at her music. Her eyes are like shattered glass. Her lips press into a faint smile as her manicured fingers dance along the keys.

Mister M inclines his head toward the display. "Sorrel Montgomery. She'll be graduating next week." I nod along, eyes transfixed on her. She looks ethereal. The music emanating beneath her fingers is nothing short of magic. It should make me excited. And it does, in a way. It would be a dream to get to play an instrument. She may even get to travel the country like June said.

A feeling twists in my chest. Envy. It's an ugly trait—or so my instructors tell me. I'd love to try the piano. A voice in my head tells me I could do it. A deeper voice tells me *I could do it better.* I startle, clamping my fingers tight by my sides.

"That could be one of you someday," Mister M says, directing us back to the path. Avery nods enthusiastically, grinning like he had whispered it in her ear rather than announcing it.

The group moves forward, but I linger. Fascination isn't the right word for it. I'm engrossed. Watching every shallow breath, every hint of emotion that almost flickers behind her stormy eyes.

A note rings sour. Sorrel's head snaps up, and she finds me almost instantly. Her eyes light with something real, wedged between curiosity and confusion. The more I look, the more it twists into something familiar. She blinks a few times, eyes scanning the walls like she's taking in the room for the first time.

"Oh," Sorrel murmurs, tilting her head. "It's you." Her words are slow, guarded. Like she's not sure she's allowed to be voicing them. She rises from the bench, gliding toward me in gentle steps. "You're not supposed to—" She stops, eyes snapping above my head. It's only then that I catch the distinct tread of boots.

"We should go," Colt says, suddenly at my side. He grips my elbow, tugging me down the hall with more force than necessary. I look back at Sorrel, but she's already settling at the piano, eyes glossed over.

We've barely caught up to the rest of the pod when Mister M stops, gesturing to the door ahead like it's wrapped in gold.

"Prepare yourselves, girls. Your future lies just beyond that door."

4

TRUST IS IRRELEVANT

Man, our future looks bleak.

We've been sitting in a side hallway for well over an hour, counting the tiles and reciting the principles of etiquette back and forth. After twelve rounds, things got quiet...for all of three minutes. Brielle is incapable of sitting still, especially when she's nervous.

She leans close, whispering even though we're the only pod in the hall. "I heard tier two girls get their own rooms!"

"Oh good, I was reaching my breaking point with your snoring," June quips, cracking a smile.

"I do not snore!"

"Yes, you do," Ivy and I say at the same time. June giggles and shakes her head, half-pinned curls bouncing with the motion. "Well, I heard there's a garden."

"Really?" I don't bother hiding my amazement. "Maybe. I heard it from one of Mister K's girls last week, so I don't know how reliable it is."

Bri's blue eyes brighten. "Fresh air would be so—"

"Quiet," Avery hisses from the end of the bench, hands folded in her lap. "You'll make Mister M look bad if anyone hears you."

"They always hear us," Ivy mutters. She's slouching, dark hair falling over her face as she kicks at a seam in the tile. I don't correct her, because she's right. Especially here, where it feels like even the walls are listening.

The door at the end of the hall swings open hard. Our four pod enforcers file in, boots clicking in sync.

They always look the same. Black jackets cut close enough to keep them from snagging if things turned violent. Dark pants, dark undershirts. Even the insignia stitched at their chests seems deliberately muted, as though their power didn't need announcing. On the surface, they are uniformity personified, faceless unless you stare too long.

And yet—a closer inspection would reveal so much more. If you were really looking, you'd see Colt's default slouch when he thinks no one's watching. The scuffed toes of Ryder's boots. The small tear at the shoulder seam of Ralston's jacket. Tiny cracks in the sameness that proves they're human. Lance has no such crack, therefore his humanity remains a mystery.

Lance steps ahead of the group, beckoning to Avery. "Avery. Ivy. With us."

Ralston nods along, holding out a hand to help Ivy up. She rolls her eyes at him, standing on her own. Avery glides beside her, a practiced smile plastered across her lips.

Ryder flicks his wristband, the tiny screen flashing blue. "Great. We get the noisy ones."

"Lucky you," June shoots back.

"Mhm." Ryder stalks toward a second door. Colt gives me a reassuring nod as he ushers us forward.

The evaluation room within is practically empty. A camera blinks red above the wall, comfort and warning wrapped into one. Doctor Rook stands in the center. He's an older man, maybe late forties. Thinning hair and a permanent look of discontent, complete with a stiff white coat. I've had the misfortune of meeting him a few times before, but today he carries extra menace.

"Compliance evaluation." He snaps his fingers. "Stand on your marks." We shuffle to the colored plates that glow beneath our feet. Our cuffs light in sync. On the wall, a graph blooms for each of us: pulse, temperature, and something just labeled "compliance." I'm not sure how they measure that, and I'm not dying to find out. The doctor adjusts a slider on his tablet, and my cuff tightens. I didn't know that was something he could control remotely...or at all.

"Posture," Rook orders, stopping in front of Bri. She flushes the deepest shade of scarlet, but her slouch remains.

"Sloppy," he scribbles a note. "Fix it."

"Straighter," Colt prompts under his breath, just loud enough for Bri to catch. She straightens, form trembling, but it holds.

June folds her arms across her chest. "This is ridiculous—"

"Slouching reads like defiance," Doctor Rook says, silencing her with the flick of his wrist.

"Noted," June groans, forcing her shoulders back. My turn. I lift my chin, smooth my skirt, and fold my hands in front of me exactly like Avery would. I don't bother copying the smug little look she has when she does it; she's got plenty of that to go around. The doctor pauses, gaze intense as he looks me over. He jots something down anyway.

The drills continue, my cuff cinching tighter and tighter until heat explodes through my wrist. My feet are cramping, but I know if I shift my weight, the sensor will catch it. So, I stand straight, teeth gritted, swallowing every protest until silence floods my thoughts.

After an eternity of corrections, Doctor Rook nods at us once, turning toward the door. "Adequate," he mutters on his way out.

Doctor Kade enters next, heels making satisfying clicks against the tile. She's all soft hair and a smile sweet as tea with honey.

"Ladies," she says. "You're doing well so far, let's keep it up." She takes her place in front of the marks. "We'll test your presentation next. Smile. Don't relax until I cue. Shoulders down, chins level." Her commands start out simple, repetitive even. But when she asks us to apologize, June's mouth moves before her brain does.

"For existing?"

"For the hair." Doctor Kade's corrects, voice dripping with false pleasantry. She gestures with her pen as she speaks. "And for all you fail to be."

That's vague. When does she expect me to have the time to unpack what I fail to be when I barely know what I succeed at being?

She walks the line again, stopping in front of Brielle. "Each one of you has a deep-seated flaw." I keep my eyes forward, but I can feel a pit forming in my stomach.

"212 is overly eager, and yet under pressure, she crumbles completely." I spot Brielle out of the corner of my eye, biting her lip. "219 masks discomfort with impolite humor." June grins like she believes that's a compliment. Doctor Kade crosses to me in three clicks of her heels.

"And 214—" She studies me for two seconds too long. "Is a prime example of controlled divergence."

"Controlled divergence?" Ryder parrots from where he's lounging by the door. "Is that like lying?"

"It's a skill," Doctor Kade says without looking at him. She steps closer, tilting my chin upward with a fingertip I can't flinch away from. "You're very good at pretending. People will mistake it for composure. Tread carefully. The board loves a disguise, until they don't." She releases me, pivoting on her heel and gliding to the door with the same grace she entered with.

"Beautiful work, ladies. I'm sure you'll make us proud."

We're split after that. Bri and June are led to one room; I'm left waiting outside a door at the end of the hall. The bench is cold even through my skirt. I fight back a shiver, focusing on the wall ahead. The cuff at my wrist pulses with my heartbeat, something it only does when the rate grows too unsteady. I coax my breathing into something that resembles calm before anyone can notice.

A high-pitched scream rings out from somewhere down the corridor, reverberating against the thick walls. I jerk my head in the direction, but the hallway's empty save for a handful of enforcers and med techs, none of which acknowledge the horrific sound.

Footsteps hit, fast and pounding. The double doors at the end of the hall burst open, rattling against their hinges.

A young man barrels past, suit jacket half-shrugged on, a tablet clutched in one hand. He crosses the hall in long strides, racing something no one else can see. But when his gaze catches on mine, he nearly stops dead. His eyes are the richest blue I've ever seen, familiar yet so foreign.

He shakes his head, hard, and presses on. At the threshold, he slows his pace just long enough to snap. "Clear this hall!"

The med tech beside me nods, clutching her clipboard tight. With the swipe of his badge, he's gone, vanishing don the corridor.

Unease grips my chest. There's something about the way he moved, desperate and determined all at once, that sets me more on edge than I already was. A feat I didn't think was possible.

The med tech clears her throat. "214?"

I stand quickly. "Yes, ma'am?"

She pushes the door open, and I follow before I have any more time to unpack what just happened.

The room beyond is small. Pale walls, no windows. A single table lined with crinkled white paper waits for me.

"Sit," the doctor commands. He's younger than the last, eyes tired and hooded, white coat sagging like a burden. The nametag at his chest reads *Doctor Noxen—Sedation Specialist* in half-faded print. I hop up, feet dangling over the edge.

His stethoscope is ice against my back. I shiver as he murmurs, "Deep breaths."

Mister M leans against the far wall, arms crossed, watching on with bored contempt. His presence fills the space like a shadow. Why he would choose to be in my room over anyone else's is beyond me.

The doctor sets his tools aside and wheels a tray closer, flashing me a mild grin that stops just short of his eyes. "Let's chat, shall we?" He pats my knee, and I force myself not to flinch. "How are you feeling, 214? Excited for today?"

"Yes, sir," I say instantly, praying it's the right answer.

He jots something down. "If you're anything like Avery, I'm sure you'll make us proud." Of course she's already been through here. That or Mister M has been raving about her all day.

Likely both.

I force myself to sound certain as I recite one of the

many lines I've been drilled on. "Thank you, sir. I strive to reflect the advancement program's excellence."

His smile falters for half a second as he turns away, fiddling with a covered tray.

Behind him, Mister M lets out a quiet laugh. "Was that sincere, 214? Hard to tell with you sometimes."

Heat crawls up my neck, but I bow my head enough to look like a concession. The doctor doesn't intervene. Instead, he steps closer, lifting the lid off the tray in his hands.

A single glass sits in the center, filled with liquid so black it swallows the light. My stomach twists. I've been through six months of training, but nothing could've prepared me for this.

"Do you trust the organization?" he asks, voice sickeningly smooth. My throat constricts. My head spirals into a flurry of wrong answers.

Trust is irrelevant when you don't have a choice.

The thought cracks the surface, then drowns beneath 183 days of training.

"Yes, sir," I whisper. "I do."

"Prove it." He offers the glass; the liquid inside sloshes, thick and threatening.

I stare at it too long, hands shaking as I reach for it. My heart pounds in my ears, a loud, unyielding drumline.

I don't know why. Of course I trust the organization. I'm lucky to have been saved. It's just...I don't know. I guess it's just that it's never been my choice before.

"Hurry up," Mister M says lazily, eyes locking on mine. "Unless you'd rather tell the doctor you don't trust us."

No. That's actually the last thing I'd like to tell the doctor right now.

I raise the cup to my lips with trembling hands. The liquid smells metallic, yet disturbingly sweet. A voice in my head begs me to stop, but I squeeze my eyes shut, choking the vile drink down in one gulp.

It's just as awful as I imagined. Worse, actually. It coats my tongue like tar, sliding heavy down my throat. Heat spreads fast, filling my lungs, and sagging my limbs. My vision tunnels, reduced to the doctor's fixed smile, Mister M's mocking hazel eyes, and the pulsing cuff at my wrist.

My spine stays straight, my chin high, even as everything slips away.

5

NEW GAME, NEW RULES

The darkness that follows is anything but sleep.

I'm in a room that's simultaneously unending and collapsing, golden walls shrinking around me until I'm suffocating. Glass rains down from nowhere, a thousand glittering shards cutting the air to bits.

Someone is screaming. The sound bends and echoes until it doesn't even sound human.

I raise my hands to shield my face—

Except they aren't mine.

Pale, bloodied fingers stretch upward, trembling at the motion. A faded red hem brushes past my vision, soaked through and torn.

A warm hand seizes my wrist. I hear a boy's voice, sharp and urgent: *"Look at me—now!"*

It pierces my eardrums, then dissolves into an endless static that ceases all thought.

I jolt against nothing. My body doesn't move, but my chest heaves like I've run a mile. The warmth against my wrist is gone, replaced by the cold metal cuff biting against my skin. The surreal world leaks like water through my shaking hands.

My eyes crack open to bright white.

Sleek white walls, bright white lights. A cold, unfeeling bedroom.

And him.

Mister M leans against the doorframe like he's been waiting hours for me to stir. His smile curves without an ounce of warmth.

"Up," he demands. "You've wasted enough time."

I push onto my elbows, head still spinning. My legs feel like wet sand. Whatever was in the dark drink still claws at me, sagging impossibly heavy in my veins.

"Slower than Avery," he observes, as if this is some game I don't know the rules of. His gaze skims over me, wholly unimpressed. I must look dreadful—hair mussed, collar crooked, cuff blinking a vivid orange that denotes me as unsteady. "Messy doesn't suit you," he murmurs, straightening the crease of my collar himself. "And when you look bad, I look worse. Do you see the problem?"

I nod, heat rising in my cheeks.

"Then fix it, 214. Quickly." He leaves me with that and turns, expecting me to follow.

I do, because that's what they've taught me.

I'm apparently the last one awake, which I don't find very comforting.

The rest of the girls are gathered in a small sitting room that sits just beyond the door I emerged from. It's simple, practical, and incredibly drab. A gray sofa, two even grayer armchairs, and a small coffee table on a shag rug. The wall to my right is consumed by what I can only describe as a giant half-translucent mirror. Its looming presence is unsettling, though I can't place why. The back wall has an oversized glass door and a badge scanner. The door to the rest of the wing, I think.

On my left, there are identical wooden doors, each bearing a golden plaque marked with designations. 219, 216,

276. Juniper, Ivy, Avery. Only one door sits on my right, 212. Brielle. Each door is also equipped with a glass viewing window. I fight back a sigh. No privacy, even in sleep. Not a surprise. The organization says the only girls who need privacy are girls who have something to hide.

I have nothing to hide. *Nothing important, at least.*

It's clean. Intimidating. Like a stage I've stumbled onto without being handed a script. I resist the urge to retreat into my room, moving on uncertain legs and settling into the nearest chair. Brielle flashes me a warm smile, but her eyes are locked on Mister M, who's taken his place at the front of the room.

"Now that sleeping beauty has decided to grace us with her presence, there are matters to attend to."

He wants a reaction. I don't give him one.

"This is your common room. You'll treat it with respect and keep it spotless. The enforcers aren't your maids, and you don't want to find out what happens if I find you abusing your freedoms." He strides to the mirror, tapping it a few times. It flashes clear, revealing a small office on the other side. "And I will *always* find out."

If his goal was to make us more wary of him than we already are, he's doing a fabulous job.

"Six months," he says, prowling down the line. He pauses briefly on Ivy, who's still splayed out on the floor. He toes her ribs with his dress shoe, and she mutters something like "present" under her breath. He huffs, seemingly satisfied, before continuing. "That's how long you have to prove yourselves. You'll be evaluated each month. Obedience is just the beginning."

I gulp down a breath, swallowing every ounce of uncertainty that digs at my chest.

"When asked, you will perform. You will prove that my training produces excellence. Some of you will shine. The rest of you..." He flicks his gaze deliberately toward me. "Well, you'll find out soon enough."

My stomach drops through the floorboards. I can feel the color leeching from my face as I contemplate shriveling up and disappearing from sheer anxiety. I force a smile instead. He knows best, after all. He's just keeping me engaged. Eager to learn. Motivated to do better.

Yes, I'm sure that's what it is.

"In three months' time, the organization will be holding a ball for the investors and sponsors to preview our exceptional work. At least one of you will get to accompany me." Mister M stares pointedly at Avery when he says it, assessing her with narrowed eyes. I nod regardless, clinging to the fact that he said, *"at least one,"* which means the rest of us still have a chance. Impressing the investors would be huge for getting noticed before graduation. Impressing Mister M? Now that could prove a challenge.

Avery doesn't shy away, blue eyes glinting with pride. "I'll be looking forward to it."

Mister M's fingers twitch at his sides, but he merely nods. "That's all for tonight. Your workbooks are on the shelf. I expect to see chapter four ready for review by morning." He points at Avery. "You'll be coming with me."

She's on her feet in seconds, padding after him like an obedient puppy. Mister M straightens her collar, attention still locked on us. I try to keep my pulse level as he looks me over. You'd think after six months I'd be used to his judgment. Guess not. His eyes go glassy, mouth moving wordlessly like he's recounting a to-do list.

"Oh, and sedation's at nine now. If I find out any of

you"—he flourishes his wrist and points directly at Juniper—"give the enforcers any trouble, there will be consequences."

Mister M offers an amused grin, dipping into a mock bow. "Get comfortable, girls. This is your home now. Whether you deserve it or not is up to you."

6

LIGHTS OUT

The lights click down one by one until the pod is wrapped in that dim, bluish glow meant to keep us calm while the enforcers prepare to drug us for the night. In tier one, we'd wait on our bunks. Here, we all gather in our new and improved common room. Ivy and I are perched on the couch, Brielle and Juniper are sprawled out on the floor. It almost looks normal if you squint past the cameras and armed men actively filling syringes.

Brielle is carefully braiding June's curls, who's lying across the rug, grumbling and squirming but not moving away.

"You're pulling too hard," June whines.

"You keep moving your head."

"I'm trying to keep it attached, thank you very much."

Ivy pretends not to watch, twisting her own braid with precise little motions. I sit at the end, knees to my chest, staring at the silver tray Colt is setting up. Ryder leans lazily against the counter beside him, twirling a capped syringe around his fingers like it's a toy.

Brielle finishes tying a band around the half-wild braid. "Tell me something good."

My head perks up. "What, like a bedtime story?"

Brielle nods, face deadly serious. "Something about the outside."

Ryder huffs. "We're really doing this?"

29

"Ooh, yes!" June agrees, seizing any chance to stir trouble. She sits up, twisting to meet the enforcer's gaze. "Storytime. You heard her."

"Not my job." Ryder sets the syringe down, a glint of amusement in his eyes.

"Then make it your job," June says. "You've got the voice for it. Deep, brooding, tragic-hero type. I bet the ladies go crazy for that stuff." She does a finger gun at him. He rolls his eyes.

Colt huffs a laugh and sets down his clipboard. "You're stalling."

"Exactly." Juniper gestures wildly. "And it's working. So, details. Give us a good one."

"What is it like outside the program?" I ask, eyes locked on Colt as he squints to read one of the vials.

Ryder snorts. "You think we remember? We live here too, y'know."

"Make it up," Ivy cuts in. "Lie well enough, maybe she'll believe it."

"If we do this, do you all promise to take your knockout drugs quietly?" Colt says, holding one up. I cringe at his choice of words, but nod regardless. Bri echoes it.

"No promises." June smirks, making Colt narrow his eyes. "Fine." She holds her pinky in the air. "But this better be good."

"Deal." He looks up, eyes searching the ceiling panels for the words. "Once upon a time..."

June's eyes widen in satisfaction. "Yes! Commit to it."

Colt rolls his eyes but continues. "Once upon a time, there was a city settled under the grandest sky." He pauses. I try to picture it, stretching miles in either direction. It's hazy, but it's there.

"More," I blurt before I can stop myself. "What does it look like?"

"Bustling during the day, quiet and pitch black at night. Full of stars you didn't need to earn to see." He cracks a small smile as he says it.

Brielle leans forward, chin propped on her knees, soaking up every word. "What else?"

Ryder groans. "You're terrible at this. Stars, really?"

Colt shrugs. "That's all I've got."

"Add some animals or something," June demands. "Bedtime stories need animals."

"Fine. Uh—birds. Big ones. Loud in the mornings, annoying as hell. Like someone I know." He tosses a look to June, who glares at him, but cackles anyway.

Brielle smiles, small but certain. "I want to see them."

"Me too," I add, thinking of the ones on the dining hall mural.

"You won't, not here," Ryder mutters.

"Good! I think they're creepy." June shudders. She crooks a finger at him. "Your turn. You're not getting out of this."

Ryder groans, but he finally gives in. "There were… trees. Tall ones. Big enough to climb. With leaves so thick they blocked the sun when you wanted shade. And in autumn—" He pauses, searching for the words. "The ground turned gold." Ivy looks up, eyes alight.

I try to picture it, but all the gold I know is etched into plaques or locked in glass cases we're not allowed to touch. Never something that falls from a tree.

June cocks her head. "Not bad for a liar."

Brielle whispers "Gold," like the word itself is magic.

For a moment, we're not subjects and enforcers. We're

just restless kids, waiting for sleep in the low light of the evening. The silence lingers far longer than usual. I revel in it, content to replay the story. A perfect sky, a golden tree I could climb, a loud bird to chase June around a garden.

The tray clinks as Colt lines up the syringes. He clears his throat, head bowed in quiet apology. "Sleeves up. If we delay any longer, Mister M is going to come in here and blow a gasket."

Two hours later, I'm still reliving the story.

Sedation should drag me under, just like it does for the others, but it can't. Not fully, at least. My vision blurs at the edges, my limbs grow heavy, but I don't sleep.

I drift in and out, softened yet restless, never quite able to escape the in-between. I count everything. There are eighteen panels along the ceiling. Nine cracks spanning various expanses of the wall. Twelve wrinkles along the hem of my pink uniform dress hanging in the corner.

Enforcers make their rounds like clockwork. Countless sets of pounding boots litter the hall, reverberating the walls so hard that I'm shocked anyone actually stays sedated. Only one set is in our pod. It's Colt tonight, I think. The footsteps that pause just outside my door are too light to be Ralston, too careful to be Ryder, yet too reckless to be Lance. The door creaks open. I stiffen on instinct, ready to give the performance of my life. Shallow breathing, soft sighs, the whole nine yards. Truly a sight to behold.

My cuff, however, is a depraved, evil traitor.

It chirps once, flashing orange to indicate a heart rate spike.

"Maysie?" Colt calls. My eyes are closed, but I can tell he's still near the doorway.

I try to force out a sigh, but it sounds more like a squeak. My eyes shut tighter as if that might fix it.

He sighs. "I can hear you."

"No, you can't," I whisper, pressing a hand over my eyes. "I'm asleep."

"And I'm Doctor Kade," he says, putting on a painfully bad impression.

I let out a small, stupid giggle.

He breathes another long sigh. "Are you feeling all right? Any nausea? Dizziness?"

I shake my head.

"Ryder must've screwed up your dose," Colt grumbles, more to himself than to me. "Can't trust the guy to tie his own boots. This is partially my fault for even handing him syringes."

He's trying to make me feel better, I think, but the pressure in my chest hasn't eased. I could tell him the truth. That it's not the dosage. That it never works, but then I'd have to explain why. Which wouldn't be good, considering I don't know why. It just feels…wrong. I feel wrong for being wrong inside.

Redundant, maybe. But truer than anything I'd ever let myself feel.

It's hard to lie, though. The organization knows what's best for me. They just want to help me. An acute tug of guilt sends an ache down my spine.

"I'm sorry," I whisper into the darkness, secretly hoping the world will send me a sign. Something. Anything to tell me I'm doing the right thing.

"Not your fault," he says quickly. "I won't log this, but

you should get some rest."

Colt slips out the door without another word. I'm alone again. Counting the seconds. Savoring the stories.

Wishing for a sleep that may never come.

7

YOUR POTENTIAL

We're herded into an unfamiliar room just after breakfast. Mister M says nothing of the schedule change as he points to a row of white padded chairs. The room is packed with them, all neatly lined in groups of six. At least seventy girls are already seated, all dressed in the same pale pink uniform dresses with their pod numbers embroidered just above the heart. A large screen consumes the stage at the front, displaying the organization's silver crest. Faint, classical music emanates from speakers hidden above the panels.

We file into the row, sitting in descending number order. Mister M finds a place along the wall, quickly swept into conversation with a tall mentor I don't recognize.

The music cuts mid-phrase, replaced by the crackle of a speaker.

"Watch," a voice booms over the room.

The screen flashes, then blossoms into brilliant color. There's a girl in a gold dress clutching a microphone in one hand. Her voice is honey-sweet as she thanks an unseen crowd, curtsying so deep she's practically bent in half. The camera cuts to another girl, greeting a row of official-looking people with a vacant smile plastered on her face. Another twirls across a ballroom floor, beaming radiantly in silk as a crowd watches on in adoration.

A voice drifts over the footage, warm and over-rehearsed. "Each of you comes from hardship. We've brought

35

you here because you deserve more; a chance to be perfected."

The screen changes again. More girls: waving from balconies, clinking crystal glasses, playing classical instruments.

"Many of our graduates find placements in elite households or positions in performance venues. The most exceptional travel, representing our program as ambassadors. All living lives of exceptional influence and grace. You are here because you have that potential. We will shape you into what you were meant to be." The voice drones flat. "The world won't offer you a third chance. Be grateful for your second. Be obedient, be pliant, be eager to be corrected."

Whispers and gasps ripple across the space.

"Wives, performers, ambassadors; all roles crucial to a unified society. No matter what the program decides for you, you'll serve proudly."

I stay silent. These are things we know, of course. We've been repeatedly told what we are here to accomplish.

But to see it—to really see girls outside these walls—it sparks something in my chest, bright and undeniable. Because that could be me.

It will be, with any luck.

Well, luck, hard work, and trust in the organization to steer me right. Brielle tugs on my sleeve. I offer her a warm smile, squeezing her fingers.

"That'll be us," she whispers.

"I call being the blonde one."

"Already taken," June whispers over my shoulder, bouncing her auburn curls with one hand and winking at us.

I giggle, a sort of peace settling over my chest. Graduation has never felt so attainable.

It's equal parts exhilarating and overwhelming.

I won't let myself be scared of it. For today, I'll focus on hope. I must. They say without something to guide us, we're just drifting. Hope is a fragile tether—pull too hard, and it'll snap. I'd be a fool to give up just because the path is uncertain.

So yeah, I'll keep hoping. I'll dodge every catastrophic mistake and perform perfectly until I walk the stage at graduation. I'll take my first step back into the outside world with confidence.

I'll become exactly who they want me to be.

8

DRILLS AND SKILLS

My toothbrush fell in the toilet this morning. That's how I know it's going to be an awful day.

It feels incredibly silly. Forbidden, even. Mister M once told Ivy that superstition is a gateway to disobedience. I'm not sure how those two things could possibly correlate, but it sounded threatening coming from him.

The instructor for our afternoon classes never showed up. It's not unusual for an instructor to be late, but after fifteen minutes, Mister M decides he's done twiddling his thumbs, grabbing Avery by the arm and motioning for the rest of us to follow.

Juniper jokes that we're being dragged away to a dungeon, but if that were true, Avery would've been left behind.

We're led to a practice room, barren save for a white line taped to the floor. Six red X's lay across it, perfectly spaced. We move wordlessly onto them, awaiting his next instructions.

Mister M strides to the front, hands in his pockets. When he reaches the center, he just stares. He spends almost a full minute studying every inch of our forms before speaking.

"If any of you are fortunate enough to accompany me to a public event, I'll need a way to control you." I grimace internally at his choice of words, keeping my face impassive. He brandishes a pen from his suit pocket. "I'm going to teach you a series of non-verbal cues. By the end of this, you'll be performing them in your sleep." He gestures for Avery, who steps forward.

"Avery already knows the routine, and she is kind enough to demonstrate. Aren't you, lovely?" he purrs, hazel eyes practically sparkling as he looks her up and down.

"I'd be honored to." She beams. He taps his pen once against his clipboard, and she dips into a deep curtsy. Head bowed, posture perfect. He motions for us to repeat it. It looks…slightly less graceful. When I hit the deepest point, I glance over at Ivy. She hasn't moved an inch. Mister M pinches the bridge of his nose, turning back to Avery.

He taps the pen twice this time, watching her expectantly. Her shoulders go tight, but she masks it with a polite smile.

"I am lucky to be saved. I am grateful for the opportunity to be corrected. I will strive to reflect the advancement program's excellence in all that I do." The words are a mouthful, even for her.

Mister M's jaw ticks.

Avery bites her lip. "I'm sorry, I—"

"You told me you'd have it ready by now." Mister M steps forward, gripping Avery's chin, forcing her face inches from his.

"I will," she squeaks.

He sighs, turning back to us. "We'll focus on the non-verbal cues for now, since *someone* is clearly still waking up."

Avery dips her head, face rife with discomfort. Being corrected is new for her, so I decide not to stare. The high road, considering if it were me, I have a sneaking suspicion she'd be rubbing it in.

He flicks his wrist once, and Avery straightens, folding

her hand with polished grace. He hums in approval. "Posture correction. If you're performing as you should, you won't need this one."

Mister M flicks his fingers up, then snaps his fist closed. "This denotes silence. If you see it—" he turns to June. "—you'll shut your pretty little mouth and listen."

The room chills around us. June presses her lips together, offering nothing but dead-set boredom.

He teaches several more cues in quick succession. *Apologize, smooth skirt, smile.* Things that should be simple but apparently need regulation in moments of importance. I would think I'd know when to apologize, considering it's all I ever do...but I digress.

The chime sounds after our fourth round of practice. We move toward the door, but Mister M clears his throat. "Oh, darlings, we're not done. Back on the line." I stagger back to my spot, as do the others. Ivy practically drags herself to her mark.

Once he's sure we're watching, he takes his spot at the front again, sneering. "You don't have time to slack off. Even after this block, I'll be expecting you to improve on these daily. Train them. Drill them. Remember them." He smiles, cold as ice. "I won't ask so kindly next time."

9

UNDISCOVERED TALENTS

"If I don't sit down right now," June declares, "I'm going to disintegrate."

"I hate him," Ivy grumbles, grabbing a sketchbook from the row of shelves that line the wall. She pulls three chairs into a line before laying across them like her own little makeshift couch.

"Four hours, no breaks," I mutter, dragging my feet across the threshold and slinking into the nearest chair. "Is that even allowed?"

The art room offers little in the way of relief, just dim lights, four white walls, and the smell of old paint that must've seeped into the floorboards. No water, no snacks, no restroom. That last one is catching up to me, and based on the look on Ivy's face—though she'd never admit it out loud—she's likely having the same problem.

I could ask one of the pod enforcers for an escort. And I would, if one were here. It strikes me as strange. To my knowledge, we haven't been left without at least one enforcer at any given time. Two in the day, one at night—though Ryder sleeps through his shifts, so I'm not sure that counts.

Regardless, they are notably missing in action for the time being, so I'll just have to wait. June grabs our sketchpads from the shelf, tossing mine haphazardly across the small table. To my dismay, the motion bends the cover and about a dozen pages. She mouths an apology before hiding behind her book. I roll my eyes, but flip to a fresh page.

"Do you think Mister M would get us new paintbrushes if we requested them?" Brielle asks, sifting through the cup of broken supplies as if it might yield a miracle.

"No," June and I say in sync. I slap my hand over my mouth as she giggles.

Enrichment is the least of Mister M's concerns, as he reminds us daily.

Enrichment is indulgence. The only thing you should be "indulging" in is extra drills.

The back of my neck tingles as his words echo through my head. Most days, I hear his voice in my thoughts more often than my own. It's a little frightening, but Doctor Kade assured me it just means I'm "eager to please."

"What's the assignment?" I ask, glancing at Brielle. Typically, I'm the one who keeps track. Or rather, I make one of the pod enforcers check the schedule for me.

"Survive," Ivy mutters, wearing her sketchbook like an eye mask.

"I don't know," Brielle runs her fingers along the strands of her blonde braid, worrying her lip between her teeth.

"I don't need an assignment. I'm creating a masterpiece." June waves a half-crushed oil pastel wildly above her head. "I shall call it 'ode to drills.'" She brings it down hard, creating a long black smudge across the page—and her sleeve. She laughs and keeps drawing.

"Poetic," I tell her, trying to peek at the self-proclaimed magnum opus. "I'm sure Mister M will appreciate your continued dedication." Her smile only widens as she grabs for a green marker. I take a set of colored pencils and stare at the blank page.

Art is not my thing. It's not really any of our "things" for that matter. But it's *really* not my thing. I doubt my half-finished still lifes would capture the attention of... well, anyone. And yet, we're dropped here every day like clockwork while Mister M drags Avery off to private lessons.

She's the most promising musician in the whole advancement program, or so we've been told. June jokes that our ears are "too unworthy" to be graced with her skills. We should be focusing on the things we're good at; learning a performance aptitude that might actually impress the investors.

My cuff flashes, evidence of my mental overstep. I suck in a deep breath to center my thoughts.

Poise. Obedience. Purpose.

Mister M has our best interests at heart. He wants us to succeed. More than that, he wants us to be perfect. It's not my place to question him.

I take a yellow-colored pencil and sketch a crooked daisy at the corner of my bent page. I'm halfway through the last petal when June kicks my foot. I jerk up, and she raises her eyebrows, keeping her head low as she whispers.

"Do we know that guy?"

"What guy?" I ask, furrowing my brows.

"The one lurking over there." My head snaps up, eyes colliding with a sharp gaze of icy blue. It's the man from advancement day; the one who was sprinting down the hall like his life depended on it. He looks the same, albeit calmer. Same dark suit, still clutching a tablet as he stares at me. I didn't even hear him come in. His posture is so rigid. Honestly, it looks painful.

"Hi?" My voice is polite, but the hint of a question pokes through.

"Good evening," he responds stiffly, tugging on his sleeve with his free hand. Bri gives him a small wave, chewing on the inside of her cheek.

"Do we know you?" June's voice is so blunt. Rude, actually. I step on her foot under the table. She scowls at me.

"What? We were all thinking it."

"No." He inclines his head my way. "But I know you." My heart skitters, but I don't show it. He takes a gander around the room, gaze catching on Ivy. "Is she—"

"Dead?" Juniper interrupts. "No. At least I don't think so. We haven't looked in a while. Bri, can you check her pulse?"

Brielle grimaces. "Not funny."

"It's kind of funny," I say, hiding my smirk behind my fist.

"Kinda," Ivy echoes from under the sketchbook, proving her vitality. The man just stares at us for a moment. Then, he takes a step toward me, cocking his head to peer at my work from the angle I have it sitting at. He's exceedingly tall, so it doesn't take much.

"The flower's crooked," he observes.

"I like it that way," I tell him, smiling like the picture of innocence. He purses his lips, nodding as though the thought has never occurred to him.

"Interesting."

"Thank you," I manage. He may have meant it as a compliment, but I have no idea. He's so calm, so still. So very different from the man I saw that day. After an uncomfortable amount of prolonged eye contact, he takes a measured step back.

"I should be going. Thank you for this...educational experience." He runs a hand through his midnight hair. Magically, it doesn't muss the careful styling. "I'll be sure to inform your mentor that your art supplies appear to be older than I am." He pivots on his heel.

"Wait," I call out before I can stop myself.

"Hm?" He flicks his gaze over his shoulder, ice spears piercing my soul again.

"You never told us what we should call you." He looks at me, expression unclear and stormy. For a moment I think he's going to ignore me.

"Mister V," he offers with the faintest nod. Then he's gone. Vanishing into the void of the training wing.

Once she's sure he's gone, June leans in. "That was strange, right? I'm not going crazy—"

"You're always going crazy," Bri giggles.

"You know what I mean." She shoots a glare at Bri then turns to me. "That was weird, right?"

"Oh, totally," I say, searching for the still-missing orange pencil. "How did we not notice him come in?"

"I was too concentrated on my life's work," she proclaims, turning the sketchpad to face me. It's an amalgamation of squiggles and regret, but I offer her a polite clap. She tips an invisible hat my way.

"He was like a statue," Bri whispers.

June laughs. "Yeah. A statue with unresolved trauma and a metal rod in his back." She sits up straighter, trying to fake his strained posture.

I frown. "A statue who claimed to know who we are."

"Pretty sure he only claimed to know you," June corrects.

"Oh my god, you're right." I clap a hand over my eyes, shaking my head to erase the memory. "I don't like the way he looked at me."

"He liked you," Brielle says, making swirls of blue paint to imitate the sky.

I scoff. "Liked me?"

"He talked about your daisy."

"He *insulted* my daisy."

"Same thing. He noticed. That's rare."

She's not wrong. Why did he notice me? Not just notice—he said he knew me. The strange man I've only ever seen darting down halls and silently judging... knows me?

Unsettling.

"Something tells me we'll be seeing him again." June folds her arms with a grin. "I vote we call him tall, dark, and grim."

"Perfect!" Bri gushes.

I roll my eyes. "I'm not calling him that."

"Suit yourself." June moves to pat me on the back, knocking at least half my supplies onto the ground. I huff a half-curse, and of course, she giggles. My legs are like lead, too stiff right now to do anything but sit, so I reach down and prod around. I flinch as my fingers brush something cold and dust-caked, wedged between the floorboards and a supply cart. I pull it up to find a book, bound in black with real paper crinkling out at the edges, a far cry from the laminated training textbooks we're used to.

"Ooh! What is that?" June leans in, already reaching for it.

"It's a book, I think." I flip it over, brushing a thick layer of dust off the textured cover. A silver-etched creature with wide-webbed wings and pointed teeth stares back at me with midnight eyes. The title threads through its lines in a looping script of faded silver. *Creatures of the Night: Tales of the Lost and the Unnatural.*

My heart kicks as I study the strange thing. The pages are worn thin—half-ripped, half dog-eared. There's a name scribbled out inside the cover, gouged flat into the paper in black whirls. It starts with an E, but the rest is a mess. Elli maybe?

Over it, a newer stamp of red ink: VH-6, still crisp against the seemingly ancient artifact.

Brielle scoots closer, curiosity flickering beneath her politeness. "What's it say?"

I skim the first paragraph aloud, careful to keep my voice low:

Creatures of the night are defined by what they've lost. Memory and warmth. Restraint and control. They are said to wander until the dawn reminds them what they once were.

"Creepy," June whispers.

"Poetic," I correct, forcing a small laugh so they don't notice how freaked out I am. "Probably meant to teach us not to lose control. See? Moral lesson. Everything here has one, so it must be fine, right?"

"But how did it get here?" Bri whispers.

I flip the page to reveal strange sketches. Girls with black eyes and hands dripping ink. Men with sharp teeth and flowing cloaks. Creatures with wings that stretch from corner to corner in long bony arcs. I trace the figures, trying to make sense of it all. "Maybe it belonged to a past pod."

"Then where are they now?" June asks.

"Graduated," I say, too quickly. "Obviously."

"We shouldn't be touching it," Brielle whispers, jabbing a finger into my shoulder.

"Then they shouldn't have left it out," I say, flipping to the next page and sliding it between us. It's not defiance. Not exactly, I hope. I'm still a good girl. I'm still going to graduate. This changes nothing. It's just… curiosity.

And curiosity isn't rebellion unless you get caught.

June hums. "A few pages couldn't hurt, right?"

Bri fiddles with her fingers, finally letting herself peek. "I still don't get it. It's a book about nighttime?"

"I think it's about animals," I correct. "Or—monsters?"

"Let me see!" June says, pulling it toward her and flipping through the pages. "Look. They're alphabetized. Banshees, bats, demons, ghosts, owls, vampires—"

"It's official!" I cut her off before she can list us to death. "Anything with a table of contents can't be that bad." It sounds a little less teasing than I wanted it to, but Bri looks reassured.

"Fine. But just a few pages, then we put it back. Okay?"

I cross my fingers high enough for her to see. "Promise," I whisper, knowing I'll find a way to read every last word.

10

DON'T FIGHT IT

Wake up

    Wake up.

        Wake up!

My eyes snap open, but the world doesn't shift into focus. I'm facedown on white tiles, freezing and gasping for air. The floor tilts as I stagger upright, each motion unsure.

A long corridor of doors surrounds me. Lemon antiseptic assaults my nostrils with every rigid pull of breath, twisting my stomach tight with nausea. Everything is bathed in white. Clean. Cold. Clinical.

Like everything I've ever known.

And yet...wrong.

My legs betray me. One step. Then another. Each drags me farther until I'm captive to the sea of nothingness. More doors, each bearing plaques tarnished beyond recognition.

Before I know I've stopped, I'm reaching for a golden door handle. The moment I make contact, it turns scarlet, dripping to the ground like fresh blood.

My hands are soaked with it. A soundless scream shakes free from my burning lungs. My hands tremble as I drag them down my uniform, unable to look away from the crimson seeping into clean fabric. The door before me vanishes, but the one to its right rattles until it fractures, sending jagged fissures down the middle.

It splits just wide enough to reveal a girl with matted auburn curls and familiar green eyes staring straight through me. A dark ribbon is tied across her mouth, pulled so taut she can't possibly breathe. Her form crackles at the edges, phasing in and out as if the universe doesn't know if she's real. There's no time to decide. The door slams with a force that sends me tumbling back. My mouth opens. I'm screaming again. And again. And—

Laughter roars from somewhere beyond, low and thick. My knees hit tile before I can register I'm falling. The sound only swells.

"Careful, little star. The world's already watching," a deep voice purrs.

I'm on my feet in a second, skidding impossibly fast down the twisting hallway…and going nowhere. Eyes. There are eyes everywhere. Studying me with hunger and horror and something I can't place.

A door falls off its hinges, slamming to the ground. Two faceless figures are on the far end of the room, voices bleeding down the corridor. Their silhouettes are hazy, shadows in human form.

"She'll break if you push further!" one says, urgent.

"Nothing unbroken can be rebuilt," the other responds coolly.

They dissolve into smoke.

Every time I run, the hallway stretches further. More doors. Always more doors. I fall into the handle of another.

The room beyond is empty save for a mirror that's cracked at the edges. When I blink, I'm in front of it.

The girl staring back isn't me.

Deep brown eyes find mine, burning bright—almost feverish as she takes me in. Her hands twitch at the hem of her skirt like she can't coax them still. Her hair is more gold than brown, falling in waves she's tucked precariously behind her ears. A lopsided smile sits on her lips, hazy and wrong.

Then I see it.

Stark against her bloodless skin is a bruise curling around her throat in black and blue swirls. My breath shudders. I reach for my neck, but there's nothing save for my hammering pulse. When I look back, the mark remains, spreading now, blooming darker across her neck like I've awoken it.

Her lips part. Her eyes darken. Seven words ring crystal clear through the glass.

"Don't fight it. They'll take you, too."

The room dissolves. Another hallway replaces it in a blaze of familiarity. A figure looms at my back, shadowed and too close. My gaze falls, and I'm left staring at my uniform, spattered in ruins of arterial dark. My mouth opens before I give it permission, lips forming words I didn't choose. Barely a whisper, shaky and raw:

"Don't remember me in red."

The figure reaches, but I'm already moving. Heat surges down my arms in waves faster than my mind can follow. Every scrap of sense tells me to cower, to duck, to hide. But I can't stop running. The hall collapses, hurling me forward.

The lights flicker. Someone screams.

When the world reanimates, I'm braced over a piano.

A piano stained with blood.

An incessant ringing brings me back to the hallway. Sound explodes through the expanse.

Laughing. Screaming. Begging. They all bleed the same from here. I collapse to the ground, limbs dragging in protest. Cold slices through my dress as I press myself to the floor, praying the sounds will pass. But they just turn to incoherent static, growing closer and closer until my eardrums threaten to burst. A whisper caresses my ear:

Shine for me, little star.

The floor drops out.

I jerk awake, instantly aware that I'm not alone. There's a shadow in the doorway, broad-shouldered and tense. For a half second, I think it's Mister M, come to taunt me—or worse—drag me to the lab.

Then Colt shifts in the light, jaw tight, caramel eyes fixed on me like I've done something dangerous just by opening mine.

"You shouldn't be awake."

I flick a bead of sweat off my forehead, forcing my breath to steady. "Sorry."

He shakes his head fast. "Don't...don't apologize." His eyes flick to the cuff at my wrist, then to the ground. He presses a hand to his temple. "I drew the dose myself," he mutters, baffled. "It should've held."

I don't know what to say.

Colt crosses the room before I can blink and crouches low so we're eye level. His face is harsher in the dim, his usual boyish grin stripped away. It occurs to me that I don't think I've ever seen him serious. "Listen to me, sedation doesn't fail. Not like this." His breath hitches. "How long has this been going on?"

I don't respond, which seems to be the only answer he needs.

"You've been faking sleep? Why? How often?"

My stomach drops. "No!" It comes out too loud, amplifying the shame. I bite my lip and try again. "No, I—I wouldn't."

Colt studies me, searching for something in my eyes. Whatever he finds, it doesn't ease him. He scrubs a hand over his mouth, then sits back on his heels, sighing in something like defeat.

"I have to file it," he murmurs, the words heavy with dread. "If sedation can't hold you then—" He stops. Runs a shaky hand through his hair. "God, I don't know Mays. That's the shit girls get flagged for." My chest seizes. His gaze flicks to the door, then back. "You get how rare this is, right? I shadowed patrols for almost a year before being assigned a pod. And I've never seen it. Not once."

"What's going to happen?" I wring my fingers through the blanket, fighting the urge to vomit.

Colt doesn't answer right away. He presses his eyes closed. Sighs. "Diagnostics. Noxen." The name rolls bitterly off his tongue. "It'll be fine. He'll know what to do."

He pushes to his feet, forcing his tone into something that could be interpreted as reassuring. "Stay put. Don't fight the next dose if they bring it. Promise me that."

Words fail. I bob my head in the barest nod. Colt lingers a beat longer, hands flexing uselessly at his sides. Then he leaves, his shadow quickly swallowed by the dim blue lights of the common room. And once again, I'm alone with the echo of everything.

My nightmare. His disbelief.

The fact that I can still feel an ache at the base of my neck.

Don't fight it. They'll take you, too.

11

THE HOUND

A good girl doesn't eavesdrop.

The chair outside Doctor Noxen's office sits so high that my feet dangle. By design, I'm sure. Everything here is built to make us feel small and sweet and pliable. Even so, the offices on this floor are nicer than the exam rooms in the medical wing. Less sterile, more foreboding. The hallway is cramped, thrumming with machinery and littered with unmarked doors lining stark white walls. The one at the far end is slightly ajar. A ray of warm, artificial light pours through the crack, blinding compared to the dim of the hall. But light isn't the only thing slipping through.

I smooth my hair; adjust the wrinkled hem of my blush pink uniform until it looks pristine. Try to make myself small. A man's voice cuts through the murmur, but I shake my head, hard.

A good girl wouldn't listen.

Another man chimes in, low and eerily familiar. I shrink smaller in my seat, counting the seams between the tiles. But seconds pass, and the voices don't fade, and suddenly I'm not feeling like a very good girl. I slip out of the chair, soft-soled practice shoes silent against the tile. Keeping my head down, I pad to a steel bench on the other side of Noxen's door.

"I heard Carr's sending his hound after you, aye, Mav?" a deep voice mocks. A low groan answers him.

"Don't remind me, Diedrich." This time it's the voice I recognize, Mister M.

"You mean, the ghost is back to haunt us again?" another voice chimes in. Laughter follows, easy and unbothered.

"Ghost, executioner, analyst, whatever Carr's calling him this week." Mister M sounds bitter. *Who is he talking about?*

"What did you do this time?" the deep-voiced man quips, voice like sandpaper.

"I didn't *do* anything," Mister M snaps. "This whole batch is worthless." I clutch my skirt tighter, fabric bunching up in my sweaty palms. The growl in his words makes me want to melt into a puddle. "Beyond Avery, they're all liabilities."

Something in my heart cracks at that. I knew Mister M wasn't fond of us, but to hear him say it so casually hurts more than I'd care to admit.

"Maybe he'll prove useful then. If your girls can't be fixed by Carr's almighty saint, then it's their problem," one of them says, though I can't place which.

"Or better yet, it's his problem." The deep-voiced man laughs thickly. The group joins him, sharp rumbles echoing down the corridor.

Mister M scoffs. "He's far from a saint. I bet he gave himself that nickname." His voice drops lower, thoughtful. "You've got a point, though. A visit from the ghost might just clear my name." Shivers snake down my spine.

"And clear him out, if we're lucky," one agrees.

"He should be long gone by now," a higher-pitched man cuts in. "Given his track record."

The deep voice hums in agreement. "I thought so too.

Six girls lost, so close to graduation? There should be no coming back from that."

There's a long pause, giving me time to expel the breath I've been holding far too long. *Six?* I can't place it, but something about that number leaves a pit in my stomach.

"Carr seems to think he's still useful," the younger voice asserts.

Mister M groans. "Oh please, Carr just wants control."

"He's not bothering *me* right now," the deep voice cuts through. "That's all I care about personally."

"Cheers to that!" the young man agrees. Glasses clink. Their conversation turns to something else. I push myself back in my chair. Dress smooth, hands folded. Newfound secrets carved into my chest, blaring louder than any alarm.

Still a good girl.

Doctor Noxen's office is less of an office and more of an a lab. A desk is nestled in one corner, but the rest of the room is purely clinical. An oversized chair looms in the middle, with long leather straps dangling from its edges. I don't need his instruction to know that's where I'm needed. I fold myself onto the edge.

Be still. Be small. Be easy to fix.

"You woke up screaming," he says, tired eyes glued to the tablet in his hands. "Tell me what you saw."

My fingers pinch at the hem of my skirt. I open my mouth, then close it. What do I tell him? I don't even know what it was I saw. A blur of doors? Faceless voices? A girl with honey brown hair and a striking bruise who was me but also wasn't me?

No.

There's nothing I can say right now that won't make me sound absolutely out of my mind. I swallow past the prickle in my throat. I know I'm not polished like Avery, but what if I'm not even fixable? A good girl doesn't cause trouble. A good girl doesn't dream at all.

"I don't remember," I say to the floor.

He looks up. "Nothing at all?"

I shake my head, ponytail flicking over my shoulder with a flourish.

He hums. Makes a small note. "Strange. The others don't wake at all. You know that, right?"

Heat rises under my collar. I tamp it down and sit up straighter, grateful for instructions when they come.

"Hold out your wrist," he says. I offer my left, keeping my head low. He slides on a diagnostics band and waits for the readout. His lips press into a frown at something I can't read. "Even now, you're more awake than you should be. Dosage miscalculation?" The question sounds like it's for the tablet, not me.

"Sorry," I say anyway, just in case.

"Not your fault." His annoyance slides past me, directed at the metrics piling up on his screen; a puzzle with too many misshapen pieces. "Likely just an enforcer's sloppy work. I'll log it." He pulls a tube from somewhere in the wall and attaches a rubber mask to the end. "This will smooth your edges. Nothing more."

I nod because nodding is easy and right. The mouthpiece is cool against my lips. I breathe when he tells me to, deep and slow. The vapor that floods my lungs is floral and metallic, like blood-soaked lilies. It burns bright through my chest, then softens to a dull ache at the base of my ribs. My shoulders drop a fraction. I exhale a half-sigh.

"Follow my finger," he says, and I do. Left to right, right to left. "Count backward from five."

"Five…four…three…two…one." The numbers are clean on my tongue. I make them neat in case neatness counts for something.

He glances at the monitor, the crease between his brows deepening. "Recite your mantra."

"Poise. Obedience. Purpose."

"Still sharp," he murmurs. His stylus makes another line. "Unusual."

I hold my breath without being asked, hoping stillness might make me easier to solve.

"We'll try stronger." He sets the tablet aside and takes out a syringe tipped with a fine needle. "Close your eyes. Drift. Don't fight it."

Don't fight it.

I do as I'm told. The sting is quick; the warmth is slower. Blankets of haze being stacked one on top of another until I'm buried. The lamplight blurs. The chair tilts like I'm falling, but I don't flinch. My thoughts rise and fall on rhythmic waves.

A voice moves at the edge of my consciousness. "Follow the light." Something bright passes my eyelids; I mean to obey and forget to.

"Designation?"

My mouth opens because he asked, and I always answer when I'm asked. "Two… One. Four."

The stylus stops abruptly. I feel the shift in the air as much as I hear it.

I blink without meaning to. The room swirls back into frame. Doctor Noxen is a careful smear that sharpens into a stunned form. Then a person. And the look on his face screams that something has gone terribly wrong.

"You should be gone under this dose," he says, matter-of-fact, dark eyes now glinting with curiosity.

"Sorry," I whisper, because there is genuinely nothing else to offer. I comb my mind for every mistake I could've ever made to cause this.

"Don't apologize." He leans back, setting the stylus down. His tone changes into something flatter. "You said you don't remember, yet you're still fighting; that tells me you do."

My fingers twitch at my sides, cold on the metal's edge. The urge to please him and the urge to cower in a corner and cry overlap like crossed wires. "I don't—" I start, then swallow it. A good girl doesn't contradict. Or argue. Or dream.

Yeah. Things aren't going well for me.

He watches me a beat longer, then tilts his head, as if he's choosing a gentler angle. "Let me ask differently," he says, and I hate that I'm grateful for the mercy he's affording me. "Do you prefer to sleep without dreams?"

I nod slowly. *Please make me right. Please fix me.*

"Good." The corners of his mouth ease into something that's not quite a smile. "Do you know why we sedate our subjects at night, 214?"

I shake my head.

"Because sedated girls can't dream. Dreams destabilize the very structure the advancement program is built on. The structure that keeps girls like you steady." He retrieves the stylus and writes while he speaks. "You want to be steady, don't you?"

Yes. Yes. Yes. I want to glue myself to the correct answer until it sinks through my skin and takes residence there. I don't want to be fixed—I *need* to be fixed. Stable girls graduate; unstable girls disappear.

He reaches for my wrist again, checks the numbers against whatever the monitor says is acceptable. It doesn't please him. He makes another note, a single neat word.

"What will—"

My words tangle. *"What will happen to me"* is not a proper question. I swallow it back into my chest where my heart is hammering like I'm still sprinting down an endless hallway.

"Nothing dramatic," he says, as if he heard the question anyway. "We'll adjust. Different formulas, different dosages." He removes the cuff with a snap and sets it gently on the desk, metal clicking against wood. Then he pats my knee, offering me a tired nod. "Nothing you'll need to worry about. Hop up. I'll have someone escort you back."

That's it? My mind scrabbles for what that should come next: A lecture, a punishment, a veiled threat. It doesn't arrive.

At the door, I hesitate. "Doctor?" The word leaves me before I can tuck it back in. "I...I can try to sleep better."

He steeples his fingers against the desk. Tilts his head. "Sleep isn't a task you pass or fail," he says flatly. "It's a protocol. One that simply needs refining."

I lower my eyes. "Yes, sir."

"Don't fret." He swivels the tablet toward himself again. "The organization knows best."

I let the door close softly behind me. The air of the now-silent hallway chills around me, colder than when I entered. I start back toward the stairs, and Lance falls into step behind me without a word, face hard as marble.

The cuff at my wrist flashes orange, the only indication that I'm still spiraling inside. I smooth my skirt and fix my hair and practice the right kind of breathing all the way back to my pod.

If anyone asks, I'll say it was fine. The doctor was kind. I'm steady. I'm safe. I'm good. Lingering beneath the lies, the doctor's question bites at me.

Do I prefer to sleep without dreams?

Yes, I tell myself. Yes, I do. Of course I do.

I tell myself until the words sit properly on my tongue.

And I keep walking.

12

SHAME CASTLE PRINCESSES

The lecture room feels wrong when no one's in charge. Mister M dropped us off nearly an hour ago with no instruction besides, "Finish chapters four through ten in your workbooks. Be ready for a review tonight." He didn't say what time, he didn't say who with, he didn't say why. But Avery's not with us, and that tells me just about all I need to know.

The clock ticks loudly, daring us to misbehave.

Of course, Brielle takes the bait.

She balances an etiquette manual on her head like a crooked crown, arms outstretched, walking heel-to-toe across the training mat like it's a grand stage.

"Observe," she declares. "Poise. Precision. Perfection only the program's elite training can produce."

June's already giggling. "Try not to break anything this time."

"Oh please, I am the picture of balance," Brielle says. She turns too sharply, and to no one's surprise, the book slips, clattering to the ground with a *thud*. She freezes. Eyes wide, frozen mid-curtsy like the desks might report her to Mister M.

June claps. "Three out of ten. Disqualified for violence against literature."

Brielle bows low. "Thank you for your feedback. I am eager for the opportunity to improve."

I laugh. I can't help it. It feels good. Real. Like maybe

we're still people under all the polishing. Weird people, but people. My eyes land back on June, who's now stacking etiquette manuals like bricks on the floor around her.

"What are you doing?" I ask, leaning over.

"I'm building a fortress of shame."

Brielle snorts. "Ooh! Put me in the east wing."

"Sorry, that's reserved for mentors with repressed emotions."

"Sooo, all of them?" I shake my head, still smiling, and toss her my textbook. "What wing are we in, then?"

"Denial," June says. "Obviously." In the far corner, Ivy hasn't moved. She's got her head down on her desk, likely asleep.

June peeks over her ever-growing book wall. "Hey, sleeping beauty! Wanna rent a room?"

Ivy doesn't even stir.

"Hard pass," June mutters. "Respect."

Brielle flops dramatically onto the floor, stretching her fingers toward the ceiling. "Okay, but seriously… where is Mister M?"

"Bleeding out in the north stairwell," June says. "Probably tripped over his own ego."

"I bet he locked himself in his office trying to write the perfect insult," I add.

Bri giggles. "Or spilled something on his fancy coat and died of embarrassment."

The door creaks open, freezing us in place. Juniper's arms are suspended mid-stack. Brielle's splayed with one sock half-off. Ivy's snoring lightly. I sit up a little too straight, which only makes me look more guilty.

Mister V steps into the room with a folder carefully tucked under one arm and a raised brow that could double as an accusation. His jacket's buttoned, gloves tucked in one hand, eyes flicking around like this was not his intended destination.

He takes in the scene with a level stare: the scattered workbooks, Brielle's cardigan strung between two chairs like a finish line, and of course, the looming shame castle. His gaze lands on each of us in turn. Longest on Ivy, then me.

"Is this the new etiquette curriculum?"

"Independent study." My answer is automatic. Automatically stupid, but automatic, nonetheless.

June salutes from her spot on the floor. "Extra credit points, please."

"Where is your mentor?" he asks, lips pressed in confusion.

"Lost in the vents," Bri claims, waving her hands wildly as if his absence were thrilling folklore.

"Ascending to his final form," Juniper adds. Mister V turns to me, eyes narrowed.

I shrug. "I heard he took the day off to scowl at himself somewhere quieter."

He raises a brow, unimpressed by our display. "And none of you thought to report his absence?"

"Technically," I say, dragging out the word. "We built a support system."

"Shame castle. Very effective." Juniper pats the book tower.

Brielle points at me. "She's the mayor. I'm the head of foreign affairs."

Mister V exhales, a long, suffering sound. "This room looks like a daycare for the terminally well-spoken."

"Thank you," June beams.

"Not a compliment." He steps forward, picks up the etiquette manual Brielle dropped, turns it upright, and slides it back in front of her. "I'll inform Mister M that you've all advanced to theatrical improvisation. I'm sure he'll be thrilled."

Juniper snorts. Brielle slaps a hand over her mouth. Mister V turns, studying me with haunting blue eyes. They're like two oceans. Not the cute kind with little creatures; the deep kind that drowns people who swim too far.

"Don't you usually de-escalate them?" he asks, tipping his head.

"I got distracted."

"By rebellion?"

"By architecture." I nod toward June's tower.

He hums a non-judgment that feels like secret judgment. Clears his throat. "Well, I suggest you clean that up before someone less tolerant arrives."

June leans in. "He means Mister M," she says.

Mister V doesn't deny it; he simply disappears down the hall. We stay deathly still for three more seconds.

June gets to her feet. "Do you think he secretly liked it?"

"No," Brielle says.

I grin. "Maybe."

13

OBSERVATION DAY

"Do you think we're being sent to the dungeon this time?" June asks as we round yet another flight of stairs.

"Maybe," I whisper.

"Impossible. Dungeons are in basements," Ivy says, rolling her eyes.

"Quiet," Mister M barks, glaring at us from the landing. "Today is important, or have you already forgotten?"

I haven't. The announcement came at breakfast, along with temporary uniforms and a laundry list of rules that no sane person could possibly remember. Doctor Kade called it "Observation Day," a chance for investors to preview our progress and experience the facility's "top-notch conditions." Strange, considering we've been led up four flights of stairs to a room we've never seen before.

Mister M levels us all with a hard stare at the door. "Let's not turn today into a lesson, hmm?" He strides inside, not bothering to see if we're following. He knows he's trained us better than that.

The observation lounge is lovely. A little too lovely compared to what we're used to. It's...unsettling. Maybe that's the wrong word; it's suffocating, in a way I can't quite place. I probably shouldn't think that—even in my own head.

A long, carpeted aisle runs down the center, splitting the room in symmetrical halves of tables adorned in cream tablecloths. Towering bookshelves frame the walls, lined with untouched books that somehow aren't dusty. Harsh sunlight pours through arched windows that reflect nothing but the too-bright midday sun. We must be on a high floor, considering we can't see anything but sky. Sometimes I wonder how far we must be from the nearest city. Since we never see movement outside, I'd guess pretty far. There are no birds in the morning, no stars when day dips to night.

June waves to a tall girl from pod five, who crinkles her nose and turns back to listen to whatever lecture her mentor's giving. There are around six other pods here. It feels full, yet the walls echo with every sound that dares to be louder than a whisper.

We take seats around a central table set with porcelain teacups painted with flowers. June grabs for hers immediately, but Mister M clears his throat.

"Later," he hisses, pointing to the stack of books in the center. She takes one begrudgingly and passes the rest down. Avery opens hers immediately, looking at Mister M like he's about to hand her a medal for it. He turns to me instead, settling a hand on my shoulder and leaning down.

"Be on your best behavior today," he whispers, squeezing my shoulders tighter than necessary. I blink a few times, ready to tell him I'm on my best behavior every day. Then I hesitate, because I'm not entirely sure that's true these days. I nod meekly, flipping open the book, only to find it blank.

I barely have time to process before photographers are flooding in, wielding large cameras that click and flash at alarming rates. My head spins, little pops echoing as I reorient. Mister M snatches the book out of my hands, setting it flat on the table and pointing to another page.

"You missed a line here."

"It's blank."

"I have eyes," he hisses through his teeth, still smiling. "Fake. It."

I could say something snarky. Instead, I smile and thank him for the correction, fighting back a laugh as June flourishes her wrist, writing dramatically across the blank pages. Doctor Kade instructs on poses from the corner. Each slightly more absurd. Fix Brielle's ribbon, pretend to clink teacups, laugh politely at something Mister M didn't say. The photographers grow closer. Men and women I don't recognize who seem to care about nothing but snapping as many photos as humanly possible.

Avery plays her part well, eyes glued to her blank book like it's the most fascinating thing in the world, but they hardly pay her any attention. They're incredibly interested in Mister M, who hovers far too close to me.

A couple strides into the room, their steps light as the air itself. The woman has striking hazel eyes, with gold hues that catch the light as she inclines her head. They're beautiful, yet I can't help but think they'd be far more beautiful if they weren't boring into my soul. The man looks severe: set in harsh lines, square shoulders, and a no-nonsense glare that makes me straighten on instinct.

Mister M freezes before he remembers not to, pressing his palms to the table.

Doctor Kade beams. "Mr. and Mrs. Ashford, we're so pleased you could make it."

The woman hums, still staring at me. "This group is truly exceptional, Selene. We are so pleased with the progress we've been observing." She turns to Doctor Kade. "Our son has always had an eye for refinement."

Mr. Ashford nods. "Discipline suits him."

Mister M inclines his head, all grace and control. "It's an honor to have you here," he says.

This, I realize, must be his parents. It's written all over them. The jawline, the posture, the green-brown eyes that only warm when they want something. Mrs. Ashford glides close, straightening Mister M's collar with gentle fingers.

"You remind me of your brother at this age," she says fondly.

He stiffens, smile pulling tighter. "High praise, mother."

"He made us proud too," she whispers, fingers ghosting against his sleeve as she pulls away, following her husband out. Mister M exhales once they're gone, turning back to us with the polished, calculated grace that reminds me why he's terrifying. It's hard to know where the act ends and the man begins. If I were smart, I wouldn't concern myself with trying to find out.

Not that I have the time to.

Expensive perfume wafts through the space, followed by voices too unguarded to belong to anyone here. A sea of well-dressed figures spills onto the carpet in waves, eyes everywhere at once. I don't let it distract me from my ever-important task of pretending to be busy.

"They look very content," one whispers, nodding around the room like he's assessing art in a gallery.

"Oh yes, and so calm," a man cloaked in gray chimes in, waving to a table in the corner. The girls don't respond. They're too "focused," flipping through pages of their likely blank textbooks.

A woman near the back bristles, pressing herself close to a stocky man in a navy suit. "It's all a bit eerie, don't you think?" she murmurs to the woman beside her.

The other woman giggles, shaking her head. "Nonsense.

I wish I could get my daughter to be this docile."

"That one's posture is to die for," a woman in pearls re-marks. The weight of many sets of eyes lands squarely on my shoulders. She drifts closer, pressing her hands to her chest. "And what about you, dear? Do you like it here?"

I blink. Look at Mister M. Blink again. Freeze. My mouth unfurls to say yes, but nothing comes out.

"Of course she does," Mister M answers smoothly, his hand falling to Bri's shoulder. "They *all* do."

Laughter follows, soft and polite as though he's said something charming. Heat crawls up my neck. I knew the right answer, *so why couldn't I say it?* The pages of the book blur as I force myself to stare at it.

Doctor Kade rounds our table, ready to dazzle her way out of my slip-up. "Any other questions?"

A soft-voiced woman perks up. "Do they ever ask to go home?"

Doctor Kade laughs softly, placing a hand on my shoul-der that reminds me I should be smiling. She tilts my chin with the other, lifting my eyes to the investors.

"Why would they? They're already home."

14

THE HEIST

By the two-hour mark, the novelty of this experience has severely worn off. The investors have cleared out, half the pods have been dismissed, but Doctor Kade claims the photographers need a few more pictures of our group. Mister M floats around the table, barking orders under his breath and posing ridiculously. I'd laugh if I weren't exhausted.

I never thought I'd be eager for sedation. Especially sedation that doesn't work. But I need time to think. Or to breathe without someone telling me I'm doing it wrong.

I lift my teacup again, smiling through a sip of tea-colored water that tastes faintly of metal. It's gone cold. Though I'm not sure it was warm in the first place, considering it's not tea.

Ivy rests her head on her hand, eyes fluttering no matter how hard she fights to keep them open.

She wasn't always this tired. If I remember right—which is admittedly unlikely—Ivy was a completely different person at intake. Feisty, sharp, almost as spirited as June. I think she's being over-sedated, but no one will give me a straight answer. Mister M claims she's lazy; Doctor Kade says she "presents better subdued."

Her hand slips, head conking the table. She jolts up, wincing.

Mister M rolls his eyes, thrusting a textbook her way. "If you can't look alive, at least keep the book in front of your face. We don't need them thinking you're bored, now do we?"

"We *are* bored," June whines as she writes the principles of social etiquette for the fourteenth time.

"Then be bored quietly," he says, fixing his jacket for the third time in a minute. "And photogenically, if possible."

"That won't be necessary," Doctor Kade interrupts with a syrupy smile. "We're finished for today."

June cheers, ignoring the glares it earns her. I push to my feet before Kade can change her mind and keep us here.

Avery follows, swaying slightly. Her smile slips. It takes me a second to notice she's gone pale. Sweat beads on her forehead. Her eyes don't seem to be moving right...or at all.

Doctor Kade notices first. "Avery, dear, are you all right?"

Avery blinks slowly, turning to Mister M. "Did someone turn off the music?"

A shiver runs down my spine, because there wasn't any music.

"She's fine," Mister M says, but he's not looking at her anymore.

Doctor Kade steps forward, pen-light already raised to check Avery's pupils. "Take her to diagnostics."

His jaw ticks. "Now?"

"Now."

"You're all right," he murmurs to Avery, fingers brushing her sleeve as he guides her out. "Let's get you checked."

Doctor Kade turns to the side door we entered from. Ralston and Ryder are posted there, wristbands blinking blue with fresh orders. "Escort them back."

June tugs on my sleeve as we fall into a loose line. "That was weird."

Bri joins us, eyes wide. "She's probably just sick, right?"

"Probably," I say, since it's the only thing that makes sense. I mean, she certainly looked sick.

Maybe she drank too much fake tea.

The enrichment hall reeks of lemon disinfectant, so overpowering it makes my eyes water. A pair of gray-uniformed enforcers turns the corner ahead, pushing a cart stacked with cleaning supplies and covered bins. One tips his chin toward us in greeting.

"Clearing out?" Ralston asks, nodding to the cart.

"Deep-clean." The enforcer shrugs. "Some board member complained about the air quality or something. Boss freaked. Now he wants the whole hall spotless by lights out."

Ralston tilts his head. "That so? About time someone took a broom to this floor."

"Yeah." Ryder laughs. "Who knows what's lurking under all the dust."

My spine stiffens, because I can think of one thing that was lurking quietly until a few days ago.

The book.

I wasn't finished with it yet, so I stashed it behind our pod's stack of sketchbooks. But if someone finds it there—

This is bad. Whether or not the book belongs here, it wasn't given to us, and I have no good excuse as to why we would have it. My chest burns with the foreign desire to do something I know is stupid. But I force my legs to move on.

We drift deeper into the enrichment hall. Ryder jokes about the poor enforcers stuck on maid duty. Ralston smacks him in the back of the head. June laughs like it was the joke of the century. I trail behind, trying to convince myself that this is totally fine and I didn't just walk past a ticking timebomb that I don't have the tools to defuse.

My eyes catch as we turn the corner. The door to art room 3-A is wide open, and more importantly, vacant. I'm moving before the rational part of my brain has time to catch me. My flats echo on the hollow tiles, which only makes me move faster. The shelf is waiting, as overstuffed and messy as we left it. I dig around our row, almost toppling a stack of recycled workbooks in my escapade.

Wheels squeak as a cart rattles down the hall. My fingers move faster, pushing past dusty piles of materials from girls that must've graduated years ago. I shove the rest of it aside, snaking my arm into the crevice behind. The book gives me a papercut as I grab it, but I'm so overcome with relief that I don't have it in me to care.

Bootsteps sound nearby. I shove the book under my cardigan and fold my arms tight, which makes me look exactly as guilty as I feel.

Ryder pokes his head into the doorway, huffing an exaggerated sigh of relief when his eyes find mine. "If you were trying to give me a heart attack," he says, stepping into view and leaning on the doorframe. "Congratulations. Mission accomplished."

"Sorry! I uh, thought I left something."

He nods slowly. "Your common sense? Your survival instincts?"

"I—" My pulse kicks as I try to conjure up any excuse.

"Relax. Turning you in isn't worth the effort, or the lecture I'd get for losing you in the first place. Whatever you're doing—"

"I wasn't doing anything."

He eyes the shelves, then me. "Right. Well, whatever you're *not* doing, finish not doing it faster. We gotta go."

I nod eagerly, ever-so-grateful to be caught by the world's laziest enforcer. We have to run to catch up, but Ryder offers an easy smirk as we fall into step behind the group. Ralston turns, raising a brow at us.

Ryder shrugs. "Bathroom break. Happens to the best of us."

"You couldn't have waited five minutes?" His eyes briefly flick down to where the book is nestled against my chest, but he's too respectful to let his gaze linger for more than a moment.

I shake my head. "Sorry, it won't happen again."

Ralston nods, unconvinced but not pushing. He checks the schedule on his clipboard as we cross back into the pod hall. "Your uniforms should be laid out on your beds. Change quickly and wait in the common room. Afternoon lectures start in fifteen minutes, and if you're late again, we aren't covering for you."

"Ryder will," June laughs. "If we bribe him."

Ryder scoffs. "Bribe me? With what?"

Ralston opens the pod door, rolling his eyes. "I'm serious. Make it quick."

"Yes, sir." June mock salutes, not moving.

He cracks the smallest of smiles. "Go. Before I drag you."

She giggles, almost knocking me over as she rushes into the room. The book shakes free from my arms, sending me scrambling to catch it before it hits the tile. My heart rate spikes, cuff flashing in warning as I regain my grip. Bri gasps, eyes wide, pointing like the book might bite.

"May! How did you—"

June clamps a hand over Bri's mouth, dragging her by the arm toward her room and fighting back a laugh. She tips her head toward my door, reminding me that I should already be moving.

My door shuts behind me before my brain can even register I've moved. I stash the book under my mattress before collapsing to the bed. Thoughts tangle as my mind fights to catch up with what I just did.

I snuck away from an enforcer, lied to the face of said enforcer, and stole a book that may or may not belong here...*emphasis on may not*. Then—to top it all off—hid said contraband in my room, of all places.

That has to be, like, a million levels of bad, right?

No.

I think of the markings, the notes, the little drawings in the margins. This book was clearly important to someone. I didn't steal it. I just...kept it safe.

Curiosity isn't rebellion unless you get caught.

That's what I tell myself, anyway.

15

DANCE, DANCE

"Would any of you like to guess why we teach ballroom basics as part of your training curriculum?" Doctor Kade stands before us, white coat abandoned in favor of a lacy straight-cut black dress that brushes her knees. Her hair is pulled back in an updo that makes even her sharpest features look delicate. She's devastatingly beautiful, and the way she carries herself screams that she knows it. She claps once, loud enough to echo against the hollow walls of the ballroom.

"To torture us?" June jokes, chin tipped up with a hint of defiance.

"Hilarious as always, 219," Kade's expression doesn't change. "But no. Poise is about more than just standing still. It's about retaining grace even in motion. You are training to be public figures. Naturally, you'll need to know how to look effortless when every eye is on you. Depending on your placement, balls, charity galas, and ceremonies may be commonplace." Doctor Kade prowls down the line, lightly correcting our posture. Her gaze lingers on me long enough to make my skin crawl. "Beyond these walls, every moment of your lives will be a performance."

My breath catches on that, and I feel immediately foolish. *Of course, I know why I'm here.* If I'm given the chance, I'll do everything in my power to bring pride to the organization. But every moment seems a little excessive.

A lot excessive.

I don't want to doubt Doctor Kade; she's supposed to know what's best.

"It seems your mentor is absent." She sighs. "This is rather unfortunate. You'll need to see the form before you attempt it." Her gaze sweeps the length of the room before landing squarely on Ryder. "You."

Ryder points to himself, eyes wide as saucers. "Me?"

"Yes, you." She beckons him forward. "Help me demonstrate."

"I don't—" His protest dies under her raised brow. Ryder mutters something that sounds suspiciously like *"you've gotta be shitting me"* as he shrugs off his black uniform jacket and stalks forward like a man sentenced to the gallows.

Kade extends her hand. "Hurry, please. We don't have all day for this." I glance over to June, who's stifling a cackle behind her hands with every ounce of restraint she can muster. Ryder grumbles again, then awkwardly sets his hand against her back.

"Lower," she corrects, moving it firmly into place.

She waves her hand at Colt, who fiddles with the wall panel, hitting various buttons until the metronome falls into rhythm. Kade glides into step like she's been waiting her whole life for this. Ryder stumbles after her, boots too heavy, posture far too stiff for this kind of grace.

"See?" Kade says, pleasant as ever. "Even your enforcers can manage basic form."

"Manage is generous," June whispers, the sound muffled behind her hand. I cover my giggle with a cough. Bri tries to do the same and nearly chokes. Even Ivy's mouth twitches as she feigns indifference.

Kade spins Ryder clean across the floor, heels clicking.

He spirals out of her grip, boots tangling, cheeks flushing crimson as he fights to right his balance. Kade waves him off with a sweet smile, and Ryder bolts back to his post, muttering obscenities under his breath.

"Partners," Doctor Kade orders, as if this were a normal thing to witness. "We'll start slow. For now, just try to match the rhythm and stay on your feet. 219 and 214, start as leads. 212 and 216, follow." June starts to open her mouth, but Kade waves her off. "No excuses."

Brielle nudges my arm, clearly nervous. I nod idly, trying to match where Ryder had put his hands. She tenses when my hand finds the small of her back, then she mutters an apology under her breath. I take a steadying breath, trying to picture the steps.

It can't be that hard, right? I mean, Ryder could *almost* do it. Brielle's murmuring again, but I don't catch any words. I set my eyes forward and push every thought I have deep into the depths of my soul, where it will hopefully remain until lunchtime.

We begin exactly on the music's cue-in chime. My body straightens involuntarily, then I'm moving. Step, step, together. Step, step, turn. I let the pattern carry me. Bri stumbles, eyes darting between me and her feet like the floor's about to vanish beneath us. I coax her through the steps, murmuring the counts. I lift my arm so she can twirl, but panic seizes her face. Something—or someone—hits the ground to our left. June, if I had to guess. I can't look. My body's entered a strange sort of survival mode. Only, I'm not just surviving. We've hit nearly every mark, and Bri is somehow still upright.

Bri's arms fall away the moment the last note fades. I startle free of the waltz's trance, nearly trip over nothing.

Mister M is here, clapping slowly as he paces the space behind Doctor Kade. He offers a smile that's a little too wide to be natural, eyes fixing on me. I avert my gaze, hoping to smother my curiosity with something that vaguely resembles sweetness. Avery's beside him, eyes low.

She moves like she's not sure she's allowed to take up space. I try to imagine why the ever-perfect, ever-smug Avery could be feeling blue—and come up short. She's worse than yesterday, and I didn't think that was possible.

Mister M holds a hand out to me, shooing Avery off with the other. "Switch partners. Avery with Ivy, Juniper with Brielle. And you—" I'm already halfway across the floor, but he points at me anyway. "—are with me."

I cross to him slowly. Too slowly, apparently. He waves me on, impatient.

"Closer." When I hesitate, his voice drops into something dangerous. "Don't make me ask twice." My feet move before my thoughts catch up. His smirk is wicked as he takes my hand in his. "That's better."

The music starts again, and I'm immediately swept into the rhythm. He's good. Disturbingly good. Whatever they taught him at mentor school—or wherever he learned to boss us around—did a marvelous job. I hold my own, but it's anything but easy. He's moving much quicker than the pace Doctor Kade set, practically floating across the floor. When we finally slow for a moment, I'm overcome with relief at the chance to breathe. That is, until I realize what he's doing.

He stops us deliberately in front of Avery, who's stumbling through the motions with a very stiff Ivy. The smile that spans his lips is cold as ice.

"It seems *one* of you has been practicing." He looks me

up and down before continuing, eyes flicking across each of them as he says: "While the rest of you waste my time." Avery opens her mouth to say something, but he's already pulling me away, resetting our position.

Mister M's full attention falls back on me as the music kicks up. "You're a natural," he says.

My face falters; a smile would be the appropriate response, but it seems to be less of an observation and more of a dig. "Perhaps there's more to you than I thought."

The way he says it makes my stomach ache. I wrench my jaw open anyway and give him the proper response.

"Thank you, sir. I'm glad my talents are well suited." It feels like a lie, but he flashes me a look that says I gave him exactly what he wanted.

"Makes me wonder," he continues. "If you're trying to steal the spotlight." Mister M huffs a chuckle under his breath, gold-flecked eyes locked on mine, unblinking.

I shake my head too quickly. "No sir."

"Liar." He presses his face impossibly close, breath hot against my face. "You want to be the star, don't you? You want to be seen. To be chosen. To prove you're not just another number."

My chest tightens. Because I do. Of course I do. I've spent six months being told I'm nothing but average. Passable. Boring. The chance to actually be *good* at something is nothing short of a dream. The truth of it sears through me. My eyes go wide with a glimmer of hope I'm too slow to mask across my features.

"Admit it." He grips my waist, pulling me forward until our chests touch. The sudden jolt knocks me off balance for a split second, but I catch myself. Miracle of miracles, really.

"I just want to serve the organization and prove myself

worthy. All other rankings or measures are meaningless to me," I recite, gliding through the motions.

"Fascinating," he drawls. "I don't recall teaching you that, little star." He sinks his fingers into my waist, deep enough that pain shoots up my side. I cringe, biting my lip to keep from yelping. If I'm being honest, I don't remember learning that, either.

He grins, all pristine white teeth and bad intentions. "How else do you plan to surprise me?"

"I don't know what you mean."

"Lying again?" he says, clicking his tongue. *"Tsk tsk."*

"I'm not—"

"You can't lie to me, darling. I know you better than you know yourself."

I hope he knows how wrong he is about that. He may be my mentor, but he doesn't know me. In fact, he hardly even looks my way unless it's convenient. Frustration twists in my chest as I stare at him.

"This is fun, you know," he says, scanning my face for a reaction. "I like seeing the way you think, the way you feel, what makes you tick."

He slows long enough to trace a finger down my cheek. I bite back the wrongness of the warmth in his hands.

"I thought I had you pinned. Perhaps I was mistaken." Mister M yanks me forward, and I feel my composure give way.

"Is this a game to you?" I recoil, forcing space between us. He only tightens his grip.

"Everything within these walls is a game, darling." He flashes a haughty smile and sweeps me into another twirl. "You just haven't learned to play."

16

WEIRD DINNER

As soon as ballroom basics ended, Mister M went back to pretending I don't exist, which is perfectly fine by me.

Dinner starts out quiet, the way it always does. We find our unofficial assigned seats and settle in. Mister M at the head. Avery on his left, an empty chair on the right. Ivy and June sit on Avery's side, with Bri and I opposite. Bri used to sit next to Mister M, until he made a comment about her manners being abysmal. She cried, I spoke up, and the consequences were far from worth it.

Whatever Mister M was served looks good. Meat of some kind, real mashed potatoes, steamed broccoli, fresh bread. Our entrée on the other hand, is…unfortunate. It's supposed to be soup, I think. If soup were made with fewer ingredients and more self-loathing. Like whoever cooked it directly imbued it with sadness. It has no scent, and the flavor profile is so confusing that no amount of words could capture the abhorrent feeling every bite inspires. June's not liking it either, if her mock gagging is any indication.

"Do you think the enforcers get better food than us?" I whisper not-so-quietly across the way. June chuckles, then tilts her head, genuinely pondering it.

"I'm not even sure they eat," she whispers conspiratorially, glancing between them with narrowed eyes.

"True, they could be battery powered." I raise my spoon in agreement, my focus catching on Colt. He smirks, then shrugs, keeping the mystery alive.

"Caught you staring," June sings, sticking her tongue out at me.

"Was not."

"You were," she whispers, jade eyes glinting. "It's fine May. He's pretty, for an enforcer. Plus he's got the brawn." She flexes her arm and pulls one of the dumbest faces I've ever seen.

I smother a laugh, about to fire something back when Brielle pokes my shoulder, nodding toward Avery.

She's frowning into her soup, swirling it with her spoon and sending little ripples across the surface. The bowl is still full, which would be unsurprising if it was anyone else. Without warning, she drops the spoon. It clatters into the bowl, sending droplets exploding outward. They fly right at her face, then veer, pattering harmlessly onto the tablecloth.

Mister M's head snaps up. He grips her hand and asks if she's all right.

Avery's lips start moving wildly, words spilling too fast and frantically for me to decipher. She's leaned in close to him, face deadly serious, whispering like the air itself will swallow her if she stops.

"I can't—" Her whisper spills into a cry, wide eyes darting to the ceiling and lingering like she sees something we don't.

I follow her gaze, finding nothing but symmetrical white panels. Avery turns to Brielle, bright eyes feverish. Bri shrinks into her seat, looking nervously between Mister M and her lap.

For a moment, Mister M's smile falters. He bends down, closer than he ever does in public, command slicing through the silence. "Stop."

Avery flinches but keeps whispering.

"Stop it," he snaps again, harsher. His hand clamps the back of her chair, knuckles going white. "Do you hear me? Stop."

The entire table goes still. Bri bites her lip, staring into her soup. June and Ivy freeze. I keep my eyes trained on her. He squeezes her hand again, and Avery's whispers die out. Golden strands fall over her face as she drops her head in her hands with a muffled cry.

Mister M straightens slowly, smoothing the front of his jacket. "Eat," he says pleasantly, as though nothing happened.

My spoon jolts with static when I touch it. I fight the urge to wince. Instead, I drag it up to my lips and choke down a bite of lukewarm soup.

Behind the blind obedience drilled into my psyche, an ache swells in my chest. It's not hard to get on Mister M's bad side, but something is still seriously wrong with both of them. Avery's eyes are too wide, her lips bloodless where she presses them together. Mister M is smiling again, but the way he looks at her makes my blood run cold.

It's rude to stare, but I do it anyway.

Brielle leans in to whisper something, but her spoon catches as her arm brushes the table, clattering to the floor and tipping the bowl. June reaches across to catch it, but most of it still splatters onto Brielle's pink uniform. Mister M's head flicks up again, hazel eyes wide with fury. His jaw tightens as he stares at the mess. I hesitate, but the fear plastered on Brielle's features tells me I need to do something. Now.

I pretend to reach for her, tipping my full glass of water into my lap. Just as I'd hoped, the glass rings out clear as a bell as it falls against the wooden table. I wince; the water is absolutely freezing against my skin.

To say Mister M is irate would be a grave understatement. He glowers at me, at Bri, at Avery, at June and Ivy, who haven't even had a chance to screw up yet. I offer him my most polite smile.

"I'm sorry, Mister M. I must've slipped."

"Slipped," he echoes, unconvinced.

Colt steps forward. "I can get her a towel—"

"No," Mister M snaps. "She'll sit in it." His eyes narrow on me, watching the steady drip pooling beneath my chair with disdain. I keep my hands folded in my lap, now soaking and clammy. Brielle bends over to get her spoon, mouthing a meek "thank you" in the process. On the way up, she smacks into the underside of the table, crying out before she can stifle it.

Mister M's gaze darts around the room. I follow. There are eyes on us. Many eyes. Other pods, other mentors, even a few instructors at a table in the corner. He forces an exasperated sigh, slamming his palm against the table and standing.

"Dinner's over," he announces, jaw clenched like he's physically restraining himself. "Sedation's at eight.

Consider it a mercy." He storms out, snapping his fingers at Colt and Ralston, a wordless announcement that we're now their problem.

Ivy rises first, tossing her black braid over her shoulder. "Best dinner I've ever had."

17

SOMETHING'S WRONG

A scream shatters the dark.

I tear free from my half-sedated haze, breath caught in my throat, skin slick against the sheets. For a moment, I think it's another nightmare, but the sound comes again. Higher, sharper, too loud to be imagined.

I almost trip as I stumble out of bed, clambering to the glass window on my door. Mister M sent our sedation an hour early, but it must be after midnight by now. No one should be up. At the very least, no one should be screaming. I press my face to the panel, letting my breath fog the glass. I can barely see the hallway beyond our pod from here, but it looks empty. Something rattles the wall. I crane my head to the left to look down the row of doors that connect to our rooms. My breath hitches when a dark silhouette of chaos comes into view.

Avery.

It's Avery.

Two enforcers in black coats drag her out of her room, one on each arm, pulling so hard her body jerks between them like a rag doll. She's thrashing wildly, bare feet kicking at nothing, face streaked with tears and fury. The glass muffles most of her words, but I catch fragments. She's screaming that she didn't mean to. Begging for Mister M. Demanding to know what's going to happen to her.

My heart bashes against my ribs. They wrestle her

through the common room. She flails, landing a solid kick before a syringe plunges deep into the crook of her arm. The effects wash over her instantly. She goes slack, body falling limp as they lift her between them and disappear into the shadows of the training wing.

I can't move. I can't breathe.

Where are they taking her?

My knees threaten to give. My body locks against the glass as I clutch my head in my shaking hands. It doesn't make sense. Nothing here ever does. But Avery's perfect. Composed. Talented. Nothing like the girl out there fighting like an animal.

I raise an unsteady hand and knock against the wall that connects Juniper's room to mine. Nothing. I don't need to knock on the other wall; I can hear Brielle's rhythmic snoring from here. My thoughts are skidding out of control. They say sedation keeps us safe, keeps us calm.

But she was definitely not sedated. And I can't stop thinking that there's no way anyone could sleep through this, no matter what drugs they give us. The common room sits empty now, eerily serene in the dim blue light. But the image won't leave me. Avery's wide eyes, her sobs, her voice breaking on his name.

His name.

Does Mister M know?

If he doesn't, he'll know soon enough. I know they've been arguing, but there's no way he would've wanted this. *Would he?*

I don't know how long I stay rooted in place. Long enough for my lower back to throb. Long enough that I don't care to move when the sound of bootfalls grows closer. Colt makes his rounds like all is well. Shoulders loose, pace easy. But when he sees me at the glass, he slows. He cracks the door open, looking me up and down.

"Maysie," he says under his breath, gaze flicking over his shoulder. "You aren't supposed to be up."

"Avery—she…" I try to describe what I saw, then stop dead. Because I have no idea what that was.

His gaze doesn't falter. He shakes his head, gesturing at the bed. "Go lay down. Please."

"I just…Avery—"

"I know." His words are clipped, tone thick with emotions I can't decipher. His eyes hold mine, steadying me. "I know. But you need to trust me on this. Get back in bed."

"She didn't do anything wrong. She was fine a week ago. And this morning. And—"

"Please, Mays." He slips through the door and grabs my arm. His eyes are so pale in the dim light that I can barely make out the warm hues of brown in his irises.

"Does Mister M know?" I whisper, hoping I don't already know the answer.

"I don't know," he admits quickly, eyes flicking toward the hall again. "But shift changes are happening any minute. They can't see you up." He frowns. "Bed, now."

"She didn't do anything wrong—"

"I know," he says, too quick to be a lie. "Trust me. I know."

The cuff warms against my wrist, light flashing as I slip from the target heart rate.

"Just trust me," he repeats, softer. "Please."

I stumble back, legs hitting the back of the bedframe with a dull *thunk*. Colt lingers in the door for a moment, gaze downcast.

"If anyone asks tomorrow." His throat bobs. "You didn't see that."

I open my mouth to beg him for answers. To tell him that I did, in fact, see that. But he's already gone, bootfalls fading down the hall. My back meets the bed as I collapse down, utterly drained from whatever just transpired. I tug at the covers, trying to remember the relaxation techniques that Doctor Noxen taught me. Empty the mind, steady the soul.

But my mind is chock-full, and my soul is anything but steady.

I can't make sense of it. She was perfect, and it wasn't enough. Avery did everything she was supposed to, and more. Before today's incident, I was half-convinced she was a robot built by Mister M to make the rest of us feel bad.

But it wasn't enough.

A slew of terrifying thoughts floods my head, but one sticks out, jagged and wrong. It rattles against my skull, making my eyes blur. The room shifts in and out of focus as I wriggle under the blanket, palms damp with sweat because I don't get it.

If obedience isn't enough, if it can't save us, then what can?

18

THIS GUY AGAIN?

Sleep finally drags me under, only to spit me back out.

I drift between half-baked nightmares of places I've never seen and hours of counting the cracks in the ceiling, just to make sure I didn't miss any the last seventeen times I checked.

Regardless, the world is normal when I awaken. Calm, even. There's a noticeable lack of screaming.

I creep out of my room a few minutes before the chime. Ryder, our valiant nighttime patrol, is asleep on the floor. Slumped against the wall, boots crossed at the ankles, head tipped back. His jacket is bunched up behind him like some sort of makeshift pillow.

I brush past him, sweeping into the bathroom. The auto-lights hum to life, fluorescents too bright to be pleasant at this hour. I cross to the shower panel and punch in my designation to start the countdown.

If the showers weren't remotely timed to be exactly five minutes, I would lock myself in the stall and soak until my skin goes raw and the steam erases every memory from last night.

I shake my shoulders in a feeble attempt to loosen the tension pulsating across my back. The sleeve of my night-gown catches on the counter; I tug it off and toss it into the blinking slot that swallows our laundry. My shelf folds out from the wall, summoning me with its blinking red light. I brush my teeth and slip on a waterproof cuff cover. Only then does my cubby open so I can retrieve my shower caddy. Everything is measured here, down to the soap I'm permitted. It's a familiar comfort.

Not very comforting today.

By the time I'm finished in the shower, the pod is waking up. Doors click, chimes sound, uniforms rustle. June's standing in front of the long mirror, plucking pins from my designated bin. She glances up, eyes catching mine through the reflection.

"You're up early," she grumbles, sedation hanging heavy on her words. "Everything okay?"

"Fine," I say, nodding too quickly. June sidesteps so I can use the sink. I gesture vaguely at the pins that continue to disappear into the disaster of a bun she's constructing. "You eating those?"

"They're eating me." One flies out of her fingers, clattering onto the floor. "Help."

I giggle, handing her a handful more and turning back to my station. The plaque above my head glistens, beckoning.

A little reluctant, I mumble through the mantra.

Poise. Obedience. Purpose.

It doesn't settle the ache in my chest.

Ivy appears in the common room as I finish up in the bathroom, having clearly just shoved yesterday's uniform on. She's dragging a brush through her sleek black hair, dark eyes scanning the room like she knows something's amiss. Her gaze drifts toward Avery's door. Still closed. Slate-still.

"Is she—"

"She's fine," I say, forcing my voice level. "Probably in diagnostics."

"Or in hiding." June jokes.

Brielle elbows her. "Or with Mister M. Maybe he realized she works best in the middle of the night—y'know, like a bat."

Creature of the night. Nice, though it feels a little too real today.

"Right," Juniper drawls, rubbing her side. "Or maybe Mister M realized she's not getting enough compliments and threw a tantrum so loud Carr tranquilized him." She pretends to flip a coin. "Fifty-fifty."

Bri's eyes go wide as she digs through her cubby.

My palms itch until I drag them down my skirt.

Colt's voice from last night clicks into place. *If anyone asks tomorrow…you didn't see that.*

I shouldn't have seen it. I shouldn't have been awake.

I wasn't, I tell myself. I'm a good girl. An obedient girl. I was certainly not a witness to my friend being dragged from our pod in the middle of the night when I should've been sedated.

I angle my body away from Ivy's questions and straighten a stack of workbooks that doesn't need straightening. "The enforcers are running late," I observe.

"Also tranquilized," June says, aiming a finger gun my way. I roll my eyes.

Someone knocks on the pod door. My spine snaps straight. No one here has ever had the decency to knock.

Mister V strides across the threshold, taking in the room with cataloging eyes. He stops mid-stride. His gaze flicks down. Then up. Then down again. Right at Ryder.

I expect him to snap. Or freak out. Scoff, at the very least. But he just stares, silent and stiff as marble. He nudges Ryder's leg with the tip of his dress shoe.

No response.

He nudges harder. Ryder startles with a noise somewhere between a snore and a curse. "Oh. Morning," he says, unbothered. "Didn't hear you coming."

"I gathered," Mister V says dryly, folding his arms.

Ryder scrubs a hand over his face. "Must've nodded off. Happens sometimes." He flicks his wristband. "Too bad this thing doesn't have an alarm built in."

Mister V exhales through his nose. "Get up."

"On it, boss."

"I'm not your boss."

"Noted." Ryder rises slowly, brushing dust from his uniform and tossing us a hazy grin. He shakes his jacket out and moves for the door. "Daytime crew should be on their way up. I'll show myself out."

Mister V shakes his head, then turns to us, eyes landing on me. "Your mentor is unavailable," he states, even as a level. "In his absence, I'll be overseeing your schedule for the day."

June's face lights up. "Do you prefer 'omnipotent overseer' or 'benevolent dictator'?"

"Mister V will suffice."

"Where's Avery?" I blurt, pressing a fist to my mouth as soon as her name escapes.

He nods like he expected this, pressing his lips together for a moment. "She's undergoing a specialized review. I wasn't informed of her return date."

Specialized review. I can't help but wonder if they bothered to tell her that. Based on the screams? I bet *not.*

"Figures," June says, folding her arms and sticking her tongue out. "I bet they're using her as a case study."

Mister V says nothing, but his fingers twitch by his side. "With that out of the way, your schedule will continue as normal. Your enforcers should arrive shortly for vitals and cuffs. Then breakfast and morning lectures. You'll be informed if anything changes." He slips out without another word.

June turns to me, grinning wildly. "This just got interesting."

19

APTITUDES

The world keeps turning. Breakfast. Lectures. Diagnostics. Lunch. More lectures. *Man, do these people love to lecture.*

Monotonous or not, today's been a breeze. Turns out, without Mister M around to bark orders, things are actually pretty peaceful.

Mister V is different. He doesn't glare when we whisper or snap when we misstep. Better yet, his feedback is genuinely helpful. Even Colt and Ralston seem calmer with his presence.

So yeah. That part has been great. Mentally, on the other hand, I think I'm seconds away from exploding. I shouldn't still be thinking about Avery. If Mister V says she's fine, she's fine. But it doesn't sit right with me.

"You have art?" Mister V cuts through my spiral, already reaching for his tablet again as if to double check. "Again?"

"We have art every day," I tell him, confusion prickling the edges of my words.

He shakes his head. "That's not how it works." He glances back at the screen, brows furrowed. "Wow."

"What?" June asks, trying to peek at the tablet.

He pulls it back. "Nothing. Just—no art today. We're taking a trip to the practice suites."

I'm equal parts intrigued and perplexed at that. "The practice suites?" Bri asks, like it's a foreign country. "We're allowed to go there?"

"You should already be going," he corrects, gesturing for us to follow. "This way."

A maze of halls later, we arrive in a section of the wing that smells like lemons. Each door lining the corridor is labeled by a gold plaque. "Movement," "Flute," "Voice," "Piano."

Piano.

The tug I feel toward it is visceral.

Each door is equipped with a slim glass viewing window; most of the rooms beyond are vacant. The only noise is a mentor yelling sequences at the end of the hall. Oh—and someone who's definitely never played the flute before. I'll be choosing to tune out both.

I keep my focus on Mister V, resisting the urge to touch anything. The tablet on his hip pings. He casts a quick glance at it, then sighs.

"Get to work. Start with your aptitudes, rotate if needed." Mister V waves us off, unclipping his tablet and swiping it open. No one moves.

Bri gives me a nervous nod, as if to say, "Your turn, do something."

"Mister V?" I ask, unassuming.

He doesn't look up. "Hm?"

"We don't know what they are."

He pauses. Surveys me with a blank look. It makes me feel a little stupid for asking, but his expression only twists further into confusion. "You weren't informed?"

I look at Bri. Bri looks at June. June looks at Ivy…who ignores all of us. Four variations of "no" chorus through the room.

Mister V looks genuinely baffled for a moment, then sighs, rubbing his temple like the thought physically hurts.

"This pod is a disaster." He waves us forward just as his tablet chirps again, twice this time. Irritation bleeds through his composure. "I have to handle this. Pick something. Rotate. Don't break anything."

Ivy huffs as Mister V hurries away. "How are we supposed to know what to pick?"

"Pick what looks fun?" I offer, already grabbing the golden handle to the nearest piano room. She groans again, but I'm already past the threshold. The room is simple. Four gray walls with nothing but a well-loved walnut piano and a set of gray chairs. A screen is mounted where the music stand should be. I raise my wrist and press my cuff to the scanner on the lid.

The screen chirps, then stutters, flashing a deep blue.

USER: VH-6

[ERROR]

The screen cuts out, then flashes again.

[USER CLEARED]

SELECT MODE

I hit the top option without reading it, initiating a ten second countdown.

My skirt swishes as I settle on the bench. The screen blinks again and a series of keys light up, pulsing red. I place my fingers where the light tells me. A soft voice guides.

"Left Hand. Play C-E-G"

I do. The system hums its approval. A new sequence populates.

"Right Hand. Play C-D-E-G-C"

I hesitate but follow. The rhythm comes easier than I expected. My fingers stumble once, then find their place. The screen pauses, stutters, then skips ahead. The voice returns:

"Module three unlocked: Intermediate chords. Begin"

I blink. *That was fast. Maybe too fast?*

The system doesn't wait for me. More lights. New patterns. My hands fly to keep up. It's not perfect, but it doesn't feel foreign, either.

The door creaks, but I can't bring myself to turn around. Thankfully I'm not in suspense long. Bri leans over until her hair brushes my shoulder. "Woah! I didn't know you could play." She plops beside me on the bench, taking in the screen with amazement.

I give her a nervous chuckle. "Neither did I."

Ten minutes later, Mister V is ghosting the doorway like he never left, watching us intently. June traipses behind, bumping Mister V out of the way with her hip and whispering something into Brielle's ear.

Bri taps my leg with a pleading look, then presses her lips to my ear and whispers that it never hurts to ask. I swallow my nerves and give him the most honest look I can muster. "Could we go to the garden?"

He considers it a long moment. "Five minutes."

June gasps like he just offered us a pony. "Twenty?"

"Fifteen. Final offer."

"You're an angel." June beams, mock bowing to him.

"Incorrect."

The garden is quaint. Too quiet for the chaos we bring.

It's more like a courtyard, walled in by high stone borders entangled with ivy and lined with hedges trimmed to perfection. A narrow path winds between flower beds and low benches, curving around an oversized fountain that frames the center. The trees are tall and even, with lush leaves trailing each branch. Above us, the sky is hazy, swirling with all the colors of the sunset. The faintest gold bleeds through near the horizon.

Mister V beelines for a bench under a shady tree, popping a file open and brandishing a pen like this is the highlight of his day. June immediately plops down on the nearest patch of grass. The enforcers take posts by the door. Colt slips off his jacket, pressing his back into the stone wall and smiling faintly at the sky.

"Why did you bring us here?" Ivy asks, kicking a rock down the path.

"Because you asked," Mister V says, not looking at her as he turns a page.

June props up on her elbows. "We ask lots of things."

"You asked nicely," he replies, so dry it might be funny if it weren't also true.

She grins. "Don't get used to it."

The other girls disperse, but I find myself drawn to Mister V, who's still scribbling away, eyes scanning each page with fervor. I want to admire his work ethic, but all I can think is that there's absolutely no way whatever he's studying necessitates this kind of interest.

"Why do you take so many notes?" I lean over, trying to peek at the file. He pulls it away, the corner of his lip twitching faintly.

"I'm afraid that's above your clearance," Mister V says, not looking at me. I click my tongue. He doesn't seem to care one way or the other about my presence, so I lie back, sinking into the cool, trimmed grass. The sun has mostly set; blurs of brilliant pink disappear over the walls with each passing moment. I frown. Even as the sky darkens, it remains vacant. No clouds, no stars. A barren void of listless night. It's pretty, but something about it stings.

I wrap my arms around my chest, whispering words only meant for me. "Are stars real?"

Mister V startles. He blinks a few times, casting his eyes to the sky. Something like hurt crosses his features.

"I'm sorry," I say quickly, but the pressure in my chest tells me it may not be enough.

Gray flecks fester like storm clouds around his irises. "It's fine." He shakes his head, turning back to his notes. "It's just…not the first time I've been asked that."

He offers nothing else.

"I think they're real," Bri says, sliding down next to me and stretching her arms wide like she can hug the whole sky. "Just hiding."

Juniper hums from somewhere in the grass. "Maybe they're scared of us."

I smile, plucking a blade of grass and twisting it between my fingers. "Wouldn't blame them."

No one speaks after that. The garden crawls back to its equilibrium of calm, allowing me plenty of breathing room for reflection. Avery's probably fine, everyone else is fine, and we're still on track for graduation.

Beneath my attempted reassurances, my fingers ache with a need so strong it makes my heart skitter. I can't explain it, but something about playing just felt right. More than right, it felt like the answer to a puzzle I didn't know I was solving.

If that's the case, I need to find a way to play again.

20

WASTED TIME

Mister V lets us stay outside far longer than fifteen minutes, only coaxing us back in once it's too dark for him to work. We're led back to the common room, given nothing but advice to "check the scheduling board" before he disappears.

Little does he know, Mister M hasn't updated said board since we were first assigned to this room. We've collectively decided to finish our workbook reflections, since they just-so-happen to be endless and painful, and having to do them first thing in the morning is a drag.

Quite frankly, it's a drag no matter the time of day.

Ivy has gone rogue. She's standing at the one-way observation mirror with half of a soap bar clutched in one hand, drawing something I can't quite make out from this angle. The rest of us are pretending not to watch while absolutely watching. She takes a step to the right, and the full picture of her masterpiece comes into view.

"Is that...?" I squint, tilting my head. "Wait. Is that Mister V?"

Juniper cackles, flopping down on the rug. "Oh my god, it is."

I've got to hand it to her. It's uncanny. Sharp cheekbones. Shadowed eyes from staring at a tablet all day. The picture of mentor angst. Ivy proceeds to add a crisp suit and a stack of papers the size of a small child.

"Oh no. No, no, no." Brielle covers her eyes. "We are so

dead if anyone sees that. Like extra-sedated, mindlooped, lab-scrubbed kind of dead."

"I think it's flattering," I offer, stifling a giggle behind my hand. "She made the suit tailored."

"He's judging me through the drawing," Brielle hisses. "Stop it, Ivy!"

June leans closer. "Give him devil horns."

"I'm not doing that."

"Coward," June teases.

"We're going to be dissected," Brielle groans, collapsing against the cushions like she's accepting fate.

Ivy steps back to admire her work. "I made the folder bigger. It looked unrealistic."

"Unrealistic?" I echo. "You drew the man in soap!"

"I'm practicing perspective."

"You're planning our demise," Bri snaps back. I bite the inside of my cheek to hide another laugh. I should stop her.

I really, really should stop her.

But Ivy is alive in a way she hasn't been for weeks. Her eyes shine. Her lines have genuine energy. Whether it's enough to make up for the consequences we'll face if someone sees it…is to be decided.

Juniper folds her arms like a pouty child, slipping into the most terrible impression of Mister V. "Elegance is a weapon. Unfortunately, you're all unarmed." I wheeze, pressing my head into my hands.

Bri clutches a throw pillow in a final attempt to disappear. "We are so, so doomed."

The door slams open, almost thrown off its hinges by the angriest man humanity has ever laid eyes on. June flings herself into a chair. Brielle drops straight to the floor. Ivy steps back from the panel, admiring her handiwork with a grin. I flip my workbook open, feigning innocence.

As suspected, he doesn't buy it.

Mister M strides into the room with a look that could bleach paint. His eyes catch on the soap V instantly.

"What," he seethes, lethal. "Is that?"

Nobody breathes. He crosses the space in three long stomps and stops directly in front of the mirror. The sketch stares back at him with impeccable posture.

Bri lets out a yelp as he gets close. "Please don't kill us!"

Ivy shrugs. "It's art."

He scoffs. "You think this is a game?" There's a long-drawn stretch of silence as Ivy holds his gaze, unwavering. I'm so tempted to throw his words back in his face. According to him, everything's a game. Unfortunately, if I say anything of the sort, I'm fairly sure he'll kill me...or explode. Maybe both.

With evaluations a week away, we don't have time for him to do either.

"No, sir," I finish for her. His eyes shift to meet mine, rage blooming in his irises.

"Then why the hell is Harrow's face etched into my goddamn observation window like he's the patron saint of wasted time?"

Juniper winces. "Well, when you say it like that."

He turns, hands in his pockets, eyes darting between us as he decides how painful this is going to be.

"Who started this?"

"Group project?" June tries.

"My idea," I add, not meeting his eyes.

"Liar." His voice is so low it might as well be gravel. "I'll ask again, who—"

"I drew it," Ivy says, staring him down.

Mister M smirks, vicious and terrible. "Cute. Real cute. You just bought yourselves a week of reconditioning." Brielle's face pales. Ivy's finger twitches the tiniest bit.

My heart stutters. "Wait—"

"Save it." He raises a hand in dismissal. "No common room access. Early sedation for a week. And Carr will see all of you, starting tomorrow."

"What?" Brielle blurts before slapping her hands over her mouth. She's near tears at the mere mention of Doctor Carr. He's the head physician of the program, not to mention the man directly responsible for our resets. That makes him equal parts savior, executioner, and terrifying dictator.

"That's not fair. We didn't even do it!" June is on her feet in a second, brows furrowed at the fireball in a suit.

"Should've thought of that before you vandalized my pod. This space is a privilege. One you *parasites* clearly aren't ready for."

I hold my hands up in surrender. "It wasn't vandalism! We—"

"Tell it to Carr." Mister M flicks his wrist like he's swatting a bug. He's already halfway to the door, but I know exactly what sick face he's making. He pauses at the threshold just long enough to let the weight settle.

"Clean it up. Or leave it as a warning, I don't care," he spits, flicking his fingers at us. "Bunks in ten. Some silent reflection will do you all some good." The door slams, leaving us in stunned silence.

After an eternity, June's slow exhale slices through the tension. "Well. That escalated."

"We're going to die," Bri groans into the throw pillow.

"I think it was worth it," Ivy muses, splashing water on the panel and wiping it with her sleeve.

"Totally." I turn, already stacking the workbooks in size order, the way he hates, because order is the only defiance I can afford tonight.

The moment the enforcers finish their sedation rounds, I dig the black-bound book out from under my mattress. It falls open to the page I left off on last night. The dim blue overheads illuminate little, but I manage. Nothing here ever truly goes dark. Darkness is unguarded, dangerous, far too private for the organization to allow.

Since last week's heist, this has become my little ritual. I read the pages until my eyes blur, then challenge June with fun facts the next day during enrichment. Not exactly a fair fight, but we've made quite the game out of it. Bri pretends not to listen. She thinks our fascination has tipped too far into rebellion.

I think if the book were truly so bad, it wouldn't be here at all. It even has a stamp, that has to count for something. Part of me does get a little freaked out if I think about it for too long, but I convince myself it's fine.

Mostly because the alternative means admitting that it's very much *not*.

Some pages are more intact than others. Many have ink too smudged to read, others have doodles in the margins. The last few are missing entirely. This page is one I normally skip, though I can't say why.

Two towering figures frame either side, surrounded by endless halls that distort and overlap without reason. The creatures are dressed in black, inked so deep you can hardly make out the masks that conceal their faces. Between them, a girl kneels, drawn so faintly she's almost a part of the background. The corridors converge behind them at a vanishing point that looks just a little too much like a door.

I run my thumb along the text, careful not to smudge it any further.

The Wardens.

Guardians of the dark.

Said to protect the weak, yet few who live beneath their rule ever glimpse the daylight. They carve passageways without end, shielding themselves from what they cannot contain. When a Warden removes its mask, the face beneath is always different.

I hurry to turn the page, but my eyes catch on a note I've never noticed before. Barely there, written along the bottom margin in careful, flowing strokes:

Not all monsters live outside.

Huh. One page is enough for tonight. Maybe enough for a while. My fingers tremble as I tuck it back under the mattress, trying to coax my mind toward something else—anything else. The rush I feel when I play piano, Ivy's weirdly accurate depiction of Mister V, the perfect stillness of the shady trees in the garden. Things that are easy and safe and don't make my pulse climb high enough to set off my cuff.

My mind finally settles on Mister M, replaying his smug face and his hopefully shallow threat.

21

TOO YOUNG FOR THIS

It was the furthest thing from a shallow threat.

Reconditioning dragged on for days. Tedious drills, Doctor Carr's clipped orders, countless needles. The kind of punishments made to wear you down piece by piece. Even Juniper's jokes ran dry by day four. By the time it was all over, soap V was a distant memory. One I never want to repeat. Ever.

In better news, there's an investor event today. We're not privy to the details, but I'm not too pressed. It just means Mister M has been gone all day and will hopefully be too tired to check on us once he's finished. Most of the mentors, enforcers, and instructors are absent, as are half the girls. Which means instead of lectures and mock evaluations, we get bookwork and extra enrichment.

Not a bad trade, all things considered.

I reach for another pen. I'm not drawing anything particularly useful, just looping soft spirals into the corner of the page, trying to make them look like the trees in the garden. A challenge, considering I've only seen them once. They keep coming out too rigid to be natural.

June's chewing on the edge of her pen. Brielle's painting a pastel pink sky that she's already wipedoff twice. Ivy has her head down on the table, curtain of black hair fanned over her face, snoring lightly. Other groups are scattered around the room, all at various stages of the "creative process." I don't need to look to know that no one's making anything frame-worthy today.

The instructor hasn't looked up in ten minutes. He's flipping through a beige bound book; feet kicked up on a rogue supply box.

"Okay," Juniper says, loud enough to count as reckless. "Real talk. How old do we think Mister V is?"

I glance up. "Why?"

"Because he walks like he owns the floorboards. That's not a thing you do unless you're, like, thirty."

"He's not thirty," Brielle says, frowning. "He still has that—I don't know. That too-perfect skin thing."

"True," June agrees.

"Maybe he was born here," I offer. "Grown in Carr's lab."

"Right, like a prototype." June draws out the words, gesturing with her hands. "Beta version of the perfect mentor. It explains the gloves."

"And the posture."

"And the ability to appear out of nowhere."

June gasps, delighted. "Plot twist. He's actually a vampire."

Brielle's eyes go wide. "Oh my gosh, don't even!"

"Not possible," Ivy groans against the table. "That would make him interesting."

June throws her hands down. "No, no, it totally tracks. Have you ever seen him sleep?"

"I've never seen his reflection, that's all I'm saying!" I agree, sticking my tongue out at Bri.

Bri grimaces. "You guys are going to get us all killed."

"Please," June says, sounding cocky. "What's he gonna do? Materialize out of thin air?"

Worse.

He strides right through the door.

"Ladies," Mister V says smoothly. The blood drains from my face.

We're so dead.

He folds his arms, gaze sweeping over the four of us with surgical precision. I can't tell if he's amused or furious. "Glad to see the enrichment is keeping your minds active," he says. "Though I'm not sure creative slander counts as personal development."

"It wasn't slander," June retorts. "We were just…analyzing."

Mister V raises an eyebrow, then clears his throat like he's about to speak.

"How old are you?" I blurt. *Stupid.* I shouldn't have said anything, but now I need to know. Mister V pauses, just long enough to twist the moment into something uncomfortable.

"Nineteen," he says, pointed. "Is that disappointing?" The silence answers for us. Brielle looks stricken. June's mouth opens, then shuts again. I just sit there, trying to re-wire everything I thought I knew.

He's nineteen.

"How old were you when you got here?" June asks.

"Fourteen."

Brielle gasps. The breath gets sucked right out of my chest.

Fourteen?

He was a child. *Probably a well-dressed child.* But still.

Mister V's eyes find mine. He looks tired. Or maybe he's always looked like that, and I never noticed. "Carr will be thrilled to know his advanced subjects are debating monster lore. Truly, this is what the program was built for." He cracks something that could almost be mistaken for a smile.

It takes me too long to realize he's joking. Joking. Like that's something he knows how to do. He pauses like he's waiting for a response, but I'm too stunned to force anything out.

"Well, don't let me interrupt." He nods goodbye, and strides out. We're once again left sitting in the too-bright light, surrounded by dried up markers and the acute feeling of dread.

"I thought he was, like…" Brielle trails off, wiping the smudgy clouds off her painting again.

"Older," I finish, offering her a towel.

It's not that I don't believe him, it just feels wrong. It shouldn't be possible. He said it like that was normal.

June exhales so hard her whole frame sags. "He's kidding. He has to be kidding."

"No." My voice dips quiet. "He's not." And suddenly, none of it is funny anymore. I stare down at the page I was drawing on.

The trees don't look like trees anymore.

They look like bars.

22

BOYS WITH CLIPBOARDS

I spent my evening waiting for a manual cuff sync after I tripped over June's feet on the way to dinner. For advanced tech, they are such a pain.

I'm back in the common room by nine, and to my immense joy, there's still no sign of Mister M. The girls are already here. Ivy's laid out over the couch. Bri and June are cross-legged on the rug, whispering conspiratorially. Bri waves when she sees me. I slide down across from them, pressing my back against the leg of one of the chairs.

Colt's leaning against the far wall, pretending to work. Technically he's supposed to be doing some kind of logging, but he's been staring at his clipboard blankly for about fifteen minutes. Probably assigned to keep an eye on us. Definitely bored.

"Okay" Juniper starts, kicking her legs up onto one of the chairs. "I've been thinking. If Mister V really is nineteen, then what the hell does that make Mister M?"

I tilt my head. "Maybe like—"

"Eighty-seven!" Brielle cuts in, a little too excited.

Juniper snorts. "On a good day."

"No," Bri says. "Not human years—in demon years. Like dog years, but for evil."

I smile despite myself, thinking of the creepy creatures from the night book. "Wait, so that means one human year equals, what? Nine demon years?"

"Which makes him twenty-one," June declares, "and emotionally seventy-four."

I hum. "Still feels generous."

"You guys are terrible at math," Colt mutters, pretending to write something on his clipboard. I can see it from here; the man's page is utterly blank.

Mister M must be close to Mister V's age. He moves like he's older, like he owns the very ground we stand on. But little things give him away: the petty cruelty, the need for control, the little gleam in his eye when someone calls him sir. Something tells me he's still growing into this role.

June hums. "You think they trained together?"

"Probably," I nod. "There's only so many of them. Carr must pick them directly, right?"

Brielle frowns, picking at the little fibers in the rug. "I don't know… They act so different."

"I think that's the point," I say. "If every mentor was like Mister M, we'd probably all be dead by now."

A thought nags at the back of my mind. Maybe they didn't get to choose at all. *But that can't be true.* They must choose to become mentors, right? I blink away the discontent bubbling in my stomach.

The conversation shifts, less playful now. It's like we're all sitting with the same thought, trying not to touch it.

Brielle cracks the silence. "Do you think all the mentors are that young?" My heart stutters. I glance at Colt. He's silent, still leaning against the wall, dark eyes weary.

"I think," I start slowly, hoping my next words sound coherent. "They make them young so they don't know better."

"Like us." The colors leech from June's face. "Easy to train."

"And easier to replace," I whisper, fear settling over my chest.

Brielle presses her palms to the floor. "But why would someone choose this? To be a mentor or an enforcer. To live here and take care of us. It can't be easy, and there have be better options, right?"

"They probably didn't pick," Juniper mutters, bitterness creeping on the words. She turns to Colt, eyes narrowed in curiosity. "All right, spill. How old are you?"

He blinks. "Me?"

"No, the other enforcer in the room."

Colt scratches the back of his neck, suddenly aware of four pairs of very judgmental teenage eyes. "Eighteen. Nineteen in…four months, I think."

"You think?" I echo.

He shrugs awkwardly. "Dates get weird here."

"Are you telling me we're surrounded by teenage boys with state-issued weapons?" June groans.

His hand flies to the holster at his hip. "It's not really— The stun rods, I mean. They're mostly for show. I'm not even sure mine is char—"

"You're barely older than us!" Brielle blurts.

Ivy lifts her head, interest piqued. "They said I was seventeen at intake. We've been here for at least"—she lifts her fingers like she's going to count them, then slaps a hand over her face—"an eternity. So we're probably the same age."

The thought makes my head spin.

"I'm sixteen," June declares, face twisting with delayed concern. "I think."

"I don't even remember my intake age!" Brielle cries. I bite my lip, because I don't either.

"Everyone needs to slow down," I say before Bri can hyperventilate. "This is insane." I square my shoulders toward Colt. "So, are all the mentors and enforcers young?"

"Define young."

"Under twenty-five?"

Colt nods slowly.

"That's gotta be like—a huge liability, right?" I add, trying not to look at him. "Teenagers being trained by teenagers while being watched by—you guessed it— teenagers. Why would anyone think that's a good idea?"

"'Youth ensures obedience,'" he quotes, too neatly to be spontaneous. "Carr loves that line. Says the trick is catching us before we start thinking for ourselves. Bright eyes, steady hands, clean slates."

"Cute slogan," June huffs.

"Yeah," Colt mutters. "Until you've lived it."

I shake my head. "That's kind of messed up, right? Like, even for them?"

Colt lifts his hands like a shield. "Hey, I didn't design the program. I just passed the damn tests."

"What tests?" I ask.

His face shudders a little. "Doesn't matter." But it does. *And we all feel it.*

June sounds gentler now. "Did you…sign up?"

He doesn't answer right away. He takes a long, deep breath, rubbing the back of his neck again. "Sort of."

Sort of.

I glance at Brielle, then at June. I don't like the implications of this. Belief-altering statements make my stomach hurt.

June sits up, serious. "So let me get this straight. We're being shaped by boys who probably still flinch when Carr raises his voice." She points at Colt. "Watched by barely legal enforcers. Surrounded by instructors who never interfere. Drugged, monitored, and evaluated constantly. But the only real involved adults in this whole place are Carr and the other doctors?"

Colt folds his arms but doesn't correct her.

"Yeah," I whisper, "I think you just about summed it up."

Bri leans forward again, voice small. "Do you think Mister V ever had a choice?"

I want to say no. I want to believe he didn't. That he was dragged into this, same as us. But I think of the way he stands and watches, so stiff it hurts to look at. The way he deflects everything we throw his way. The way he looks at me with icy eyes that see too much.

"No," I say softly.

But it scares me more to think that maybe he did. Because if you chose this…

If you walk into these halls and say yes, what kind of person does that make you?

And what kind of person do they turn you into once you do?

23

MISSING IN ACTION

I slept through the chime. Not just the wake chime, but rise and line-up as well. I'm still groggy when Lance appears at my door, barking orders and bellowing about the consequences of oversleeping. I shake my head, ready to argue. Then, I remember what today is. I jolt up, mutter an apology, grab the uniform he's waving around, and bolt for the bathroom.

Of course I chose today to sleep in. I've been nervous about evaluations all week, and the constant change of sedative doses Noxen's been trying has run rampant over my sleep schedule. Nothing's worked, which has only amplified my nerves.

Two minutes later, I'm in line, tugging on my white flats while Brielle ties a ribbon around my ponytail. Ralston has my wrist in one hand, fumbling with the cuff that's refusing to sync. It's been doing that a lot lately, harboring a personal vendetta for no good reason. Lance disappeared to find the manual. Instead, he returns with the velvet box that holds our designation pins, passing it to Ralston and instructing him to forget the cuff for now.

"Left side of your chest, make sure it's pinned straight." Ralston calls us one by one, reciting the numbers like a checklist. "Brielle, 212. Ivy, 216. Juniper, 219. Maysie—" He stops. Frowns at the box. Then flashes a nervous glance at Lance. "Where's 214's?"

"She won't be needing it," Mister M calls as he steps across the threshold. I can't even process his words as I take in the sight of him. He's always polished, but today he looks downright immaculate. His suit is perfectly tailored, with a blazer the deepest shade of crimson. His chestnut hair is styled tighter than usual. It makes him look older in a way, more distinguished. The mischievous glint flecking his hazel eyes reminds me that he just said something incredibly disconcerting.

"Sir?" I clasp my hands behind my back to keep from fidgeting. Mister M watches me for a long moment, gauging my reaction. I give him nothing, because no answer is safe when it comes to him.

"You'll be sitting this one out." His smirk widens. I press my lips into a frown. He chuckles. "Don't look so ungrateful little star, there's always next time."

"Why?" My voice is hardly above a whisper, but he flashes me a look of contempt like I just yelled in his face.

"Because I said so," he sneers, gripping my arm. I catch June out of the corner of my eye, the look on her face mutinous. Bri bites her lip.

I just shake my head. "But my scores are almost perfect. I haven't done anything wrong—"

"Exactly," he says. "You're too comfortable. Too proud. I'd rather you step back than falter in front of the board and make me look careless. Stable girls graduate; perfect ones draw questions." He smiles, faint yet cutting. "You want to graduate, don't you?"

He's contradicting himself in the same sentence. I step closer, ready to push. "I can do it!" Regret seizes my stomach. I soften my voice into something pretty and pliant. "I want to graduate. I want to show them my—"

"Work in the art room," he interrupts, plastered smile back in place. "I'll send someone to escort you." He waves me off without another word, turning on his heel and herding the girls out. Bri flashes me a sullen look over her shoulder, bottom lip pouted.

I give her a reassuring smile and mouth "good luck" to both her and June, who hasn't moved from her spot. She gives me a disheartened mock salute and makes her way out, followed by Lance. Ralston flashes me a small look of sympathy as he shuts the door behind them.

Then I'm alone. Left with a thousand questions and a still-broken cuff.

When Ryder comes to pick me up, it isn't hard to convince him Mister M had ordered me to stay in one of the piano rooms. I felt sick to my stomach lying, but if I had to spend the whole day in the art room by myself, I think I would actually lose my mind. Ryder simply shrugs and drops me at the door with some terse words about staying put.

The practice suites are dead quiet today, and we didn't pass a single other girl on the walk here. Which means either every single other girl has an evaluation, or this is a really intense game of hide and seek and I didn't get the memo. My bet's on the former, which only twists the knife more.

The schedule marked today's evaluation as mandatory, which I know for a fact means Mister M had to do far more work to keep me out of it than to just let me try.

The more I think about it, the more absurd it feels. He'd rather put the other girls in front of the evaluators. Ivy, who hasn't completed a single movement sequence. June, who recites her introduction like it's the first time she's seeing the words. Or Bri, who can't curtsy without shaking. I'm not supposed to question my mentor. I'm not supposed to question the system that saved me. I'm grateful. I'm obedient. *I'm so lucky to have the chance to improve.*

So, I do as I'm told. Well…partly. I lock myself away in a practice room and play until my fingers go numb. I fight to convince myself that it's better this way, I haven't gotten to touch a piano since Mister V's visit last week. The bitterness that bites at me when I think of all the other girls who get routine time in their aptitude is startling. But I can't help it, piano time may be the only time I feel like myself.

The system is excellent. There's no shortage of songs, and I don't have to bother with turning pages or picking music. The screen flashes, and another piece begins. It's one I've heard before, slow yet grand. Every note intentional, every measure bigger than the last. I can't hide the smile that consumes my features at the last note. I pause for a moment, eyes closed in small victory.

A polite clap coming from the doorway frightens me so badly that I about fly from my seat. My head flies up in surprise, meeting a calm set of icy blue eyes.

Mister V.

He's leaning in the doorway, the picture of perfect cool; notably not dressed for evaluations. His dress shirt's untucked, gloves slipped awkwardly in his pants pocket. A massive stack of files tucked under his arm. The tablet clipped to his belt is going off like mad. I don't think I've ever seen Mister M's do that.

"You scared me," I confess, keeping my tone polite. "I honestly didn't think anyone would be here today."

"You're astonishing," Mister V states, ignoring my statement. It's odd, his face doesn't bear the kindness that sort of compliment would typically bring. He takes a few steps toward me, inclining his head. "How did you learn to play so well?"

"The system taught me," I say. "It really wasn't that hard." He says nothing, eyes still trained on my face. It feels like he's waiting for something, so I continue. "It feels nice to play. Easy." His face remains unchanged at this. I blink at him a few times, unsure of what he wants from me.

"What are you doing down here?" he asks, passive.

"Just practicing. I wasn't ready for evaluation today." My cheeks warm in embarrassment. He nods, but the way his eyes settle on me feels off. I grip the hem of my dress nervously, trying to mask the awkwardness of it.

He hums. "I wouldn't fret over it, evaluations are mostly for show anyway." He's lying, but I nod regardless.

"Do your girls have evaluations today?"

Stupid question. I'm pretty sure every girl but me will have an evaluation today.

And if they perform well, they may get a chance to attend an event or perform for investors. Performances could lead to promising placements after graduation. Something I won't get by sitting on the sidelines. I bite back the bitter taste in my mouth, smiling pleasantly like I know I should. My eyes settle back on him. He's watching me, calculating. Not responding.

"Mister V?"

"Did you know your aptitude is listed as harp?" he asks, distant.

How? I've never even touched a harp. A frown spreads on my lips before I can catch it, and it takes a few blinks to bring my expression back to the pleasant neutral that's expected.

"I've never played the harp," I confess.

"I know." The way he says it makes me suspect he could recite my entire seven-month history faster than I could, backwards and forwards.

"May I stick around for a while and listen? It's been a while since I've heard someone with your skill." I have no idea how to respond to that. I nod curtly, swiveling back to the piano.

Mister V strides across the room, settling in an oversized gray wingback. He flips through a stack of files, bringing one to the top and running his fingers over it gently. "214" is printed in bold letters. My stomach turns, bile rising in the back of my throat.

Why does he have that?

Evaluations are happening now, for everyone else at least. Girls being graded, praised, corrected. I, on the other hand, was told to stay out of the way. I wasn't even good enough to try.

So why is he here? Why is he watching me?

He's reading, but his eyes are glossed over, like he already knows what the file says. I force myself to breathe. To smile like a good girl. Smooth my skirt. If I can't get answers, I can still give him a performance.

"Do you have any preferences?" I say, delivering the line as politely as I can. He almost smiles, snapped out of his haze. *Bingo.*

"Something up-tempo would suit you." He's by my side in a second, fingers flying across the screen as he flips through songs. It takes him a while, but I know the exact moment he's found the one, his eyes lighting up with both recognition and something deeper.

The songs Mister V picks are perfect. Light, up-tempo,

very motivating. He claps after each one, offering gentle corrections and suggesting similar works. My fingers ache desperately for a break, but I'm in no place to refuse him. We're deep in conversation about composers when his tablet springs to life again, pinging wildly like it's scolding him. He lets out a deep sigh.

"Duty calls. Thank you for your time. You truly are…" He trails off, shaking his head more to himself than me. "Unique." He gathers his files, shoes clicking quietly against the wooden floor as he slips out.

Alone again. Somehow with even more questions than before. Evaluations are a huge deal; girls and mentors alike spend weeks preparing for them. And yet, he was here. *Watching me.*

The adrenaline that's been powering my performance has dwindled. My fingers throb like they're about to fall off, my back aches from holding proper position for hours on end. I pull myself to stand, shutting the piano lid gently as if I could shut my wild running thoughts with it. The light clicks off behind me, and I slip into the hall. It's a ghost town, which means everyone's either resting, or still in evaluations.

No enforcer is waiting for me, which I guess means I should walk back on my own? That's what an obedient girl would do… *I think.*

Two turns in, I'm entirely lost. The corridors grow colder, less familiar. Full of cameras that actually blink and walls that might be breathing. Thankfully, the enforcer who's supposed to be off-duty this evening is lurking at the end of a side hall.

Colt's stationed outside an unmarked door, eyes trained

on his wristband. An idea pops into my head. I'm in front of him before I have time to change my mind.

"Hi," I say, uncertain.

"Mays." He startles, then smiles, caramel eyes lighting the way they always do when he sees me. "What are you doing down here?"

"I was in the art room," I lie, fiddling with the ribbon around my waist. He nods, assessing me slowly. Hesitation grips my system. I almost move past him, but my desire for answers overpowers my second thoughts.

"Do you know Mister V?"

His brows furrow. "Uh...yeah. I know of him, I guess. Why?"

"Who is he?"

He laughs, uncomfortable. "I'll ask again, why?"

"He just happened to show up today, while everyone else was in evaluations. He said he wanted to listen to me play." I fold my hands to keep from fidgeting.

Colt cocks his head. "Play? I thought you were in the art room?"

"Oh—yeah. The art room," I correct half-heartedly. "But that's weird, right?"

"Maybe. I think Carr calls it 'supplemental support' or something," he says, his eyes trained on the wall behind me like it's suddenly fascinating.

"What does that mean?" I ask, trying not to sound desperate. Colt shakes his head, like it's not worth even trying to explain.

"It means he shows up when something's off." Something in my chest pulls tight.

What does that mean?

"Off... like failing?"

"Off like different," Colt corrects. He doesn't say it like an insult, but it's anything but comforting. Being different doesn't do a person any good here.

"Do you think he's trustworthy?" I ask.

"No." Colt flicks his eyes between me and his wristband. He pushes off the wall, gives me a dismissive nod, and moves to swipe his ID badge on the metal double doors. He holds them open for me, caramel eyes swirling with unspoken words. I turn to leave just as his fingers ghost my shoulder.

"Maysie." I look back to find his face twinged with concern. "Just...be careful."

"Why?"

"Because if he's around, it means Carr's looking for something."

24

WHATEVER COMES NATURALLY

We don't discuss anything about evaluations at breakfast the next day. We haven't discussed much this week, for that matter. It's strange, to say the least. I can't shake the feeling that something's changed. June doesn't doodle in her notes anymore. Brielle doesn't paint sunsets, not since Mister M told her that her works were a disgrace to the arts.

Morning classes pass quietly, each minute indistinguishable from the next. I used to find comfort in routine. Now it's like I'm drowning in it.

Lunch and enrichment are much the same. We're well into afternoon classes when I finally feel my humanity catch up with me.

The afternoon lecture is long and predictable. A speech we've been given a thousand times. The girls around me sit upright, nodding intently, smiling graciously at the appropriate beats.

I smile when the instructor glances my way. I even write notes. Nothing important, just a few phrases that sound clever if you don't know what they mean. I'm being obedient, just like I've always been.

That should be enough, at least for today.

A knock interrupts the *riveting* presentation. The instructor turns in irritation as an unfamiliar enforcer steps across the threshold. His eyes flicker directly to me.

"214," he says gruffly, beckoning with a lazy wave.

"You've been requested." *Requested?* That's a new one.

A few heads turn. Brielle's eyes widen; June's mouth forms an "O." I rise quickly, smoothing my skirt. I don't ask where I'm going, or who requested me. Mister M would surely be mortified if I did.

He leads the way through a maze of corridors I don't recognize, stopping in front of a wooden door. I linger counting to ten before tipping the handle and pressing on.

I can't tell if the room beyond was truly intended to be a room, or someone converted a supply closet. It's carpeted in gray, illuminated by soft lamp light yellowed with age. Two uncomfortable chairs in one corner, an upright piano in the other. It smells stale, like no one bothered to air it out for my visit. Surprisingly, there are no cameras, at least not ones I can see.

Mister V, of all people, is here. Perched on one of the chairs like he's afraid if he gets comfortable it'll bite him. Dark hair styled immaculately, cream sleeves rolled to the elbows, gloves folded beside a stack of files. His legs are crossed, one hand resting lightly on the chair's arm. He's not broad like the enforcers, but he's certainly toned. His gaze levels me in a second.

"Maysie."

My heart stutters at the sound of my name, but I force the right response. "Mister V."

"Come in. Sit." He gestures with his pen. I make my way slowly, every step deliberate. "You don't have to look so nervous. This isn't a test," he adds. He sounds calm, dare I say mildly pleasant.

That doesn't make me feel any better. Not after what Colt said yesterday.

"What is it then?" My voice sounds almost level even as

I speak out of turn. I shouldn't question him. It isn't what a well-trained girl would do.

"A check-in, of sorts. More of a benchmark than anything. Your mentor's record-keeping is," he clears his throat, "unreliable, at best." He flips open the top file and sifts through the endless pages of notes that I'm really hoping aren't all about me.

"I had a full diagnostics panel two days ago," I blurt, too quickly. If Mister M was here, he'd be livid.

"I know." He plucks the results from the file and lays them neatly between us; proof that he doesn't need me to tell him anything. "We'll skip biometrics." He sets the page aside. "Just some questions. No wrong answers."

Uh-huh. Sure. I nod through his lie, holding my politeness by a thread.

"What's your biggest fear?"

Oh. I wasn't expecting *that*.

My pulse quickens as I sift through my mind, grasping for the perfect answer. The kind Mister M would drill into me: mediocrity, disappointing the board, getting paint on my white uniform.

Polished lies. Safe lies.

The words that tumble out of my mouth instead are far from a lie.

"Answering that question." My eyes go wide with my own stupidity. *Why on earth did I say that?* My heart pangs with the sense that I'd just handed him something I can't take back.

A genuine smile flickers across his face. "Honesty," he remarks. "Unusual."

I press my lips together. "I'm not sure it was smart."

"No, but it was true."

I look away, cheeks hot. Mister V's still watching me, the weight of his stare prickles against my skin.

"There's a month until your next evaluation," he continues. "I've been asked to ensure you excel."

I freeze. "Asked by who?"

Mister V closes the file with a quiet *snap*. "From now on, you'll have daily private instruction. Piano. Posture. Speech. Whatever I deem necessary."

"Piano? Yesterday you said my aptitude is harp."

"It *was* harp," he interrupts dryly. "I changed it."

"You can just do that?"

"I'm allowed certain…discretion. Most people prefer not to notice." The chill that runs down my spine tells me he doesn't just mean music.

That's not a good sign. It can't be, right? I shouldn't press any further. I shouldn't—

"Why me?" I say anyway, wishing I could kick myself in the face.

"Someone sees something in you." Mister V is already on his feet, crossing toward the piano in slow steps. His hand brushes the polished edge, eyes going distant for a moment before slipping back to me.

"I'd like you to play something." He's not asking, but he's not commanding either. It's a little strange to hear something so casual from him.

"What would you like to hear?"

"Whatever comes naturally."

The bench is cool against my palms. I lower myself carefully, focusing on anything but the man looming a foot away. This model doesn't have a system attached, so I'm on my own. My fingers hover over the keys, but the notes don't come.

Natural? That's what he said. A little disorienting considering nothing feels natural anymore. But I can start with something simple; a piece the system assigned me before I completed all the lesson modules. It's a bore to play, but pleasing to an untrained ear. The melody flows, muscle memory carrying me through with surprising ease. Mister V doesn't move, but his attention drifts. He's fiddling with his pen, twirling it over his gloved fingers again and again. At first it's nothing, until—

Two taps of his pen, rough against the edge of the lid.

My mouth opens without permission. "I am lucky to be saved. I am eager for the opportunity to be corrected. I will strive to reflect the advancement program's—" I choke on the phrase too late. The words die in a coughing fit as I struggle to grasp what just possessed me.

My head jerks up, horrified. Mister V is staring at me, judging my reaction.

"I—I didn't mean—"

"You startled," he says simply. "Your training kicked in. That's all."

Humiliation burns so hot I can't breathe. "Was that—"

"Wrong? No, but it's good to know what's written into you." His icy blue eyes bore into my soul like he's dissecting me from where he stands.

My thoughts tangle, loud and incredibly unhelpful. I should want to be well trained, I know that much. But something about losing my autonomy like that makes my skin crawl. For a moment, I felt like a puppet.

"Try again," he says, slipping the pen back into his pocket like nothing happened.

This time, my hands choose differently. My fingers slip into something deep and somber—nothing like anything the system assigns to me. The melody unfurls without invitation, slick under my touch. Notes dominate the air like they always belonged right here and nowhere else.

It feels like remembering.

Which is weird, considering that's the one thing they don't want me to do.

Every bar sends a fresh ache rippling through my chest. When the final chord fades, my fingers fall docilely to my lap as if they hadn't just become sentient and betrayed me. Something rustles beside me.

Mister V's not looking at me anymore. He's clutching my file in one hand, flipping through the pages at an alarming speed.

"Mister V?"

He exhales a hard breath, startled. "Do you—" He stops. Tenses. Shakes his head so hard it looks painful. "Forgive me," he says, too quickly. "We'll pick up tomorrow."

"Did I do something wrong?"

"No. You're fine." His gaze flicks down again. "I'll have someone escort you back."

I feel guilty for not dropping it, but I can't *not* press. I clear my throat, trying not to sound rude when I ask: "What was that? With the song—I mean. What happened?"

His jaw ticks. "It's an older song. You must've learned it before."

"Okay—" I say, queasy. "What does that mean?"

"It means," he murmurs, still cycling through the pages like he's missing something monumental, "that there may be more to you than you realize."

I'm starting to get sick of people saying that.

25

REGULATION WHITE

It's supposed to be a reward.

That's what Mister M says, bright as the sun itself as he saunters into the common room, two crisp white boxes balanced on his arms. Bri lights up, but something about the masked cruelty cracking his features freezes me to my seat.

"Special delivery," he beams. "Custom uniforms. Approved by the board this morning. Recognition for notable progress and top-tier performance." He pulls dresses out one by one, pointing out their features.

Brielle's dress is blush pink, trimmed in silver thread with a tiny microphone pin glittering at the collar. June's is a striking storm blue with a lightning bolt stitched over her shoulder—the symbol for movement attitudes. Unfitting, considering she barely scraped by in drills last week. Ivy's is pale green, her name barely visible in a looping, polite script above the breast pocket. She runs a hand along it like she doesn't believe it's real.

They're beautiful. Real dresses made to be seen and admired.

"And of course," Mister M purrs, reaching for the second box. "I didn't forget about our wildcard."

Wildcard. What a strange sentiment coming from the man who's spent months calling me boring.

He lifts a single dress and lets it drop. Plastic-wrapped and regulation white. Entirely plain save for a pin of my number, clipped haphazardly on the chest.

"I wasn't quite sure what to choose. Without an evaluation, I'm not sure where you fit." He offers me a smile that's anything but sympathetic.

The room goes still. Heat crackles up my spine, flushing my cheeks scarlet with humiliation. My mouth opens before I can think better of it.

"That's not fair." My words are soft, but he hears me. Mister M pauses, long enough to make it clear that I've done something wrong. He doesn't need to inform me; I'm sure talking back to my "perfect mentor" breaks at least five rules. I should shut up, but my heart is pounding at me, screaming that I can't take this silently. I stumble forward, keeping my eyes on the dress. "I never got an evaluation."

He inclines his head, amused. "Oh?"

"I was scheduled, then pulled for no reason. You fought to keep me out."

The other girls shift uncomfortably behind him. Brielle clutches her dress like a shield.

Mister M exhales like I've said something adorable. "Darling, you weren't *ready*. It would've been cruel to let you fail so publicly. I did you a favor."

"I would've passed," I say, louder this time. "I've been perfect, you said so yourself—"

"There she goes again, the little star. You're being a bit entitled, wouldn't you say?" Mister M's voice dips, bitter. He gestures toward the dresses with the flick of his wrist. "You've been here for months. You think a few good rehearsals render you deserving of this?" My fist clenches so hard I might draw blood. He steps closer, inches from my face. Overpowering cologne assaults my nostrils as he towers over me.

"Let me be clear," he says, words sharp yet sweet, a dagger coated in honey. "This isn't about fairness. The board doesn't care who almost earned it. They care who performs. And you—" He tilts my chin up with one finger. "Didn't."

I bend to pick up the dress. The plastic crunches against my fingers, loud and patronizing. Even through the bag I can tell how stiff it is. My eyes find his again. He's still looming over me, an expectant look twisting his face.

I bite the words out. "Thank you, Mister M."

He bristles, cocking his head. "Say that again."

"What?"

"Say it properly. Say it like you mean it."

I don't mean it. I'll never mean it when it comes to *him*. But he's still not moving.

Fine. I plaster on a fake smile and bow my head in resignation. "Thank you, Mister M."

"That's better." The smile that graces his face is equally fake. "Go get changed. I don't want to hear any more drama from you." He turns, already brushing his hands over Brielle's sleeves and whispering niceties he never would've wasted on anyone besides Avery.

Bri's eyes catch mine as I turn away, and I can see the guilt that tugs at the edge of her lips. I offer her the barest smile before slipping into my room.

By the time I finally work up the courage to change, I'm already on the verge of tears.

The dress doesn't fit—not a surprise in the slightest. The waist is too tight. The hem sits at least two inches higher than regulation. The rough fabric is so thin that it's practically translucent. It scratches my ribs and clings wrong at the shoulders. The sleeves don't even match in length.

I smooth the skirt once to keep my hands busy, though it does nothing for the wrinkles. I bite my lip to choke back tears I want to spill so desperately.

He knows I've been working harder than any other girl in that room. If he would've put me in front of an audience, I would've done well.

And still, it wasn't enough.

I look at the number pin again. It's the same one I was wearing when I first arrived in the advancement program. A symbol that I had been saved, that whatever the organization decided was wrong with me before had been wiped clean. It was a marker so Mister M could tell us apart before he decided on names. A marker that was supposed to be temporary, now being used to take what little dignity I had left.

Poise. Obedience. Purpose.

My fingers curl into fists. I have to blink rapidly to keep from seeing red. Again.

Poise. Obedience. Purpose.

I force the words through gritted teeth. This is for the best. It's for my own good. It must be, because I'm not sure I can bear the alternative.

Poise. Obedience. Purpose.

I center myself. Repeat it one more time. Then I force my hands to unclench, straighten my spine, and walk out of the room like I belong here.

Even if I'm the only one who still has to prove it.

Colt is waiting at the pod door, leaning back against the wall like this is some casual stroll and not the aftermath of my public humiliation. He offers a little wave when I appear.

"Ah," he says with a smirk, eyeing the disaster of a uniform. "Back to the classic. White goes with everything, y'know." He pushes off the wall, eyes glued to my face. "We're headed up to the practice suites. You have a private lesson, I think?"

I nod meekly. "It's with him." I don't bother saying Mister V's name. Colt pats my arm.

"Don't worry about it. I'm sure this is routine." He's lying, but it's enough to fizzle out a drop of the anxiety bubbling in my chest. I kick at a seam in the tile, not caring if it scuffs my flats.

"If it helps," he says lightly, "I've seen worse uniforms."

I glance at him. "You have?"

"No. But I thought it could help."

A laugh slips out before I can stop it. Real and small and lovely. I stop, turning my full attention to him.

"Why do you think Mister M kept me out?"

"I don't know," he admits with a soft shrug of his shoulders. "He keeps going on and on about your attitude. It sounds like a load of nonsense to me."

Attitude?

Mister M has hardly been around since Avery left for her "specialized review." When he is present, he spends his time barking orders or insulting anything and everything he can tear apart. He won't speak to anyone in the dining hall, and if he shows up to morning inspection, he's already seconds away from blowing a gasket. So yeah, I'm not sure I'm the one with an attitude problem.

In fact, the only private conversation we've had in the last two weeks was when I asked him if I could practice piano more often. After I told him about Mister V taking us to the practice suites, he waved me off with a terse speech about wasting his time.

There's no way he would've pulled me for that...*right?*

What kind of psychopathic behavior is that? How on earth would that be what's "best" for me?

Colt clears his throat. "Apparently, he's not the only one you've got riled up."

"What's that supposed to mean?" I ask as he pulls us into a side alcove, out of view from the cameras and roaming eyes.

"Ryder said you caused a meltdown," he says, a smirk playing at his lips. "After Mister V heard you play, he stormed right into Carr's office."

"He *what?*"

"Yeah. Rumor has it he was in there for a while. And now—boom. Private instruction. Ralston says he's never seen Carr approve something that fast without a fight."

I raise an eyebrow. "What do you think happened?"

"I think you're good. Real good. And I think he saw something in you they didn't prepare him for." Something blooms in my chest, caught between pride and horror. I open my mouth to respond, but nothing comes out.

My gaze falls to my shoes, but he clears his throat. "Hey, Mays."

I can't bring myself to respond. Heat crawls up my cheeks, but I offer the smallest murmur of acknowledge-ment.

"You look great," he says, like it's the simplest thing in the world. "Don't stress it, yeah?"

Something in me snaps. My shoulders fall, and suddenly I can breathe again. I hadn't realized how badly I needed to hear that.

"Okay," I say quietly, finally mustering up the confi-dence to meet his eyes. There's so much warmth there, so much glittering honesty that things almost feel okay. He gestures to the practice suite door.

"Be brave, oh musical one," he says, giving me a little two-finger salute. I slip into a mock bow, chest still fluttering with nervous energy. I'm still not sure what private instruction even means.

But I guess it's time to find out.

26

FOLLOW THE CUES

The air changes as I step across the threshold, frigid and teeming with possibility. It's at least double the size of the common room, with lofty ceilings and echoey wood flooring. A unique sight, considering most of the training wing is tile. A long black velvet curtain lines the back wall. Furniture-wise, it's sparse. A polished grand piano covers much of the back corner, surrounded by three high-backed chairs. There's a desk toward the back, with a chair on either side like it's used for meetings. The middle is barren, presumably for running drills and sequences.

Mister V is leaning over the desk with his sleeves pushed up, dark brows drawn tight. A large canvas looms above him like a threat. It's simple, with sleek black lettering that reads *"I am becoming my best self."*

He glances up at the sound of the door. Deep blue eyes sweep over me inch by inch.

I'm not even sure he's noticed he's doing it.

At first, I think I've done something wrong again just by walking into the room—then I realize what he's looking at.

The uniform.

It's still damp from where I scrubbed the stained hem in the sink. The sleeves still sit uneven, despite my best efforts to pin the longer one up.

His jaw flexes as he takes me in. Then, he nods toward the center mat. "Stretch. I'll be right back."

I blink. "Aren't we—?"

Mister V is already gone.

Confused, I lower myself onto the mat and start working through the warm-up sequence. It's harder in this awful fabric. The dress bunches at my ribs when I bend, and clings awkwardly at the waist when I sit.

He returns without a word, holding something folded in his hand. It's a deep gray, with fabric that looks strange for a uniform. Softer. Worn in.

He sets it on the edge of the table, then gestures toward the curtained wall. "Get changed."

I hesitate. "What is that?"

"Training dress," he says with a nod. "The instructors are out today. And Ashford wrote you off the schedule. That leaves us..." His eyes flick to the watch at his wrist. "Six uninterrupted hours."

My mouth goes dry. "Six?"

"I'd like to complete a full benchmark. Movement, etiquette, speech, musicality. For that, you'll need to be comfortable."

I eye the dress again, closer this time. I can't help but wonder where it comes from. It's not my place to question it, though. I should shut up right now and go change before he has the chance to take it back and tell me this is some strange drawn-out joke.

Unfortunately shutting up isn't my forte.

"I've never seen one like that."

"You're not meant to. It wasn't made for the advanced wing."

Oh.

I don't ask how he has it.

I don't ask why he brought it. I slip behind the curtain.

I'm shocked to find a space that looks like it was made for changing. There's a small bench, a mirror, and a stack of folded towels that smell faintly of lavender. I lay the strange dress across the bench and begin to change, carefully folding my white uniform and setting it aside in case it decides to retaliate and bite me for carelessness.

When I slip the new one on, I flinch.

It's soft. Like, actually soft. No scratchy boning or zippers or anything meant to punish me into pretty posture. It moves when I do. The waist hugs without digging. The neckline sits right. It's a near-perfect fit.

Except for the straps. They pinch a little, just like my intake uniform would before I adjusted it with a safety pin. It's not bad, just tight. Poetic, in a way. A quiet reminder that one part of me is always just a little off.

Still, it fits better than anything I've worn. Which only makes it more confusing as to why he has it.

Mister V's waiting when I return. His eyes widen for a moment before he catches it, smothering whatever emotion was flickering with cool composure. He strides past me and sets a bottle of water on the bench.

"How's that?" he asks, not looking at me.

I smooth the dress down. "Comfortable. Thank you."

"Good. Let's begin with movement sequences. How many do you know?"

"All four," I say, trying not to sound too proud.

He lifts a brow. "There are twelve."

My jaw hits the floor. For a moment all I can do is stare at him.

"Do you know all the social scripts?" he asks, now confused.

"There's more than one?"

"You don't—" He cuts himself off, inhaling sharply before continuing. "You have drill blocks every day. Do you mean to tell me you spend three hours a day running the same four sequences and a single social script?"

I shrug. "We mostly run cues."

Or sit around waiting for Mister M to show up.

I don't tell him that part. He seems boggled enough already.

He gestures to the center of the floor. "Let's start there then. Show me each cue."

I do. Mostly perfect, though I stumble slightly through the recitations. Mister V doesn't correct me. His stylus flies across his tablet as he takes pages of notes, his focus on me more than a little unnerving.

"This won't do," he says the moment I finish. "I'm going to teach you a new set, all right?"

"Why?" I ask before I can think better of it. I literally just proved I know them.

"Because it seems your mentor is setting you up to fail."

I almost laugh. "That doesn't make sense. He wouldn't waste time training us if he wanted us to fail." My head spins as I defend a man who doesn't deserve it. "I assure you, the last thing Mister M would tolerate is us embarrassing him."

"Mister M thrives on performance," he says, eyes rife with irritation that isn't directed at me. "Every mentor's cues are slightly different. He designed his to be impressive, but they won't hold up under pressure. You need cues that work even when your mind goes blank—*especially* when your mind goes blank."

My mouth opens in protest, but I've got nothing. He's right. I can normally pull off the cues when we practice them in enrichment or the common room. But when Mister M quizzes us in drills, every ounce of training goes out the window. I give him a curt nod.

Mister V sets the tablet down and moves to stand in front of me. His thumb brushes against the cuff of his jacket, a movement so minor I barely catch it. Icy blue eyes catch mine.

"This," he says, repeating the brush motion. "Indicates breath reset. In for four, out for eight. Chin up, shoulders back." I correct my posture subconsciously. "Good. Your breathing is one of the most crucial things to regulate. If I see you having difficulty, I'll cue a reset."

I nod, not sure what to make of it. Mister M says the cues help us shine. As far as I'm concerned, there's nothing shiny about needing to breathe. He moves again, tapping his index finger against his thigh.

"Hold," he explains. "If it's cued: stop speaking. Reset your stance and wait for it to drop before continuing." *Simple enough.* That one's closer to Mister M's.

He taps his leg twice this time. "Performance on, you're being watched," he says simply. My breath shudders. *I thought we were always being watched?* I follow him anyway.

Mister V teaches six more after that. Three recitations, all much simpler than Mister M's, plus signals to mirror his stance, curtsy, and retreat. The last one felt silly, but sometimes a graceful departure is the best move. Once I've mastered them, he nods, the only indicator that he's satisfied.

He steps closer to me, close enough that I can see the soft shadows under his eyes. "You don't have to obey every cue. That's the point. But you'll know what I'm telling you when we can't speak. Use them to ground yourself."

Choice. That's new.

I press my lips together and nod, somehow empowered. I don't *have* to obey the cues. He said it like they're a favor, not a method of control.

Mister V is confusing. One second, he's as hard as stone, the next I think I understand him completely. The mask he wears rarely slips. Which makes him just as terrifying as Mister M.

"What's next?" I ask. He grabs his tablet, swiping through without looking at me.

"Water break. Then we'll start on speech."

I make my way to the bench, wiping a bead of sweat from my forehead. I'll never get over how nice it feels to learn something new without someone barking at me every step of the way. I look back over my shoulder to tell him as much, but he raises a hand.

"Don't thank me yet. You still have five hours."

V was right, we had a lot to cover. He gave me breaks when I asked, explained corrections clearly, and took notes like this truly mattered to him.

"Maysie," he calls when I'm almost out the door. "Keep your head up, all right?" He's not correcting me. It's…encouragement? Maybe. In his own way. I don't have a good response, but I volley something back anyway.

"You too, Mister V."

The corner of his lip twitches as he turns away, gathering his files.

On the walk back to the common room, I can't help but feel lighter. Hope threads in my chest, burying a seed in a patch of dirt I had thought was long dead. Maybe that's what

I am. A seedling. Something small, just waiting for the right time to grow. I think of Mister M. Of his constant digs and demeaning new nickname and the way he loves to make me feel small. Only today, I don't mind it as much. Maybe—just maybe—with time, I could be something better than passable.

Not a star though. Stars burn.

"You missed the best drills block ever," Bri calls before I've even crossed the threshold, waving her hairbrush in the air. "Ivy bet that Ryder couldn't do sequence eight."

June starts cackling behind Ivy, who grabs one of the throw pillows and tosses it at June's face. She catches, pressing it against her mouth and laughing harder.

I settle on the couch. "I'm guessing it didn't go well?"

Bri snorts. "He tripped and almost took Mister M down with him."

I gasp. "He didn't."

"He did!" June's half-cry half-laugh is muffled by the pillow she's smashed against.

"Change the subject," Ryder grumbles from the corner. He's sitting against the wall, boots kicked off, pressing an ice pack to his ankle.

Bri turns to me, eyes alight. "How was your lesson?"

"Oooh, yes!" June calls, throwing her legs over my lap and tossing the pillow back at Ivy. "Was he terrifying? Sarcastic? Menacing?"

"Not really." The words taste strange as they leave my mouth. Maybe it's because I'm not sure if it's a lie. He's undoubtedly terrifying, but not for the reason he should be.

I'm not scared of *him*. I'm scared of what his presence might bring.

27

THE EXECUTIONER

"Diagnostics at dawn, what could be more exciting than that?" June says, flopping onto the third of the six metal beds that line the back wall. Lance snaps his fingers at her, pointing further down the line with a scowl.

"Bay five, 219."

"But that one's cold!" she whines, folding her arms like a toddler.

"They're all cold," I correct, moving toward bay four. The techs crowd around me, connecting electrode pads to my temples and wiring my cuff to the monitor.

"Can we hurry this up?" Ryder rocks back on his heels, hands tucked in his pockets. "It's freezing in here."

June cackles. "Says the one in a giant coat."

"Enough." Lance cuts her off. "We have places to be."

Mister M strides in, pacing down the line as he recounts the same dry speech he always gives. "Clean diagnostics breed stability. Composure under stress is one of the most important skills one could wield. Stable girls are grateful for their chance to be here." He nods to the techs. "Proceed."

A female tech taps my shoulder. "Eyes forward." I barely have time to obey before the first shockwave crashes through me. Colors pulse behind my eyes in a familiar pattern. White. Red. Green. Blue. Repeat. Always that order. Always six times. When the gift of sight returns to me, I'm acutely aware of pod 5 filing in. An oddity, considering we're always paired with pod 8 for diagnostics.

Mister K's girls are younger than us. Louder. Always ready to pick fights with each other. Two are missing from the last time I saw them. The little redhead who was always crying, and the freckled girl who tripped June in the hall last month. Something strange in my stomach twists at the thought. Are they in "specialized reviews" too?

I've never considered where girls who get flagged go. You'd think they'd be sent home, but if our pasts are dreadful enough that we need to forget them, would we even be wanted back home? I catalogue the thought for later, unsure of who I could ask without sounding too curious.

I draw my gaze back to Mister K's girls. Three of them drop into their bays without a word, wrists up. The fourth lags. She's the smallest, with curly brown hair that usually bounces around her shoulders when she walks. There's nothing bouncy about her today. She drags her feet, inching forward as a pod enforcer with a ridged scar across his cheek shoves her along.

Another wave pulls me under. I suck in a deep breath, imagining my emotions in a tunnel like they taught us— long tunnels, pulling the feelings deeper and deeper until they can be buried in the dirt.

Minutes pass. More sensations. The taste of iron.

A buzzer booms from across the room. I pry my eyes open to find the small girl shaking, her cuff alternating from red to orange like a flame. Mister K is pacing, arguing with one of the techs.

"Do not call him. Don't you dare—"

Brielle gasps loudly beside me. "What's happening?"

"Eyes forward," the tech repeats. I exhale nervously, but obey. Images flood my vision next. Birds. Sky. Glass. Ballroom. Fire. Blood. It's always been the same images, some-times distorted or out of order, but never changing. The door swings open just as the last one fades.

Mister V slips urgently through the door. His ice blue eyes lock on me for a moment, then cut away. He moves to-ward the panicking girl, gaze fixed on the monitor. She's shaking harder now, tremors casting jagged spikes on every monitor.

"The sequence will reset," Mister V orders. "Focus."

"I can't," she cries. The test can't even reset before the alarms shriek again. She reaches for her mentor, who's pre-tending not to see her.

"Control it," Mister V snaps, urgent. "You're fine. Breathe."

The cuff shrieks, flaring red. She's hyperventilating now, wrists catching on the restraints with every motion. The whole bay rattles. One of the monitors cracks along the edges.

"She's going to get herself flagged." Brielle's whisper ripples through the chaos.

Panic runs like a current through my veins. My vision tunnels. *Stop looking. Breathe. Focus.*

She screams again, loud enough that even the lights overhead stutter, throwing us into darkness once. Twice. Ev-ery sound echoes off the tile in waves. Pressure builds in my ribs, too piercing to ignore. I can't watch what happens next.

"Stop!" I blurt before I can think. "You're scaring her—just *stop!*" The techs freeze for half a second; that's all it takes for my own pulse to trip dangerously. An electrode pad tears loose from my temple as I jerk forward. The shock catches me mid-breath; the world flashes white as pain sears across my skin. My cuff screams yellow.

The alarms surge again. It takes me a heartbeat too long to realize they aren't for her anymore. Sounds dig into my chest, biting like teeth.

"214!" someone barks.

Mister V's head whips toward me. "Stand down!"

Shock and fear rip through me like static fire. Monitors flash, everything grows unbearably hot. The strap across my chest tightens with each breath as the light on my cuff pulses faster. Yellow. Orange. Brighter. Hotter. Heat slicks down my spine. I can't think straight. I can't breathe. I can't—

"For god's sake," Mister M snaps, cutting across the noise as he rushes forward. "Eyes forward, 214." He plants himself beside my bay, voice clipped. "Don't move." Restraint rolls off his every syllable. His hand hovers near my wrist, not quite touching. Every muscle in his arm tenses.

"You're fine," he says, too fast. "You're fine, do you hear me? Breathe. Now."

I have to get it together. I can't get flagged. Not here, not now. I force a single, stuttering inhale. Then another that catches halfway. The cuff flickers orange, pulsing in warning.

"Again," he orders sharply, because command is the only language he speaks.

I do. Inhale. Exhale. Match the rhythm. Survive the emotion; survive the day. The monitor steadies. The color shifts from yellow to green. Only then does Mister M exhale.

I still feel like I'm drowning.

"Control re-established," a tech announces.

Mister V turns back to the girl. She's not screaming anymore; her breath comes in ragged pulls as she fights the restraints, every motion labored.

"Run it again," her mentor says, voice taut. "She was just nervous, if you—"

"I can't."

"She's not unstable! You can't just—"

"It's not my choice." Mister V presses two fingers to his temple, pressing his eyes shut for a single second. Then, he waves a hand. Two black-clad enforcers stride forward and take the girl by the arms, hauling her upright in one efficient motion.

"I'm sorry!" She's shouting now. "I'll do better. Please!"

She reaches for her mentor, still begging; Mister K turns away, fists clenched. The enforcers wrestle her out, leaving Mister V standing eerily over an empty bay, stylus hovering still over his tablet. He shakes his head as if reentering his skin, and exhales through his nose. "Carry on."

The machines whir back to life, and the cycle continues. Mister M smooths his jacket and falls back to his spot like nothing happened. But—just for a moment—I swear I see his fingers twitch against his sleeve.

The rest of diagnostics is silent. I keep my eyes on the wall until the tests end, pretending everything's fine. If I can't hear the bad thoughts, they aren't there. I'm still a good girl. I'm still going to graduate. I'm going to be fine.

Just fine.

When the monitors chime with completion, I thank the techs and wait to be dismissed. Instead, Mister M's shadow falls over my bay.

"You're coming with me." He doesn't wait for a response. His hand closes around my upper arm, firm enough to make it clear this isn't optional. The other girls watch on with wide eyes.

"Why?" I whisper, not really wanting the answer.

"Doctor Noxen wants a closer look," he says, words smoothed in a way that barely masks the strain beneath. "We can't have another...disruption."

I almost ask what that means, but his grip tightens just enough to answer.

"Don't make a scene, little star," he murmurs, leaning in close. "You've embarrassed me enough."

"She's yours," Mister M says as he shoves Noxen's office door open. I try to fight the tremor in my hands and fail miserably.

Doctor Noxen glances up. "Unstable?"

"Momentary lapse," Mister M replies. "Fix it."

Their eyes meet, two predators exchanging a problem.

Unfortunately, I'm the problem.

"Sit," Noxen says, still not looking at me. "Let's see what we're dealing with."

Mister M releases my arm harshly, slamming the door behind him. I cringe, rubbing the spot where his fingers burrowed into my skin. Left with no other choice, I lower myself into the chair, fighting to ignore the overpowering scent of citrus-coated metal. The restraints click shut on their own, just tight enough to serve as a reminder of my place. I keep my eyes on the floor until Noxen's form drifts into view.

"Elevated pulse, residual tremors, minor burns from feedback," he murmurs, scrolling on his tablet. "And of course, a tendency toward dramatics."

"I wasn't—"

"No need," he interrupts, gesturing to the monitors overhead. "The data speaks."

He nods to a tech wielding syringes like blades. My arm

is prepped and prodded without ceremony. Blood vials fill in slow, rhythmic pulls, darker than I'm used to. I don't ask what they're testing for; I'm not sure I want to know. I count them because counting is the only thing I can control. Five, all filled to the brim.

Don't think about the girl. Don't think about the heat. Don't think about the fact that everything is going wrong and all you can do is sit here and count.

"I had a dream," I blurt, desperate to escape my thoughts. Regret shivers down my spine, but relief burns my lungs. One less secret. That has to count for something.

Doctor Noxen looks up from his tablet, impatience painted across his face. "We discourage preoccupying dreams," he says. I ignore it.

"It was a hallway. White walls. Medical. I was wearing red, I think. There was someone with me."

"Vivid imaginations aren't uncommon among girls with your sedation resistance," he says calmly, but his face flashes with—interest? It's gone before I can fully identify it. "Your neural activity spikes when stimulated by poor resting habits. It's concerning, but nothing we can't correct."

Nerves bubble in my chest. "But it was—"

"Stable girls don't dream," Noxen interrupts. Which feels a little redundant, considering we aren't supposed to dream at all, stable or otherwise. He taps his stylus once. A nervous tic, or a warning. "I'll check the ratios again. Once the dosage is balanced, it will subside."

I'm not satisfied. My mouth opens again without permission. "I asked the person with me to not remember me in red."

Doctor Noxen folds his hands, unmoved. "Where are you going with this, 214?"

"Was I ever in that hallway?"

He tilts his head. "You've been in many hallways."

"That one felt real."

"Real and true are not the same," he replies. "You would be foolish to believe that dreams are anything more than nonsense."

"It didn't feel like nonsense."

"Hm." Noxen narrows his eyes. "Perhaps the dosage isn't the problem after all."

My heart skips. "Then what is?"

"You."

I fight the urge to throw up and collapse right here and now.

Thankfully, I don't get the chance.

Doctor Noxen dismisses me with a flick of his stylus. "You may return to your pod." I'm almost at the door when he adds, "And 214—do try not to make a scene next time. This visit could have gone very...differently if your mentor hadn't stepped in."

I force the door open and slip into the hall, wiping my damp palms on my skirt. Mister M is waiting in the corridor, back against the wall, eyes scanning his tablet like he'd rather be anywhere else.

"He said you're fine. That's a relief." His words sound like praise until I hear the tremor underneath. He masks it fast, face twisting into something darker, crueler. It fits him far better than concern ever could.

"You scared them," he adds, quieter now. "You scared *me*."

He steps closer, close enough that I can feel the tension radiating off him.

"Don't do that again," he murmurs. The warning isn't

loud, but it vibrates through me.

I hesitate.

His face darkens further. "Do you hear me? You don't get to make scenes. You don't get to embarrass me—and you certainly don't get to go around getting yourself flagged." He grabs my arm, yanking me until our chests are almost touching. Any remnants of concern are buried beneath his unwavering need to terrify me. "Do you understand?"

I nod meekly, planting my feet so he can't trip me.

"Say it."

"I understand." It sounds like I'm choking, but he nods like it's close enough.

"Good." He straightens, smoothing the crease of his sleeve as if nothing happened. "You're due in lectures. Keep your posture. Eyes forward." He walks ahead before I can answer. I try to follow, but my heel catches on an uneven seam in the tile. I gasp on instinct, arms flailing as I fight for my balance.

Mister M turns, annoyed. "God, 214." He grabs my arm again, dragging me down the hall with more strength than a man like him should wield. "Stop shaking. You're safe."

I stumble into step beside him, trying to remember when I stopped believing that.

28

PRECISION ERROR

I would trade anything for a jacket right now. The posture studio is so much colder than the rest of the training wing, both in sparsity and temperature. It's equipped with slick white floors that show every speck of dust. Floor-to-ceiling mirrors frame the front wall, warped just enough to make me feel a little too small. A posture tracking harness clings across my shoulders, spine, and hips.

TURN AND FLOW DRILL: MOVEMENT SEQUENCE FOUR

The system announces.

BEGIN

My breath stalls a moment too long before my body remembers it's supposed to be moving. Three steps forward. Pivot. One arm raised to shoulder height. Step back. Curtsy. Reset.

Every motion is timed to the metronome pulsing through the harness. We're focusing on rhythm today, which means no music. V said it'd be good for me. More "practical." It's been less than an hour, and I can "practically" say I hate it. The silence nips at me, shifting the sequence in my head even though I've done it a dozen times today. I move into the half-turn, my left foot dragging a beat behind. My whole body tenses for a split second.

That's all it takes.

The harness tightens. The sensor by the mirrored wall flashes red.

ERROR: SEQUENCE VARIANCE FLAGGED.

My breath catches. Great. My second day of private instruction and I'm already proving I'm not worth the effort. Behind the observation glass, Mister V closes his folder.

He stands, and I have no idea what to expect.

Footsteps echo across the vinyl floor as he enters the studio. His expression is unreadable, hands tucked carefully behind his back. He stops just short of the red sensor, still proclaiming my failure with its vicious glow. Without missing a beat, he lifts the tablet from its dock. Swipes up. The logs bloom to life on the screen: timing, posture variance, and of course, the deviation count flagging my mistake.

"You missed the half-turn," he says mildly.

"I know."

"Late by half a second. Tension in—"

"I know!"

He watches me for a long moment, the blue of his irises hardening like fresh ice. He taps the tablet once. The red light vanishes as the error log disappears completely.

Just like that, it's gone.

"Why did you do that?" I ask, too quickly to stop myself. He doesn't answer right away, still studying me like I'm a problem to be solved.

"Because the official report says you were perfect."

"But I wasn't," I correct, biting my lip.

V gives me a measured look. "No, you weren't."

"That's not something a mentor would do," I whisper. His eyes flick down to the cleared screen, then back to me.

"Isn't it?"

I shake my head, slow. "You're not a mentor." He raises a brow as if he's waiting for me to continue. The pieces click together painfully slow. "You're the hound."

"Is that what they're calling me now?"

A faint smile tugs at the corners of his lips. He sets the tablet back on its dock, not waiting for me to respond.

"Fitting." V steps forward, taking his time to carefully reset the harness on my shoulders. "Take a deep breath and start again." He moves toward the observation door, hands behind his back once more.

At the threshold, he offers me one last glance, eyes set in a flash of icy determination. "Don't make me fix it twice."

In the sixteen days following, he fixes it far more than twice. V covers every slip, trip, and stumble without a word. My mistake-avoidance count is off the charts these days.

I keep thinking it's because he has to prove something to Carr, but as an "analyst," wouldn't he want to point out my failures instead of covering them up?

I try to appreciate his intervention. To tell myself it's fine to accept his help as it's offered. I don't have another choice, anyway. In fact, intervention may be an understatement at this point. Mister V never seems far. He drops in on my lectures. Reviews all my workbook reflections. And lately, he's been attending our group review blocks, to Mister M's obvious displeasure.

Today is no different. It's our pod's turn for drills review with the designated instructor, a tall, brawny man with the coolest mustache I've ever seen. He barks the sequences one by one, quick to correct if we falter even a fraction.

Mister V stands along the back wall near the enforcers, arms folded, singling me out without saying a single word. The light in this room is so bright that I get a clear look at his hair for the first time. It's not black, at least not entirely. It's the darkest shade of brown, deep and rich. The realization nearly throws me off balance, but I manage to correct quickly enough that the posture harness doesn't notice.

Next sequence, Ivy pivots the wrong way, just enough to confuse my feet. The room freezes around me as I trip forward, knocking into her and tripping both our sensors red.

ERROR: SEQUENCE VARIANCE FLAGGED

The system calls it twice, distorting and overlapping. The instructor steps forward to submit the log, but V clears his throat. "216 was out of spacing. The error should be marked as such."

He's blaming my fall on Ivy?

That's impossible. There's no way the instructor is going to agree.

Mustache-man presses his lips together. "That's three strikes, 216. I'll be seeing you for review block this week, and Rook will want to review your behavioral profile."

I was wrong.

Flagged. She's getting flagged. For my mistake.

Ivy sighs, like this is all some minor inconvenience. But her left eye twitches as she retakes her mark. June's gaze is snapping all around the room, confusion and pity etched on her features as she tries to work out what just happened.

I clench my jaw, trying and failing to force down the guilt climbing up my throat. A mistake on my record would burn, sure. But it wouldn't have cost me. Not the way it will cost Ivy.

29

YOU'RE SPECIAL

"We have art today," Bri grumbles, flipping through her workbook. "But I'm guessing you'll be missing it?"

"Again," Ivy murmurs, her voice hardly audible from where she's splayed out on the floor.

"I don't know," I admit quietly, twisting the cap of my chewed pen so I don't have to look at them.

We're sitting in an abandoned classroom, doing busy-work until Mister M decides to grace us with his company again. If this were any other day, it'd be a blessing to have some time without him. Today? Things feel different. There's a noticeable chill in the air, a shift you'd only be able to see if you knew our pod. We aren't supposed to be tense or stressed when it's just us.

"Don't know," June echoes, clicking her tongue. "You have private lessons every day, sometimes twice." She pretends to count on her fingers. "Colt may say we're bad at math, but I feel pretty good saying you'll be missing art again."

I battle back the unease that's currently laying cinderblocks along my spine. I'm used to June being mad; she gets mad about pretty much everything. But not at me. The girls in my pod are like my sisters, ones I've known for my entire renewed life. We have an unspoken pact, a closeness. Sure, we squabble plenty. But we don't...fight, or whatever this is.

I let my voice soften into something that's hopefully unthreatening. "Yeah, I guess you're right."

"I guess," June says, rolling her eyes.

"You're mad at me?" I didn't mean for it to sound like a question.

Genuine shock washes over her features. Frustration replaces it. "Yeah, Maysie. I am." Her fist clenches. "I'm happy for you, or whatever. But I think I can speak for everyone when I say what happened today was absurd." She looks to Brielle, who bites her lip.

My apology slips automatically. "I'm sorry. You know that I didn't—"

"Apologize to Ivy," June bites out.

I open my mouth to tell her that I did, but a sharp pang of guilt strikes me down because I *hadn't*. I bow my head to Ivy, fighting back the tears that want nothing more than to well up and humiliate me further.

"I'm so sorry, Ivy. I didn't—"

"I'm used to it," Ivy calls from the ground, which does nothing for my guilt.

June starts flipping through her etiquette textbook wildly, marking random pages with flourishes of red. I cringe, both at the severity of the color and the fact that she'll be in a world of trouble if someone finds her defacing it.

"We're supposed to be in chapter—"

"You're starting to sound like Avery," she snaps, bitter, "and we all know what happened to her."

Bri puts her hand on June's shoulder. "June, that's not—"

June shrugs her off. "No. I'm not going to apologize when it's true."

"You think I enjoy this?"

Ivy rolls her eyes. "I do."

June points at her. "Even Ivy sees it! And oh, by the way, yes. I do think you enjoy it. Who wouldn't enjoy getting daily private lessons or having their mistakes covered up for no reason at all. I bet you enjoy every single second you don't have to spend rotting here with the rest of us." She throws her arms out wide, looking positively exasperated. "Admit it!"

"No!" I stand. "That's not fair. You know I have no control over any of this!"

June's eyes widen. Bri gasps. My chest burns with the gross realization that they didn't think I'd defend myself.

My heartbeat spikes. I want to scream at her that no, I absolutely don't want this. I want nothing more than to be normal. I wish I were still the girl Mister M loved to call boring and passable. I wish I could reach out and shake her until she understands what V's presence means for me. I'm not some little flower getting extra help because the organization is just so infatuated with me.

No.

Something is wrong with me. I'm different. So different that they feel the need to assign me to the man Mister M called "The Executioner." Correction: call doesn't do it justice. It's not a playful taunt or silly nickname. He is just as the name indicates, an executioner. A man that even mentors fear because he can end a girl's time in the program with nothing more than a snap of his gloved fingers.

But they don't see that. Even after what we saw in diagnostics. All they see is a girl getting advantages handed to her for no reason.

Something like guilt flares in my chest. I know it's unfair. I know she has every right to be upset. I just wish she wasn't directing it at the only person who has no control over the matter.

June takes a step toward me, fury still clouding the jade of her irises. "That doesn't make it right."

I match her step. "What do you want me to do about it? You think I can just waltz into the boardroom and demand—"

"Break it up!" Ralston commands from the doorway, his gaze landing squarely on me. "Maysie, out."

June laughs bitterly. "Perfect timing. Enjoy your little vacation, May."

30

DON'T CORRECT ME

Colt is waiting for me outside, leaning against the wall across from the classroom like he's been there a while. He straightens when I step out, clipboard tucked precariously under his arm.

"Private instruction tonight," he says, offering me a little thumbs-up.

I roll my eyes. "Oh good. Because that always goes swimmingly."

He shrugs, falling into step beside me as we start down the corridor. "It's better than drills."

"Debatable." I keep my eyes down, watching the way his boots hit the tile. Normally, our walks are filled with random trivia, stupid jokes, or a vent about Ryder's inability to keep his bunk clean. Once, he even detailed a conspiracy about Doctor Rook secretly living in the vents and crawling around at night to spy on people. Tonight? It's quiet. I don't know how much he heard of what went down with the girls, but I can tell he knows something's off.

He tosses me a sidelong glance, face twisted with discomfort. "You okay?"

"Peachy."

"Doesn't look like it."

"Then stop looking," I snap, feeling instantly guilty. I'm not mad at him. I'm not mad at anyone, really. Well—I'm kind of mad at Mister V. And Mister M. And Doctor Noxen.

Now that I think about it, I do have quite the laundry list of people to be angry with, but Colt isn't one of them.

He sighs under his breath but doesn't push. For a while, it's just the two of us and the echo of our steps. The practice suites are on the other side of this floor, and he doesn't seem to be in a particular hurry.

We pass the row of glassed-in display cases of shined plaques and trophies I'll never touch. Proof of the program's accomplishments and all the girls who came before us. Their faces have been scrubbed from memory, leaving nothing but their obedience etched into the metal.

We span another stretch before I can't take the quiet anymore. "Do you like your job?"

He falters like he wasn't expecting that one. "Like's a big word."

"Okay. Do you hate it?"

"That's a different big word." He scratches the back of his neck. "Some days I'm glad I'm here."

"And the other days?"

"The other days, I'm still here." He shrugs. I don't know what to do with that, so I don't say anything else. We stop outside the practice suite. Colt reaches for the handle, then hesitates.

"You want me to stall?" he asks quietly.

"Would it help?"

"Probably not."

"Then don't."

He opens the door and ushers me in. Mister V, king of timeliness, is already inside, flimsy notebook in hand. He doesn't look up, just flicks his fingers toward Colt in wordless dismissal. The door shuts with a muted click, leaving us alone.

I drop onto the bench harder than I mean to, hands flattening against the keys in a sour burst of sound.

"Rough day?" V asks mildly.

"What do you think?"

He studies me from across the room, still as ever, pen poised above the page. I can't stand the silence, the way it feels like he's waiting for me to reveal myself.

"You can't keep doing it," I snap before I can stop myself.

"Doing what?"

"Covering for me. Fixing things." I strike a single note, a loud G. "Every time you do, it just makes them hate me more."

"They don't hate you."

"No?" I slam another note. "Then why are they treating me like this?"

His pen doesn't move. "If you want answers, Maysie, ask me something I can actually give you."

I huff a humorless laugh. "Fine. What happened to the girl you flagged? The one from diagnostics."

His gaze doesn't falter, but his jaw ticks. "I can't disclose other subjects' information."

"Of course you can't." I press another key, holding it until it sours. "Fine. How long have I been here?"

"In the advancement program?"

"Yes."

He taps his pen like he's counting. "Two hundred twenty days, give or take."

The number rocks me. It feels like too many and not enough all at once. "It doesn't feel like two hundred days."

"It's not supposed to."

My mouth runs dry. "When will I get to leave?"

His expression doesn't shift. "Ask me something I can answer."

"That is something you can answer."

"Not in the way you want."

I grip the edge of the bench. "Fine. Do you ever regret it?"

"Regret what?"

"Coming here. Becoming this…" I wave a hand at the room, his tablet, the cameras overhead. "Whatever this is."

Silence. The pause sits for long enough that I'm starting to worry I've offended him. My stomach cinches, but I don't backtrack.

Finally, he blows out a slow breath. "Ask me something else."

The only question that comes to mind feels silly as it escapes my lips. "How old am I?" It shouldn't matter, but it feels wrong not knowing.

His gaze lifts to mine, startled. "You're seventeen."

"They said I was sixteen at intake," I start, half-lying. "But I guess I'm seventeen now." It's not that I don't believe him; it just doesn't feel possible. Seventeen years of a life I can't remember living. Two hundred and twenty days of being told that's somehow a good thing. A foreign burst of anger takes root in my chest. "Funny how I know the number, but not the year. Not the day. Not a single piece of any of it besides 'seventeen.'" I brush some non-existent dust off my skirt to keep my hands from shaking. "It doesn't seem fair."

The silence is jagged. He shuts the notebook slowly, setting it aside and leveling me with a long look.

"You're seventeen, Maysie. It isn't fair, but I can't give you back the time they've already taken."

The brutal honesty of it sends my head reeling. I want to beg him to tell me more—to ask why he won't do anything about it if he honestly thinks it's unfair. Instead, I press my hands back to the keys. The notes come out uneven, fingers weighed down by by my warring emotions.

"I know all this is a lot," he says after a moment. "I'm trying to make things easier."

"Then stop trying to protect me," I whisper. "If you really want to help me, then stop making it worse."

V leans back in his chair, resigned. His stormy blue eyes roam over my face, assessing me like he's deciding if it's worth the effort to argue.

"Please," I add, faltering.

His face falls, and he sighs. "Fine."

I offer a small nod, wishing away the pit in my stomach. I don't need his help. I just need to stop making the kind of mistakes that need saving in the first place.

31

CAREFUL WHAT YOU WISH FOR

I normally don't mind group review block, but today's is rife with dread. It's not a formal evaluation, but Doctor Carr is here, trailed by a team of scalpel-ready specialists who look eager to do more than just observe.

Mister M is running us through the movement sequences. He doesn't bother taking notes, not unless we make a mistake. V is here too, presumably to monitor me. He lingers near the door, arms folded, face passive. A spectator, nothing more.

I'm halfway through movement sequence ten when I lose the rhythm. A stutter in my footwork. Not catastrophic, but obvious. Enough to draw eyes, enough to ruin the performance. I hold still for half a second, concentrating on nothing but my shallow breathing. I wait for the override, for the quiet voice that always cuts in when I mess up. When things "glitch."

I wait for him.

But V doesn't move. His eyes flick to mine briefly; his thumb brushes along his cuff in a gentle cue. *Breath reset.* Then it's gone. His head dips, studying the floor.

"How embarrassing," Mister M scoffs, flashing me a sick grin. I suck in a breath, in for four, out for eight, just like V taught me. It centers me, but heat still prickles my skin like a simmering flame. I finish the sequence, slower now. My pulse pounds in my ears, so loud I can't hear the rhythm, but I keep my chin up.

Carr regards me with a cold stare. "Noted." My cuff pulses hard against my wrist, flashing orange. Mister M ignores me, snapping an order to start another drill.

V never speaks. He doesn't lift his eyes from the ground for the rest of the session.

Catastrophic mistakes face-planted into: one.

Meanwhile, I complete every other sequence, hitting every mark with my head held high. It won't matter, though. No one remembers when I succeed.

Only when I fail.

32

CONSEQUENCES

I don't cry.

Not when I receive the summons during dinner. Not when Lance and Ralston drag me out of evening lectures in front of everyone. And certainly not when I'm dropped on the ground in Doctor Carr's exam room like trash. My knees slam on the pristine tiles, metallic scent flooding my senses instantly. I cough, stifling the scream I'd much rather be emitting.

"Why do you think you're here?" Carr asks, not looking up from his notes. I keep my mouth shut. I don't have an answer that won't make things worse.

There's always a right answer, but it isn't always an honest one.

I cast my eyes toward Mister M, who looks painfully amused, tapping his leg in a cadence that is eerily similar to the rhythm I stumbled over earlier.

"Don't look at me, little star." He wags a finger at me. "This is all your own doing."

Carr stands. He opens a drawer and retrieves a silver tray. Two vials. One syringe. A long metal rod I don't recognize. I've been poked, prodded, injected, sedated, sliced open and stitched back together, but I've never seen a device like that.

"Sequence ten," he says plainly. "Complete lapse in form. Two missteps. One extended pause. A slip-up like that in front of the board would have been devastating."

"I fixed it—"

"You broke immersion," Carr interrupts. "You reminded me you were human."

He says it like it's a crime. Like the only thing they can't seem to control is the very thing wrong with me.

If that's true, maybe I deserve the punishment.

"I am human."

"You'll feel better once we've corrected that."

He crosses the room, motioning me to the exam table. I move on shaky legs—not fast enough. Lance is on me in a second, depositing me on the table like I weigh nothing. Two med techs buzz around me, falling into a routine they've no doubt done countless times. Containment cuffs on, restraints fastened, sleeves rolled. In seconds, my legs are immobile.

"This won't take long." Doctor Carr flips my arm roughly, positioning the needle over my already scarred skin. Ghosts of past bruises color the crook of my elbow.

The sedative is darker than usual, almost gray. It burns like a line of fire when it enters my bloodstream. It's quick. Efficient.

Awful.

I sputter; the room goes sideways. Everything goes dark even though my retinas are blinded by the surgical lights above. I buck against the restraints. Someone—Mister M—I think, grips my shoulders, forcing me back on the bed. He runs a hand along my cheek, too gentle for the motion to belong to him. He laughs softly, moving to trace the scar at my temple.

"Don't worry, little star, we'll put you back together again."

My blood ices over. A thick static floods the room, warping and contorting everything until I can't tell what's real anymore. I wait, but the welcome embrace of sedation doesn't come. My vision doubles, triples, spins. But I don't pass out.

I don't pass out.

Maybe I'm not supposed to.

My body convulses violently, then locks. I can't move.

I can't scream.

I can't even blink.

Oh my god.

"Paralytic engaged," Carr murmurs, dropping my arm to the bed. "Subject appears to be conscious." He turns back to the table, and I think I can almost see him grabbing the second vial in my periphery. Or maybe he's not moving. Maybe nothing's moving.

I can feel everything. The light still burns my now unfocused, unblinking eyes. My fingernails are frozen, permanently dug into my palms deep enough to draw blood. Pain seems to be the only thing the drug hasn't drowned out. That and Mister M's hot breath against my neck as he looms over me.

"She's conscious, all right." Mister M runs his hand along my cheek again. "I can see it. She's trying not to cry." He laughs. It's light, as if this form of torture is a delight to him. Carr ignores him, pressing the metal rod to the base of my neck.

The world explodes behind my eyes.

Fireworks. A million colors surge wildly in my skull, leaving nothing but pain and chaos in their wake. Memories flicker, stretch, distort, and vanish too quickly to digest. Glass raining down, distant laughing, a uniform stained red, the metallic taste of iron, flowers in a garden.

Nothing.

Everything slips away.

I don't know how long it lasted. I don't know what he stripped from me. I don't remember when Mister M left. All I know is by the time it's over, I can't tell where the pain ends and I begin.

The paralytic wears off like thawing ice, returning me to my body in drips. When Doctor Carr finally dismisses the techs, I feel like I could sleep for a century and still wake up exhausted.

Carr unhooks the monitors one by one, coiling their cords and setting them gently on the trays, as if neatness could pass for mercy after what he's done. "Poise," he says low, soothing like a lullaby.

The monitors stutter and die as he peels the electrodes from my temples. "Obedience."

I watch in my periphery as he lifts my limp arm, sliding the containment cuff off and replacing it with my daytime monitor. "Purpose." It clicks shut around my wrist; a sound without sensation.

"Three words," he murmurs. "That's all it takes to make the chaos stop. The body forgets pain when it remembers purpose."

The pain isn't gone.

His thumb drags along the recalibration scar at my temple, slow and deliberate, pressing just hard enough to pierce the haze still coating my senses.

"You were made to be perfect, 214. To be calm. To be

obedient. To show the world what beauty looks like when it's controlled."

I try to sort the words in my brain, but they muddle, dissolving into vapor.

Doctor Carr studies the steadiness of my pulse, the tremorless still of my fingers. "All better," he says softly, running a gloved hand along my cheek, brushing away the streak of blood near my mouth. "You truly are one of my finest works."

My throat tightens around the breath still locked in my chest.

Carr straightens, smoothing his sleeve. "Poise. Obedience. Purpose. You'll remember now, won't you?"

The mantra works its way under my skin, words stark against the blur he's made of my thoughts. My head simmers, slowly melting away everything beyond the three words I've been taught to live by.

My eyes fix on the steel panel that makes up the ceiling.

In it, I see me.

At least, what *should* be me.

The girl in the reflection is hardly familiar: blood on her teeth, bruises beneath her eyes, irises dulled from months in shadow, even though it couldn't have lasted more than a handful of hours. Enforcers move to wheel me out; I can't bring myself to look at them. I keep my eyes on the girl above, wondering if she could truly be me.

"Sleep now, 214," Doctor Carr says, smoothing my hair back. "The world's a kinder place when you stop fighting it."

The sting of the lie is the last thing I remember as I plunge into darkness.

33

RESIDUALS

I don't remember how I got to my private instruction block.

We're running sequence three—I think. Measured steps, breath control, balance. Easy. I could do it sedated. *I've done it sedated.* But my bones don't move the way I desperately need them to. I reset, taking the mark with slurred steps. This time, my vision doubles, causing a slip that slams me into the mirrored wall. It reverberates, cracking something wide inside me. I push myself up so fast my head spins.

"I'm sorry," I say quickly, stepping back to the line. "I'm fine."

V doesn't respond at first, but I can feel his eyes on me. He closes the folder in his hand and strides forward. "You're not fine."

Obviously.

"I just need to run it again—"

"You've run it six times already. You're stumbling. Your timing's erratic. Your fists are clenching." I look down. He's right. My fists are drawn so tight that my fingers don't feel like they're connected to anything.

"I can't focus," I whisper. "Everything's itchy and too loud. I feel like I'm watching myself from outside. Like I'm not actually in my body."

V nods. "Residuals."

"That's what you call them?"

"That's what they call them." His voice is flat as he steps

closer and reaches for my wrist. When I flinch, he stops. "Carr's blend was too aggressive."

"Did you know?" I slur. Vertigo seizes my sight again.

"What?"

"What he was going to do to me?"

"No." His answer is immediate, honest. "If I had, I would've intervened sooner." The lights overhead buzz too loud. The mirror warps in my periphery. My hands twitch again as the tingling sensation intensifies.

The part I've been too horrified to admit tumbles out. "I was awake."

V's grip tightens on the folder. "What?"

"I heard them. Doctor Carr. Mister M. I couldn't move... but I felt all of it."

His eyes widen, genuine shock floods his features before he can mask it.

"I waited for you," I whisper. His jaw tightens, but I don't stop. "I thought maybe you'd come. That if I held out long enough—"

"I didn't know."

"You always know," I snap. "You see everything. You know everything. I can't even flinch without it ending up in your notes."

He doesn't argue.

That tells me all I need to know.

"I thought I was dying," I whisper.

He steps closer, hand outstretched. I back away too fast. My foot catches, sending me tumbling backward. I throw my hands back to catch myself, but there's nothing. I crash into the mirrored wall again, shaking like a leaf.

"I can't feel my arms," I gasp. "They're not working. I don't—" My stomach flips. I double over and vomit onto the floor. It's loud. Violent. I'm choking and crying and shaking all at once. My knees buckle. My hands hit the tile, numb and utterly useless. V catches my shoulders before I slam face-first. His grip is strong and fast, anchoring me. My breath comes in ragged pulls as I cling to him.

"I thought you'd come." My voice is a wreck. "I thought you'd stop them."

"I should've been there," he says, hoarse. Unfiltered devastation lingers on his face.

"I'm not okay," I heave.

"I know." He presses his hand against my back, breathing hard.

"I can't feel anything."

"I know." He steadies me. Lifts me up carefully. "You're not practicing today. You're going back to your room."

"I can't—"

"You can. I'll file the override for you." He helps me to the hallway, hand shaking against my back. His grip is feather-light, like he's scared the slightest touch will snap me in half.

It might.

I make it seven staggering steps, just far enough to breach the hall, then the floor disappears.

Colt pushes off the wall, grabbing me before I hit the ground. "Hey! Maysie. Shit—hey. Stay with me." His voice is close, panicked. I can't answer. My head lolls. My eyes flutter. He gathers me up like I'm weightless and starts back toward our pod…or medical. I don't know my way very well, and I can't really see. Somewhere behind us, I think I hear V.

He's still apologizing as we turn the corner. I don't get the chance to tell him that it's okay.

Mostly because it's very much not.

34

WORTHY OF TRYING

I prod at my half-eaten muffin, searching for more chocolate chips. It's the only thing they're good for when they've grown this stale.

It's evaluation day again, and this time, I'll actually be worthy of trying. Four long weeks of working almost exclusively with V have left me exhausted, but I just have to manage for today.

Since the whole "residuals" incident nine days ago, I've mostly been left alone. V's been trying to make it up to me, in his own way. He pulls me from classes often, pushing my training until I can hardly stand. Then he offers breaks, helps me through my workbook, or lets me play whatever I want on the piano. It's hard to thank him after everything, but I can't deny it's been helpful.

The breakfast table is quiet, as is most of my life nowadays. Not much to talk about, I suppose. We used to dream about graduation, the world outside, freedom. Now I consider myself lucky if any of the other girls even give me the time of day. The realization of it stings. Hope is a slippery, fragile thing, and sometimes I'm not sure I have the strength to keep holding onto it.

I don't have the luxury of worrying about the future anymore. I just have to perform today.

Brielle taps my shoulder hesitantly, fingers hovering a beat too long.

"May?" Her voice is meek, eyes downcast on her bowl as she pushes around something that claims to be yogurt.

"Hm?" I try to sound light, but my cords sound strained after the four hours of torture that V disguised as eloquence training yesterday.

"Are you nervous?"

"A little," I confess, underselling it.

"Yeah, me too." She offers me a small smile. "I thought about playing sick if we're being honest."

"Not a bad idea. Is it too late to try that?"

Before she can respond, Mister M clears his throat from the head of the table, ready to kill the mood. I've barely spoken with him these past few weeks. He only makes the effort to pay attention to me when I've done something wrong. Granted, about everything I do is wrong in his eyes. He sends a spine-stiffening smile my way, sickly fake. So very him.

"Brielle, 214, do you have something you'd like to share with the table?" I cringe at the use of my number. I can't quite remember when he decided I wasn't even worth the name he gave me himself.

"No, sir." Bri's apology is quick. She shifts in her seat, biting her bottom lip. I nod in agreement, not averting my eyes from his.

The sneer he sends back is small, as if it were only meant to be seen by me. By design, I'm sure, the dining room is too crowded for him to break character.

"Then stop prattling. It's unbecoming and horribly irritating." His hands grip the table, knuckles whitening. "Besides, you have nothing to talk about. Or have you forgotten what today is?"

We shake our heads slowly, as does Ivy. She hasn't spoken a word all week, at least not while I was around, which thankfully isn't much. I used to dread the attention I would get when V pulled me away from social blocks or enrichment. I felt like I was missing out on everything. Turns out all I was missing was the slow, painful unraveling of our collective sanity.

"Good." Mister M releases the table, holding his crystal glass up to his lips. He takes a long, drawn-out sip before meeting my eyes again. "You don't want to find out what happens if you step out of line. Do you, 214?" His gaze is fierce, but I hold it anyway.

"No, sir. I look forward to making you proud." I plaster on a pretty smile that he clearly despises.

"I find that hard to believe."

"I don't." V approaches, tablet clutched in one hand. *I swear this man materializes from the shadows.* He looks immaculate today, not a single strand of dark hair out of place, pants perfectly pressed, tie perfectly set. He's the picture of a perfect mentor. *Something he's not.*

"Pardon?" There isn't enough fabric in this facility to veil the threat behind Mister M's words.

"I don't believe I need to repeat myself," V says, perfectly calm.

"You're looking awfully sharp for someone who wasn't invited to the festivities," Mister M sneers, shoulders raising in amusement.

"Funny you should say that," V retorts, a careful grin gracing his face. "I'll be escorting Maysie today." He gestures for me. I shift to stand, my muffin discarded on the table. But a rage-filled glare from Mister M keeps me planted in my seat.

"I don't believe I called for the hound," Mister M

seethes through gritted teeth. "Perhaps you should stop sniffing around where you don't belong."

"You flatter me." V's tone suggests otherwise. He removes a note from his pocket, tossing it Mister M's way. "Carr's orders. Surely you understand?" Mister M grabs the note, unfurls it, then simply tosses it onto my plate.

"You really are a dog." He waves me off. "You'd better hope 214 performs perfectly today. I'd hate to see what Carr does to a hound that can't fetch."

The slightest clench of V's fist tells me the comment struck too close—and that he can't afford to show it.

I'm on my feet before I decide to be. June narrows her eyes, and I immediately hate myself for how quickly I ran to V's side like a coward. He settles a hand on the small of my back, guiding me out without so much as a glance.

"Where are we going?" We hang a left at the enrichment hall past the piano rooms, the posture studio, and everywhere else I thought we might be headed. V's quick, weaving through the halls like he could navigate them blindfolded.

"The board values presentation," he says simply. We hang another right, and it clicks. *The dressing rooms.* I think of the fine dresses the other girls were wearing. Uniform standard, yet vibrant and pretty. I wasn't brought anything else to wear.

Shocker.

The worn regulation white dress I've been wearing for three days straight is starting to fall apart at the seams. I did everything I could for it—I even scrubbed it in the bathroom sink this morning, but it's far from finery.

We stop short of the only open door down the stretch. The room is incredibly small, just a full-length mirror and a small chair with a lavender dress draped over it.

"I have an errand to run. Get changed quickly, I'll send an attendant to fix your hair." He slips through the door, letting it fall shut.

Sensing his urgency, I make quick work of changing, taking a moment to admire the short satin dress he selected for me. It's uniform standard, but polished. Not too flashy, not too boring.

I zip the side, reveling in how blissful it is to wear something clean. The attendant arrives shortly after, arranging my hair in an up-do that's elegant yet soft, with ringlets that frame my face. I wait until I'm sure she's gone to peek at the mirror. A challenge, considering it frames most of the back wall.

Sure enough, it's perfect.

I hate the smile that falls over my face. I'm comfortable, and that's a danger I can't afford today.

Frustration builds behind my eyes as my emotions twist. I ball my fist, grounding myself before I do something I can't undo. I'm eager and terrified by the opportunity I have no choice but to want.

If this is what being chosen feels like, I'm not sure I'd survive what happens when I'm not.

35

NO REST FOR THE WEARY

I take my place on the line. I'm last, which feels so incredibly fitting.

Carr hasn't arrived yet. A blessing, truly. One that will certainly be short-lived. The exam room itself isn't a surprise, thankfully, since V snuck me by a few days ago to preview the space. He claimed it wasn't cheating since the other girls had evaluations before, which was a good enough answer for me. The pristine white tile is colder than it appeared, and the mirrored walls are significantly more disturbing now that I'm actually in front of them.

I don't make eye contact with the men seated around the semi-circular table, opting to gaze just above. Chin up, soft smile. The picture of a pretty, pliant girl, exactly what they want to see.

I count them out of habit. Five in my periphery. Two are instructors; I'm not too sure about the others. They look important, and worse, impatient. V lingers near the door, hands clasped behind his back, face carefully blank. He doesn't flinch. I'm not even sure he's breathing.

A ghost. Fitting.

Carr enters, needing no introduction. He's dressed in a pressed white lab coat, clipboard tucked under one arm, pen uncapped and ready. He takes his place in the center, with Mister M trailing close behind. He looks tired, but present. Arms crossed, shoulders tense. Doctor Carr turns his back on us, facing the table.

"Gentlemen. Thank you for taking the time to be here today." They all nod ceremoniously. My eyes land on V once more, but he doesn't so much as twitch.

"Let's begin, shall we?" Carr strides to the front of the line, his face eerily unreadable. "Juniper, designation 219. Movement sequence six."

"Yes, sir." June's shaky, not a strong start. Sequence six is one of the simplest drills, a few steps, a curtsy, and a pivot turn. But she falters, almost falling face-first.

"Balance is off. Try again," he orders. She does. It's better, but not perfect. No one claps when she finishes, and I see the slightest downturn of her lips when she realizes there's nothing to celebrate.

"Brielle, designation 212. Social aptitude, script 4."

Bri begins reciting, but her words are over-rehearsed. Skipped phrases here and there, even a few beats of silence. She laughs nervously at the end. Carr shakes his head, scribbling more notes furiously in the margins.

"Ivy, designation 216. Movement sequence two." Ivy doesn't react. In fact, she's as still as the dead. Staring at the wall like it's moments away from sucking her up. "216," Carr repeats, less patient now. Her head turns slowly, methodically as she studies him.

"I don't know that one," she says quietly, eyes fluttering like she's struggling to hold them open.

"Shame. We can discuss it in my office later." He snaps his fingers at Lance and Ralston.

"Take her downstairs, please," Carr orders. Ralston's eyes flash with pity, but he obeys. Loud boots click against the tile floor as the enforcers charge forward, hauling her out before she has the chance to protest. Though I'm not sure she would've. My stomach drops at how easily she accepts her fate.

Juniper looks like she's about to vomit. I don't acknowledge it, keeping my eyes trained forward. Under the polish, my chest constricts so tight I'm not sure I'm breathing.

"She's slipping," Doctor Carr states, not a question.

"Ivy was just nervous," Mister M offers quickly.

"There's no excuse for that, and you know it."

"Of course," Mister M concedes. It may be the first time he's ever sounded small.

"214. Movement sequence eight." He gave me the hardest one. *Figures.*

I take a step forward, smile wide, but not too wide. Chin up. I try to picture the harness from the posture studio. My chest stays lifted as I curtsy to the panel. I hit every angle, every step, every turn. Graceful. Precise. Perfection. Or at least something close. Doctor Carr nods, just once.

"214?" *He's going off script.*

"Yes, sir?" I respond, cautiously level. My heart pounds in my ears. He didn't stop to ask anyone else questions. My left hand betrays me, trembling. I tuck it behind me, holding painfully still. Masking it all with a graceful smile.

"What do you think of your position here?" Carr asks. Mister M doesn't miss a beat, tapping his pen twice against his clipboard.

The statement. The stupid gratitude statement. My mind stumbles, trying to sort the sentences. *I am grateful for the—I am corrected to be—no. Wait. Lucky? Lucky to be corrected.* Maybe? I don't know. I'm not feeling very lucky right now. I suck in a breath, resetting my posture to stall for time.

V's form catches at the corner of my eye. He brushes two fingers against his thigh. A cue. *His* cue. The phrase floods my brain so fast I could cry.

"I am grateful to reflect the program's excellence," I say, bowing my head. Mister M's jaw tenses.

"What is the purpose of excellence?" Carr asks. My first answer gave me confidence. This round, I don't need time to think.

"To reflect the integrity and objectives of the organization." I make a mental note to thank V for those extra lessons. Carr nods again.

"And whose integrity do you reflect?"

"My mentor's." No hesitation. *I might survive this.*

"Which one?" A trap. One I know the right answer to, even if it isn't *right*. My eyes flick to Mister M, who narrows his gaze. He knows exactly what corner I've been backed into.

"Mister M has overseen my progress," I state, clear and sweet. "But both have helped me immensely." It doesn't sound hesitant, but it feels like I'm swallowing glass. V's expression doesn't change, which at least tells me I haven't messed up royally.

"What do her progress notes reflect?" Carr asks. This question isn't for me.

"Average at best," Mister M states, sounding bored. "As far as—"

"I wasn't asking you," Carr snaps, turning to the back wall. V's shoulders tense for a moment, but he takes a small step away from the wall, reporting with ease.

"Remarkable. Near-perfect scores in posture, movement, and etiquette. Very gifted at piano. Known sedation resistance. No other irregularities to note." He offers me the smallest nod.

One of the members, a tall man with silver cufflinks,

raises a hand. "Piano?"

"Yes," V answers smoothly, like he practiced for this in the mirror. "Her aptitude scores place her in the top percentile. Top rank, to be specific." A murmur ripples down the line.

The man glances toward Carr. "Then why wasn't she included in the music rotation?"

Carr does not look pleased. "That roster was finalized during the previous evaluation."

"With lower scores than this?" the tall man presses. "The investors' ball is next month. They'll expect to see the strongest subjects."

"I'll see that it's amended," Carr says tightly. From the corner of my eye, I see Mister M's jaw tense.

"Excellent progress, 214. Let's hope it continues." I fight the urge to collapse into a puddle of triumph and pent-up anxiety. Catastrophic mistakes avoided: eighteen. *I'll take it.*

Carr pivots to address the group. "Girls, you're dismissed." We move for the door, holding our line, skirts swishing in sync.

"Ashford, stay a moment." Mister M's face pales. He runs a hand through his hair and turns back with a tight smile. Doctor Carr nods to V, who follows us out, shutting the door behind him.

The other girls are already halfway down the hall, whispering to each other. I want to follow, but for a moment all I can do is breathe. For the first time all day, I don't feel like I'm drowning.

V exhales slowly, like he, too, has been holding his breath since we stepped into that room.

"You did well," he says. The tension that usually coils

tight through his shoulders has slackened. His jaw is unclenched, his fists uncurled.

"You're not smiling," I murmur. "Should I be worried?" He huffs, a gentle sound that might be a laugh if he weren't exhausted.

"If I smiled every time you impressed me, they'd start to suspect something."

I blink, unsure of how I could possibly respond to that. "Impressed?" I muster, cocking my head with the laziest hint of a smile. He nods, meeting my eyes. For the first time in days, he *really* meets them.

"You weren't perfect. But you were undeniable." It's a compliment, somehow. We start down the corridor. I want to revel in the silence, but like always, I have too many questions.

"They didn't say my name," I whisper. "Just the number. They called Brielle by name. Juniper. Even Ivy."

"I know."

"Why?"

He hesitates, and I know there's something he doesn't want to tell me. He clicks his tongue. "Because your name's not in your file." I stop dead in my tracks. So does he.

"What?"

"I mean that literally, Maysie. Your official record lists your designation, 214, but the field for your name is redacted." My stomach knots.

Why?

"That can't be right. Even the new girls—"

"Have names," he finishes. "I know."

"So it was erased?"

"Maybe. Or it was never entered. Either way, someone made a choice." Something icy snakes down my spine. *I do not like the implications of that.*

A strange sense of unease settles in my chest. "Wait—then how'd you know my name?"

He gives a faint shrug. "You told me."

"No, I didn't."

"Are you sure?"

I shake my head. I'd know if I did. I open my mouth to say so, but he's quicker.

"I'm not them," he says softly. "I don't need your file to know who you are." The words knock the breath from my lungs. He takes a half-step back, like he knows he's said too much. "Get some rest. They'll be watching you closer now."

36

TRIUMPHANT

Two hours later, we're back in the common room. There's no fanfare, no relief, just the over-loud thrum of the vents and an unease that won't settle. Today was everything I wanted it to be. I showed Carr and the board. More importantly, I showed myself.

So why does it feel so wrong? I thought I'd feel unstoppable. Instead, I just feel hollow. Because while I flourished—

They fractured.

Brielle's cross-legged on the sofa, nervously tugging threads loose from her hem. Ivy turns a page she hasn't read. The cuff at her wrist glows a steady green that feels wrong. She was dropped off an hour ago, bandages wrapped on both wrists, black hair half-clipped back with pins she hasn't bothered to remove. June's sprawled on the rug, baring her teeth like she's daring the ceiling to collapse on her.

"Well, cheers to me!" she says. "Lowest score in the wing. Not that anyone's shocked. Bet Carr's already penciling in my funeral notes."

"Junie—" Brielle starts, but June cuts her off with a crazed laugh.

"No, really. You should've seen their faces when I almost ate the floor. Pure delight. Like 'oh good, another screwup, put her on the chopping block.'" She claps in mock applause. "I'm killing it."

"Don't talk like that," I whisper. She's been off since we left the evaluation room. She didn't crack any jokes at dinner or tease Brielle when she tripped over her shoes. She keeps staring at things that aren't there. Almost like—

No.

I don't let myself go there.

This is nothing like Avery.

June is fine.

She tilts her head, jade eyes glinting. "Why not? If they could take Avery, they could take any of us. Might as well be me."

A shiver runs down my spine. A stupid, hopeful part of me still tries to believe Avery is truly just in a specialized review, but my confidence shakes with each passing day. I worry my lip between my teeth, anxiety pinching at my skin. A question I'd never be allowed to ask surges behind my eyes. *If something happens to me, would anyone know?*

I tamp down my terror to focus on June. "Please, stop it," I whisper, reaching down for her hand.

She pulls away, lacing her fingers through her auburn curls and tugging until a strand snaps. "You think I haven't tried?" she chokes out. "I breathe and it's wrong. I stop and it's worse. What am I supposed to do when there's no way to win?"

The lights flicker overhead, stuttering back to pale blue. "I can't do this anymore," she tries to laugh, but it breaks into a sob halfway through. "I just can't."

The wave of emotion that floods the room sends my head reeling. Brielle curls tighter into herself, tears welling behind the cardigan sleeve she has pressed to her face. Ivy remains still. An unblinking, unfeeling version of herself. I'm not even sure the words are reaching her.

"It's okay," I coax. "Everything's going to work out. Graduation will be here before we know it, then we'll get to marry rich guys or something and never have to see Mister M again." The joke falls undeniably flat. I shudder at my own half-lie, wishing graduation didn't feel eons away.

She claps a hand over her eyes, then pulls it away like it burned her. "Yeah, right," she mutters with a sigh.

Ralston clears his throat from the doorway. He steps in with a clipboard tucked under one arm, a tray of syringes balanced in the other. Colt follows close behind, stiffer than usual, kicking the door shut with his boot.

"Early evening protocol," Ralston says, a little worse for wear. "Line up."

Brielle rises first, obedient, tucking her hair back and rolling her sleeve. Colt's already waiting, hand hovering near her elbow like he's preparing to guide her through glass. He murmurs something low—too soft for me to catch—as Ralston administers the injection.

Ivy stands next, wordless, rolling her sleeve in one clean motion. Colt doesn't touch her, but he doesn't look away either.

Then Juniper.

She takes her time standing, dragging her feet across the rug. "Tuck me in after, too?" she grumbles when she finally offers her arm.

"Quiet," Colt snaps, harsher than I've ever heard him. He grips her elbow harder than necessary, holding her steady until the needle's in. His jaw is tight, eyes on the cuff until it flashes back to green. Only then does he release her. Ralston places a steadying hand at June's back, guiding her toward her room.

My pulse is in my throat as Colt steps in front of me, the

brown of his eyes so pale, he almost doesn't look real. He pushes my sleeve up, fingers brushing too close to the cuff. The needle pricks. Cold races down my arm. My vision blurs, but it won't last. It never does.

"You okay?" My words are so soft they barely form. His eyes widen in surprise.

"No," he admits. "But it's fine. Try to rest, all right?" The honesty of it sends a chill down my spine. He grips tighter, thumb pressing against my elbow as the cuff hits green.

Ralston returns, tone clipped. "Rooms. Lights out."

One by one, we file to the back, shuffling into our glorified cages. I fall back onto my bed, trying to pinpoint where things started going wrong—

And deciding it must've been long before this place erased my identity and dared to call it salvation.

The sedation haze wavers within the hour, leaving me alone with my thoughts.

A truly dangerous thing.

I chance a quick glance to the camera on the wall, relieved to find it dormant. My hands twitch as I dig beneath my mattress, producing the forbidden book and slipping back under the covers. I haven't read it in weeks, but if I don't get out of my head soon, I'll drown in a sea of my own thoughts.

I flip through the pages, tracing the creatures with my fingers, savoring the paper's roughness against my skin.

On the last page, my nail snags on a tear I didn't catch before. I pull it back to reveal another sheet caked to the back, sticking under a mountain of black ruin. With careful fingers, I pry them apart.

Black smudges fill the empty space in wild strokes, like something was written and crossed out until there was no space left. Whoever had this book before me left only one line, outlined again and again to the point that the paper wears thin under spatters of ink.

A monster only becomes dangerous once it remembers its name.

37

DRILLS HALL

I didn't expect to be patted on the back for my performance. I'm too calloused to hope for even a "good job" from Mister M.

Still, I hadn't expected *this*.

Lance shook me awake long before the chime. He offered no explanation as he led me down two flights of maintenance stairs and deposited me in front of a huge set of cracked double doors.

The faded plaque read "drills hall." The sight of it was nearly enough to drown me in my own terror. The drills hall is a place of legend. The kind that makes a girl want to shut her mouth and never open it again.

An enforcer dressed in black dragged me inside by the arm, slipping a containment cuff on my left wrist and pointing to a spot on the line. There are nine other girls present, all of them wearing brightly colored wristbands.

I've seen them a few times before. They denote girls who are slipping. Flagged. They haven't been removed from the program yet, but they aren't like the rest of us. They're unstable, unsafe, and emotionally unregulated. Instead of lectures, they attend drills hall. Supposedly, it's to train control under pressure.

In reality, it's the ultimate punishment.

Only, I don't have a wristband. I don't have any documented flags. According to V, I'm about as close to a perfect subject as one can get.

But I'm here.

Because Mister M wanted me here.

Because I performed too well under the guidance of someone who wasn't him.

The whistle screeches, sending my thoughts scattering.

"Sequence nine," barks the instructor. He's a burly man I don't recognize, with a long scar that runs from his jaw to the base of his neck. "Go."

My limbs know this routine better than my head does. I worked this drill in private instruction at least a hundred times.

To mess up now would take effort.

I guess I shouldn't speak for the others. A girl beside me stumbles on the first pivot. Another turns the wrong way. A third forgets the sequence entirely and gets a shock pulse from her cuff for it. I don't flinch. I finish on time with a smile on my face. The picture of obedience. The instructor doesn't even glance my way.

By the seventh repetition, the girl to my left is sniffling. The one on my right has stopped blinking entirely. I know that look. It's the same one Brielle gets when she stumbles in lectures. Panic masquerading as stillness.

I'm not sure I'm blinking anymore either. Just panting. And sweating. It's awful. Grating. Miserable. But I won't let it get to me. I suck in a deep breath—

The whistle slices the air.

"Again."

I obey, mouthing the counts to stay conscious. Heat billows behind my eyes, sending tingling sparks down to my fingertips.

I complete every sequence flawlessly. And still, I'm

made to run it again.

Two hours later, I'm sat on an uneven bench in the hallway. The white uniform clings to my back with sweat. My hands tremble enough to make the water bottle in my fingers crinkle with every squeeze.

The girl beside me has blood on her knee from a bad fall that the instructor scolded her for. Her lips are cracked, but she's made no effort to sip from the water they handed us.

She doesn't look at me when she says, "You're not like us."

I blink a few times in an effort to make the room stop swaying. "What?"

"You're not flagged." She shakes her wrist twice, drawing my eyes to the black band. "Why are you here?"

I could tell her the truth. That this is punishment, not protocol. That I did everything right, and it wasn't enough for my power-hungry mentor, who supposedly wants what's best for me. Instead, I choke down another sip of water, forcing my breathing to steady.

"I don't know."

The door at the end of the hall snaps open with a fervor. I don't look up, but I can feel the shift in the air. Followed by the distinct click of shoes that aren't built for patrol.

Mister V.

He's not supposed to be here. He was scheduled for private instruction today. Where I should've been at least an hour ago.

He must've been called away, probably responding to whatever chaos is always befalling his tablet. That's the only conclusion I can make, and the only one I'll accept. I mean, the man is a walking pocket watch; there's no way he waited over an hour before questioning where I was.

I let myself glance at him. His jacket is half-buttoned, his hair slightly ruffled. The tablet in his hand is vibrating nonstop with alerts, screen flashing red again and again like a heartbeat. His eyes scan the hallway. The benches. The girls. Me. He freezes, taking me in. Then he moves. Fast and controlled, but a far cry from the calm way I've grown so used to. He stops dead in front of the instructor.

"214 wasn't authorized to be here. I'm removing her," V says, voice steel. The instructor shifts his stance, wildly uncomfortable.

V moves to kneel in front of me, tension radiating off him like heat. His eyes rake over my face, the hair stuck to my neck, the tattered white uniform, the dried sweat on my collarbone.

"You shouldn't be here," he whispers, like he's forcing each word out past something sharp in his throat.

"I passed," I say, though it doesn't feel like an achievement; more like drowning with extra steps.

"You shouldn't have been made to."

I look away, because he's right, and looking at him feels like admitting to it. "It's fine."

"No, it isn't."

He stands, extending a hand to help me up, deliberately ignoring the half-dozen enforcers staring at him like he's grown a second head. I don't let myself relax until the incessant beeping and tension of the drills hall fades.

V takes a left down a side hallway that leads God knows-where. I don't question him, because I'm not about to ruin the first half-decent thing that's happened to me all day.

38

GHOSTS

We stop short of a wooden door tucked between an old rehearsal room and a diagnostics lab. He pushes it open to reveal what I suppose could be classified as an office.

Maybe that's too generous a term.

It looks like a supply closet someone shoved a desk into. Half the size of Mister M's, maybe smaller, but it's well used. Two cabinets loaded with files and supplies line one wall. A small desk with a half-pushed-in chair occupies the other. Along the back wall, a full-size armchair is askew, too big for the space.

V doesn't say anything as we step in. The lights in the hall were so harsh that even with the lamplight on, the office feels dark. He doesn't guide me, but my feet move anyway, toward the strange chair in the corner. It's unlike any of the furniture I've seen in the training wing. Not structured to guilt you into good posture or cold enough to make you shiver.

The leather gives a little beneath me, worn smooth along the seam of the right armrest, like someone used to sit here often. I fold my hands in my lap, spine painfully straight. I wait for him to demand a debrief, but V brushes right past me. He crouches near a cabinet and pulls out a bottle of electrolytes, setting it gently on the desk. My fingers close around it.

"I'm sorry," I murmur.

He looks up from whatever he's sorting through. "For what?"

"I don't know. For being sent there. For not being... better."

He stands and crosses the room, leaning against the desk with his arms folded so tight that tension draws through his shoulders. For a moment, he looks baffled. "I'm not upset with you."

"But you're upset."

"Yes, but not with you."

That somehow makes it worse. I blink hard, staring at the label on the drink. "Then who—"

"I don't think that's a question you really want answered."

I twist the cap and take a slow sip. He watches me for a moment, and I think he's about to dismiss me back to Mister M's torment. Instead, he stays right where he is, not even bothering to glance at his blinking tablet or my open file.

"I would've come for you sooner," he says quietly. "If I could've."

I look up, startled by the shift in tone. His eyes are darker now, hardened.

"There was a situation," V says, not elaborating. "But I should've been there."

I nod once, not sure what to say. I'm not mad at him, but I don't have any comforting words to assuage his guilt.

"Thank you," I manage. He nods back, almost reluctant. "Can I ask you something?" I say before the silence settles.

"Yes?"

"Did you ever have a pod like Mister M?"

His expression shifts, eyes darting away. "I did."

"Was it…like us?"

Pain rakes over his features. He presses his lips together, a silent war of how much to tell me waging behind his icy eyes. "No," he answers finally. "They were louder. Messier. We were in a different wing of the program, with different protocols." He presses a hand to his mouth. "Not as polished as this one, but they were mine."

Another wing? There's more than one? Something about the way he says it makes the back of my throat ache. I nod slowly, pressing the bottle to my lips again just to give my hands something to do.

"You must've been good at it," I tell him, mustering up every ounce of honesty I can manage through my exhaustion.

"I was trying to be." He doesn't say more, but I don't need to ask. I already know his past here doesn't have a happy ending.

I just wanted to hear it from him. I never know what to believe, but I guess this means it's true.

V, the best mentor I've ever observed, lost six girls. His entire group. And somehow that landed him here, in a different wing, sentencing girls to death at noon, then teaching me piano at one.

Makes perfect sense.

The silence settles between us, and this time, I let it. His office is warm, and my legs are still sore from drills. The chair shifts slightly under me, worn with a softness that doesn't belong here. I tip my head back, cherishing the peace of this singular moment.

"I'll be fine," I whisper, succumbing to exhaustion. My eyes flutter shut. V doesn't respond, but he doesn't move to wake me either.

It all feels…familiar.

I tell myself it'll only be a moment. Once my heart rate settles, I'll scrounge up a good excuse for Mister M and return to my pod before anyone knows I was gone.

Or not.

Overpowering cologne permeates the walls, strong enough to nauseate. Sure enough, the door swings open to reveal everyone's least favorite vulture. It may just be the exhaustion talking, but I don't have it in me to be afraid of him right now.

V stiffens, not turning. "Can I help you with something, Ashford?"

"Didn't know you were hosting therapy sessions now," Mister M says, stepping inside without invitation. "Should I book one for myself?"

"If you think it would help," V answers, eyes still on the file in his hands.

"Wow." Mister M plasters on a smile. "You're bold today."

"You're reckless most days," V says, swiveling his chair. "What's your point?"

"My point," Mister M replies, tilting his head. "Is that you should be thanking me. You're lucky I'm the one who found this…" He gestures around the room. "Intimate display. Carr would have a heart attack if he found out his precious hound was out collecting strays."

V huffs a laugh. "Impossible. Carr doesn't have a heart."

Mister M turns to me, hazel eyes glinting. "You shouldn't be here."

"I didn't—"

"She's recovering from the punishment you had no right to authorize." V cuts me off without so much as a glance.

"Recovering," Mister M repeats, eyes trailing over me. "Funny. She seems refreshed to me."

I've never wanted to step on someone's foot so bad in my life. My heart leaps to defend itself, but I quell it. I know better now. Clearly, the price of speaking out is more than I can afford without a plan. I drop my gaze and let him think what he wants.

He laughs softly at this. "You always look like you're waiting to be told what to do. It's almost endearing. I've trained you well."

The dig crumbles my resolve in an instant. "Waiting," I tell him, "doesn't mean listening. There's a difference."

"You'd know?"

"I'm learning," I say with a polite smile. "From the best."

He studies me for so long that I almost flinch. Instead, I double down, offering V an exaggerated nod. "Thank you for all your help, sir. I'm so grateful for the opportunity to improve. I look forward to private instruction tomorrow." The last words wipe the smile clean off Mister M's face.

He waves me on, impatient now. "Let's go, little star. I'd hate for you to think you have a choice."

"Of course, sir." I nod, holding my exhausted legs steady as I move to the door.

Mister M smiles like I've handed him a crown. He glances at V. "See? She still knows who's in charge."

I offer him a poison-dipped smile. "Do I?"

39

MELODY MOCKERY

The piano has been my only real company for hours. The steady weight of keys beneath my fingers is the closest thing I have to control, and I cling to it.

V is seated in the corner, head tipped back against the wingback, eyes closed. His stillness is deliberate, the kind that says he hears everything. It's not threatening. At least, not anymore.

Colt leans against the wall, arms crossed, standing silent guard. It feels grounding to have him here. Unlike Ralston or Lance, his presence isn't suffocating. He doesn't fidget, only glancing at me between songs like he's ensuring I haven't disappeared.

The gentle melody winds down beneath my hands, final notes dissolving into the walls. My fingers twitch for the next phrase, desperate to continue. But I lift them, taking in the silence like it's part of the show.

"You're doing well," V says, eyes cracking open. Colt catches my eye and gives me a small, lopsided smile and a little thumbs-up. It's peaceful, for all of three seconds.

A heavier presence fills the doorway, dripping with unadulterated malice.

Mister M.

His smirk sharpens at the sight of me, a direct target in his line of fire, but his first words are for Colt.

"Enforcers have no place in lessons," Mister M says

lightly, eyes cutting to me. "Especially this one."

Colt hesitates, jaw tight.

Mister M flicks his fingers in annoyance. "Dismissed."

I keep my head down. My mouth shut. Colt's eyes find mine for a moment, helpless and too apologetic. Then he steps back. The whisper of boots echoes down the hall as the door clicks shut.

The room feels smaller without him. The balance tips, not in my favor.

"She's a natural, isn't she?" Mister M muses, already moving on. "I just knew the piano would be perfect for her. And as always, I was right."

V's mouth curves, but it isn't a smile. "Oh yes. Brilliant foresight—especially given you filed her as a harpist. She's playing now because someone fixed your mistake."

The air between them chills. Mister M's eyes flash, the grin faltering for just a heartbeat before he smooths it back into place. He circles the room like a shark.

"Let's put that theory to the test, shall we?" He stalks to the piano, nudging me to the side of the bench with nothing but a flick. A keypad populates on the screen. Mister M pops a long code into the system, pulling up a piece I've never seen before. Dense, black, far too complicated for sight-reading. My throat closes.

He's going to humiliate me. *Great.*

"I don't know this one," I try, knowing it won't work.

"That's the point," he says smoothly. He leans close enough that his lips brush my ear. "Play it."

My hands hover helplessly over the keys. "Sir, I—"

He cuts me down instantly. "Do. Not. Embarrass me." Mister M turns on his heel, strolling toward a wingback in the corner.

I swallow hard, turning back to the piano. My palms sweat against the ivory. When I press the first chord, the sound rings perfectly, as if my body has played it a thousand times in secret.

I can't stop. It's like I'm back in the check in room with V, only worse. The melody is dark and alive, tearing at me while I strain to contain it. My left hand rolls with flourishes I've never learned; my right aches with ornamentation I don't remember choosing. Every note is a desperate cry.

I can feel Mister M's grin from across the room. "There it is," he murmurs, pleased. "Something real at last." Nausea claws at my throat from the possessiveness in his tone.

I risk a glance up. V is watching me intently. His mask is cracking, anguish written in his eyes before he forces them shut again, jaw locked tight. The sight steals my breath.

The bridge rises, twisting me inside out. Every note drags out pieces of me I didn't give it permission to touch. The lights flicker overhead as the melody swells one final time. I lift my hands, breathless. I can't bear to look at either of them.

Mister M claps mockingly. "Beautiful, little star, but unrefined. All that passion, and for what?" He laughs. Turns to V. "She knows it better than she thinks, wouldn't you say? It's like it's in her bones."

My fingers twitch. I wish I could slap him.

V says nothing. He steps forward, pressing a bottle of water I didn't know he was holding into my palm, gloved hand lingering just long enough for me to notice the tremor in it.

"Small sips," he coaxes. "You did well." He meets my gaze for half a second, enough for me to catch what he won't say aloud:

You survived. Don't give him more.

V schools his features back into something distant. "Posture review tomorrow," he says briskly. "Don't be late." The door shuts behind him, leaving me alone with a man I'm ninety percent sure is a deranged psychopath.

Mister M rises from his chair, his smirk etched in cruelty. "Don't let his words flatter you, 214. You're the last girl I'd put in front of investors. Pretty music means nothing without substance, and you don't have it yet." He prowls closer, enjoying himself far too much. "But that can be trained. Broken out of you. Carved, if necessary."

I wring my hands in my lap, bracing for what's sure to be a long lecture. His gaze cuts into me like he's already choosing where to dig next.

Before he has the chance, an ear-splitting ping explodes from his tablet. I gasp, covering my head on instinct. Mister M curses under his breath, snatching the device from his belt. His eyes skim the screen, urgent.

"Shit," he mutters, already moving.

Against my better judgment, I follow. The hallway tilts with his pace, my legs scrambling to keep up. He veers left, sharp enough to nearly send me careening into the wall. We round another corner, now face-to-face with the source of Mister M's panic. She's sprawled on the floor, fingers clawing through her hair, a scream tearing through the air so loud the walls tremble.

Juniper.

40

DOWN FOR THE COUNT

This is wrong. All Wrong.

June is on the floor of the art room, thrashing wildly. Her nails tear at her scalp like she's trying claw something out of her own head. I want to move toward her, but Mister M is frozen in the doorway, blocking me.

She's surrounded by black-clad enforcers, blank faces stark against the chaos. They're shouting codes, moving to form a barrier without daring to touch her.

"What's happening?" Mister M demands. He stands tense at the threshold, arms folded tight to his chest. I can see a twitch of his fingers against his sleeve. A nervous tell. *I didn't know he had those.* My stomach lurches at the sight.

One enforcer risks a step forward and gets knocked back by nothing but the force of Juniper's scream. He staggers into the wall hard enough to rattle the cabinets.

"We don't know!" Ralston snaps from the corner, eyes panicked. That doesn't make sense. They're here to protect us. They're trained for everything. Why don't they know? "She just collapsed and started—"

"Useless," Mister M spits. His eyes cut to Juniper, calculating. "Restrain her!"

What is wrong with her? I know she wasn't feeling well after evaluations, but I didn't think she was breaking down. A pang of guilt sears me. I would've noticed if something was wrong.

Right?

She jerks up, back arched, screams rising into a pitch that makes my teeth hurt. I clap my hands over my ears, but it doesn't stop. My body tenses, head pounding so hard I might collapse. Whatever's happening to her is making me violently ill.

Doctor Carr pushes past, shoving me sideways without so much as a glance. He's already snapping orders. "Hold her down! Don't let her—"

"She was stable this morning!" Mister M is shouting now, resolve shattering. "What did you do?"

Carr doesn't answer. He's too busy jamming a needle into June's arm. Then another. Then another. Thin glass vials roll across the tile. None of it works. Her convulsions worsen, her eyes roll back. Blood streams from her nose.

"I don't belong here!" she shrieks, practically unrecognizable. Her eyes lock on me, burning red from bursting blood vessels. "They're lying to you, Maysie!"

I stumble back, spine slamming the wall. My heart claws at my ribs. That's not Juniper's voice. *This isn't her. It can't be.*

Except it is. And she's looking right at me.

The lights overhead sputter violently, plunging us into darkness again and again. The floor quivers beneath my feet, rippling like water. I don't know if it's the room or just my head, but the world tilts on its axis, bending like it wants to fold in on itself, consuming me in the process.

"Terminate!" Carr bellows, sweat beading on his brow. "She's too far gone—end this before she brings the ceiling down!"

"No—restrain her!" Mister M shouts, pitched higher than I've ever heard it. He's frozen, arms folded, desperately working to mask his terror.

I can't wrap my mind around it. There are six grown men in here, dancing around June like she's a bomb about to detonate. And June is…I don't know.

I've seen girls break. Crying after drills or fainting during diagnostics. This is something else.

She isn't breaking.

She's exploding.

The enforcers surge together, four of them forcing her limbs to the floor. She shrieks again, the sound so piercing it feels like it's inside me, burrowing under my skin. I swear my vision doubles. My stomach flips. I gag, doubling over violently.

"Please stop!" My palms slam into the tile, stinging. "Don't hurt her!"

Her gaze jerks to me again, eyes wild. "It'll happen to you too!"

"Get her out of here!" Carr's voice rips through the storm.

The weight of an unsteady enforcer crashes down on me, driving my arms back at an unnatural angle. Pain lances through my shoulders.

"Stay out of this, 214!" Carr snarls, not sparing me a look. He tosses a syringe to the man pinning me. The cap pops off. The needle finds the crook of my arm before I can pull away.

"No!" The cry tears out of me, raw and pathetic. I kick at the man, but he's stronger, pinning my leg with his knee. Something far stronger than a sedative floods my veins. A metallic taste coats my tongue. My limbs sag as I thrash, weak.

June bucks against the enforcers. She's screaming, but the sound fractures into choking, then wet coughing, then something that doesn't sound human. My vision blurs, tunneling and swimming all at once.

"She's not responding!" one guard shouts.

"Stronger dose," Carr orders, frantic. "End it—now!"

Everything burns. My head is spinning so hard I can barely formulate thoughts. Only one tears through: *Why is this happening?* I can barely lift my head, but I try. Through the blur, I see her eyes, deep green and bloodshot. The veins of her arms are raised, pulsing against her skin so bright they almost look silver. Her mouth is still forming fragmented screams. The second injection slams into her, and her body stiffens.

Then collapses.

All that's left is the dripping of paint water, the scrape of an enforcer shifting back, and a dozen sets of panting I can hardly hear over the static of my thoughts. I try to say her name, but the sound is lost to the darkness pulling me under.

The last thing I see is Mister M, standing clear of her, face pale as chalk.

And Juniper, limp. Surrounded by the wreckage of her own storm.

41

LET IT ACHE

I wake up cold.

Not a simple chill of the air. The kind of cold that seeps straight into bone. I reach for my blanket and find a metal chain. I tug instinctively—no give. My arms and back throb, but I can't place why. I try to force my eyes open, only to be hit with a light that sears my retinas.

I am certainly not in my room.

Antiseptic fills my lungs as the thrum of the med bay closes in around me. It's familiar—which is odd, considering there isn't much to recognize. No furniture occupies the space beyond the bed I'm chained to and the monitors beside it. An enforcer waits by the door, avoiding my gaze like I carry a plague that's only transmissible through sight.

My head reels as I sink into the flimsy pillow. The lull of sleep creeps at the edge of my mind, only to be trampled by approaching footsteps. I flutter my eyes open, already preparing for whatever lecture Mister M has in store for me.

"You're dismissed." The calmness of the order both startles and reassures me because that is *not* Mister M.

The guard vanishes without a word, leaving only V—a tray balanced in one hand, folded blanket in the other.

"Mister V—" My voice scrapes out in a pained whisper.

"Shhh." He sets the tray in my lap, grabbing the small water cup from it. "You shouldn't be speaking yet." He holds it to my mouth. The cold rush of water surges through me until I feel like I can breathe again. V sets it down, pulling a key from his pocket and working on my wrist restraints.

"What are you doing here? What's happening?" I rasp, not yet confident in my ability to talk without sounding like I've been run over.

"Try to eat something." V frees one of my wrists, gesturing to the small plate on the tray. When I don't move, his lips press into something between a frown and a grimace.

I wave him off and run a shaky hand through my tangled hair. My fingers snag on something unfamiliar, a ridge of skin pulled too tight. It's a small scar, about an inch behind my right temple. The soreness radiating under my touch makes me wince. It's new.

V doesn't seem to notice. He's muttering, more to himself than to me. "It's so damn cold down here, and they wonder why girls keep getting sick."

Wrongness clamps down in my chest. It roils fast through my body until my vision snaps taut, pressure slamming against my eyes.

"June—" My breath stutters. "What happened to her?"

V stills. His eyes flick to the camera in the corner. Then back to me.

"She's—" The word catches. His jaw goes tight. His gaze finds the floor. Whatever he was about to say retreats behind his eyes, sealed away.

"She's getting the help she needs," he says instead, voice careful.

My head throbs. I try to picture June's face and get nothing but static. I press my fingers to my temple, rubbing at the aching skin.

"Something's missing. Every time I think about it, it—" I falter. "It goes fuzzy."

"That will pass," he coaxes. The phrase lands wrong, a jagged edge I can't ignore.

Not because I know it's a lie—but because he does.

His face is calm. His posture perfect. But his eyes won't stay on mine. He's looking at his tablet, his shoes, the blank wall, anything but my face.

"You're lying," I whisper.

His jaw tenses. "I'm protecting you." He presses a hand against my forehead. "Let me."

I try again to reach for the memory. June on the floor. A sound ripping the air to bits, too animalistic to be a scream. Tiles smeared with…blood? No—paint, dripping to the floor in crimson ribbons. My stomach pitches, and the image collapses in on itself. V's hand finds my shoulder, light but grounding. "She's getting the help she needs," he repeats, firm. A line in the sand that tells me it's not up for discussion anymore.

His eyes find the monitor. "Three doses," he murmurs. "That dosage is reserved for full shutdown."

He says it as if it scares him. Like he still doesn't quite believe it.

I shake my head, wading through the muddle of thoughts. "Three doses—of what?" My words are slurred, but audible.

Not audible enough to be acknowledged.

"Eat," he asserts instead, gesturing to the tray. I flash him a look of annoyance that goes unnoticed. "It'll make tomorrow easier."

"Slow down!" I snap, heat rushing to my face. "Sorry. This is all just a lot. What do you mean tomorrow?"

"The investors' ball. Despite your recent condition, the board requested you to perform." He's frowning again, which only serves to confuse me further.

"That isn't until—"

"It's tomorrow." He grabs the cup of water, offering it to me again. I pluck it from his hands, taking a long sip so he'll back off. His words finally land.

"Wait, how long have I been asleep?"

He exhales slowly. "Two weeks. You were over-administered containment sedatives."

I choke on the water. I was drugged. Not just drugged. I was overdosed and sent into—what? A coma for two weeks?

What did they do to me?

"Cruel, isn't it?" he murmurs, eyes distant. "The world doesn't wait—" He stops. His eyes find mine, raw and unarmored for a single breath. "Even when we need it to." He adjusts his tie, fingers curling tight around the fabric like it's suffocating him.

"I don't understand."

This is too much, I need to think—or breathe. Both, probably.

"You won't," V says softly. "That's normal. But dwelling won't change the past. Your only job now is to rest so you can wake up tomorrow ready to perform."

The dismissal stings.

What an easy thing for him to say. I don't think he cared about Juniper. Or maybe he did, and this is just what "caring" looks like on him. Bile creeps up my throat as my memories shift further from my grasp.

"I can't!" I whisper-shout, exasperated. "I'm not ready!" Tears blur my vision. One of my only friends is gone, and he's acting like her disappearance is a virus I can just sleep off.

V doesn't flinch; he studies me with disappointment, like I'm failing whatever invisible test he's set forth.

"You just have to fake it. That's what the rest of us do," he retorts, folding his arms. I wince, watching the way his face falls in exasperation. "No one here has any idea what they're doing. The ones who claim otherwise are either lying, arrogant, or already broken."

"I can't do it." My response is automatic, but I've never been so sure of anything in my life. "I don't—"

"Enough," he exhales, hard. "You're not ready. I get it, but you don't get to give up here. You've worked too hard." He says it like a fact, not a compliment. It doesn't make me feel any better.

"Rest. I'll handle it." He takes the half-eaten tray from my lap, setting it aside before helping me ease back against the bed. He slips a syringe from his jacket pocket, holding it low, clearly hoping I won't notice. I narrow my eyes.

"I won't do it if you absolutely don't want me to," he says carefully, holding his free hand up in surrender. "But when the enforcers come to move you tonight, you'll need to be perfectly still. You don't want them dosing you again." He tries for a reassuring smile, but it's hollow, doing nothing to ease the tension between us.

My fingers dig into the blanket. "You don't need to. It won't work."

"This one will," he says calmly, as if my body's already agreed.

"How would you know—"

"Because I do."

My lungs constrict. After a long moment, I offer my arm. "Just—make it quick."

I don't trust him. I *can't* trust him. But I can't let the enforcers touch me again, so I'm choosing the lesser of two evils.

V tears an antiseptic packet open. The cool swipe raises a shiver along my skin. I grit my teeth until my expression goes slack. I've done this too many times before to whine over it.

But when the syringe catches the light, I forget I'm supposed to be breathing. It's unlike any sedative I've ever seen. The liquid is amber, not blue. Thick and dark and swirling like something alive.

"Wait—"

The injection hits its mark before the protest can leave my lips. My muscles sag, breath locking in my chest as ice snakes down my body, replaced all too fast by insurmountable heat.

Then memory.

A piano chord, ringing dissonant. Hands guiding mine. Something warm, someone familiar.

"Don't rush the third measure. Let it ache first."

Glass clinks. Monitors beep. A distant voice calls a name I don't recognize.

Not Maysie. Not even 214.

"Chin up, dove."

A gold ribbon slips from my hair. Turns red.

A chandelier sways above me. Or maybe I'm swaying.

"You're stabilizing," a soft voice tells me. I lift a cup that isn't in my hands. My dress digs at my skin, too tight across the shoulders.

Don't look at him. You'll remember.

A chair. A book. A hand brushing mine.

"Tell me the ending,"

"It didn't have one."

"Then it isn't over."

The floor tilts. My knees hit tile.

"Don't remember me in red."

The chandelier crashes.

And the world shatters.

The lights flicker—

White.

Red.

Gone.

My world slams back into view. I jerk against the blankets, still restrained. Heat is still coiling around me—a fire taking residence mere inches from my skin as if it's afraid to touch me.

V freezes, the blanket caught mid-motion between his fingers; I catch it in my periphery. A hitch in his breath, a flicker in his eyes like he felt it too.

Is that supposed to happen? I try to ask, but my throat doesn't move.

Neither does the room. It's quiet and clean, as if nothing's wrong. Only, something is. There's a weight behind my eyes now that couldn't possibly be caused by the strange drug.

Recognition.

Of what, I don't know.

"Are you okay?" V asks softly. He's watching me too closely. Not like I'm sick; *like I'm about to say something important.*

I try to meet his eyes, but they smear into a haze of blue fog. A sinking feeling floods my chest. Hot and cold. Painful and serene. I'm an anomaly. A figment of my own imagination made flesh and bone. I can't even tell what's real beyond the boy watching me with wide eyes and a face flushed with concern he can't mask fast enough.

"You saw something, didn't you?"

I try to nod, but my head is cement.

The drug is winning now.

He exhales slowly through his nose, gaze dropping as he tucks the blanket into place. "It happens sometimes," he says. "Memory fragments. Carr says it's nothing."

Carr says. Not him.

He stands slowly, eyes lingering on my face like he's seeing it for the first time. His fingers brush the edge of the wrist restraint, resting there for one extra second like he's forgotten how to let go.

"Get some rest now. I can't afford to lose you again."

42

THE LIE, THE COVER

V appears in my doorway early the next morning, shadows looming under his eyes. I can't tell if it's pride or concern that crosses his face when he sees I'm already up. I decide not to tell him that I was up the second the sedative wore off.

Not just up—totally wired. To the point I couldn't sit idly by until the overlords who run the chimes decided it was time to wake. I thought about reaching for the book still tucked securely under my mattress, but I doubt stories about creatures that tear themselves apart would do anything for the ache burrowing beneath my skin.

"Good morning, Maysie." He offers a curt nod. "It's a relief to see you back where you belong." A rehearsed response, one he'd never use of his own volition. The facade he wears today is wrinkled at the edges. His eyes dart around the room like he can distract me from it.

There's an intricate dress tucked over his arm, a shade of blue so deep it would put oceans to shame. V looks me up and down, fingers brushing his thigh and tapping twice. I realize he's waiting for me to respond.

"Good morning," I muster. It's polite enough, passable. "Where's Mister M?"

I don't really care, but I feel obligated to ask.

"Your mentor is dealing with a..." He pauses, eyes darting to the corner again. "Situation. I've been asked to prepare you for the ball tonight in his absence. You've been resting for some time since your fall." His jaw tenses, and I know he wants to say more. We stay like that for a moment, unspoken emotions tangling thick.

"My fall?" I ask, breaking the awkward silence with an equally awkward question.

"Yes, I do hope you're feeling better. It must've been a nasty one, for you to be gone so long. Poor thing." The words are painfully fake. So exaggerated that it sounds more like something Mister M would say. He taps his leg again, two steady beats. *A cue of some sort, I just don't remember which one.* His eyes are fixed above me. I follow his gaze, unsettled to find my room's camera whirring, blinking a steady red. The one in my room has never been active.

Then it clicks. The performance. The lie. My cue. *Someone's watching us.*

I nod in acknowledgement. His shoulders drop, just a fraction, and the act continues. V strides forward, holding the dress out.

"We have much to do," he continues. "Get washed up and dressed. Your prep session isn't until later, but I trust you can make yourself presentable."

"Yes, sir." I brush past him, grabbing the dress in a flourish.

"I'll be waiting outside. Be quick about it." He disappears without another word, leaving me with my instructions.

The morning hours are consumed by private lessons on etiquette, drills on dancing, dress alterations to the exquisite gown that already fit me perfectly. No time to process. No room to breathe. I don't even give myself time to think until

I'm finally left alone with V in the practice room.

V is hovering above the bench, flipping through the end-less catalogue of songs, only stopping to point out ones he thinks the investors would like.

I clear my throat. "So, I fell?"

"Not my idea," he sighs, pressing a hand to his temple. "Ashford is an idiot; I can't believe Carr let him pick the nar-rative."

"What kind of fall takes someone out for two weeks?" I almost want to laugh at the insanity of it. He shakes his head, equal parts baffled and annoyed.

"I'm sure everyone else is wondering the same thing." His jaw sets. "There's no helping it, though. What's done is done. Should anyone ask you, that's what you'll say." He taps my shoulder three times as he rattles off the points. "You fell. You don't remember much. You're all better now." He brings his other hand down to cup my shoulders, squeez-ing lightly. "Don't forget to tell them you're so very grateful to the organization for helping you."

I whip my head around, not bothering with the formali-ties. "And why would I say that?"

"Because that's what they want to hear. You need to be perfect tonight." V shakes his head. "Better than perfect, if possible."

"In case you haven't figured it out—I'm not perfect!" I snap at him, déjà vu flooding my senses. My jaw locks as droplets of rage prickle my vision. V pulls his hands away with a jolt, wincing as if he's been burned. Heat shoots up my spine, clawing deep. I brace my hands against the piano, concentrating on nothing but my unsteady breathing.

What is wrong with me?

"I'm just a girl, V. I'm not a doll or a robot or—"

"Oh, trust me, I know." He glances toward the door, pressing a palm to his temple. "I don't get it. You shouldn't re—" His jaw snaps tight, an internal war waging behind his tired eyes.

I lean forward, trying to sound level when I ask, "Shouldn't what?"

He exhales a tight breath. "Stop asking questions you don't want answers to."

I swallow. "What are you hiding from me?"

No response. The soft ticking of the metronome serves as the only reminder that time hasn't stopped completely. My mouth opens again to protest, but before I can muster any words, I notice he's not looking at me anymore. His eyes are trained on his watch. He snaps straight, jerking his head toward the far corner of the ceiling.

The camera. Far larger than the one in my room. It looms in the corner, the light atop it blinking a vicious red.

I would love an explanation on why the cameras are suddenly so interested in me, but considering no one even bothers to tell me what's for breakfast, I find it unlikely that I'll ever find out.

His whole demeanor changes in an instant. That polished mentor facade slides right back into place. The easy smile. The rehearsed charm that feels a little too labored.

"Shall we?" He gestures to the piano.

The shift makes my stomach twist. But I nod like the good girl the cameras want to see, taking my place back on the bench. He leans down, sifting through the digital sheet music with exaggerated flair.

"A charming waltz. This one's a fan favorite." His voice carries loudly enough for the walls to hear. I scan the piece in an attempt to note the key details. It's challenging, but nothing I haven't done in the past.

I start to play, but my fingers tremble. Trembles build into tremors, my hands slipping from the keys before scrambling for their placements. V cuts me off before I can even finish the first page.

"Again."

Wrong note.

"Again, Maysie."

The outcome is the same. Uneven chords creating a clumsy, half-hearted melody. It's awful. You would think I've never even seen a piano.

The notes melt together as I stare at the measures. The beloved instrument that has become my safe space is mocking me.

"I can't—"

"Yes, you can." His words are clipped with warning. "Stop shaking." He brushes his thumb against his sleeve. *Breath reset.* "Try again."

I force my hands to obey, but all that follows is a mess of sound and panic. There's no tempo, no grace to it. V's look of disappointment is unmistakable.

"You said I should fake it," I blurt, unable to stop myself. V's eyes lock on mine, gaze so intense I want to tear my eyes away.

"It's how you survive," he replies carefully, like every word poses unique danger.

"And if I don't?"

The look that spreads across his face is indescribable. A sort of cold determination that makes me shiver. "Then I'll have to fake it for you. One way or another, we're going to get through this."

I freeze.

I don't even need to know what that means for it to terrify me.

"Do you understand?" he asks softly.

No.

I nod, not trusting my voice.

His expression flickers something close to regret, but I don't have time to study it before his tablet pings. He turns on his heel, unclipping the tablet and walking calmly to the doorway. "You're almost ready. Run it until I come back for you." Unease settles in my chest as the door shuts behind him.

I stare at the keys, hands shaking. My throat is sandpaper. The red flashes of the camera's indicator haunt my periphery, mocking me.

Something tells me I'm anything but ready.

43

THE INVESTORS' BALL

A private dressing room is a luxury I never thought I would be afforded. The break from all the hustle and noise of the training wing is an unexpected gift.

At least it would be if there wasn't a girl in the next room over sobbing her eyes out.

Not exactly a comforting indication of what tonight might bring.

The attendants fuss around me, fumbling with hairpins, expensive perfumes, and enough glittery eye makeup to cover this place top to bottom. One passes me a pair of long black lace gloves, which I slide on with ease. The contrast is brilliant against my pale skin and the sapphire of my dress. They help me into a lovely pair of open-toe black heels. I take a moment to admire them before realizing how pointless they are when they're immediately tucked beneath the floor-length gown. The skirt itself is light, swishing around my ankles.

"I trust you practiced?" V slips through the doorway, light as the air itself. He's fiddling with the cufflinks of yet another perfect suit. It's the deepest shade of charcoal, with a tie the color of sapphires. It matches my dress too well to be unplanned. I want to scoff at his indifference after all he's put me through today.

Practice doesn't even do it justice. I rehearsed that piece until I could play it inside and out, facing forwards or backwards. I bet I could play that stupid waltz better than the composer himself. Snapping at him for never coming back to pick me up feels appropriate, but a taste of his own medicine sounds far better.

"I practiced until it was perfect, sir." The smirk that plays on my lips is sickly sweet. "Thank you so much for giving me this opportunity, Mister V, I hope I can bring great pride to the advancement program tonight."

His brow twitches. He presses his lips together, matching my energy with an over-enthused: "Excellent." I roll my eyes at how absurd it sounds coming from him.

V gives me a once-over, admiring what I know were his choices. Mister M would rather die than dress me in anything nicer than a potato sack. A regulation white one, of course. The chime signals our departure, and I drift to his side, the satisfying swoosh of my dress echoing in the small room. Before I can step past him, he catches my arm, pulling me in close enough to whisper. "You better muster up a better act than that. For both our sakes."

The wide hallway that leads to the presentation hall is downright stunning. Soaring ceilings, marble floors. Decorated immaculately in warm blues and pale yellows. The organization's silver sigil adorns everything. To the untrained eye, it would look like a palace. It makes me feel important, in a way. Until I spot a pair a few paces ahead.

The girl is hauntingly beautiful. She's walking a step behind her mentor, spine straight, expression vague. The gown she's wrapped in is cream, making her look like an angel...or a ghost. Her amber eyes are eerily blank, mouth curled in the faintest of artificial smiles. She doesn't see me, or anyone for that matter. She simply moves forward on cue.

I falter a fraction, fighting not to gag on the bile of dread clinging to my throat. V tightens his grip on my arm.

"Smile," he whispers through his teeth. I offer a fake one that's hopefully convincing.

We reach a set of ballroom doors that are impossibly tall and sickeningly grand. A pair of enforcers open them with a nod, ushering us in like royalty. The sight laid before me is nothing short of nauseating.

It's huge, easily triple the size of the practice hall we use for ballroom basics. The space swells with music and applause and endless conversation. I recognize almost none of the faces, but I can tell they're important. Investors. Board members. Even some instructors. They look like cold, calculating predators cloaked in finery. My eyes are everywhere in seconds, but there's too much to take in.

"Keep your chin up," V murmurs. "Remember what you are."

I glance sideways at him. "And what's that?"

His smile stops short of his eyes, glinting with an ounce of honesty. "Something they think they own."

My heart flutters. I don't have a chance to respond—not that I need to. We're immediately swept up into the crowd. It's obvious V has been to these gatherings more than a few times.

To my surprise, he's quite popular. Everyone seems to want an audience with him. By the time we've reached a refreshment table, I've recited enough practiced responses to make my head spin.

"You're doing well," V says, pressing a tall glass into my hand. He hesitates, then swaps it for a different one. "Don't drink that," he adds, grabbing one from a different row for himself. I don't even get a chance to ask why before another couple approaches. A tall, burly man with a peppered beard offers me a kind smile, and the woman I presume is his wife does the same, struggling through a half-bow in her structured red gown. She pulls V into a tight embrace. He remains charismatic, but the subtle clench of his fist tells me he's not enjoying the contact.

"So lovely to see you again!" she chirps, pulling back to look him over. "You really must attend more often, darling. It's always such a pleasure."

"The pleasure's all mine," he returns with undeniable charm. Her attention shifts to me.

"And look at you! I haven't seen you out in forever." She takes one of my hands in hers, squeezing it tightly. "You're looking positively radiant. Blue has always been your color, you know!" The strange woman gushes at me. My brows rise in confusion. I chance a sideways glance at V, which goes unreturned. He clears his throat, a painfully fake smile tugging at the corners of his lips.

"Actually, Mrs. Devon, this is Maysie. A new advancement," he says, words rehearsed. "Her mentor was preoccupied, but I couldn't let her miss a night as important as this."

Mrs. Devon purses her lips in a tight frown, looking me up and down again. She lets out a small giggle. "Surely you're joking with me. I'd never forget those eyes."

"I assure you, I'm not." V looks wildly uncomfortable as he pats my shoulder. "You should hear her play piano, though. It's truly remarkable." He takes my arm in his again, guiding me away from the now-perplexed woman.

"I'll be looking forward to it! Toodaloo!" she calls after us, giggling and grabbing another glass.

V leads me off to the side, not daring to say a word until

we're safely out of earshot.

"What was she—" I start, but he shakes his head dismissively.

"She's drunk," he states plainly. "Ignore—"

"But what was she talking about? With my eyes? And the dress and—"

"I promise to explain everything later, but right now you have to focus on getting through this."

I take a shaky breath. Nod. "Promise?"

"Promise." It's sincere. He turns his back on me, releasing my arm in a fluid motion. "I'm going to see if they're ready for you. Stay out of trouble." I flash him a shy half-grin and lean back against a marble pillar.

"Stand up straight," he calls, half-glancing over his shoulder.

V weaves through the crowd. I'll bet it's ten times easier when you aren't having to guide someone in a floor-length gown.

Something rustles beside me. I snap my head up, gaze catching on a girl half-hidden behind a tall pillar. When she chances a step out of the shadow, I nearly leap out of my skin.

Avery.

Her once-bright blonde waves fall limp around her chin, stick straight and brittle. Her eyes are shadowed, with irises that appear more gray than blue. She's dressed in white, giving her pale skin an almost translucent flush. There's a fresh scar at her temple, delicately stitched and mostly covered with makeup. A polite smile plays on her lips.

"You're looking lovely, 214." Her voice is faint. I reach for her hand, but she steps back.

"Avery," I breathe, losing any semblance of words. I bite

my lip, using the sharp sting as clarity. "Where have you been?"

She hums softly. "I needed some maintenance. I am grateful for the opportunity to be corrected."

A shiver snakes down my spine, raking through me until I can't feel my toes. "I'm glad you're okay," I manage, though I don't believe it. It doesn't take a doctor to see something's amiss here. She smiles impossibly wider, blinking at me.

"I'm better than okay, 214," Avery beams, pressing her gloved hands to her chest. "I'm perfect." She steps forward, taking my free hand in hers. "You'll understand soon."

I want to press, but my words stall. Anyone could be listening. There's a presence at my back that I politely ignore as twisted curiosity gets the better of me.

"What are you—"

"They're ready for you," V interrupts, threading his arm through mine and practically yanking me away from Avery. I'm still trembling, squeezing the hilt of my glass. Cracks spread up the delicate stem. My finger slips across the side, slicing a gash across the tip. Panic creeps up my throat. The glass slips, but V manages to snatch it from me, tossing it haphazardly in a nearby trash can.

"I'm sorry, I don't...I—"

"It's all right, you're okay." His tone is soft, sympathetic. He grips my arm tight, guiding me gently around the edges of the crowd. V casts a nervous glance back at Avery, who is still dissociating in the corner, right where I left her. He squeezes tighter when I try to shift out of his grip, using his free hand to blot the blood from my finger with his jacket sleeve.

"I don't know what she said, but you need to snap out of

this. Right now." Unease is etched into his features. He stops, turning me to face him. "Hold it together until you're safe. Then you can fall apart."

He's right, and I hate him for it. Crying right now wouldn't do me any good. In fact, it could do me a whole lot of bad. I exhale deeply, ready to play the part so I can get out of here. As we approach the front of the seemingly endless ballroom, a raised stage comes into view. About a hundred patrons mill around it, clinking glasses and laughing. V steps aside, motioning me forward.

"You can do this."

"I know." I flash him a hint of a smile, one I can't be certain is real. That doesn't mean much; I don't really feel certain about anything anymore. I climb the short steps and find my way to the bench, ignoring the low whispers and numerous eyes on me.

The keys are cool to the touch, centering. It lasts for all of two seconds as my eyes find the display.

Dismay claws at my ribs as I look over the sheet music. It's not the waltz I spent all day honing.

No. Because why would it be?

Why would absolutely anything go as planned here?

For a place that thrives on structure, this is a gross oversight.

No, it's not the piece I practiced. It's the haunting ballad Mister M forced me to play. The one that echoes through my brain when a room grows too silent. The one that made V look like he'd seen a ghost.

I suck in a deep breath and do what I do best. I play. Slowly, at first. One measure at a time, until the song consumes me, entrancing me into its story so tightly that I can hardly make out the pained expression on V's face. By the time the song reaches its climax, the music is flowing out of me like a storm, raining a perfect stillness over the room. Every patron near the stage has turned to face me. I can feel their judgmental eyes and too-tight smiles. Heat surges down my spine, but my heart rate holds steady. Terror should be biting at my heels; instead, somehow, this may be the freest I've ever felt.

It's exhilarating.

That is…until the lights go out.

44

TAKING CREDIT

The room is plunged into darkness.

Terror seizes my core. I already felt trapped in a room full of predators. Hard enough to face in broad daylight. But in the dark? Now that's just downright unfair.

There's no screaming or clapping. No sound at all beyond a spatter of shocked murmurs.

Darkness stretches for one heartbeat.

Two.

Then, with a loud *pop*, the lights spring to life, revealing a sea of faces whose expressions range from bewilderment to concern to amusement. V doesn't hesitate. He starts clapping. Firm, fast, and loud. Others soon follow suit, until the room is doused in applause. I stand on jelly legs, offering the best curtsy I can muster.

My victory is short-lived.

Mister M swaggers in from God-knows-where, dressed in a full crimson suit, with a crisp black tie and a cocky smirk to match. He claps slowly, clearly relishing the attention. When he reaches the stage, he pivots to face the still-stunned audience.

"Wasn't she lovely? It's such a privilege to have been the one to train her. An honor to call her mine."

I almost laugh at the absurdity of it. Here he is. The man who has done positively everything in his power to ruin my every opportunity and tear down my hopes and dreams has decided I'm now worthy of his affections. To top it all off, he's patting himself on the back for merely standing in the same room as my "success."

I wait for V to argue, to snap back with something dry and witty. But he's quiet. He presses his lips together, as if to tell me he's holding his tongue, and I should as well.

Mister M turns to V, face etched in cruelty. "Thank you for babysitting, Harrow. I'll take it from here."

I open my mouth to protest, but V shakes his head, shoulders tense. Frustration and hurt linger behind his eyes.

"Dance with me, won't you?" Mister M outstretches a hand. The only thought that dares cross my mind is how much I would love to spit in his face. Unfortunately, there are a few too many people lingering a few feet too close. I offer him a curt nod.

"I'd be honored," I hear myself say. He wastes no time taking my hand in his and pulling me away from V. His hand finds my waist possessively as we assume a starting position. As always, his timing is impeccable. We join the dance floor just as a new piece begins. It's melodic and floaty. A little slow for my liking, but nice.

Well…it would be. If I were with someone else. Anyone else, actually. I'd rather twirl around the dance floor with Doctor Carr than be stuck with Mister M. But here we are. Three steps. Glide. Turn. Repeat.

"Incredible work, 214," he starts. My stomach dips. Even here, he won't use my name. "You know, I almost believed you were sincere." He smiles like it's praise. My expression falters. He clocks it immediately. "Don't fret, little star. No one else noticed." He slows long enough to brush a hand down my cheek. "Still, it's a shame. Such ugly lies for a pretty girl."

My heart flutters at the half-compliment, before I remember who uttered it. Now repulsed with myself, I draw his arm up, forcing my way under it in an incredibly stiff turn. He catches my waist again, tighter this time.

"Now, now, you're supposed to be following my lead." He lets out a chuckle that turns humorless halfway through. "You seem to forget that more and more each day." Mister M pulls me back more forcefully, throwing my body into the moves like he used to in ballroom basics. For a moment, I allow myself to be pulled around like a rag doll in hopes it'll get this over with faster. It only displeases him further.

"Feeling mad, little star?" he taunts.

"Do you want me to be mad?" I retort through my teeth.

"It's certainly more fun that way."

My heel lands on his foot. Half on purpose, half because he's moving us impossibly fast. Mister M's teeth grit, but his smile only widens. He tightens his hold until my chest slams into his. Our foreheads almost touch. I try to wrench back, but his grip is firm.

"That's more like it." He drags a thumb down my cheek. "Defiance looks good on you."

He's still watching me as the sound fades. There's another wave of familiarity in the gold dancing in his irises. I will myself to look away, acutely aware of the figure approaching us. An older man claps Mister M on the back, balancing a sloshing glass in his other hand.

"Ashford! That was quite the performance. Your parents must be proud. Such a shame they couldn't make it."

Mister M bristles, smile flickering so briefly I might've imagined it. He laughs politely, squeezing my arm tight enough to sting and guiding me in front of him like a shield.

"They're attending a board dinner," he says evenly. "Optics, priorities, all that. They trust me to make a suitable impression." If he's trying to hide the strain in his voice, it isn't working.

The investor nods anyway, oblivious. "Ah—yes. Send them my regards."

He takes his leave. I brace myself for whatever command Mister M has loaded up to bark at me next, only to find his gaze fixed somewhere behind me. No doubt on the girl he's abandoned in the corner.

"Shouldn't you be with Avery?" I ask innocently. There's a pang in my heart as her name escapes me. I don't feel pity for him; not really, at least. His jaw tightens.

"Don't."

"It was an honest—"

"Don't," he repeats, gripping my arm. "Don't presume to know me. Don't presume to know her. Don't feel pity for a situation you know nothing about." The corner of his lip twitches as he casts a look across the ballroom. There's a sharp inhale. A sigh. Then he shifts his gaze back to me. A cold smile spans his face. "Let's go. There's more patrons I'd like to show you off to."

Hours pass, even if the clock claims it's only been twenty minutes. The attendees seem to be multiplying. We finish with one couple and suddenly there are eight more. I'm the talk of the town after my light-altering performance, which is…not what I was going for.

On the bright side, I don't have to take the lead. Mister M is more than eager to do all the talking. Most investors regard him with familiarity. Hugs, compliments, fond stories of past gatherings. I smile when required, dance when asked, but my eyes stay alert. Scanning the room for anything and everything. I spot V a few times as he works his way through the room.

I'm not surprised Mister M can perform this well; he was built for empty smiles and haughty laughter. Something tells me he's been attending these sorts of gatherings since he first learned to gloat. Which, if I had to guess, was about five minutes after he learned to talk.

V's skills, on the other hand, are admittedly startling. People seem to flock to him. They hang on his every word, though he speaks few. He offers easy smiles. Laughs too loud to be natural. Drinks when others lead. He casts me a few sidelong glances, cueing subtly as he speaks. *Mask up. Reset. Mirror stance.* Things Mister M would never catch.

Enforcers are milling everywhere. Posted along the back walls. Lingering by the stage. Some are intermixed in the group, accompanying girls and investors alike.

"—rebuilt remarkably." Mister M's stray words catch. I haven't been paying attention, but a strange tug in my chest tells me this is important.

"Hm?" I ask, curiosity piqued.

"Nothing," he says dismissively, swatting the air. "Be a doll and fetch Mr. Yoshida another drink. One for me as well." I nod, stepping back. He catches my shoulders as I turn. "Hurry back. Wouldn't want the little star getting lost."

45

EAVESDROPPING

I'm barely halfway there when a woman steps into my path. She's older, dressed in a gray satin gown and long black gloves. Gilded hairpins are worked into her hair in a halo, so bright and tightly situated it almost looks like a crown. Her face is set in confusion.

"You look terribly familiar," she says, cupping my face in her hands and tilting my head up. I cringe, but don't wrench away. She shakes her head. "My imagination must be getting the better of me again, forgive me." She casts a sidelong glance around the room. "You'd better get back to your mentor. It's not safe for you to be wandering alone."

Not safe?

She's gone before I can open my mouth to ask why. I sigh as I make my way to one of the many refreshment tables, spotting a familiar face.

"You look like someone just pissed in your shoe," Ryder says, hovering at the end of the table like he's planning to swipe something.

"A woman said I looked familiar," I confess, hoping he'll offer some kind of insight.

"Weird," he counters. "She's probably drunk."

"What makes you say that?"

He makes a vague gesture around the room. "They're all drunk."

"Fair. Which drink should I get for Mister M?"

Ryder shrugs. "Whichever one makes him look the douchiest."

I chuckle, grabbing two glasses from the end of the table. The liquid is crimson, the color of Mister M's obnoxious suit. *Perfect.*

I return to find him gone. The man from before is nearby, a lone wolf in a pack of chaos.

"Have you seen my mentor?" I ask, offering Mr. Yoshida the glass.

Mr. Yoshida takes it with a deep nod. "Thank you, deary." He tilts his chin toward a narrow wooden door tucked between banquet tables. "I recall seeing him follow a woman that way."

I should leave it alone. Find V, or go back to Avery and wait the night out unless Mister M decides he needs to do more gloating. That's what the obedient version of me would do.

But something in me strains against the thought. A flicker of curiosity—or defiance; they feel the same after being drugged for two weeks.

Before I can talk myself out of it, I'm already moving.

The door groans open. The corridor beyond is dim, illuminated by wall sconces that flicker faintly as I pass. Only one direction to go. My shoes click loudly, but I don't have to venture far. Stark voices echo along the tile ahead of me before I even reach the turn.

"...second time's the charm." Mister M. His cadence is unmistakable.

"Maverick, surely you cannot be sincere."

"Oh, but I am," he replies, light as air.

Every instinct inside me screams to leave. Get back to

safety before he finds me and makes things worse. Against my better judgement, I press a hand to the wall and edge closer. I'm far too curious to leave now. And curiosity isn't rebellion unless you get caught.

"She doesn't act a thing like the Ellington heir I remember."

The what?

"That's entirely the point, Ms. Amani. The program is built on reformation."

Avery. She's talking about Avery. Although I wouldn't say she acted like much of anything this evening.

"Yes, I suppose." Ms. Amani's voice is laced with concern. "But do her parents know?"

Mister M—*Maverick*—chuckles, the sound of someone who enjoys being the smartest man in the room. "Know? I assure you, they are more than satisfied with her progress. Our team of doctors have been updating them regularly."

Parents? She has parents watching her progress? Parents who care? Something like jealousy burns inside me. I force it down, remembering that her parents knowing only makes them more complicit. They know what this place is doing to us, and they still gave up their daughter for the chance of "perfection."

"Oh, I see," Ms. Amani says, definitely not seeing. "Well, you should be pleased with yourself. She played beautifully tonight. Though I must say, it was a rather dark display compared to what we normally see at these sorts of festivities."

"Indeed. It was an academy classic. A piece from her roots."

Piece? Avery couldn't have played tonight; she could hardly stand up straight. And no one else in my pod was in attendance except—

Oh.

Oh God.

They're not talking about Avery.

Before I know I've moved, I'm running. Heels clattering against the tiles in unsteady strides. My steps aren't my own. My mind whirs. Buzzes. Goes blank.

Detonates.

Everything is wrong.

Wrong and bad and loud and—

Colt. I need to find Colt.

Or Ralston. Or V. Or anyone who isn't Maverick.

I need answers, and I need them right now before my brain explodes. A stray tear hits my cheek. I flick it away.

I'm being stupid. So stupid and rash, but I don't care.

Twice.

I've been through the program twice?

How is that even possible?

I want to believe I misunderstood. I misheard them. I'm reading too much into silly things.

Or more likely, I'm naive, memory-wiped, and blind.

I turn another corner, spotting the same marble pillar I passed two minutes ago. The back hallways are so confusing. An enforcer approaches. Older, with cropped hair and a scowl plastered on his features.

"Where are you headed?" he asks, eyebrows raised in suspicion.

"I have to go find out if my whole life's been a lie!" I don't say.

"I'm feeling ill," I lie, rubbing my hands against my dress. "I need to use the restroom."

"Where's your mentor?" He's pressing now, physically

blocking me from pushing further into the hallway.

"Preoccupied with another girl from my pod." Another lie. Still unconvincing.

Fine. If I can't lie to his face, I'll switch tactics.

I force myself to double over, coughing violently. It burns, but in a way, it's comforting to get the feelings out, even if it's just for show. Cry. Gag. Repeat. When I look back up, the enforcer is shell-shocked, watching me with confusion and a dash of fear. He steps aside, he's speaking harshly into his comm now, looking me up and down. I stride past him, slipping down another hall. He's unlikely to know my name or designation, so as long as I can get far enough from here, I shouldn't need to worry about backup arriving. I've almost completed a full loop around the back hallways before it dawns on me. Without an escort, I won't be able to get back into the training wing.

Seeing little other choice, I force composure and step back into the ballroom, scanning for any familiar face. But I see none. Besides Lance, who's still standing behind Avery in the far corner. Yeah no. *Not an option.*

I chance another step forward, but a firm hand finds my elbow. I wrench away, expecting to come face-to-face with Maverick. Instead, it's V. Face painted with concern as he takes me in. It hits me that I must look like a wreck from fake crying, gagging, and sprinting down the halls in impractical heels.

"Maysie?" he says, brows furrowed. "What's wrong? Where's Ash—"

"Is it true?"

He pauses, really confused now. "Is what true?"

The words die in my throat. I bite my lip, holding back tears as I grab his arms, squeezing tight enough to leave marks. His face flashes with panic. He runs a thumb along his cuff, cueing a breath reset. I follow, shakily.

"Maysie, you need to talk to me. What's wrong? Is what true?"

"Is it—" My words trail into a coughing fit. A real one, this time. He pulls me toward the door, shielding my face with his arm.

"It's fine. You're fine," he says. His other hand is on my back, guiding me into the hallway with hastened steps. Once we're tucked in an alcove, he spins me to face him.

"Talk to me." It sounds like a command, but his icy eyes are softened with concern as they meet mine.

"The program?" I manage, though it sounds like a question. My cheeks heat. "Maverick said— He said—" V winces as soon as I slip Mister M's real name. "I've been here before." It's hardly a rasped whisper, but he hears me.

Confusion. Panic. Guilt. The rate at which the emotions flicker across his face should win some kind of award.

That's the only answer I need.

I take a step back; he matches it.

"Maysie, I..." He trails off as bootfalls grow closer. He tosses a haphazard look over his shoulder, exhales slowly, then grips my wrist. "Not here."

We're moving again. He's dragging me down the hallway, breath labored.

"Wait!" I bite my lip to keep from crying. I root myself in place, gripping the gilded wall for any kind of anchor.

"Es—Maysie." He exhales hard, tripping over his words. "Please. This is not the time to be stubborn." V pulls again, but the walls I've constructed in my mind might as well be true concrete. Panic seizes me again as the steps grow closer.

"No. No I can't. I—"

"Maysie, please. You can scream at me. Question me. Fight me. Hate me. I don't care. But you can't do it here."

That sobers me enough for rational thought to return. I pry my feet from the floor and let him guide me out. I'm still mad, still confused, and very, very angry. But staying here won't get me any closer to what I need.

Answers. I need answers. And I need them now.

46

NOTHING OUT THERE

When he finally releases my wrist, we're in his room. Not his office—his room. I always thought it'd be polished, like him. Ordered, precise, nothing out of place. Instead, it's chaos. Folders spill across the desk in uneven towers, their corners dog-eared and bent from overuse. Loose pages litter the floor like he stopped caring where they landed. Multiple half-finished mugs of tea sit abandoned. The curtains hang stiff around the window, the sunset beyond a hazy pink.

The lower shelves against the wall are in ruins, the center panels cracked through the middle like someone drove their foot through them. I don't need to ask. I know with near certainty who did it. Mister M's temper leaves fingerprints everywhere. I can't stop wondering why V made no effort to fix or hide it. He left it there, broken.

It makes the whole room feel fractured. Like him. Like me. My mind is battling with too many desires all clawing their way to the forefront: I want to leave. I want to know. I want to breathe.

I force my head up.

"You knew who I was before tonight?"

He freezes, but he doesn't speak.

"You did." My chest tightens. "And you didn't say anything. Why? Why didn't you tell me?"

He exhales, long and strangled. "Because you weren't ready."

Not ready. The words slice me like a blade.

Not ready when I'm being dressed up and paraded around like a trophy.

Not ready when the ground feels like it's giving way every time someone says they've seen me before.

I laugh, but it comes out broken. "Not ready? I'm standing in front of strangers who look me in the eye like they own me. And you think I'm not ready?"

"Maysie—" The cuff on my wrist buzzes. His eyes flicker there before snapping back to me. He runs his thumb along his sleeve. *Breath reset.* I bite back the training.

"You're spiraling," he says, soft and steady, like if he stays calm, I'll follow. "Breathe. In for four. Out for eight. Stay with me."

I can't.

Not when my skin feels like it's turning inside out. I stumble toward the window. Anger drowns my thoughts with every step. He grabs my arm, but I shake him off.

"No! You don't get to smooth this over. Not after you lied to my face!"

"I didn't—" He huffs in exasperation. "I just—you have to stop, Maysie. You'll get flagged."

"Why am I here? What is this place?" My questions tumble out in waves. He raises his hands in surrender, face set in panic.

"You're here because this is the only path for you. You were given another chan—"

"I don't want another chance!" I cry, words tripping over themselves. "I want to leave!"

His jaw tightens. "Don't—"

"I mean it!" My chest feels like it's caving. "I want to go home, V! Why won't you listen to me?"

"You can't—"

"You're lying." My cuff screeches against my wrist, but I push through it. "Admit it!" The lamp on his desk flickers.

I stamp my heel into the carpet, shouting freely now. "Tell me there's more than this!"

Something in him breaks.

V moves like a shadow turned violent, crossing the room in a rush and slamming his fist against the window. The glass shatters in a web of cracks. The skyline dies, glitching and collapsing in on itself, revealing a sea of bare gray concrete and steel.

The truth stares back at me, raw and merciless.

"There's nothing out there!" he shouts. He turns back toward me, breath ragged. "You want the truth? There. That's the truth. This is all there is. These walls. Us. That's why you're here. That's why you were brought back."

The weight of it crushes me. My chest locks, breath tearing short. Ribbons of pain slice my mind, tangling into a web too thick to see through.

I stagger back, tears burning my skin. "You're lying."

"I'm not." His breath stutters. "I wish I was." My cuff presses, sinking its metal pronged teeth deep beneath my skin.

V doesn't move. His hand stays pressed to the ruined pane, trembling. His eyes close like he can't stand to look at me.

"No," I whisper, though I don't know who I'm arguing with. Him. The window. The cuff screaming on my wrist. Myself. All of the above. "That's not true. It can't be true." The walls draw closer, threatening to crush me.

"Maysie," he pleads. His hand slides off the cracked pane. He looks like he's aged a decade in a minute.

"I can't—" My knees buckle. I hit the edge of his desk, sending papers skidding across the floor. Numbers, names, reports. Proof of everything I don't understand. The broken shelf gapes at me from across the room like an open wound.

"I can't live like this," I rasp. "Not if this is all there is."

His mask slips entirely. The elegant control, the careful restraint, gone. He steps forward like he might catch me, but stops short, fists tight at his sides.

"I was trying to protect you," he says hoarsely. "I didn't—"

The door bursts open. For a split second, I think it's Carr himself—come to drag me God-knows-where. But it's Colt. He takes in the scene rapidly, and when he catches sight of me, he doesn't hesitate. He crosses the room in hurried strides, drops to one knee, and pulls me into his arms. I choke a sound that's half-protest, half-relief.

"Hey— Hey, it's okay, I've got you." He braces his hands on my shoulders. The warmth of his grip cuts through the static in my veins. "Breathe. Just breathe with me, all right? In. Out."

I try, but it falls out in shallow sobs.

V hasn't moved. He's frozen by the ruined window, shoulders rigid as if the concrete beyond demands his full attention. Colt glances up at him, fury detonating in his eyes. He pulls me closer, steadying me against his chest.

"I've got you," he murmurs again, firm against the storm raging in my head. "You're not breaking on me, you hear?"

"There's nothing," I whisper into Colt's shoulder. His arms wrap tighter like he can shield me from it all.

Behind us, V says, "We need to get her to—" Colt raises a hand to silence him.

"Mays— Hey. Look at me."

I can't. My chest is on fire. The lights overhead are sputtering like the power's on the fritz. His comm crackles on his shoulder, but he doesn't even reach for it.

"You're burning up," he mutters, more to himself than me. He presses my wrist into his chest, pinning it between us. The skin at my wrist sears against the fabric of his uniform. It chirps once, then slows as the signal muffles.

Colt scoops me up, arms hooking under my knees and back like I weigh nothing at all. "We're leaving."

"You—" My voice breaks. "You're supposed to—"

"I'm supposed to do a lot of things," he mutters, already turning for the door. "But I'm not going to let them throw you in the lab." V opens his mouth, but no sound escapes. He makes no move to stop us.

Colt shoulders through the hall like a soldier in enemy territory, head down, pace fast but measured, comm still prattling alerts.

"Stay quiet," he breathes against my hair. "I'll get you out."

His comm shrieks again:

"Status: Enforcer C19. Report the spike."

Colt shifts me higher against him and keeps walking. "False alarm," he says flatly, tapping the comm with the arm he has wrapped around my back. "Subject's stable. I've got it under control."

A lie, terrifyingly natural.

The corridor is wide and cold. Countless cameras blink overhead in sync. Colt masks the annoying cuff with every step, offering an easy smile to passing enforcers.

"Nothing to see," he calls, voice laced with soft demand. "Move along."

And somehow—they do.

By the time he kicks my door open and eases me onto the edge of my bed, I feel as though I'm seconds away from passing out from lack of oxygen. Colt drops to one knee in front of me, running his thumb along the cuff.

"You're fine now," he murmurs. "They're not coming."

I want to believe him.

The room's quiet, save for my ragged breath and the faint tick of the ever-present cuff. I don't know how long it stays that way. Eventually, footsteps pad closer. Slow. Deliberate. The doorframe darkens, and V fills it.

He's still flushed, dark hair mussed like he dragged his hand through it too many times, eyes like fissured ice. Unease flickers in his expression as he takes in the scene.

"Protocol dictates she should be in medical," he says, though it doesn't look like he believes it—more like he needed to say *something*, and the only thing he has to fall back on is the protocol he's made to enforce.

Colt doesn't even look up. "Protocol doesn't know a damn thing about her." The words hang, electric in the tense air.

"You're risking more than yourself."

"I'll take it," Colt fires back. "Better me than her."

For a heartbeat, I think V might drag me out himself, cuff or no cuff. But he's frozen, every line of him pulled taut. He's staring, but I can't hold his gaze. Not after what he said. Not after what I saw. My fingers twist in the blanket until I lose circulation. V finally steps into the room, toward Colt.

"Take your hand off the cuff."

Colt's head snaps up, face set in pure rage. He cocks his head as if to say, "Try me." Instead, he levels V with another glare and says, "If she spikes again, you'll lose her. You really want that on your conscience?"

The silence is *brutal.*

V's gaze cuts back to me—just for a second—then he turns away, jaw tensed. "I'll file the report," he says tightly. "It'll read as stable. See to it that yours says the same."

The door shuts, and the air collapses around me. Colt's hand is still warm over the cuff, the only thing keeping me here.

"You're okay," he says. "I'm not going anywhere."

Just when my breath starts to fall back into rhythm, the door opens again. Ryder—of all people—peeks in, curiously amused. "Oh damn. This is gonna be good."

Colt huffs a low, disbelieving scoff. "Why are you here? You weren't dispatched."

Ryder shrugs, unbothered. "Ballroom's dull. Thought I'd stretch my legs. And look—front row seats to *this.*" His gaze flicks to the light still pulsing under Colt's palm. "Carr's gonna have a field day."

"You didn't see this. If you're asked to report, you'll file her as stable."

Ryder raises his brows, mock-offended. "Oh, sure. And when Carr asks how she didn't get hauled to medical, I'll just say—what? Colt cuddled the problem away? Yeah. I'm sure that'll fly."

"Do it."

Ryder's grin falters. "God, you're serious. Fine. But if she explodes, Carr's going to wipe the floor with all of us, and I'm far too pretty to die."

His words tip me over the edge. A laugh bursts out of me, high and shrill. I press a hand over my mouth, but the sound claws out anyway, too loud in the suffocating quiet.

Colt panics. "Mays!" He runs a hand along my back. "Stop. Look at me." I can't. The laughter wracks my chest until tears blur my vision.

"Maysie." Colt's hand shifts, firm on my wrist, the other bracing my shoulder. "Breathe. You're safe."

Safe—that finally hits. The laugh dies in my throat, leaving me trembling, breath coming in ragged pulls. Colt breathes a long sigh of relief.

Ryder looks wholly unfazed.

"Stable," he mutters with a mock bow. "Glad I could be of service." His eyes cut toward Colt. "Don't make me regret this." He leaves as casually as he arrived, still chuckling to himself. Colt follows, but returns moments later, dragging a chair from the common room. He plants it beside the bed, close enough that his arm rests on the edge of the mattress. Every time I close my eyes, I see the window again. The shards, the glitching skyline, V's shout splitting the air as it tore me open. *There's nothing out there.*

My body aches with exhaustion, but sleep is a luxury I've never been afforded, even in my darkest moments. I roll onto my side, curling toward the wall, and the tears I've been holding back finally break loose. Relentless in their wake, quiet sobs rake through me, dragging months of pain to the surface.

Colt shifts closer, hovering close enough to anchor me with his presence. "They won't take you," he says, steady. "Not while I'm here."

I almost laugh at the absurdity of it. He's just one enforcer. One boy with scarred knuckles and too much stubbornness. He can't stop them. Not if they decide I'm broken. But he says it like he believes it. Like he'd fight the entire system bare-handed if it came to that.

I bite the inside of my cheek until the taste of iron drowns an oncoming sob. "Why?" I whisper, hoarse. "Why are you helping me?"

"Because you're not like the rest of them. And I...I can't watch them strip you down to nothing." The words sit heavy between us. Dangerous in their honesty. I bite back another wave of tears.

"I'm just like the rest of them. Don't you see?"

"I know what I see," he says sharply. "I see someone fighting like hell not to drown in their rules. I see someone who thinks, who feels, who lives. And I won't be the one to hold your head under. Protocol be damned."

My chest still hurts, a dull bruise now, replacing the relentless panic with something that may never fully heal. I curl tighter into myself, pressing my damp face into the pillow.

"This place—" I whisper, each syllable fracturing. "This place is poison." A rogue tear slips down my cheek. The words burn at the back of my tongue like venom, begging to be spoken. "It's killing us."

Colt rubs my back until my breathing evens, and I'm suddenly overcome with exhaustion. My skin prickles with the weight of everything I've seen. Worse, everything I can't unsee.

In the fragile edge before sleep takes me, one thought stutters on loop, jagged and sure: If V's right, if there's really nothing out there, I have no choice.

I have to fight for what's left.

47

EVERYTHING'S FINE

I don't remember when Colt left. Worse, I can't remember if I fell asleep on my own or if he sedated me. After last night, I'm not sure I'd be mad if he had. In fact, if he had gotten his hands on whatever magic sedative V claims works on me, I'd applaud him.

Lance wakes me well before the morning chime, setting a gray diagnostics shift on the chair and snapping that I have two minutes. I brace my hands on the bed and prop up on my elbows. My pillow is smeared with makeup. The sapphire dress is still clinging to me, all popped seams and wrinkles. My hair is a mess of pins.

I don't have time to fix it. My hands are at my back in seconds. I work the zipper down until the gown falls, pooling around my feet. I toss it over the chair, more than a little relieved to be rid of it. I hardly have time to splash some water on my face before Lance is back, ushering me down the hall.

The rational part of my brain tells me I *should* be panicking. But for whatever reason, I just can't. Whatever happens will happen.

I just have to be ready when it does.

Lance knocks on a tall metal door. I stiffen reflexively. My mind runs quickly down the mental list of who could be on the other side. We're too far into the medical wing for it to be an instructor or mentor. And I doubt any board member would step foot in here. Which leaves Carr, Rook, Kade, or Noxen.

I'm not particularly fond of any of them.

"Come in," a feminine voice calls from the other side.

Doctor Kade greets me with a grand smile. She's seated by the desk, blouse sleeves rolled to her elbows as she scrolls on her tablet. "There you are," she says warmly, like I've kept her waiting. When our eyes lock, her lips press into a small frown. "I heard you had a rough night."

I freeze mid-step, because "rough night" doesn't quite cover it.

Before I can speak, she waves her hand in a dismissive little flourish. "Nothing too unusual. Investor events can be overwhelming."

She doesn't even know the half of it.

Kade gestures to the padded chair, her tone so light it would be impolite to refuse. "Let's check you over."

I sit, waiting for the oncoming lecture.

Her hands are gentle as she connects the cuff to the system, humming softly under her breath. After a moment, she tilts her head, satisfied. "Already stabilizing. That's promising." She scrolls through a series of metrics, nodding briefly at each one. Numbers rise and fall across the screen in meaningless waves. "Stable across the board. Exactly what we want to see."

Wow. This place never ceases to amaze me.

I'm stable.

Twelve hours ago, I had a monumental freakout. Bad enough to make the man I'd consider the epitome of calm shatter a window just to make a point. Bad enough to make an enforcer put his life on the line to keep it hidden.

Yesterday, I was a trainwreck.

Today? I'm exactly what they want to see.

Catastrophic mistakes avoided: Twenty-three? Twenty-nine? I'm not sure. It's easy to lose count when the rules keep changing. If this truly is all a game, it's absolutely, positively rigged.

I suck in a long inhale. "So…I'm fine?"

Her smile deepens, warm enough to singe. "Of course you are. You're a strong one, Maysie. Resilient. Always have been."

Anger swells in my chest when she speaks about my life so flippantly. I nod before I even realize I'm doing it, like the trained girl I am.

"Good girl." She pats the back of my hand. "Keep this up, all right? Graduation is closer than you think. And you never know who's watching."

The phrase chills me to my core, but she's already turning back to her tablet. "You may go."

Lance is waiting outside, rigid and alert, hand on his stun rod like he's waiting for someone to leap out from the walls and attack. His gray eyes flick to me, unreadable, before he sets a measured pace down the corridor.

I trail after him, trying and failing to scrub Doctor Kade's smile from my mind before it imprints itself in my nightmares.

We've gone only a few paces when another figure blocks the hall.

Maverick.

Disgustingly crisp crimson jacket. Loosened tie. Hands in his pockets like this is a leisurely stroll and not a well-timed ambush.

"Come," he says smoothly. "You've earned a reprieve. A

walk in the garden. Consider it a reward for last night's performance."

I hesitate.

His brow arches but his smirk remains. "Don't keep me waiting, little star."

Lance stiffens, but he knows better than to interfere. He turns on his heel and strides away, mumbling something about schedules.

Maverick's hand settles lightly at my elbow, steering me through a side door. The air shifts instantly into something too humid to be natural. The garden is lush—roses trained up trellises, a fountain arcing in flawless symmetry, hedges clipped within an inch of their lives. It's pretty.

Pretty for a lie.

Now that I know the truth, it's easy to see past the facade. If I tilt my head just right, the edges of the simulated sky above flicker, tingeing green in some places. No fallen petals litter the ground. When the vented wind blusters the space, the leaves don't so much as rustle on the trees. Even the scent is wrong. The subtle notes of flowers and dirt are almost overpowered by lemon disinfectant.

It's gross.

It's gross and I feel like an idiot for ever believing otherwise.

"Radiant," he says, breaking the silence with venom-dipped praise. Gravel crunches beneath our steps as he guides me down the path. "That's what you were. Everyone saw it." His grin curves wider. "And when the lights went out? Inspired." Maverick huffs a laugh, flicking a speck of dust off his jacket. "For a moment, I thought you'd done it on purpose. How very Ellington of you."

The name knocks my composure loose, triggering a

landslide in my chest. My pulse falters, but I force my face still. Not quick enough. His eyes glitter, then sharpen with realization.

He knows I know.

But he doesn't know *what* I know.

"You know, I was proud. For once." He leans closer, breath grazing my ear. "They saw you flourish, and they knew you were mine."

I pull back. Scoff.

But his grip only tightens. "That's how this works. Your brilliance, my reflection."

"I don't belong to you."

He laughs, amused. "Of course you do. Everyone belongs to someone. You'll learn that soon enough."

I ignore that.

We round the fountain. The water arcs delicately before cascading into a pool of crystal and deceit. He stops, turning me lightly by the arm until I'm facing him. His smile is wicked as he takes me in.

"Don't fight me, little star. You'll lose." Maverick's thumb brushes the edge of my sleeve. "Always have, always will."

I think I'm going to vomit.

"Stay close, do as I say, and I'll make sure you stay untouchable. Even Harrow won't be able to interfere."

Yep. Definitely going to vomit.

It wouldn't be the worst thing in the world. Then, at least, something out here would be real.

As lovely as that would be, I resist the urge. I hold my tongue, waiting.

He doesn't wait for a response. His hand lingers at the small of my back as he guides me toward a stone bench.

"Ten minutes," he says, rolling his wrist in indifference. "Consider it a privilege. A stroll in the garden, while the others are stuck in drills. Don't squander it."

Privilege isn't the word I would use for it.

I take the minutes regardless.

48

SOMETHING GOOD

The common room feels wrong without her. The rug is too empty, the couch too firm. My eyes keep flicking to the corner where Juniper would be sprawled out, running her mouth until Ryder threatened to sedate her early. Every shadow that dances in my periphery feels like it could be her. But it isn't. And something tells me it won't be ever again.

"Tell me something good," Brielle whispers, voice trembling like she's afraid no one will answer.

The thought of speaking a single word right now tears a hole in my heart. June's plaque has been removed. Her room's been scrubbed pristine. No one will tell us when or if she'll be back. Every time I try to recall what happened that day, the memory slips further from my reach.

The other girls are just as unsteady. We're stuck in a stage of suspended grief. The well hasn't dried—so we just keep sinking deeper as the water grows colder, with no one in sight to offer a rope.

Ivy shuts her eyes, midnight braid slipping over her shoulder. "An endless sky, blue that dips to pink at sunset."

I close my eyes tight, but all I see is shards of glass and an empty void.

"Trees with pretty gold leaves. Ryder said that once." Bri's cheeks are stained with tears. "I want to see them."

Ryder leans over the counter, folding his arms tighter

with a nervous glance. "You wouldn't just see them," he says quietly. "You'd hear them. Wind weaving through the branches."

The sound hits me like a memory I don't own. Wind, untamed and alive. My chest ripples at the thought of air that hasn't been filtered through dusty grates. The taste of oxygen that's mine alone, untainted by the program.

Colt clears his throat. "Morning rain. The kind that makes you want to stay in bed."

Rain. I clutch the couch cushion like I could wring water out of it. I imagine it pouring through my bones until it washes out every drug, every order, every obedient thought they've ever burned into me.

Brielle blinks fast, fighting tears. "Stars," she whispers. "Real ones." Her hand finds mine.

"No rules," I rasp, interlacing my fingers with hers. "No labs. No tests. No one deciding what's best for us. Just—" I squeeze my eyes shut for a moment. "Just us. Somewhere far away, where none of this can follow."

Brielle's mouth wobbles into a shaky half-smile. Colt's jaw is tight, hands braced on the counter. Ryder stares at the floor, his usual smirk nowhere to be found.

Even the act of pretending feels wrong now, but we're close enough to touch. Close enough to keep saying it, to keep making it real. And for one fragile second, I let myself believe in the story. Even as everything I thought I knew crumbles to ash.

They've spent so long trying to train the truth out of us, but all they did was prove that some things can't be erased.

49

GOING DOWN

Another day, another sterile white hallway. Colt strolls beside me, too casual to be pulling me out of drills for a meeting with Doctor Carr. And yet, he's whistling a listless tune like we're traipsing through the garden. He won't give me details; I doubt he even has any to give. *"Enforcers aren't privy to subject intel. They're hardly even privy to the breakfast menu,"* he had told me when I pressed.

There are no containment cuffs today. No sedative or scratchy diagnostics shift to wear. Plus, Colt's alone. It should make me feel relaxed. *Key word: should.* I just can't get past the fact it can't be a coincidence that Carr wants to see me two days after my monumental freakout.

"For real though, where are we going?" I ask for the eighth time. He keeps his eyes forward, but I know he heard me.

"You're nosy," he mutters, then sighs. "It's just a meeting. Nothing weird, okay?" He's lying through his teeth and he knows it. He grips the ID card on his belt tight, which only cements it further. *Something is going down.*

I glance sideways at him. "You're not a great liar."

He cracks a grin. "Yeah, well. You're not great at staying out of trouble, so I guess we're even." My lip curls involuntarily at that. We round another corner, winding further down the unfamiliar halls. He's walking slower now—stalling without realizing it.

"Should I be nervous?" I ask, pretending it's a joke.

He lifts a brow. "You're always nervous."

"Not always."

Colt snorts. "You bit your spoon during breakfast."

"That was unrelated."

"Mm. Sure." He smirks. I try to smile, but it doesn't stick. A seriousness settles over the space, and he finally brings his gaze to mine.

"Hey. You're not in trouble, all right? Nobody's dragging you to a lab this time."

"This time," I echo.

He winces. "Bad phrasing, sorry." He changes the subject. "You ever been in this wing?" I shake my head. He gestures around the barren hall. "It's nicer. They've got padded floors. You may even get an upholstered chair."

"Are you trying to reassure or warn me?"

"Little of both." He gives me a half-shrug, motioning to the right.

We stop outside a grey door, no marking beyond a single red light blinking above the frame. I'm the last one here, if the loud, arguing voices are any indication.

"Colt—"

He squeezes my hand. "Just do what you always do. Smile. Breathe. Don't give them a reason to call me in. It would really suck to drag you out." He flashes me an almost-smile before tapping his ID on the scanner. I cross the threshold into the chaos as he takes his post outside, anything but prepared for whatever's beyond.

The air in this small conference room is frigid, both in temperature and mood. I catch what must be the tail end of a very long argument as I step in. Doctor Carr is seated at the far end, tapping his pen against the table like a metronome. V is pacing on the left, a file crushed in his hand. *Mine, I assume.*

"This is senseless. She's not ready," V snaps, folding his arms.

Carr doesn't even flinch. "Oh? But you approved the metrics yourself."

"Not for a custom trial," V says. "That wasn't in the documentation."

"I sent the addendum last night."

"You buried it in the fine print." V sounds exasperated, but I don't miss the twinge of guilt weighing down his words.

Maverick scoffs from where he's lounging. "So read better."

"Did you even read the addendum, Ashford?" V snaps toward Maverick, who cocks his head for a moment, like it had never occurred to him. A sickly-sweet smile spreads to the edges of his lips.

"Unlike you, I don't have time to play analyst all day," Maverick sneers. "Some of us actually have girls to mentor."

Yikes doesn't even begin to cover it.

I contemplate whether I should slip back into the hallway and make a run for it. V slams his palm against the table.

"Mentoring girls into oblivion doesn't make you qualified." He's seething now, knuckles white against the crumpling folder.

Maverick tilts his head. "Says the ghost they pulled out of retirement."

"Because someone had to clean up after you."

"You're real smug," Maverick says, "for someone whose

last room got scrapped."

V turns to him slowly, eyes icing over. "And yet here I am. Still working while you wait for your family name to open doors you never earned."

"Working? Yeah right," Maverick spits, folding his arms tight. "All you do is lurk, sticking your nose where it doesn't belong."

V looks like he might explode. Then he smiles, which is somehow worse. "When the board talks about legacy, they don't mean yours. You're a placeholder until the next Ashford can spell their own name. At least Prescott—"

"Oh don't even. You wouldn't know a thing about—"

"Boys, enough." Carr raises a hand like he's swatting flies, voice flickering with restrained pleasure. "One of you is under review, and the other's on probation. If you're done proving why, I'd like to salvage what's left of your reputations."

It only now occurs to me that I've stepped into a room full of vultures. It's like I'm in the middle of a very polite war. Death threats dipped in syrup being hurled both ways while Carr watches on in amusement. I get the feeling this isn't the first time they've done this.

Maybe not even the hundredth.

"What's all this?" I ask before one of them has the chance to strike. Three sets of eyes are on me in an instant.

Carr turns to me with that slow, unsettling smile. "A calibration trial," he starts. "Customized to your development. You'll be observed, of course, but it's nothing you haven't handled before." My stomach coils. I'm used to doctors talking me in circles and calling it medicine. Used to being told nothing more than what's "necessary." But this doesn't sound great.

V speaks quietly. "She hasn't had prep. Not for this."

"She doesn't need prep," Maverick says, stepping closer to me. His jaw ticks. "She can handle it, can't you, little star?"

I glance between them, patience already wearing thin on this dogfight. I turn to Carr. "What kind of trial?"

Carr waves a hand like it's unimportant. "Emotional stimuli, memory association, standard measures. You'll follow instructions, and we'll log your response rate." He says it like it's normal. But something about the way V has gone rigid tells me it's anything but.

"What happens if I fail?"

"You won't," Maverick says instantly, glancing toward Carr. "He wouldn't risk another failure on his record."

"You forget yourself, Ashford," Carr remarks. "Your family's reach ends at that door. In here, you answer to me." Carr spares a quick glance at both of them before settling on V. "Enough wasting time. All involved parties have signed the procedure. It will continue as scheduled." V opens his mouth in protest, but Carr's faster, turning to me with stiff precision.

"Go on," Carr says, flashing me a clinical set of white teeth. He gestures toward the adjoining room. "We'll start when you're ready."

50

THE FLARE

V stops me at the threshold, holding out a pair of metal containment cuffs. He doesn't meet my eyes as he adjusts the sensors with careful fingers, like he's handling something delicate. I've seen what these cuffs do; there's nothing delicate about it.

"Just relax," he murmurs under his breath. "You've done this before."

Have I?

My pulse kicks.

V doesn't wait for my response. Not that I had one to give. His fingers graze the inside of my wrist again. This time, I don't flinch. The second cuff blinks a brilliant orange. It sends a shock through me, searching for my pulse. Then another. On the fourth try, it turns green. Safe, supposedly.

I don't feel safer.

He looks at me now. Really looks. I brace for whatever it is he's holding back. Warning? Doubt? Something worse?

"Maysie—"

"I'm ready," I lie. I don't know what he has to say right now, but I don't want to hear it.

V sighs. His lips part like he wants to say something else, but he steps back, ice eyes lingering on mine.

The screen flashes as I step under the sensor. 214. Not my name. Never my name. Why even give me one if no one uses it?

When the door opens, I step in without waiting for permission.

I don't recognize the instructor on the other side. The badge on his hip is still shiny. He's likely new. He doesn't meet my eyes. That's fine. I don't want to see his.

"Baseline calibration," he announces. The lights shift to stark white, bright enough to be surgical. The vents above kick on, emanating the scent of copper and chemicals.

"Sit."

I sit.

"Stand."

I stand.

"State your designation."

"Two…fourteen."

Again.

"214."

Again.

"…214."

Each repetition rubs like sandpaper. He continues the pointless questioning, circling me like a vulture. I don't miss a beat, but the numbers don't sound like numbers anymore.

Carr's voice crackles through the intercom. "Baseline established. Initiating auditory stimuli: Set A."

My stomach twists. I don't know what that means, but it can't make this any better.

Sound blooms around me. At first, it's nothing but static. The thrum of an old speaker warming up after months sitting idle.

Then, footsteps. Heels on tile, moving in measured steps.

One-two. One-two. One-two. Then faster. Uneven. Overlapping.

Someone playing piano.

A scale played wrong. A slew of notes plunked out of tune. Keys slammed gracelessly like a toddler with rage in their hands. My head jerks at the first chord, but it keeps playing. Offbeat, off-key, relentlessly grating.

Tension courses through my hands in waves. I strain against the cuffs, metal fasteners digging into my skin until I feel the sting of blood.

"Repeat your designation," the instructor barks, eyes wary.

I try. I really try. I open my mouth, but nothing comes out. I hear the numbers in my head, loud and clear.

214, 214, 214, 214, 214.

Two. One. Four.

Nothing.

The sound doesn't stop. It loops, layering and warping into something unrecognizable.

Laughter.

Jagged and piercing, ringing right behind my ears. I spin before I can think. The room's sealed tight. I know that.

I still check. And it's still locked. The instructor is in front of me again. "Repeat your—"

I tune him out. I can't think. I can't breathe. The cuffs click tighter, red prickling at the edges. Override mist releases overhead—a cool cloud that's supposed to clear my head.

It doesn't.

I taste metal. And sugar. And smoke. My hands tremble. My skin crawls. The room bends around me, everywhere and nowhere all at once.

What's happening to me?

The lights flicker.

Once. Twice.

The piano stutters. The laughter grows closer.

My chest burns as though it's been scrubbed raw. I try to speak, to say anything, but my voice catches on whatever's clawing through my senses.

The instructor steps forward.

"Repeat—"

My pulse tears out of me. It slams into him, knocking him clean off his feet. He careens into the far wall, sliding down with a *thunk*, not moving anymore. The glass behind him shudders, trembling from a force I can't see.

I gasp, but no air fills my lungs. I don't breathe—

I *ignite*.

The cuffs dig impossibly deeper into my wrists, fighting to restrain something that's already broken free. I stumble backward, but the room moves with me. Tilts. Shudders. Vibrates.

What's happening—

I can't stop it.

I don't even know what *it* is.

Did they know this would happen? I think of the way V looked at me, the words he said.

You've done this before.

I'm losing control. But that's not fair. It's not possible. No one told me I had anything in me to lose control of. A voice inside me whispers I wasn't supposed to be like this.

I'm not like this. Right?

The mist streams in again, faster. My eyes sharpen on the observation glass. Three figures, completely frozen. I'm alone in here. Alone with this—thing—in me. This heat. This pressure. It's not stopping, and if it doesn't stop soon, it's going to kill me.

I spin toward the mirror. The girl who stares back at me is glowing, white-hot light streaking through her veins like a current. The ceiling pulses, then warps.

No—no, that's not right.

I blink, but it doesn't fix it. Air whooshes in my ears even though I'm not moving. My hands aren't mine anymore. They're shaking. Flickering. Splitting in two.

A light above me bursts; glass rains down in slow motion. I throw my arms up, but nothing hits me. The pieces still, hovering in midair. In every shard, I see a girl who isn't me. Or maybe she's not a girl. Maybe she's not a person at all.

What am I?

Another pulse strikes harder. The mirrors rattle, hairline cracks spreading violently. The instructor groans from the corner, barely conscious. I don't remember hitting him. I don't remember doing anything.

The seal breaks. The door flies open.

Enforcers. Four of them. Full gear. They see me—and stop dead. One raises his stun rod. Lowers it. His hand trembling at the motion.

They're afraid of me. *Why are they afraid of me?*

I didn't do anything. I didn't—I didn't mean—

A woman stumbles in behind them, a med tech. I know her. She checks vitals before diagnostics. She always smiles at me. She sees me now—

And runs.

Air surges beneath me. I'm not touching the ground anymore. I'm floating. Collapsing. Falling without motion over feet I can't feel. Carr doesn't move behind the glass. Neither does Maverick. I can't make out their faces, just the stillness lacing their frames. *Did they know?*

The third figure snaps. He slams his fist against the glass, eyes wide and icy and furious. He shouts something I can't hear over the ringing in my skull.

Another bulb bursts overhead.

I flinch—No, I jerk, a full-body spasm. Heat sears down my spine in waves, snagging on every vertebra.

An emergency door to my left bursts open, half-concealed by shadow.

No. *No*, he shouldn't.

But it's too late. The enforcers make no move to stop him as he charges toward me; they stay pressed to the walls, frozen in terror. The mist coils in ribbons around him; he strides through it like it's nothing.

My body spasms again. I can feel it now, every wrong part of me trying to tear itself free.

He's too close.

I try to scream. To tell him to leave, to run, to get away from me, but the words melt on my tongue.

"Please," I choke, but it's not loud enough.

A pulse bursts from me, hard enough to crack the tile beneath my feet. Another light explodes. Something hits him—one of the shards, maybe? He stumbles, clutching his shoulder with a wince. But he doesn't stop.

He doesn't stop.

Why isn't he stopping?

The cuffs restrain nothing. The heat sizzling down my arms is burning straight through them. My vision is completely fractured now, casting the world in wild hues dipped into endless shadows.

He's still moving. He's going to die in here.

I'm going to kill him.

Oh God—what am I doing?

"It's okay, you're okay." V's voice rubs like velvet. Steady. Calm. All wrong. His face is carved out of shattered composure and fear. Not for himself.

For me.

"You have to stop," he continues, concern dripping onto the glass-coated floor. "Your body can't sustain this. You'll tear yourself apart."

I open my mouth to scream, but my jaw isn't working. His hand lifts slowly, reaching for something on his belt. A syringe of swirling amber.

"Please," I beg again, hopeless.

V's eyes flicker with dread. He takes my wrist in his hand, pressing my skin firmly just above the cuff. "Breathe." He orders, with a softness that anchors me. Or breaks me. I can't tell which. But I feel it, square in the center of my chest.

His name is already rising in my throat before I can think better of it. I don't know why I know it.

But I do.

"Vincent—"

The metal door wrenches off its hinges, blown to pieces. It explodes outward. Into the hallway, into the chamber, into the last scraps of myself that felt human.

Vincent should retreat. He should run. Should flinch, at the very least. But he doesn't—he lunges. The needle finds my arm.

And I fall. Hard.

Not down. Not asleep.

I fall inward.

51

COME BACK TO ME

There's no floor here. No ceiling.

Only the weightless release of being stripped from my body piece by piece.

I can't breathe. My lungs aren't collapsing; I'm not gasping for air. My chest simply doesn't exist anymore.

Am I dead?

No, this hurts. Dead people don't.

Light cracks through the dark in flickers, phasing into visions that don't belong to me. A bustling dining hall. Pale arms adorned in long white gloves. A girl with red velvet ribbons in her hair. Piano keys cracking under pressure. A shapeless scream that doesn't have a mouth.

And a chandelier—

A chandelier imploding on itself, sending glass hurling to the ground.

I feel it hit me.

One piece. Then another. Every shard strikes true, cutting cold and sharp and wrong, and somehow I know this isn't happening.

The ceiling bends and warps like it did in the testing room, only now, it's above a ballroom. There are mirrors everywhere, tall and thin and impossible. I'm reflected in each one—but I'm never the same girl twice. I shift. Blur. Multiply into forms I don't recognize.

One version of me sits at a piano. Another holds a glass

with blood streaking down her palm. One is running barefoot down a hallway.

Which am I?

Displaced noises bleed through, warping the very
essence of time. Laughter that sounds like knives. Music
with no melody. The staggering end of a line with no path
forward.

None of this is mine, and yet it feels like it is.

My hands lift involuntarily, and they're glowing. Veins
of light spider under my skin, sparking like wires shorting
out. It occurs to me that I'm going to explode. I can feel it.

I'm dying.

Oh God—oh God. *I'm dying.*

I start to scream but nothing escapes. It reverberates inside my ribs, shaking loose every truth they've ever buried.

I see a white dress soaked in something too red. I see a
clipboard. A number. A new name written on top of the old
one. I see my parents as nothing more than faceless figures,
turning away.

I see him.

Vincent.

Too close to me, eyes too human for someone who's
supposed to be one of them. He's kneeling. One hand
steadying me, the other cupping my cheek. His face flickers
as he speaks words I know he's not allowed to say.

"You're still in there."

I try to say his name. I try to ask what's happening to
me. Why I remember things that didn't happen and see
things that can't be real and why every part of me is unraveling.

I feel the remains of my consciousness slipping away.
His hands tighten, but it's already too late. My world col-

lapses into startling white, and I'm falling again. Only this time, he can't catch me.

Surrender thrums in my bones, bringing a levity to my mind that I don't deserve. Darkness tugs, and I stop resisting. Sensations drain away, leaving only the echo of the girl I once was, and the one I couldn't be.

Somewhere far beyond, his voice reaches desperately for me. A final plea bleeds through the static. Not attached to a number or barked like a command. Spoken low, like a secret to be cherished.

"Come back to me, please, Estelle."

BITS AND PIECES

The world is thick.

It presses against me from every side. My eyelids are heavy. So heavy that the thought of opening them can't even begin to form. My body doesn't answer when I beg it to move. Every breath drags slow, foreign, like someone is breathing for me.

Fragments of voices miles away leak through the fog in broken threads.

"...*not safe...training wing...*"

Maverick. His voice, obvious even when blurred, cuts into me.

"...*reset...again...*"

Reset. The word digs tighter than the straps, phantom bands biting into wrists I can't feel. My chest fights, but nothing stirs. I'm locked inside myself.

"...*won't...survive another...*"

That voice is Carr's. Flat. Final. I can't tell if it's real or if I've dreamed it.

"...*fifty days...*"

Fifty echoes again. Then again. Each one farther away. Fifty days until—what?

"...*Harrow...oversee...*"

Harrow. Vincent Harrow.

They said his name. I know it.

The sounds blur together after that, far and muffled. My

mind claws for them, but my consciousness lulls back toward nothingness.

I can't move. Can't open my eyes. Can't cry. All I can do is listen. And the words don't leave me.

Not safe. Reset. Survive. Fifty. Harrow.

The darkness welcomes me home.

53

THAT WASN'T YOU

I don't know how long it's been.

I don't know if I care.

I don't even know if I'm real.

I'm in a bedroom—not one I recognize. The bed is too forgiving. With sheets soft enough to disappear into and a pile of pillows that might swallow me whole. I don't deserve it. I don't deserve to improve or graduate or be free.

Everything aches. It feels like I've been sucked through a straw and spat out. Every time I close my eyes, I see it again. The heat tearing out of me. The instructor's face warped with terror as I threw him into the wall. The mirrored walls splitting apart under the force of something I can't possibly be capable of. My stomach pitches so violently I think I might be sick. Instead, I curl in on myself, wishing I could disappear. Minutes tick by like seconds as I wallow. It takes far too many to realize I'm not alone.

Vincent sits at the desk, file spread open in front of him, pen lying useless across the page. His shoulders are hunched, his eyes shadowed, like the act of sitting upright is taxing him greatly.

I shift; my blanket rustles. His head lifts impossibly fast. The look he gives me is expectant, but not impatient, like he would've waited there all night if I hadn't moved.

"Why am I here?" My voice barely rises above a ragged whisper.

He stands slowly, crossing the space between us. Careful, deliberate, eyeing me like I might fracture all over again if he moves too quickly.

"You survived. They don't know what to do with that." His hand hovers above my arm. "But you're still breathing."

Tears sting before I can blink them away. "I shouldn't be."

He kneels in front of me, lowering himself until we're eye level. His hand settles gently against my arm. Even through his gloves, so I can feel every ounce of his warmth.

Vincent's eyes soften. "Don't say that."

"I didn't even know I could...I didn't mean to—"

"You weren't yourself," he says, low and urgent, like he needs me to believe it. "You were pushed too far, and your body reacted to survive. That doesn't make you a monster."

"I hurt someone," I whisper, nails digging into my skin. "I destroyed everything."

"No." He shakes his head. "You were out of control, yes. But you are not what happened in there." His hand tightens against my arm, like he could hold me together with nothing but sheer force of will.

A sob tears out of me before I can stop it. I bury my face in my hands, waiting for him to pull away. But his presence lingers, silent and solid, until the onslaught of guilt eases enough for me to hear him again.

"This is your new room. From now on, you'll have private instruction only," he says finally. The words themselves are a blow, even as he fights to soften them.

I shake my head until it aches. "I don't want this."

"Neither do I." His thumb brushes against my shoulder, a fleeting comfort. "But you're here. That's all that matters now."

"I don't deserve to be," I whisper. His eyes close briefly, like the words physically wound him.

"Don't you dare say that." Vincent takes a hard, shaky breath. "You deserve to live, Maysie. Even if you can't believe that yet."

Another sob rakes through me, leaving me in tatters. I don't fight it. I'm not sure I could if I tried. He stays with me until my breathing steadies. Then he exhales, the sound ragged. "I need you to meet me halfway. Rest. Cry. Pull through this. Whatever it takes. If you let yourself fade, I can't hold them back."

I want to tell him I'll try, but I don't want to lie. I can't hurt him right now—not when he looks at me like he can see past the monster I've become. I can still feel it. Buried in ashes just beneath the surface is an anguish unlike anything I've ever experienced. Beneath that, a desire carved deep, begging me to succumb to it. I shut my eyes tight, press my lips into a thin line. No matter how hard I try, I can't respond.

Vincent doesn't press; he pushes to his feet, pausing when he reaches the door. His next words are barely a whisper. "I'll fight every day to keep you here. Just promise me you won't give up before I have the chance."

54

ROCK BOTTOM, STILL DIGGING

Days follow. Three? Five? Twenty?

It doesn't matter.

Time loses its edges. The fluorescents overhead buzz at a pitch I feel in my teeth. Meals arrive, then vanish. I barely move, barely breathe. The fog never lifts. I can't tell if I'm still being drugged or if I've just given up.

Sometimes I drift to the piano and sit without touching the keys. Sometimes I sprawl on the floor and cry until someone carries me to bed. Mostly, I float, just waiting for everything to end.

When the door opens, it's always one of two shadows.

Vincent: quiet. Always carrying tea he forgets to drink. He sets it on the desk, checks my cuff, adjusts the room temperature two degrees without asking. He speaks like the walls might crumble if he's too loud. I hear my name more in his visits than in the last year combined.

Or Colt: louder by nature, even when he's gentle. He brings warmth with him, something alive that doesn't match the stale air. He plants himself at the foot of the bed and pretends to lose at cards he deals face-up. He tells stories I don't hear.

Wake. Drift. Sleep. Repeat.

The rest is blank.

I don't remember lying down, but I'm on the bed when their

voices start. A hushed conversation that settles just outside the edge of pretending I can't hear.

"Is she okay?" Colt starts.

"No spikes today. Vitals are normal. She's not breaching red; she's not climbing out either," Vincent says, stylus striking his tablet.

"Meaning?"

"Meaning she's surviving, at baseline at least. They have her on stabilizers until she can prove she won't bring the roof down. Carr won't tell me the doses, so I can't say how much of her…withdrawal is coming from side effects."

"Carr asked me for a report," Colt says quietly.

"What did you give him?" Vincent sounds startled, but not shocked.

"Nothing yet. I'm due in his office in twenty."

"Keep it vague. Nothing he can act on," Vincent says. "Once it's in writing, it's his."

Colt exhales, nervous. "What does he plan to do with her?"

"I don't know," Vincent admits. "He keeps throwing around recalibration, but that's not a viable option, not for her." I shift under the blanket, suddenly uncomfortable.

"She can hear us," Colt murmurs.

"I know."

Footsteps creep closer. Vincent's thumb presses my wrist above the cuff—one, two, three, four—then lifts. Breath reset without the command.

"Keep fighting, please," he says, so soft it might be for him. The door whispers closed. One set of unsure footsteps fades down the hall. Colt hesitates.

"Hey, Mays." The mattress dips near my ankle as he sits without asking. "Everything's going to be okay, okay?"

I don't answer. I'm not sure I can.

His voice warms anyway. "What about a story?" he starts. "First time I saw real rain, I was five or six. The sky split open. There were these huge clouds, so dark you'd think it was the middle of the night. Then *boom*—droplets everywhere. I made my dad stick a bucket outside just to prove to me it wasn't magic." He huffs. "I still think it was."

My mouth curls the littlest bit at that. His eyes light up.

"You think that's funny?" he continues, gesturing wildly with his hands. "You should hear what I did when I laid my eyes on snow."

My body strains to laugh, but I sputter out a half-cough. The intent was there, and I think he saw it.

"There she is." He smiles, patting my leg. "You're going to get through this. You have to, y'know. I won't accept anything else." Colt folds his arms like a petulant child. I don't know if I can believe him, but I appreciate him, and that's almost the same.

The next morning, I manage to drag myself out of bed. I stumble to the shower, scrubbing at least a week of agony from my skin until I'm red and raw. The only thing in the armoire drawer is a loose regulation white uniform, pinned with someone else's number. I tug it on with trembling fingers. When my eyes finally find the mirror, I can barely hold eye contact with the fractured girl who stares back. She's still breathing, but that seems to be all we have in common.

I'm still fighting a brush through my brown tangles when Colt strides through the door. He finds me instantly, looking startled. Then surprised. Then relieved.

"Mays," he breathes.

"Hi," I croak, yanking at another knot. I yelp, fist clenching around the brush.

"Do you want help?" Colt's smile is so warm I could collapse into it. I can't form a response, but he doesn't seem to mind. He strides to the chair in the corner, then gestures for me to sit in front of it. I pass him the brush and drop to the ground, pulling my knees tight to my chest.

"I can't promise this won't hurt," he tells me. I nod, biting back a wince anytime he pulls too hard. For an enforcer trained in nothing but violence and sedation, he's almost gentle. Once he has a handle on the tangles, he runs his fingers carefully through my hair, calming the static. He clears his throat and presses a hand on my shoulder. "One braid or two?"

My eyebrows raise in surprise. "You know how to braid?"

"I grew up with sisters. Plus, I've watched you do it countless times. How hard could it be?" He fumbles, starting over at least six times. Eventually, muscle memory kicks in. The finished product isn't perfect, but he beams like it's a masterpiece. The sight of it brings a lightness in my chest I haven't felt in months. It dissipates almost instantly, and I'm empty all over again.

"What should I do now?" I ask, hating how small it sounds.

"Anything." He nods at me, then pauses. "Except sleep. You've done a *lot* of that." I offer a small smile, but my mind goes blank. What do you do when everything feels meaningless? He cocks his head at my silence, a small frown tugging at his lips. "How about cards?"

That...doesn't sound half bad. I offer him the ghost of a

nod and climb back up on the bed. "Okay."

We don't chat. We don't confess fears or spill secrets or commiserate. We just play. And for a few minutes, everything's okay again.

55

WHAT DO YOU WANT?

This morning, there's a new uniform dress waiting for me. It's a soft lavender, stitched finely with gold and complete with a piano aptitude pin affixed to the collar. I step in front of the mirror, taking in the way it clings to my form. The hem falls in a soft swish a few inches above my knee. It's stunning, even nicer than the ones Maverick had made for the other girls.

There's a knock. Vincent's here again. *Of course he is.*

He's been showing up every day, leaning in my doorway with his crisp posture and infinite patience.

He doesn't linger in the hall. He walks straight in, slow yet certain, and sets himself against the desk like it belongs to him. The overhead lights catch on the faint glint of his pale blue eyes. He looks measured, determined. Clearly not just here to check a box.

Colt strolls in behind him and settles by the wall, guard-dog casual, arms folded, watching like he's front row to something worth betting on. Vincent holds up a schedule, taps it against the desk, and speaks:

"What do you want?"

It's so direct my mind stutters. "Excuse me?"

His gaze catches mine, holding it. "Tea in the mentor's lounge?" He flicks his wrist for dramatic effect, words tipping sarcastic. "Solo sessions in the piano room? An afternoon in the garden? I can move your diagnostics. Have Colt smuggle you candy, whatever you want. Which is it?" His tone is dead serious now. There's no bite, no judgment or dry remark.

I want to laugh. *Why is he playing with me like this?*

"You can't just do that."

"Yes," he says simply, "I can." The certainty in his voice isn't for show. It's not about power. He's not trying to drown me; he's throwing me a rope, and the flash of care in his face tells me he's begging me to take it.

Colt tilts his head, a slow smile spreading over his features. "Oh, this is going to be good."

Vincent starts swapping blocks on the schedule without waiting for my answer. Garden hours slip into the space where an evaluation used to be. He moves an "Investor Presentation" off entirely. Every group drill's block disappears, replaced with piano or simply "downtime."

"What's the point?" I ask, an ache settling over my ribs. I don't deserve special treatment. Not after what I did.

"The point," he says, pen still in motion, "is that you're capable of more than sitting in this room waiting for someone to decide what happens to you." There's a softness buried in it, one most people would miss.

Something tightens in my chest. "I'm not sure what I'd pick."

"Pick one thing." Vincent sets the pen down, folding his hands on the desk.

I don't let myself think about it any longer. "I want to see Brielle."

That stops him. His eyes unfocus, running quick calculations I can't read. He knows exactly how complicated that is. How much Maverick will hate it.

"That," Vincent says after a beat, "might take work.

Colt lets out a low whistle, clearly entertained. "Oh, I like this game."

Vincent ignores him. "If that's what you want, I'll see what I can do. In the meantime—" He crosses the room to me in a matter of seconds, holding the schedule out. "You'll take the rest." I take it, and he moves his hands up to my neck, adjusting the pin slightly and straightening my collar.

"It looks sharp on you." He nods, something like guilt flashing in his eyes. "You deserved to have it a long time ago," he adds under his breath. It strikes me as odd. He nods to Colt as he passes, taking his leave wordlessly. He didn't wait to be thanked, this wasn't a grand gesture. It's expected. Bare minimum, even. And I can't really decide how I feel about that.

I stare down at the paper. Trace my fingers along the blocks. Garden hours. Music. Downtime. They're small things, but they feel...possible. For the first time in weeks, something warm threads through the numbness.

I'm not whole yet, but maybe I could be?

That's the part that terrifies me. Because he meant it. Because if I start to believe him, and it's taken away... I don't know if I'll survive the pain it leaves behind.

My new schedule starts tomorrow, which means today I'm at the mercy of whatever V and Colt have in store.

I don't have to wait long.

Colt kicks the door shut with his boot, balancing a tray in one hand and something gray folded under his arm.

"Lunch," he announces. He sets the tray down on my desk, then flicks the folded thing onto the floor. A blanket.

"What's that for?"

He smirks. "You think I'm gonna let you sit here stiff as a board while you eat? Nope. We're having a floor picnic."

"I don't think there's a protocol that covers this."

"There is now." He drops down onto the blanket without waiting for me, long legs stretched out, leaning back on his hands. "C'mon."

Reluctantly, I slide off the bed and settle across from him. The tray between us looks almost normal like this: sandwiches, fruit, bottled water. Like we're not buried underground, surrounded by white walls and locked doors. We eat in silence for a while. I stab at sliced pears that smoosh against my fork. Every bite is bland, though I'm sure it was always that way. Colt doesn't press, but words crawl up my throat—an admission neither of us asked for.

"I hurt people."

He glances up, chewing slow. "You flared."

"I—what?"

"Flared." He swallows, then sets his sandwich down. "Look, it's hard to explain. But it's fine. You didn't mean to."

"That doesn't change that it happened!" I fight back a swell of tears, holding his gaze. "You didn't see it. I was destroying the walls without even touching them! The ceiling was bending and things kept breaking and I—"

"You think you're special for that? You think you're the first girl who's ever lost control?" I stare at him. He's too calm. Too matter-of-fact for the nightmare I've been living. He tilts his head, eyes softening. "Mays, every single girl down here is here because of a flare. Brielle. Ivy. Hell, even Avery before she went all glassy. All of them. That's the price of admission."

I flinch. "Why?" The word hangs between us. Colt rubs the back of his neck.

"Hell if I know. Carr says it's in your DNA, some 'genetic anomaly.' He's been tearing girls apart for a decade trying to name it." He shakes his head. Rakes a hand through his hair. "He keeps saying it's caused by too much emotion—like that covers it. Grief, rage, panic. Doesn't matter. You feel too much, you flare, you scare someone. Next thing you know, you're down here, getting told you're lucky. Easy for them, right? Blame the girls and get the glory of playing savior."

My chest tightens. "So I really am...different."

"I mean—yeah. But different doesn't mean wrong—" He stops. Frowns. "Okay, it *feels* wrong. I get that. But you didn't deserve this—you *don't* deserve this."

"Feels like I do." I run my fingers along the rough edge of the blanket, tearing my eyes from his so I don't have to face the kindness there.

"I know." He nudges my knee with his boot. "That's the part they're good at."

That startles me. I bring my head up and meet his caramel eyes. There's so much warmth nestled in the hearth of his irises. So much life I've come to know—and so much I haven't learned. He reaches for my hand, then pulls it back.

"You're not some wild animal that needs taming. You're a teenage girl who got slammed with something she didn't ask for and is just—" He gestures helplessly, exasperated. "Just trying to keep her head above water while a bunch of men in suits decide how much of her is worth keeping."

"They told us—"

"Yeah, I know what they told you." He laughs, bitter. "You've been saved. They're here to polish you up, fix your rough edges, make you perfect little graduates. Bullshit. They don't care about making you better. They care about cutting out whatever they can't control."

Something shifts in my chest, but the hollow ache doesn't fade. "I'm never going to be enough."

Colt folds his legs under him and leans forward, elbows braced on his knees, voice laced with heat. "You were enough before they ever dragged you down here. That flare wasn't even your fault, Mays. Carr knew exactly what he was doing when he sent you into that trial." He sits back on his heels. Shakes his head. "It didn't go how he planned, but you're still here. That alone should tell you the system's rigged." His voice cracks rough on that last word. He swears under his breath.

I bite back a hundred more questions that would send us into a spiral. I need to stay in the present, at least until I can figure everything out. "What am I supposed to do?"

He exhales hard, shoulders sagging. "What you've been doing. Breathe. Fake the drills. Eat their food. Keep moving. That's all survival is. Living one step longer than the game was built for."

The memory of Mister M's words in the ballroom crashes into me.

"Everything within these walls is a game, darling. You just haven't learned to play."

A game. That's all this is. A sick, awful game.

One I've been losing for too long.

I choke down a deep breath. The sandwich in my hands blurs beneath the tears brimming in my eyes.

Colt taps my leg again, soft. "And for what it's worth? If I had the answer to what causes flares, I'd give it to you. I don't. None of us do. Carr plays God with a clipboard, and the rest of us just watch." His face falls, heavy with guilt. "I hate watching."

My whole body stiffens. The gears in my head turn and sputter, but nothing forms. Clearly, world-crushing realizations are not made to be had when you're eating sandwiches on the floor. I decide to change the subject. I glance at the blanket, at the crumbs between us, then back to him.

"You always eat like this?"

Colt lets out a small laugh, leaning back on his hands again. "What, on the floor? Only when I've got my boss breathing down my neck."

I blink. "Mister M?"

"Hell no." He lets out a laugh. "Carr moved me under Harrow last week. Full reassignment."

Colt—under Vincent? I try to picture it, but the images don't fit. Colt's all warmth and sarcastic jokes. Vincent is... well I still don't really know *what* Vincent is, but not that.

"He tells you what to do?"

"He doesn't have to. Other day I got smart with him. Half a joke, nothing big. He looked at me and said, 'Don't make me wish I'd taken my chances with Ralston.'"

I bite back a laugh at the absurdity of it. "He said that?"

"Yeah." Colt tears his sandwich in two with more force than necessary. "I shut up so fast I swear he could've heard my teeth rattle." He shakes his head, grinning despite himself. "He's got this way of making you feel like you're two inches tall just by existing in the same air. Can't decide if it's terrifying or impressive."

I stare at him, sandwich forgotten in my hands. "Maybe both."

It should scare me more than it does. That he can cut Colt down like that. That he has that kind of weight, that quiet power. Maverick has to shout, preen, posture, spin threats and lies in sugar-coated webs. Vincent doesn't even have to speak.

I've felt that look on me, the one Colt's describing. The one that makes you forget how to breathe. Colt makes him sound like a stone wall, immoveable and unfeeling. And maybe that's true for others. But I've seen him tilt, bend, break rules he shouldn't just to keep me steady. And it's confusing.

It's easier to hate Maverick. Easy to see his smirk and know it's poisoned. But Vincent… Vincent is harder to bear. Not because he's cruel, but because he isn't. Not always, at least. He gives me air when I'm drowning, then watches as the system pulls me back under. He knows what this place does, yet he stays.

And still, Vincent's been here, trying to hand back the one thing I lost: hope.

I just wish I could figure out why.

56

DAMAGE CONTROL

Today, we're in my new "enrichment room."

It's far too big for one person, but Vincent assured me no one else is using it. He's stuffed it with random things like he's trying to guess my thoughts. Sketchpads, watercolors, even a stack of novels I probably won't read. There's a small upright piano in the corner, angled toward the fake window I asked Colt to cover up. The lights glow warmer in here, but they do nothing to make the space feel like anything but another cage.

"You could try the paints," Colt suggests, nudging the sketchpad across the table. "Or the piano. Or—" He digs into the basket in the corner. "Look at this. Harrow thought you'd be into weaving? You could make a rug. I'd take it."

I give him a flat look from where I'm curled in the armchair. "No."

"Tiny coasters? Big market for those underground."

I almost smirk, but a wave of nausea overpowers it. "You're bad at this. You know that, right?"

He drops into the seat across from me, kicking his legs over the side. "All right. What's the point, then? Sit here until you get all dusty?"

"Sounds fine to me."

"Mays," he starts, eyes softening. "It couldn't hurt just to try something. You could just sit at the piano for a few minutes? Fondle the ivory or whatever it is you do?"

I shake my head. "I don't want to."

He opens his mouth again, but I'm faster.

"I came in here. Shouldn't that be enough?" The admission is pathetic, but I don't have it in me to care.

His posture shifts, and with it, his tactic. He pulls a face that's akin to a kicked puppy. "Boss-man said you had to try something." He pouts his lip and holds his hands up in surrender. "You wouldn't wanna get me in trouble, would you?"

Fine. I lean forward and make a squiggle on the sketchbook lying on the table. He hums, delighted.

"All I'm hearing is you're in an arts and crafts mood." Colt strides across the room to rummage through the craft bin again. This time, returning with a bag of something gray and squishy. "Modeling clay!" He holds it triumphantly over his head, beaming like he's just cracked the code. "You could make little sculptures of Mister M and smash them in the garden."

My head snaps up before I can stop it.

"Tempting, right?" He waves it in my face.

I push it aside. "That's immature."

"Uh-huh. I'd still help you do it." The door clicks and Colt glances over his shoulder. "The man of the hour," he mutters, stepping back.

Vincent steps in, eyes surveying the room like he's scanning for damage. His gaze flicks over me, the untouched supplies, the closed piano, then lands on Colt.

"How's she doing?" Vincent asks mildly.

"Thriving. You should see her artwork."

Vincent ignores him entirely, crossing the space until he's standing over my chair. He peers down with curious eyes. "I have news you might like to hear."

I roll my eyes, but the motion has no energy. "Hmm?"

"You're going to see Brielle." The words land like they've been dropped on my head, ringing loud through the room even though his voice stays quiet.

It's been one day. How is that even possible?

"That's not—" My throat tightens. "You can't just—"

"I can," Vincent says, like it's a fact. One that's not up for debate. He sets a file on the table, flipping it open just far enough to make a point before closing it again. "And I have."

Colt leans forward, brows raised. "Well, that's news."

I look to him. "Did you know he could do that?"

"Didn't have the faintest," he says, grinning wide. "But I'm enjoying this."

Vincent clears his throat. "It wasn't easy. She's not mine to move, but I made it happen. I'm not sure for how long, but she'll be here. No cameras. No audience. If you want it."

Of course I want it. The answer is already forming before my mind catches up.

But I can't help but feel a flicker of suspicion. "Why?"

Vincent crouches so we're at eye level. "Because you asked for something. And because you need it."

I search him for the catch. "Maverick would never—"

"He didn't have a choice."

I want to ask how, but I already know he won't give me the full answer. I glance at the oversized bin of untouched art supplies, the clay still clutched in Colt's hands, the piano keys I'm too scared to touch. He's been trying to bribe me back to myself, inch by inch. And now—this.

"You really can do that?" I ask, softer this time.

One corner of his mouth lifts, just enough to make it clear he's holding the winning card. "I already have."

Colt lets out a low whistle, still grinning like a fool.

"Damn, Harrow. Power looks good on you."

Vincent doesn't acknowledge him. His attention stays on me, steady. "Well?"

I perk up, rolling out my shoulders. "When?"

"Tomorrow," he says, just as his tablet pings against his hip. He sighs. Scrubs a hand down his face. "I have to go. Just—try to do something, all right?"

I give him a slow nod as he turns to leave. He murmurs something too low for me to catch, tugging on a pair of black gloves.

Once I'm sure he's gone, I turn back to Colt. "Where's he always running off to?"

Colt shrugs. "Wherever Carr points. Damage control, if I had to bet. That's his specialty. He's Carr's guy for the fires no one else can put out." He settles back into the chair, tossing the clay from hand to hand. "Could be anything, though. Could be notes, could be clean-up, could be polishing the man's shoes. Doesn't matter—when Carr whistles, Harrow's already halfway down the hall."

I don't bother hiding my shock. "Really?"

"Morning, noon, and night." He glances my way. "What? You think they call him the hound for his pretty coat? It doesn't matter if he looks like he's running the place. He's not. He's on a leash, same as the rest of us." His grin slips, the clay falling into his lap. "He just hides it better."

Leash. I almost laugh it off, but unease sinks in my stomach. I should feel safer knowing that even he answers to Carr, but all I can think is how tired he looked, how fast he moved when the tablet pinged—like hesitation would cost him far more than himself. He runs himself ragged on Carr's every whim.

And for what? To what end?

Colt waves a hand in front of my face, prying me from my guilt spiral. "Hey. We aren't focusing on that right now. You told him you'd try. So we're trying. Grab some clay."

I slide off the chair slowly, reaching for the bag. "Why are we doing this again?"

He rips off a piece, smushing it between his fingers. "Cause it's fun." His gaze softens. "You deserve something fun."

"Fun," I echo, staring at the clay. I want to roll my eyes again, but something lightens in my chest. "I'll be the judge of that."

57

TALKING NONSENSE

Colt was right. It was incredibly fun. Stress relieving, even. For a few minutes, I forgot how insane my life is now.

But it's a new day, which means the insanity returns, just as it always does.

Colt's wristband flashes blue just after breakfast, informing us that it's time to see Brielle.

I dodge his glances as we ascend the stairs. I should've prepared something—anything—to say to her. But my mind is blank, just a tangle of too many secrets. I can't even imagine what she's been through. First Avery, then June, and now, my disappearance. That's a lot to grapple with for one person, especially under a mentor who's decided that rules don't apply to him.

I'll improvise. It's not like I have another choice.

Lance is waiting at the door, his face vacant as I slip past him into a sparsely decorated sitting room.

Brielle's already here, sitting on the edge of a plush chaise, legs crossed at the ankles. Her cheeks are blushed the softest pink, blonde waves pinned back into an intricate updo. She jumps to her feet when she sees me, practically glowing; the picture of obedience.

Something I'll never be. Something I apparently never was.

"I can't believe it," she squeals, crossing the room in bouncy strides and enveloping me in a hug. She smells like roses dipped in antiseptic. "You're actually here!" Her smile is wide when she pulls back, almost reverent. "I heard you're graduating soon! Is it true?"

I open my mouth. Nothing spills out but a painfully nervous chuckle. Graduating. That's what she sees when she looks at me. To her, I'm a raging success.

"I knew you'd do it," she rushes on, squeezing my hands. "I told Ivy you would. Mister M said you were... difficult sometimes, but I never believed it. I knew you'd prove him wrong."

Difficult.

That's one word for it.

My shoulders tense as I let the fake smile fall. "Bri, it's not really like that."

She holds my hands up, still clutched in hers. Tilts her head. "What do you mean?"

"I'm not polished—or whatever they say this tier means." The words taste like a defeat for a battle I didn't know I was fighting. "I'm just here."

For the first time, Bri's smile falters. "But that's what 'here' means." Her voice softens, like she's correcting a child. "This is the last step. You're so close, Maysie. Don't you see?"

I shake my head, wishing I could fake excitement. "I don't feel close."

Something in her eyes shifts. The sky-blue shine dulls, replaced by something fragile. She tucks a strand of hair behind her ear, nodding like she gets it—when she certainly doesn't.

"Well, maybe it'll sink in soon," she says, her tone lightens, but the warmth doesn't return. "You'll graduate before us. That's...wonderful." Bri offers another smile, but it doesn't reach her eyes. "Try to enjoy it."

I lean forward, fighting the strain in my throat. "Bri…there's something you don't know. A lot of things, actually. About why they moved me here, why the others—"

She sucks in a hurried gasp, panic flashing in her eyes. "Don't."

"Just hear me out—"

"No." She shakes her head hard, hair slipping loose from its pin. "Don't say it. Please." Her fingers tangle in the hem of her skirt. "If it's bad enough that you can't say it out loud, I don't want to know. Don't make me know."

The words crush the breath out of me. She doesn't want the truth. She wants the dream. The hollow promise.

"Brielle—"

"I'm glad you're here, Maysie. I really am. I just—" She leans in for a quick hug, breath hot against my ear. "Hide this." Something hard presses against my ribs. My fingers find a worn cover. I don't need to look to know what it is.

Creatures of the Night.

My pulse spikes. I run my fingers along the coarse edges, heart pounding so hard I might pass out. I swallow hard, forcing my hands still long enough to tuck the book into my cardigan pocket. "Bri, what are you—"

"Enough."

Maverick's smooth voice cuts the air clean. He appears at my back like he's been there the whole time. One hand clamping down on my shoulder, the other at my neck, forcing my chin up. His smile is poised, but his eyes are daggers.

"Don't fill her head with nonsense, little star. You've caused enough damage." He releases my neck, letting his hand fall to my shoulder. I shudder, but he doesn't so much as flinch.

Brielle blinks up at him, startled. Her cheeks flush. For a moment, I swear I see doubt flicker across her face. But she smooths it away, furrowing her brows and inclining her head at us both.

Maverick squeezes my shoulders, a threat poorly buried in his grip. "It seems like you girls are finished here."

My blood runs cold.

Brielle forces a smile. "He's right. I should go." She offers a small nod, eyes skimming over me one last time before she turns to let Lance lead her out. Lance flashes one last glance at Colt, who rubs the back of his neck, pretending not to notice.

Maverick twists my shoulders hard, catching me just enough to keep my body upright while I stumble like a fool. Now facing him, he flashes me his perfect teeth; the kind of smile that makes you feel like the walls are closing in.

"You think Harrow can keep you safe from me? He can't even keep you quiet."

"And you could?" I retort, folding my arms so I don't slap him.

"Cute," he sneers, wrenching my shoulders back hard. I press my lips into a line, willing my mouth shut. He cocks his head. "Don't pout. It doesn't matter what you told her. By tomorrow, Brielle won't remember a word."

"What's that supposed to mean?"

"Don't ask questions you already know the answer to." His voice drops low, intimate in a way that makes my skin crawl. "It's unbecoming."

"I don't—"

"Maysie," Vincent calls from the doorway, eyes locked on Maverick.

Maverick laughs. "Better run along, little star."

58

TO PLAY OR NOT TO PLAY

It's been six days since I agreed to give this whole polishing thing a shot. Four since I terrified one of my only friends. Despite my ever-dwindling sanity, the routine's been the same. Colt brings me in for piano at one. We sit in silence while I stare at the keys until five, then he brings me back. I can't bring myself to even touch it, let alone pull up a song or try to play.

Time like this was a privilege I would've pleaded for a month ago. Now it feels like a gift I'm no longer worthy of.

Vincent stands at my side, hands folded behind his back, set in his typical statuesque posture. But his weight shifts every so often, betraying a body that would rather be doing anything other than watching me hurt.

I swivel on the bench and pull my knees to my chest. "What if I never play again?" I ask the ceiling, hoping no one will answer.

Vincent clears his throat, a little flushed. "You will."

I tip my chin, half in pain, half in petty defiance. "And if I don't want to?"

"Then we'll wait until you're ready."

"You're good at that," I say. "Waiting. Watching."

"You'd want me angry instead?"

"I'd prefer if you were honest."

His expression sags the littlest bit. "I'm not going to force you to play. And I'm not going to raise my voice when

305

you don't deserve it." Something shifts in his shoulders. Guilt isn't loud on him; nothing is loud on him, honestly.

"Even if I never play again?"

"If you're truly determined to never touch a piano again, then I'll move you to speech," he says, a faint shard of humor buried in his serious tone. "If you refuse to speak, I'll switch you to dance. If you refuse to stand, I'll log that you held your ground. I'll file a thousand forms if it'll keep you here."

"You think you're clever."

"I *think* I can buy you time."

Colt tips his head. "Gotta hand it to him, he's irritatingly good at this."

I keep my eyes set on Vincent. "Time until what?"

"Until you're ready," he says quickly, scrubbing a hand over his mouth. "You're going to graduate, Maysie. I won't accept any other outcome. You've worked too damn hard to give up here."

I hug my knees tighter, staring down at the lacquered bench. And I know he's right. *I can't just sit here forever.*

"I'm setting terms," I announce, surprising myself as much as them. I immediately feel silly, but I don't take it back.

Vincent's head tilts, that ever-present unreadable calm faltering. "Terms?"

"You want me to try? Fine. But I want ground rules."

His head bobs. "Go on."

Colt's boot scuffs the tile with a squeak as he steps forward, eyebrows raised with intrigue.

"One—" I lift a finger. "I want to choose when to stop. No mandatory drills or running pieces until my fingers go numb."

He opens his mouth, but I cut him off. "And two… you answer me honestly. No more half-truths, no more 'you weren't ready.'" My voice shakes, but I hold his gaze anyway. "I've been fed enough lies to last a lifetime."

My heart aches with the honesty of it. All I've known are lies. Down to the very reason for my 'renewed' existence.

"Three, you stop talking like the organization rescued us from something worse."

His gaze shifts to his shoes, then back to me. "For the record, I never said that."

"But you let me believe it."

Vincent's jaw tightens. "I did what I thought would keep you safe." He lets out a shaky breath. "I'm sorry."

There it is. A real, raw apology. One that almost no one in this place has ever offered me. I give him the ghost of a nod, so caught off guard by his painful honesty that my next point jumbles in my throat.

Colt awkwardly clears his throat. "And while we all sit in this stew of mutual rage and tragic honesty, might I suggest the garden after this? Ten minutes of pretending the air is real would work wonders for my spirit."

"I'm not done." I coax my thoughts straight and turn back to Vincent. My words are shaking now, but I don't let them fall. "Four, you will not touch me without asking. You will not sedate me. You will not use restraints."

They both stare at me for a long moment, waiting for me to make another demand. Truthfully, I have nothing—I wasn't really planning to get this far.

"That's all."

I wait for the rejection. The quiet "that's not how it works." The reality check disguised as "what's best for me."

But neither of them moves. Vincent's eyes flash to Colt,

who just shrugs.

"Sounds reasonable to me."

For a moment, the air between us thins. Vincent's expression doesn't shift, but something flickers in his ice-blue eyes. Hesitation, maybe even the cost. He files it away with a tick of his jaw, lacing his fingers tighter behind his back.

"Very well," he says softly. "Terms accepted."

I cock my head, unconvinced. "That was too easy."

"Prove you'll play, and I'll shake on it." Vincent gestures to the piano that's ten inches from my face. I roll my eyes.

"Really?"

"Really."

I let out an exasperated sigh and wring my hands. I take my dear sweet time leaning over before plunking out a few notes. It sounds awful. But it's real, and it's mine. Not the strained, bloodied keys that linger behind my eyes and around quiet corners when a room grows too still.

"Happy now?" I draw my gaze to his, startled to find his eyes alight. The small smirk gracing his face is triumphant, like this was exactly what he wanted.

"Beautiful. I'll pitch it as your graduation piece."

"You're not funny," I tell him, suppressing a hint of a smile behind my hand.

Colt coughs. "He is, but only by accident."

59

I CAN'T DO THIS

"What are we supposed to be doing?" I ask Colt as he swipes his badge, leading us down a hallway pumped with stuffy, floral-perfumed air. We're deep in the polishing wing now. The wing I'm supposedly a resident of—although I've only seen three rooms and the garden.

"I have no idea. My schedule literally says '4:30, observatory landing.'"

"Is Vincent meeting us?"

"He's not on the schedule." Colt shrugs, leaning back against the wall.

"So we're just going to stand here?"

"Unless you have a better plan."

I shrug, smoothing my hem a few times to keep my hands busy.

Distant music builds through a speaker beneath our feet. His gaze snaps over me, caramel eyes narrowing. I whirl around, following his stare through the glass wall.

Below us is what looks to be some sort of drills class.

Rows of girls move like a single machine, dresses pale as fresh snow, eyes fixed on some distant point.

They're beautiful. Ethereal.

Haunting.

One tilts her chin just so, and the others copy in perfect unison. A mentor flicks his wrist and twelve spines snap straight.

My stomach drops. I think of Sorrel, the pretty graduate Maverick made a spectacle of on advancement day.

The way she recognized me.

Colt steps forward, palm flattening against the glass before he snatches it back as if it burned him. He opens his mouth to respond, then wrenches it shut. His eyes find mine again, and he's already reaching, arms out like he's bracing for my knees to give.

He's right to. My vision tunnels, breath catching as I stumble into the concrete wall. Colt's arms are under mine in an instant. He lifts me back to my feet, letting his hand hover at my elbow once I'm successfully holding myself again. The warmth of him anchors me in a way I didn't ask for and can't push away.

I haven't even fully righted my balance before sound spills down the hall.

A feminine voice, smooth as silk laced with poison. "Aren't they lovely? This may be our best batch yet."

Doctor Kade glides past us, heels clicking loudly, tablet tucked tight to her chest. She doesn't slow at the landing, offering nothing more than a quick glance at the sea of girls below. Her eyes flick to mine for a brief second. "You'd photograph beautifully among them, darling." She turns a corner before I can respond, leaving the thought to rot inside me.

My chest constricts. Everything clicks with a soul-crushingly brutal clarity.

This is what they wanted all along. Colt had said that flares are supposedly caused by overwhelming emotions, but these girls move through sequences like dolls. Maybe that's the real trick; they bury the truth under sparkly dresses and perfect posture, and no one notices they're teaching us to hollow ourselves to dust.

"I shouldn't be here," I rasp. I don't just mean on this landing. I shouldn't be in the polishing wing at all. If I were supposed to be here, I'd already be one of them. A pretty product ready for delivery.

The thought slices through me. *Someone's keeping me out of there.* It's the only thing that makes even some semblance of sense.

What I don't get…is *why?*

"That's what Carr wants from me," I whisper, just to hear it leave my mouth.

Colt's head snaps toward me, eyes darkening. "No. Maysie, no. Don't say that."

"Isn't it true?"

He shakes his head. "If Carr wanted that out of you, we wouldn't be having this conversation."

The words lodge themselves squarely in my sternum. He's right. Carr's getting exactly what he wants. The game moves forward, even if we can't see the board.

Colt steadies me again when I sway. His voice softens, gentler than it should be when we're out in the open like this. "You're safe."

I want to believe him, but safety shouldn't weigh this heavily. My existence hangs like a burden around me, one I can't shrink away from.

When we step back, the line of girls glides on, gowns brushing the floor, smiles fixed. No one looks up. Not at each other, and certainly not at us.

I can't decide if that's better or worse. Do they know what's happening to them?

Will I know if it happens to me?

Something delicate inside me fractures in a way I won't

be able to tape back together. And suddenly it feels like nothing will be okay ever again.

The organization never wanted to fix me. They wanted to rewrite me. They *did* rewrite me. But they couldn't finish the job.

Now, I just need to figure out why. Before graduation. Before they have the chance to drag me under again and take the little clarity I've fought so hard to reclaim.

This can't be my future. I won't let it.

60

LEGACY LIES

I storm straight to the practice room, not stopping until I'm panting in front of a very concerned Vincent. He motions for Colt to shut the door, turning his full attention to me the moment we're alone.

"Maysie? What's wrong? Why—"

"The other girls. The ones in this wing—is that—was that…" The words die in my throat. I open my mouth again, but he holds up his hands.

"No. They aren't like you, if that's what you're asking."

"What about before? I've done this before, right? Back then—was I like them?" The urge to run surges in my chest, turning my stomach.

Depending on what he says next, I just might.

His words drag like they hurt to say. "I know what you saw, but you were never one of them. Not now. Certainly not then."

"But—" Anger surges behind my eyes. "How do you know? How could you possibly know?"

"Because I was there," he says slowly, eyes chilling to distant pools of ice as he takes me in.

My breath catches. "You knew me?"

"Knew you?" A strained laugh breaks from him, thin and bitter. "I was your mentor."

My jaw hits the floor. "You—*what*?"

"As I told you before. Before this, I—we—were in a different side of the program. The legacy wing."

I close my eyes and try to picture it but come up blank. I was here...but not here. And with him? My head might explode. I want nothing more than to curl up and sob. But if I let myself cry, I may never stop.

Instead, I wrench my mouth open and force a question before he shuts down like he always does. "What makes it different?"

"For one..." He scrubs a hand down his face, eyes darting anywhere but me. "The desired outcome. Legacy girls aren't made for polishing. The goal is merely stabilization. A safe reintroduction once they're ready."

"Reintroduction to what?"

"Society." He braces his palms on the piano lid, knuckles white. "If you become stable enough, you can go home."

"Home?" My voice breaks on the word.

He flinches. Presses his fist too his mouth like he's already said too much.

"You promised me the truth," I remind him, settling on the edge of the bench and pulling my knees up.

He nods slowly. "If the parents want their child back, they'll return home. If not—the organization finds them a placement. A family, a school, a job. Whatever makes them look the most benevolent."

I almost laugh, because "benevolent" and organization do *not* belong in the same sentence.

Although, aside from the last part, it sounds...humane. Unreal, actually.

"Why would they get to go home when we don't?"

He sighs. "This place may be government-run, but the funding must come from somewhere. Investors keep the lights on—for both wings. Though they only care about this one. Not everyone shares Vale's…vision." He reads the question behind my eyes before I can ask it. "Both are necessary to keeping the organization in power."

I blink a few times. "Why?"

"The public wants comfort, to know their daughters can be saved and returned. The investors want results they can flaunt. There's no value in the legacy wing without advanced girls making the system look flawless." His eyes darken as he says it. The words sound rehearsed…or learned, like a speech he's been given before.

"But what about flares?"

"Legacy subjects know about flares." He spends a long moment studying my reaction before he continues. "The lead physician, Doctor Vale, believes if you know what you are, you'll be easier to control. Carr believes subjects are only dangerous once they remember what they can do."

I stiffen; the scribbled note reverberates in my mind.

A monster only becomes dangerous once it remembers its name.

"So they know everything?"

He shakes his head. "Only what the program wants them to know. Legacy girls are shown videos of flares as—" He hesitates, this level of honesty obviously new to him. "Cautionary tales."

"They have videos of flares?"

His eyes flick to mine, then away.

"Vincent?"

He wrings his hands, still not looking at me. "Hundreds. They have an entire catalogue of documented flares." His next words fall so, so soft. "Yours is infamous."

Oh.

My flare. The moment my parents decided I should be shipped off and erased by a doctor who claims to have a cure for a problem he can't even explain. The moment whatever life I had before this ended. It's on video. Countless people have seen it, and I don't even know what *it* is. My throat burns, but no matter how many times I reshape the words, I can't force them out. *What did I do?*

I might've hurt people. *Killed* people.

"Did I..." The words fracture into static. I try again. "My flare. Did I hurt—"

"No," he breathes. His next words are slow and quiet, as if he's not sure he's making the right choice by uttering them. "You brought down a ballroom chandelier in front of four hundred people. They said it was a miracle no one died."

I what?

61

REACTIVE AND DANGEROUS

"I'm sure your parents tried to protect you—it was just too public. You were handed off to me less than twenty-four hours later, still covered in glass." Vincent shudders as he recounts, wiping his hands against his pants.

Twenty-four hours? When they took Avery, she was gone for months.

Vincent surveys me with those too-knowing eyes, finding my question. "They didn't reset you the first time. Carr attributes that to your failure."

They perfected the art of memory wiping and didn't bother to use it on me?

"I don't believe you," I hear myself say. "Why would they do that?"

He nods like he expected that. "Your parents have a lot more pull than you might think."

I'm too angry to even consider opening that can of worms.

"Why am I here now? Why can't I go back to the training wing?"

"Carr says you aren't safe anymore."

"Why not?" I demand, biting down on my lip just to focus on something.

"Maysie, I—"

"Tell me," I interject, hating the way his face twists. "I'm sorry. Just—please. I want to know. Please don't lie to me."

He sighs. "Every girl is different, but many are reactivity risks. If one girl flares, it's like"—he waves a hand—"a powder keg."

"But—"

"Your circumstances are different, so they isolated you here. Most aren't so lucky."

It clicks. Every warning, every cue, every look of panic I mistook for irritation. Suddenly, it all makes sense.

"That's why you stormed into the drills hall."

A muscle in his forearm jumps, but he nods. "Your gift is known to be…reactive. And powerful. Carr's been fascinated with you from the start."

"Why?"

"Flares draw on energy," he says quietly. "It has to come from somewhere. Once external sources are depleted, it turns inward, taking everything that keeps a person alive. Focus, restraint, the quiet voice in your head that tells you to stop. It burns through all of it." Vincent sucks in a ragged breath. "Most don't survive one." He swallows hard, fists still clenched at his sides. "You've had four."

Four. I'm a tragedy on repeat.

His eyes unfocus like he's reliving things I never want to witness. "It's not the power that kills. It's the exhaustion. The body empties itself trying to sustain what it was never built to hold."

I press forward, words tumbling so fast they scrape my throat raw. "Then what happened? What happened to them, to me, to—"

"My pod—our pod—was unbalanced. Girls with reactivity markers aren't supposed to be placed together. Between the six of you, four had known markers." He frowns faintly. "I knew it was a mistake, but all my reports went unread.

The doctors assured me it was fine. Vale said I was overre-acting."

His words devastate me, but the only emotion that dares swell in my chest is frustration. "You knew we were a risk. And you did—what? Nothing?"

"I was seventeen! What could I have done?" His voice is bitter, like he's blaming the boy he used to be as much as the man he is now. "It happened so fast. Everything was fine." He shuts his eyes like the weight of them is too much to bear. "Until it wasn't."

His hand clamps over his mouth so hard that his knuck-les pale. For one terrifying second, I think he might actually be sick. "I was told you were gone," he whispers. "I signed your termination notice." His shoulders twitch violently, sending fissures down his crumbling facade.

"When did you know?" The question slips out before I can stifle it. "When did you recognize me?"

Vincent's hand falls away slowly. He's blanched, trem-bling. "Not soon enough," he admits, the words breaking against his teeth. His gaze darts to the floor, shame burning hot in the silence. "God." A laugh escapes him, but it sounds more like a sob. "You were right in front of me, and I didn't see it."

"You didn't know—"

"I should have known. From the moment you asked about stars. From the moment I first heard you play." He huffs a humorless sound. "I've worked with dozens of girls since my demotion, but—"

"Demotion?" I blurt, instantly regretting interrupting him.

"I let six girls die, Maysie. I couldn't be a mentor any-more, but Carr said my skills were too useful to waste. He made me his 'analyst.'" His fingers twitch into half-hearted air quotes. "Flare-intervention, termination, so much damn paperwork. Temporary, he said. Just until they could figure out what to do with me."

I grimace. The way he's describing himself as property sounds a little too familiar.

He drags a shaky hand through his hair. "But once I developed a reputation, it stuck. They hand me a girl already drowning, then blame me when she slips under. Easier to call me the executioner than admit the water's poisoned."

My eyes lift again, and he's finally looking at me. Only, I'm not sure which version of me he's seeing.

"I knew something was off from the moment Carr assigned me to observe you. First, because he never just wants 'observation,' and second, your file was littered with redactions, unheard of for someone they still considered stable."

"So, wait… You've always known?"

"No." He presses the heel of his hand to his temple. Shakes his head. "Maybe some part of me knew. I just refused to believe it. I convinced myself I was losing it. That I was still so stricken with grief after almost a year that I couldn't even contain my own ghosts. It was easier to trust the lie than admit Carr would've done this—" He draws a rough inhale. "Or that I let it happen."

He falls silent, staring at the floor like he's begging to fall through it.

A thousand thoughts tangle in my mind like skittering mice. I should hate him for not seeing me. I should hate him even more for lying to me. But all I can think is that he looks like a man begging for mercy. And for some reason, I can't deny him that.

He saved me. More than once. He dragged me back from

the breaking point, knowing I'd hate him for it.

The reality singes my skin far worse than any flare. Carr had rewritten me, sure. But Vincent had rewritten himself. He'd chosen blindness over hope again and again just to survive. He drove himself insane because the alternative meant facing the fact that I was never truly gone.

"Vincent, it's okay," I whisper, holding the words taut for his sake. His head snaps back up. He's blinking rapidly like I just walked over and slapped him across the face.

The storm in his irises has subsided, leaving his under-eyes slick with something he'd never admit to. My heart splinters with every passing second, aching for him to say something. Anything.

When he finally speaks, his voice breaks like a snapped twig. "You have every reason to hate me."

"I don't," I whisper, chest throbbing. For me, for him, for the other girls. For every person trapped underground right now. I press my forehead into my knees, more helpless than I've ever felt.

Vincent's shoulders sag, his body curved in on itself so tight I'm surprised he isn't trembling. Pain clings to every inch of him and I don't know when I started looking at him but I can't bring myself to look away.

"I'm not your enemy," he whispers, so quiet I almost miss it.

"I know."

With that, his composure scrapes back into place, piece by piece, until I'm staring at a wrecked arts and crafts project. "Please don't mistake that for safety."

62

PROMISES

Vincent's too busy for piano block. Again.

He's been preoccupied for weeks. Only showing up in my room late into the night, disheveled and exhausted. Unless I have questions, he's silent. He brings along files, reports, his tablet; anything to keep his hands busy. But no matter how long it takes or how much his eyes droop as the hours drag on, he doesn't leave until I've fallen asleep. True to his promise, he never sedates me.

Forty-three of my fifty days have come and gone. Which means I've got seven left to either figure out a way out of here or concede to letting the organization send me to my doom.

Or…whatever comes after this, I guess.

No one will tell me what "graduation" means, and I'm starting to wonder if I don't want to know.

My days are filled with…nothing. Turns out, without lectures, drills, and workbooks, this place is incredibly dull. Colt and I have tried every single craft in the enrichment room, to varying degrees of success.

Then there's piano, or lack thereof. I still can't bring myself to play for more than a few minutes at a time, much to Vincent's growing dismay. He won't say it out loud, but it's clear something hinges on this—something bigger than me. I was never bold enough to believe he just wanted me to play for my own sake, even in the training wing. But the way his face falls when I beg to stop tells me we're gambling with something neither of us can afford to lose.

That leaves the garden. It may not be nearly as intoxicating as it was when I thought it was real, but it's the closest thing to fresh air. I've found my usual spot, back against the damp grass, legs kicked up on a stone wall.

I should be planning, but my head is still swimming from my session with Carr yesterday. That's the one thing the polishing wing hasn't saved me from. He's been meeting with me every three days like clockwork. It never lasts long, but he insists on blindfolding me. I can't tell what he does. My sensations blur, but I feel the ghosts of metal kissing my skin. When it's over, I'm dazed, tired, and sick.

Instead of curling into a ball and panicking about whatever Carr might be doing to me, I'm reading. I grabbed a book from the stack Vincent left on the way to the garden. A guide on animals. I find it fascinating. Colt, on the other hand…not so much.

"Guess what they call a group of crows."

"Annoying?" Colt muses, leaning back against a perfectly artificial tree. His jacket's shrugged off, leaving him in a slim-cut black T-shirt that frames his biceps.

I chuckle, holding the book above my head so he can see. "Good guess, but no. Apparently, they're called a murder."

"Almost the same thing," he brags, digging his boot into the dirt.

"Oh yeah, how so?"

"You wouldn't find it annoying to be murdered?"

"Touché." I press my heels against the wall, relishing the cool sensation of stone through my flats.

I flip the page, but I can't seem to get my mind to refocus. Uncomfortable seconds stretch into unbearable minutes for no reason other than the thousand questions I worry I'll never get to ask him.

I force my mouth to open because living with embarrassment is a whole lot better than living with regret. "Will I ever see you again? After graduation, I mean."

"I don't know," he says, though we both know it's a lie. I don't know where the organization will decide to send me, but it won't be somewhere he can follow. The thought makes me want to melt into the grass.

"In a weird way, I wish things could stay like this," I say with a shaky laugh.

"Yeah, me too."

I hate how true it is. I hate this place. I hate everything about it. But I can't bring myself to hate the people in it. Colt and Vincent are the closest thing I have to family.

And in a week, they'll be gone.

I've lost so much. My memories, my friends, my dignity. I'm not sure I could survive losing them, too.

I swing my legs down, sitting back on my heels to face him. His face is flushed, eyes darkened with the same anguish he had when Vincent shattered the window. The last time he thought he was going to lose me.

"We could leave?" I force my voice to be light, hoping it sounds like a joke.

"What?"

I flash him a half-smile. "You've got a keycard, right? We could—"

"We can't," he snaps, face suddenly stern. He reaches for my wrist, but I wrench away, back slamming against the stone.

"But—"

"You don't get it." Colt grits his teeth, breathing hard. "If you run, they'll give the order, and I'll be the one hunting you down. Pressing you into the tile while you beg me to stop, counting the seconds until you collapse." His hands knot into fists. A shaky breath slips from his lips. "And I'll do it—because I don't get a choice. But losing you like that…" He shakes his head hard. "It would destroy me." Colt's composure shatters on that last word. He rakes both hands through his hair.

I want to grab his shoulders and tell him he's wrong. That I'd forgive him, that it isn't his fault. But my chest is already constricting with the truth: He's bound to this place, leashed to the system that's slowly killing us.

"You can't, Maysie. Please don't bring it up again." He stares at nothing, hands gripping fistfuls of stiff faux grass. "Promise me." Colt reaches for my hand again, but I can't bring myself to move.

Instead, I watch a single manufactured cloud drift across the simulated sky. "I promise," I say, breathing depth into the lie.

Hoping I'll be gone before he realizes I've broken it.

63

TIMING IS EVERYTHING

Time doesn't move the same here. It lurches. Stops. Stalls. Starts again when it feels like punishing me.

I cling to it anyway, measuring anything and everything.

Thirty minutes between rotations. Nine seconds for the cameras to sweep the expanse of a hallway, two for a keycard swipe to register. It's not much, but it's mine.

No one knows I'm doing it…or maybe they do and they don't care, so long as I don't act on it. Funny how counting used to feel like the only thing I could control. Now, it feels like the key to so much more.

Big talk for someone with no plan.

The ticking clock reminds me why I'm keeping score. There are still four days until graduation, but the whole polishing wing feels different. Everyone's moving faster, snapping orders with an edge that they don't bother hiding behind their polished facades. Change is in the air, heavy enough to choke on.

Carr stopped me in the corridor yesterday. He didn't bother with petty small talk. He just tapped the side of my cuff, checked the green light, and smiled as if he'd already scheduled my funeral.

He didn't have to say anything. I got the message.

The world keeps turning. And me? I sit at my desk and count my breaths until I'm lightheaded. I try to hold them steady, but I keep losing track somewhere around thirty-nine. My pulse betrays me. My cuff buzzes at the inconsis-tency, and I almost laugh. Even breathing has rules here.

It's fine. Totally fine.

I'm just trapped underground, waiting to see if my clock runs out before I have the chance to stop counting and start acting.

64

ONE WAY OUT

Someone's running down the hall—no, a lot of someones. The catastrophe of sound is violent enough to cut through concrete. If I didn't know any better, I'd think the building's on fire. But if that were the case, I'd hope someone would have the decency to swing by and let me know.

As if on cue, Colt shoulders through my door.

He slams it shut behind him, back braced against the frame like he's holding something out. His chest heaves, pupils dilated. Sweat darkens the edges of his hair. For a half-second, I wonder if he's bleeding.

"Colt?"

He drops a clipboard onto the desk harder than he needs to and scrubs both hands over his face. His comm chirps twice, like it's tattling on him.

"What was that?" I ask, studying the rapid rise and fall of his chest.

"Briefing," he mutters. "Whole wing's in a frenzy. Ceremony prep, security sweeps…it's a mess." He looks at me, and for once, there's no grin, no boyish shrug. His frame is racked with an exhaustion so raw it makes my chest ache.

"You okay?" I ask, folding my hands to keep them from fidgeting.

"Define okay," he huffs. His eyes dart toward the door again, jittery. "Did you eat?"

"I forgot," I lie, because admitting I was too nervous to

ask anyone for food feels silly.

Colt nods, unsurprised. "I'll grab something."

His comm shrieks again, loud enough that I can almost hear the command from his earpiece. He clutches the side of his head, slipping a curse under his breath.

He's already halfway out the door when I call, "Wait! Your—" He's gone before I can form the word "clipboard." The door slams shut behind him with a scrape of boots on tile. The quiet that follows is rife with possibility.

I glance at the desk. The clipboard sits where he left it, angled toward me like bait.

I shouldn't.

It's none of my business. It's his job. His punishment if I'm caught.

But the longer I stare, the louder it calls. He's never careless, yet he left this. *For me?* No. Probably not. Definitely not. He was just in a rush. Still, my pulse kicks at the thought that maybe this is the only mistake he'll ever make.

I slide off my bed, every step toward the desk bogged down with guilt.

"Just a peek," I whisper to no one. It'll only take a second. Just to prove to myself it's nothing beyond simple curiosity, the kind that can't be rebellion unless you get caught.

I'm starting to wonder where I learned that from.

When I pick it up, I quickly realize it's in fact *not* nothing.

It's a map.

Colt, Ryder, and Lance all seem to be on rotation for graduation day. Thirty-minute intervals. Carefully planned routes, each scribbled in Colt's chaotic print. Everything has a label. Hallways, entrances, service elevators, even the restrooms. At the bottom corner, a coffee stain smears half a label: Exit B-2.

My heart trips, somersaults, and lands back in my chest with a *thud*.

Exit.

I run my finger over the blurred ink, tracing the shape of the word until it's etched in me. I don't need the whole picture, so long as I can find the door.

The map denotes several other exits, but only one appears to be relatively unguarded.

It also fails to specify where cameras might be. Which means I'd have to be fast. Or I'd need to disable them. The former is far more feasible.

I trail the route again, just to make sure I know how it all connects. The stage door would be the easiest to slip through. Then, I could take the maintenance hall all the way to the maintenance stairs, wait for the rotation, and slip past the service corridors. From there, I could make it to the exit in less than thirty seconds.

It's not much, but it's more of a plan than I had five minutes ago.

My senses return just in time for Colt's boots to echo down the hall. He's shouting codes, presumably into his comm. I drop the clipboard hard enough to thump and skitter to the window ledge just as the lock slides out of place.

Colt slips back in with a modest tray: bottled water, a wrapped sandwich, and a bruised apple that looks like it lost a fight. He kicks the door shut with his heel and sets the tray on the sill beside me with exaggerated care.

"Ta-da," he says, voice falling flat halfway through.

"Wow," I tell him. "A feast."

"Only the best." He scrubs a hand over his mouth. His

eyes flick to the desk, then back to me.

I offer him a small smile, perched like the picture of innocence on the non-window's sill.

"How was the briefing?"

He rocks back on his heels. Presses his lips together. "Brief."

"Doesn't sound like it," I press, squinting at his arm. Peeking out under his jacket, there's a deep mark marring his left wrist.

"Time is subjective." He flashes me a small smile that feels wrong, then shoves the sandwich into my hands like he needs my mouth to be busy. "Eat."

I take a shallow bite. Fighting him over food is a battle I never win.

"What's on the clipboard?" I ask, holding the sandwich up so he can't claim I'm not eating.

"Nothing," he says too fast. He steps to the desk and palms it, the muscles in his forearm jumping. The coffee stain darkens under his thumb. "Work stuff."

"I figured."

He exhales hard and slumps against the wall, letting his head tip back. The motion drags his sleeve up, just enough to bare the angry welt circling his wrist. It's not a bruise like I originally thought. It's a burn. Red and raw, raised in the shape of the thin wristband he always wears.

My stomach drops. "Colt."

His eyes raise to me, then down to his wrist. He jerks back like I somehow caused it. "Don't."

"What happened?"

"Nothing." His hand shakes when he drags the sleeve back into place. "It's just Carr's way of keeping us sharp."

"Sharp?" My voice splinters, rage dripping off the word.

"What's that supposed to mean? That's—" I cut myself off before the word *torture* spills out.

"Mays—"

"No." I slide off the sill and step closer before he can turn away. "He did that to you?" I battle down the bile constricting my throat. "Why? For what?"

Emotions flicker across his face—shame, guilt, and grief all tangled into a mess of pain. He laughs, flat and pitiful. "You think it's just you they've got on a leash?" He yanks the sleeve up to show me the damage full-on. "Welcome to the team. Yours shocks, mine burns. It's the same damn game, Mays."

The sight steals my breath. "Colt…"

"Don't make me talk about it. Please." His voice cracks, desperation where anger had been moments prior. "Because if I start, I'll say things I can't take back."

I reach for his hand anyway. The burn is hot under my thumb, skin ridged and raw. He winces, but doesn't pull away. I trace around it carefully, like I can undo the damage just by touching it gentler than the doctors ever would.

"You shouldn't have to live like this." My words hardly materialize, but he hears me.

"Neither should you." His hand tightens over mine, sudden and fierce, anchoring himself in me. His eyes glisten with the one emotion he has no reason to feel: guilt.

I want to tell him I'd rather take a hundred shocks than see one more burn on him. But the ache in my throat steals the words. I squeeze his hand, holding it steady between both of mine.

His free hand moves up to cup my face, rough palm brushing my cheek like he's afraid I'll vanish if he doesn't memorize me this way.

"Don't look at me like that," he whispers. "Like what?"

His jaw works, his thumb trembling against my skin.

"Like I'm worth saving."

I force my master planning to take a backseat. Tonight, I just need to be here. Letting him hold me above water before the impending tidal wave pulls me under one last time.

Two days. Sink or swim.

It won't be long now.

65

LAST GOOD DAY

"If you hate it that much, just say so."

Vincent doesn't smile. Or laugh. Or give me anything as I step out of the alcove, one heel still bare, the hem of dress number ten swishing around my ankles. He's standing where he's been all afternoon, arms folded, eyes unfocused like he's looking through me instead of at me.

"You already know my answer," he replies.

I huff, stamping my single shoe against the tile with more force than necessary.

"Fine," I mutter, already turning away. "Be difficult."

I slip back behind the curtain, tugging the dress over my head. Fabric catches. I yank harder. When it finally releases me, I let it fall in a pool at my feet, then kick it next to the growing pile of rejects.

No one told me finding a dress for graduation would be so hard. We've been at this for almost three hours, and I'm fairly sure I'm going to collapse before we find something that works. Which won't do us any good, considering the ceremony is tomorrow.

Dress eleven gets an instant shake of Vincent's head before I've even reached the mirror.

"You didn't even look."

"I saw enough."

Twelve is too frilly. Thirteen makes me look like a cupcake, all taffeta layers and ruffles.

Fourteen? He stares a little longer this time. Then his arms tighten across his chest, grip locking tight.

"Change."

I tug the curtain shut so hard the fabric snaps against the rail. When my gaze catches the mirror, I'm entranced by my reflection; at the slight differences that have crept in over the weeks. My hair is lighter now, more honey brown than chocolate, with golden strands that catch the light when I tilt my head just right. My nails have grown, now shaped into gentle peaks and painted a shimmering gold.

The physical changes are just the beginning. Everything feels different. My stance is stiffer, my chin tips higher, even my laugh rings clearer.

The girl who entered that testing room forty-nine days ago isn't here anymore, and I can't quite pinpoint when she slipped away. It's unsettling, especially when there's nothing I can do about it. Not while I'm here, at least.

Vincent's noticed too, no matter how many times he's assured me nothing's changed.

I clear my throat to catch his attention through the curtain. "Do you like my hair better this color? It feels…I don't know. More natural, I guess?"

"It works," he says, so flat I can almost hear him shrug.

By dress fifteen, I'm half-tempted to tell him to pick something himself. But as the tiered gold layers fall into place, I realize it's perfect. The skirt swishes just right when I turn. The bodice sits as if it were made for me. I slip out from the curtain and meet his eyes in the mirror.

"This one," I declare.

He finally smiles. It's almost startling to see something so real. "Finally."

I can't help but laugh. "Why are you looking at me like

I'm the one who's been rejecting everything? You vetoed fourteen dresses!"

He shrugs. "I wanted you to like it."

"Okay, wait—so you're telling me that if I pretended to like the first dress, you would've said yes three hours ago?"

"I could've," he says, stepping forward to adjust the shoulder seam, "but then we'd have missed all this quality bonding time."

His touch is light as he works, making sure the fabric sits right. But something lingers in his gaze, deep and distant, too strange to ignore. Like most things in this place, it's gone before I can identify it.

"Perfect," he says.

Funny thing is, I believe him. I hold the skirt out for a little spin, turning to the next order of business.

"Okay so—what's next? Shoes?"

Vincent's eyes narrow like I just threatened to set something on fire. "Don't start."

"What? Shoes are important." I lean one hip against the mirror frame, watching him pretend not to care. I toss a gesture toward the racks of shoes lining the wall. "Heels? Flats? Strappy? Barefoot?"

He tilts his head like he's weighing the choice of a lifetime, then settles on: "Something you can walk in without tripping."

"That's boring."

"It's safe."

The look I give him is all innocence, smothering the flutter in my chest. Not nerves for graduation; nerves for what comes after. The part where—with any luck—I won't be here. *Might as well make the most of our time today.*

"Fine. Then you pick."

He mutters something that sounds suspiciously like "God help me" before moving to the display, scanning rows upon rows of shoes with admirable concentration, as if this is a puzzle of footwear with detrimental consequences. His hand hovers over a champagne pair of wedges, then black flats, before he lands on soft gold heels.

"These."

I take them, turning the heel in my palm. It's low, low enough to still be able to run if the need arises.

Score.

I smile. "Subtle. Almost like you have taste." Because I can't very well say *"Cool, thanks. These will make escaping a breeze."*

"I'd say the same about you, but..." His glance flicks to the pile of discarded dresses. I laugh, knowing all too well he was the one rejecting everything I dared to put on. I turn back to the mirror.

"All right, hair. What's your vision, oh great stylist?" His lips twitch, but he covers it with a shrug. "Up. Off your shoulders."

I cock my head. "You like it better that way?" I keep my tone light, but I'm studying him in the reflection, hungry for any slip that gives me something real. The pause is long, and I swear his face flickers through every stage of grief.

He nods finally. "It's how it's meant to be," he says, like it's a fact. But there's something hiding in the space between the words. Something cryptic.

It's always cryptic with him, but this is extra-cryptic.

"Mm. Guess we'll see." I tug the shoes on and stand, giving him one last twirl. "Shoes pass the spin test."

Vincent's smile is faint, the kind you wear when you're trying not to think too hard about what you're seeing.

"Perfect," he says again, voice laced with a dangerous amount of honesty.

While he moves to hang the rejects, I keep my eyes on the mirror. My reflection stares back in silk and shadow, hair glinting in the light like it remembers something I don't.

My fingers trace along the bodice of the golden gown, careful not to displace any of the rhinestones. I wish the skirt wasn't so full. It may give me some trouble if I need to maneuver. I know better than to ask, but that's never stopped me before.

"Do you think a shorter dress would be better?" I drop casually, smoothing the layers over my knees. "Y'know… less tripping hazard?"

His brows furrow a little in the mirror. "For the stage? No. Longer is better. Cleaner lines."

I shrug. "Guess I just like being able to move."

His shoulders tense. It's there and gone in less than a breath, replaced by that cool, unbothered composure.

"You'll move just fine," he says, slipping the hanger back into place. When I pivot away from him, my mind's already cataloguing: the cardigan I asked for has deep pockets, the waist ribbon on my gown could be useful. Even the dress itself will work so long as I'm careful.

Vincent's reflection crosses behind mine. He's composed as ever, but I can feel him watching in the glass, noticing more than he's letting on. I tell myself it doesn't matter. That I don't have to care anymore.

By this time tomorrow, they'll think I'm theirs.

I'll know better.

66

THE FINAL TEST

"Are we almost there?" Colt groans, stretching his arms above his head like he's grown stiff from walking. Ironic, for a man who stands around all day.

Vincent cocks his head. "Almost is relative. We'll get there when we get there."

"Who thought it'd be a good idea to put tier three so far from everything. Isn't this supposed to be a privilege?" Colt runs a hand along the concrete wall. My eyes stay forward, but I offer him a light laugh.

My heels click in rhythm as I flutter down the hallway, both of my protectors in tow. Panic should be hitting me by now. Panic about tomorrow. About defying the system that saved me on what's supposed to be one of the most important days of my life. Any rational person with sanity left would panic.

I don't.

The only thing standing in the way of my escape—I mean graduation—is a final set of diagnostics. Five minutes or less, ideally. Vincent will attach my cuff to the monitor, I'll get shocked for a while, then the cuff will settle to its beautiful, natural green, and I'll be on my way.

Colt clears his throat as we near the door. "Should I wait outside?"

Vincent shakes his head. "Doesn't matter. This won't take long." He swipes his badge. The door slides open.

Oh.

Oh, fantastic.

Doctor Carr is here.

He's perched at the counter that overlooks the exam chair, sleeves rolled up, glasses settled on the bridge of his wrinkled nose. A smile twists his features when he spots us.

"Right on schedule," he says flatly, gesturing for me. Vincent steps in front, gaze heated. "I thought I had clearance to handle diagnostics."

"You do," Carr replies, a hint of amusement creeping in. "We have something to take care of first." He taps his screen. Vincent's tablet buzzes in response.

Vincent tears his eyes away from Carr, face hardening as he scans the message.

"No," he says, clipped. "There's no need. She's passed every diagnostic with no flags on record since her last trial." He wrings his hands in a way I haven't seen since…

No.

Surely not. *Right?*

"I'll remind you that her last trial failed. Tremendously." Carr cuts in, sharp. "We need data, Harrow. Something measurable. Some assurances."

"It's a risk—"

"It's protocol," Carr says simply. "You of all people should know that." Something sparks behind Vincent's eyes, but he stays silent. Carr rolls his wrist out. "Every girl must prove their stability before being permitted to graduate."

Stability. Failed. Last Trial.

It's happening again.

Nausea seizes my insides fast enough to make my head spin.

"It's a simple trial. Neutral stimuli, no custom triggers," Carr continues. Vincent's eyes scan the tablet again. His jaw flexes. After a long moment, he steps back, bowing his head.

He's giving up.

"Only this." Vincent's voice is so tense. Everything about him is tense, now that I look. "Nothing more."

My mind screams in rage, but cold panic overpowers it before I even have the chance to defend myself.

This is it.

They're going to run me through the trial again. The one that almost killed an instructor—not to mention almost killed me.

There's a tug on my arm. I cast a sidelong glance at Colt, now holding my elbow.

Carr nods, beckoning me closer with one finger. My feet take root, planting so firmly in the tile that I'm not sure Colt could pry me up if he tried.

I try to protest, but the sound dies in my throat. The world stills, a blurred mess of forgotten plans and boundless fear.

If he runs the test again, I'll die.

Here.

Now.

In front of Colt. In front of Vincent. Worst of all, in front of the man who takes pride in having gutted me. The man who has apparently dragged me through this entire process twice and whose face tells me he wouldn't hesitate to do it again.

Colt tugs my arm again, fingers shaking. "You don't have to—"

"She does." Carr barks at him, clearly losing patience. "Step forward, 214."

A dam at the recesses of my mind begins to buckle. I haven't had to hear my number in over a month. I forgot how dehumanizing it is to be stripped down to a designation.

But I can't falter. Not when I'm so close.

My feet stick like cement, but I manage a single step. Just enough for the signal reader above to register my presence. I wait for Carr to grab the containment cuffs that are placed neatly on the side table. But he remains facing me, watching with dead eyes and an even deader soul.

"Begin," he announces to the system. The lights dim down to the dull blue only used for late-night downtime. I suck in a breath, batting away the memories that threaten to surge. The common room. Brielle's nonsense stories. Ivy's snide remarks.

And June.

June's laugh. Her smile. Her endless jokes.

Her pain.

The pain we chose not to see until it swallowed her whole.

"Focus," Vincent snaps, low. I force my chin up, force myself to stare at the wall and see nothing. Hear nothing. Feel nothing.

There's a chime as the sound cues start.

Horrible, violent noises. Screaming. Crying. The pounding of a fist against metal. Pressure prickles at the edge of my vision. I force the sensation away. It's in my head. Always in my head. The floor stills. The heat subsides. I almost smile at the surge of control.

Carr takes another step back, watching me with so much intensity that I may as well be in front of an audience of thousands. He taps his tablet, and the sound grows louder.

Faster. Throbbing pain presses behind my eyes. I stare down at my hands as my fingertips grow fuzzy, buzzing with an energy I can't trace.

A shadow moves in my periphery. Vincent. His mouth parts, but I can't quite catch the words. Carr only smiles wider.

The room begins to spin. I gnaw on my cheek until iron coats my tongue. It steadies me enough to draw a single breath.

Overhead lights flash like white-hot lightning, striking me head-on. Heat claws viciously at my neck. I'm trembling, but I don't let myself collapse. I think I'm clenching my fists. I think I'm crying. No—I *know* I'm crying.

A blur of dark blocks my vision. It reaches for me. I can't fight it; my body is too tense to recoil. I press my eyes shut. Snap them open. The world focuses just enough for me to see him.

Colt's in front of me. Mouthing words I can't hear, shaking my shoulders. He looks stricken, like it's his world collapsing instead of mine. His eyes are searching mine desperately. I struggle to focus on every line of his face as he looks at me. A surge of rogue energy pulsates between us, throwing him back on the tile.

My arms are glowing again, angry with power that threatens to end me.

Colt's on his feet in a second. He's reaching for me again, and I know if he touches me now I'm going to burn him. The sounds are still muted, but four words force their way through, garbled and raw.

Fight this, Mays, please.

My veins turn to pure ice. Instinct takes over. I shove every spark of displaced energy into the concrete below before he has the chance to make contact. It leeches from me in streams of liquid fire, prying at my consciousness.

The floor tremors violently as the energy dissipates. Nausea floods the gaps where power was surging seconds earlier. I double over and vomit onto Colt's boots.

"Acceptable," Carr says flatly, already moving toward the door. He gives me the faintest glance over his shoulder. "Congratulations, 214."

I don't know whether I should throw my arms up in triumph or collapse to the floor sobbing. Honestly, I wish I could split myself in two just so it'd be possible to do both. I swipe a hand across my mouth and turn on my heel, facing Vincent.

"So—did I win?" It doesn't quite land as light as I'd hoped, but I can see relief trickle over his features. He nods.

"Something like that."

67

DEEP DARK NIGHT

The moment I'm settled back in my room, Vincent gets pinged away for some urgent matter.

I'm still alive, though, so catastrophic mistakes avoided: thirty-four.

I'm curled on the windowsill, legs snaking up the wall, trying to ignore the tremor that still rattles down my arms. I'd try to ignore the hammering of my heart, too, but it's the only thing helping me keep time.

I flinch when the door creaks, but it's only Colt.

He doesn't crack a joke or kick the door shut like he's trying to wake the dead. He slips inside, lets the door lock behind him, then leans against it with his hands shoved in his pockets. His eyes are tired, shaded in a way that makes him look older. More worn. The badge at his hip catches the pale light, a painful reminder of what I have to do.

I decided this morning that this was the best way. The only way forward, actually. Since he won't help me directly, this has to work.

It doesn't make it any easier.

"You should be asleep," he starts.

"So should you."

That earns me the faintest smile. He pushes off the door and crosses the room in a few long strides, settling in a too-small upholstered chair a few feet from the window. The closeness is dizzying.

He blows out a breath. Runs a hand down his face. "Tomorrow's gonna be hell."

I try to laugh, but it comes out shaky. "That's reassuring."

"Not for you." He tips his head toward me, eyes softening. "You'll be just fine."

I don't believe him, so I say nothing. His sleeve rides up when he reaches to ruffle his hair, exposing the still-red ring around his wrist. The welt carved into him like proof he belongs to this place just as much as I do.

"Does it hurt?" I whisper.

He smiles, small and so very sad. "All the time."

I bite down everything I want to say. I don't know which is worse—that I hate him for making it look easy, or that I hate myself more for watching him hurt while being helpless to do anything about it.

I slide off the sill and into the seat beside him. His arm is hot where it brushes mine.

I find myself staring. Trying to memorize what he looks like in the fake moonlight.

"Mays..." He hesitates. Shakes his head. "Nevermind."

"No. Say it."

His jaw works. "I don't get to say much that's mine. But if I don't tell you tonight, I never will."

My pulse stutters. "Tell me what?"

"That I'm glad to have met you." He looks down at his hands, cheeks heating. "Even if it had to be in this place. I don't regret it. I'll never regret it."

Oh. I knew tonight would be hard. But this? *This is unbearable.*

"Colt..."

He lifts his eyes to mine, that familiar caramel-brown

gaze undoing me. "No matter what happens tomorrow or any day after that. This is real. Us. Right now. And I needed you to know that."

My breath catches, tears heating my eyes. He means it. He means every word of it, and I'm sitting here plotting something awful.

He stands, then hesitates. "Can I—" He gestures, awkward, and the awkwardness breaks me open.

"Yeah," I say, already moving.

He envelops me in an embrace that nearly ends me on the spot. The warmth of him is overwhelming. His chin rests on the top of my head, breath shaky against my hair. He's solid heat and muscle and the kind of safety that's more dangerous than any flare. He folds around me, and for a terrible moment, I think about not leaving at all. About letting the program sharpen me down to an obedient, hollow shell if it means I get to stand here forever.

The thought dissipates, because that isn't how it works.

Tomorrow, they'll pry me away from him and send me blind into a world I don't remember, another nightmare of their creation.

If I leave, I lose him. If I stay, I lose him and myself.

The choice shouldn't be hard.

"Are you scared?" he asks, gentle.

"Yes."

He pulls me closer. "Me too."

The ache in my chest almost paralyzes me. I swallow down the guilt, the shame, the sickening urge to collapse into his arms and cry until he has to drag me to the stage tomorrow.

This is what I have to do.

I keep my left hand braced against his back, and with my

right, I move slowly, sliding down until my fingers find the edge of his badge reel. The plastic is warm with his body heat. My thumb hooks under it. With a small nudge, the loop catches.

He shifts like he's about to pull back. I hold tighter, burying my face in his chest. "Don't go yet." My voice cracks, real and weaponized at the same time.

His arms tighten around me. With a final flick, the badge slips free. It drops, silent, to the rug beneath us. I press my heel over it, pinning it to the floor.

Colt's whole body stiffens for one terrifying second, then he goes slack, burying his face against my shoulder. His breath shakes against my skin. I wonder if this is the last moment of peace I'll ever get.

"You know," he says softly. "If I could, I'd take you out of here myself. Show you something real. Stars. A sky that moves because it wants to. Morning rain."

The kind that makes you want to stay in bed.

The picture he paints nearly undoes me completely. My eyes sting, tears falling freely now.

"I'd like that," I whisper.

He pulls back just enough to look at me. His hand comes up, rough thumb brushing my cheek. His voice catches. "Don't forget me, okay? Wherever you end up."

"Never," I say. It's not a lie.

Finally, he draws back, eyes searching mine like he's afraid of what he'll find there. "I have to go," he murmurs, somber. "I'll find you tomorrow, after the ceremony. Okay?"

The certainty of his words pierces my dwindling composure: tomorrow. The last word I ever wanted to hear from him.

"Promise?" My voice wavers.

"Promise." His grin flickers in, tired but real. The kind that used to make me feel like the world wasn't built to crush us. "Look left if you need me."

The badge burns bright with shame under my foot, a culmination of guilt made physical. I swallow hard. "Left."

My hands shake, but I force myself to let him go.

He squeezes my shoulders, warm brown eyes still locked on mine. "Try to sleep."

"You too."

He laughs. "Yeah, right." Then he's gone.

I don't move until I'm sure he won't double back. Then I move my foot, crouch, and slide the badge into my palm. It's only plastic, but it feels incredibly heavy. That's probably just my guilt talking.

My gold shoes wait under the bed. I grab one, peeling the insole back with careful fingers. Thankfully, the badge is a perfect fit. I hold the lining down until the glue remembers how to glue. From the outside, it looks like nothing.

I tuck the shoes back into place, sit on the edge of the bed, and lace my fingers together to stop the tremor in them.

With my final objective done, I have nothing to do but sit here and hurt.

I would give anything to write him a note. A messy confessional of everything I couldn't say. *Thank you. I'm sorry. Please don't hunt me down. Please don't hate me. Please don't forget me.*

But there's no paper here. Nor are there enough words in the world for me to possibly tell him everything I want to say.

"I'm so sorry," I whisper into the dark, knowing it will never be enough.

68

THE GIRL STARING BACK

The mirror doesn't speak.

Not that it ever did. But this morning, it feels especially quiet. There's no plaque in the prep room. No words to tell me what to think.

No "Poise."

No "Obedience."

No "Purpose."

That's fine by me. I don't need to hear it anymore. I know what they want me to be. I know I'm not it. And I know I'm still here, despite everything.

I am the program's greatest creation.

One day, I hope to be their undoing.

The bruises from my flare have long since faded. My hair is carefully pinned out of my face. My shoulders are square.

I look perfect.

My reflection watches, waiting, like she's curious what I'll replace the mantra with. I say nothing. I meet her gaze slowly. And for the first time—

She looks like me.

That shouldn't be possible. She looks entirely different from the girl I thought I was. But in this moment, in this light? I am everything I need myself to be. And I'm getting out of here.

Today.

A painful tug at my wrist brings me back to reality. Vincent's unlatching my cuff. I blink a few times, catching him studying me.

This dress feels heavier than yesterday, but maybe it's just me.

Golden gossamer, with little rhinestones stitched in perfect arcs that catch the light with every breath. Too elaborate for me. Too elaborate for anyone, for that matter. Vincent adjusts the hem carefully, like the world might end if the fabric sits a half inch too high. His hands are steady. His eyes in the glass are anything but.

"You'll be perfect," he says, low enough that he may be trying to convince himself.

"Will you be there?"

His hands hover at my shoulders, so close I can almost feel the ghost of his touch.

"No," he says. "Not for this."

"Why not?" I turn, searching his face.

His inhale is measured, like he rehearsed this. "My part is over."

"Are you being reassigned?"

He nods, small, as if restraint could soften the blow. "Downstairs needs eyes," he says, tugging at the collar of his shirt like it's a chain around his neck. "You'll be all right."

"Will I see you again?" I ask, fighting to keep my heart steady. He hesitates, and in that pause, I already know the answer.

"Not in the same way."

My throat catches, heat presses behind my eyes. "I don't understand."

"You will." His voice softens, almost a confession. "Eventually." He steps closer, too close for any protocol to allow.

"You've done everything they asked," he tells me. "And more. You've given them what they needed."

"What about what I need?"

It stops him cold. His jaw works; he lowers his head. Then, his hand rises. A single brush of his knuckles across my cheek, so brief I almost think I imagined it.

"You needed someone to remember who you were."

"I don't," I say, desperately hoping the admission alone won't drown me on the spot.

"I do."

The words hollow me out. *Tell me then. Tell me who I am.*

"Then tell me," I breathe. But he's already pulling back, walling himself behind his stupid mask.

"He's coming." His voice steadies. The door opens, and I don't even need to turn to know who's looming. Overpowering cologne, confident steps, the faint scrape of dress shoes on fake wood.

"Ready, little star?" Maverick slides into the room like poison dressed in silk. I keep my attention on Vincent...because I can't *not*.

He meets my eyes. Nods once. "Go. Hold your head high."

Everything in me wants to refuse. To cling to him and cry because I'm not sure I can handle any of this.

But I can't give up. And I won't.

I've come too far to collapse here.

"Goodbye, Vincent," I say, tearing out a piece of myself I'll never get back. "Thank you. For everything."

He flinches. His eyes deepen, a swirling pool of anguish he can't conceal. "Goodbye, Maysie," he whispers.

The door shuts behind me.

And I feel like I've lost more than a mentor.

69

GRADUATION DAY

Maverick dumps me backstage like a sack of laundry, barking a command to stay put as he slips out through the curtain.

The small backstage area is so heavily perfumed with cloying florals that it makes my temples throb. A pale strip of light leaks under the double doors ahead, throwing shadows long and thin across the dark floor. Red Xs litter the ground in a perfectly straight line, most of which are already occupied. The other girls stand perfectly still in their gowns, eyes forward. I can hear their breathing, but not a single whisper.

Doctor Carr appears from a side door, not a gray hair out of place, white coat immaculate as always. He studies me like a sculptor appraising a piece.

"You clean up well," he says finally, dry as the dead.

"Thank you, sir."

"You've improved. Or at least, you've learned to stop showing weakness." I nod. He circles me, slow and deliberate. "I had my reservations regarding your viability after 219's unfortunate departure. And your little incident, of course."

A quick jolt of fire burns down my arms, but it's purely in my head.

His eyes fix on the raw skin where my cuff used to be. "I suppose fear can be quite the motivator."

"It won't happen again," I reply, tucking my hands behind my back. I'm not sure if I'm saying it for him, or for me.

"No," he agrees. "It won't." He stops in front of me. Adjusts a stray hair that wasn't out of place.

"When you walk out there, remember: No one's here to see you. They're here to see the result."

I don't let the words sting. "Yes, Doctor," I say, dipping my head.

His smile is empty. "Good girl."

And then he's gone.

Maverick finds his way back to my side just as the lights lower, smirking triumphantly. His posture is so stiff that I'm willing to bet his back aches simply from standing.

"Behaving yourself, little star?" He tugs me by the arm to the front of the line, flattening the shoulder seams of my dress with the flick of his wrist.

"Of course, sir," I lie, flashing him a lopsided smile. "I'm just so excited."

His eyes narrow, fingers faltering against my shoulder. I almost laugh. Even when it's fake, overcompliance makes him squirm. He clicks his tongue. "Right. Well, it won't be long now."

I clear my throat. "Ivy and Bri, are they—"

Maverick's grin sharpens. "They're fine. Better behaved than you ever were." He adjusts my hair, so overbearingly proud of himself. "Better focus on yourself, little star. We have people to impress."

That wasn't my question, but it's clearly all he's going to offer me. I peek out from the curtain, not recognizing a single face in the sea of heavy dresses and wine glasses. My eyes scan the back wall instinctively. I don't know what I'm looking for.

Well, I do.

But he's not here. He won't be here.

The sinking pit in my stomach dips ten feet further into the abyss.

Maverick ushers me forward.

I thought I was over stage fright. But the moment I step onto the platform, something bubbles up my ribs. I feel sick. So, so sick. I can't feel my face, but for my sake, I really hope I'm smiling.

Six months ago, I would've given anything to get here. To walk the stage at graduation with the promise of a new life. I can't help but feel a twinge of pride that I've accomplished my goal.

Only difference is, I'm not going to wait for the program to decide my future for me.

Doctor Kade stands at the podium, cloaked in a long white dress that makes her look equal parts angel and executioner. She flashes me a sickly sweet smile before turning back to the audience. "Ladies and gentlemen, tonight we celebrate the future. What you will witness is more than a simple performance. It is proof of what the advancement program makes possible."

Applause swells.

"These young women came to us uncertain and fractured. Some were fragile, others downright volatile. Each one arrived in need of direction. Through our methods, we have shaped their instincts into discipline, their chaos into purpose, their potential into promise." She rests her hands over her heart. "They are no longer at the mercy of their flaws, nor are they burdened by the weight of their pasts. Here, they have been rebuilt."

The crowd roars. Doctor Kade raises her hands, soaking

in the attention like this is her personal victory.

I stifle a cringe. *This is absurd.* I refuse to believe anyone's actually buying this.

Kade waits until the crowd dies down before continuing. "And so, with immense pride, I present the first among them. A young lady who has risen above every trial to become the very emblem of success." She waves me closer. I force a single suffering step, impossibly dizzy. "Please welcome, Estelle Ellington."

My lungs seize. The name rings in my ears, clear as a bell. I've never heard it for real. Only in dreams—or nightmares—or whatever they are. Something pierces my chest.

Not my name. Not anymore, at least.

My vision falters. Maverick's hand clamps against the small of my back, steadying and forcing in the same motion. His lips brush my ear, dipping to a whisper meant just for me. "Smile, little star. Your parents are watching."

The applause roars on, blind to the way my knees nearly buckle. I stumble toward the piano, letting Maverick guide me so I don't collapse. The bench gleams bright under the overwarm stage lights, beckoning my unwilling legs forward. It's waiting for me to sit, to play, to perform like the doll they've been perfecting.

I lower myself to the bench, straining every muscle hard enough to burst a blood vessel just to keep from melting into a puddle. My hands tremble against the fabric pooling in my lap.

My fingers hit their marks. My eyes find the first bar.

And I go absolutely, positively, blank.

70

DON'T LOOK BACK

I survived almost setting myself on fire. I can handle two minutes of piano.

Of course I can.

It's what I'm good at. It's who I am.

It doesn't matter that I've only ever finished this piece twice without crying. It matters even less that both times I was able to muster it, Colt had to hold my shoulders to keep them from shaking.

The shape of the keys blurs into a sea of monochrome. My fingers burn, but I compel them back to their starting marks. Well—where I think the starting marks are.

I suck in a deep breath, choked by Maverick's cologne. He's too close. I battle the nausea back. My eyes fall closed. I don't need sheet music; I just need to do this.

Only, I can't.

I can still feel them. A thousand watchful eyes waiting on bated breath to see if I'll break. An all-consuming wave of terror washes over me and suddenly my skin is too tight, my bones too shaky, my lungs refuse to inflate and—

Look left if you need me.

My eyes flick sideways before I can stop them. And he's there. Waiting in the wings, half-shadowed, arms folded tight. He doesn't acknowledge me, but he doesn't have to.

For the first time in so long, the voice in my head is mine and mine alone, unguarded and unrestrained, allowing me the only thought I need:

This time, I'll choose who I'm performing for.

The first note strikes too loud. The second steadies. My wrists tremble, but I hold them high. Black and white blur into a lattice of flawless muscle memory. My heart pounds between each chord, a metronome of terror-bound determination. Anytime my composure wavers, Colt's reassurances come in hushed whispers just behind my thoughts.

As the final note fades, the room explodes into an ovation I'm not sure I'm worthy of. I bow my head to hide the residual anxiety welling behind my eyes.

My chest aches. This performance was supposed to settle me. Closure, in a way. I don't know if I'll ever get the chance to play again.

I don't get the chance to grieve.

Maverick's behind me in a second, hand firmly on my shoulder as he soaks up the attention. He squeezes again, reminding me that I need to finish, to bow and smile like I've done something brilliant. Which I might've. *I'll never know.*

"You've been mine for longer than you could ever imagine," he murmurs as I rise. The surge of applause swallows the words for everyone but me.

"I hate you," I whisper, stepping a half-pace in front of him and dipping into a deep curtsy. When I glance back, the grin that spans his face could kill.

"Adorable," he mocks. "You'll come around."

Yeah, right.

Raging applause still thrums in my bones as Maverick ushers me into the wings, slim fingers digging into the small of my back.

"Escort her to the waiting room. I'll meet her there

later," he orders with a perfunctory nod toward the nearest enforcer, who just so happens to be Colt. He then vanishes, already soaking up the attention of investors who've slipped past the curtain.

Colt's waiting. His shoulders are squared, jaw set. But when his eyes find mine, something real flickers. Relief. Pride. Recognition I don't deserve.

"You did it," he murmurs, so rough it could be mistaken for a cough.

The sight of him brings my guilt back tenfold, nipping at my ribs. He walks me down the service hall, his stride careful to match mine. Always watching, always steady. The perfect guard. The perfect tether. My knees want to give, just to let him hold me up like he always does.

I can't. I want to, but I can't.

An enforcer calls his name from the far hall, sounding urgent. Colt stiffens, glancing toward the voice but not away from me. "One second," he mutters under his breath, like he's reassuring both of us.

The comm in his ear crackles. Colt claps a hand over it, teeth gritted, turning his head away from me for just a second.

That's all I get.

I slide sideways into the seam of shadow along the wall, holding my breath until my ribs scream. One more step puts me just around the corner where the maintenance corridor splits off. My gown brushes tile with the faintest whisper, but his boots keep moving. He thinks I'm still beside him.

For three, four, five steps. Then it clicks.

"Mays?" He halts mid-stride. The silence that follows could crush me.

I press back harder into the wall, nails biting into my

palms. Don't move. Don't breathe. A lot easier said than done when you're doused in guilt.

"Maysie," he says, louder this time. Desperate. I don't have to see his face to know what's lingering there. Fear laced with hurt, as if he already knows how this will end.

Any confidence I had in this plan dies and buries itself deep in my conscience.

I clutch my gown in both hands, willing myself to hold the silence for a heartbeat longer. His hesitation hangs taut in the air. Every passing second costs him more than he's allowed to afford. The comm crackles again. The order comes harsher this time. Irrefusable. Colt mutters a curse under his breath, devastation threaded through every syllable.

"Please don't do this," he breathes, like the words alone could drag me back. He lingers a suffocating moment longer, then he's gone, boots pounding down the hall toward orders he'd give anything to refuse.

Only then do I let myself breathe—and realize that he didn't sound surprised. Not in the slightest. My chest hollows with the truth: I didn't just slip past the program today. I slipped past Colt. My Colt. And he knew.

I don't look back.

Because if I do—if I have to see even a glimpse of my betrayal on his face—I'll never make it out the door.

And that's not an option.

71

THE HALL MAZE

I stay pressed to the shadows until the last set of boots fades down the hall. I turn, orienting myself, trying to picture Colt's map. I keep one hand on the wall as I start down the darkened maintenance corridor. It's freezing, not to mention dusty enough to cause a coughing fit I can't afford. My hand brushes the bundle I'd stashed here yesterday while Colt was answering a security call—a cardigan tucked behind some storage carts, already stiff with dust.

I pull it free, tugging my arms through and patting the panel where I stashed the black-bound book. I slip Colt's ID from my heel, holding steady even as my heart hammers in my ribs. At the end of the east service corridor, I hang a quick right, slamming my shoulder into a corner. I wince, hand clamping over my mouth to stifle the sound.

Breathe. Hold it in a little longer.

The camera flickers to life, red light alive with warning. I wait for it to complete a full sweep of the expanse before slipping to the left.

I can do this. One more hallway. One unguarded exit. Thirty paces, one swipe, and I'm gone.

Another set of footsteps echoes somewhere behind me. Too far to tell whose. I duck into a storage room, crouching between two rolling bins, counting my heartbeats until the sound fades. My knees shake so hard I can practically feel the soreness I'll experience in the morning. My dress snags on something sharp when I try to stand, but I don't make a sound.

Panic catches up to me as my adrenaline wavers. Everything's happening so fast. But I'm okay. I have to be. I focus on how far I've come. The work, the strides, the wins.

Catastrophic mistakes avoided: too many. Way too many.

When the space goes still again, I push forward. Faster now. My chest feels like it's splitting open, but I don't stop until I can see the door.

Except I don't see it.

My heart stalls. My feet root to the floor, bound by invisible vines of confusion. Did I make a wrong turn? That's impossible. I ran through this route in my head a dozen times, then a dozen more for good measure. So why—

A shadow detaches from the wall.

Vincent.

How?

His face is unreadable, but there's a knowing in his eyes that tells me I wasn't being nearly as sneaky as I thought. He moves toward me without hurry. The lack of surprise on his features makes my stomach drop. His warm hand settles lightly on my elbow, steering me down the hallway.

"This way," he murmurs.

Relief cuts through my panic before I can stop it. He's helping me. Not just ignoring the rules or covering for me— *actually helping*. We veer left, down a corridor I hadn't planned for.

"What—"

"You're off course. Lance is stationed down the way." He doesn't ask where I was headed. Doesn't ask why, either. His hand stays at my elbow, like this isn't the first time he's had to turn me around.

My mental map of the back halls grows more crossed by the second.

The east service door is ahead, the faint line of light around its frame almost glowing. My fingers twitch, already reaching. His gaze flicks past my shoulder—so quick I almost miss it—then returns to me with a weight I can't read.

I'm no more than three steps from the door when his hold changes into something unshakeable.

What—

"Not today," he says, shifting his grip up my arm.

I twist, wrenching against him. "Move."

His other hand comes up, palm pressed against my shoulder, pulling me back.

"I mean it," I snap, shoving at his chest. My heel catches the tile, so rough I almost trip. "Let me go, Vincent!"

"Not—" he starts, but I lunge again, forcing him back a step. His hand snags on my cardigan, tearing the book loose from the makeshift pocket I'd stashed it in. It hits the ground hard enough to echo. Vincent flinches, hard.

"Where did you get that?" he demands, eyes impossibly wide. The command in his tone freezes me on the spot. He never raises his voice. He takes a step forward, eyes locked on the black spine, color draining from his face. "That's not possible."

I don't answer. My lungs seize; air lagging behind raw panic.

He reaches for my shoulder, panting. "Answer me!"

I dodge, grabbing the book first and clutching it to my chest. "It's mine!"

He hesitates—just long enough. I drive an elbow into his ribs and turn. My hand slams against the cold metal of the badge reader, not quite connecting with the keycard pressed in my palm. Sparks lick across my fingertips before I can choke them down. The fluorescent lights above us sputter and burst, glass scattering across the floor.

"Breathe!" His command is quick, instinctive. "Please." He grips my shoulder again, steadying, but the flicker in his eyes tells me he's calculating. I draw a breath to fight back, but he's faster.

"Enough," he snaps, grabbing for the card. I duck. He counters, dragging me up by my arm. Power surges to the spot in an instant. He hisses as the wave crashes against his gloved fingers. A scream tears free from my lungs as he pulls me into his chest.

"Stop!" I try to wrench back, but his grip shifts, fingers firm at the base of my neck. Tears pelt my cheeks. I shove hard, nails catching on his jacket, dragging along the seam of his sleeve. "Vincent, please!"

"Enough, Estelle."

A pinch—no.

The steel bite of a needle under my skin, sunken deep before I can jerk away. White-hot fire races down my spine until every muscle locks.

"It's fine. You're fine." His words are half command, half containment as the sedative floods my veins.

My heel grinds into his polished shoe. Vincent grunts. The syringe falls from his hand and shatters, splattering amber remnants across the floor. I thrash, but he tightens his grip, pinning me in place.

The air dips cold enough to mist the breath between us.

His arm trembles with controlled fear disguised as precision, like letting go would mean losing more than the fight. Ice tamps down the heat, swallowing it whole. Swallowing *me* whole. My knees fold. His arms hook under mine before I hit the ground.

"I'm sorry. I know I broke my promise," he says, low and close enough that the words are almost in my skin. I hate that it sounds like he means it.

I try to spit something back, but my tongue sits heavy.

"You'll have a better chance," he murmurs. "When you understand what you're running from."

Turns out I should've been running from him.

I claw at his jacket, but my fingers won't close. He hoists me up and drags me down the hall, ignoring my incoherent protests. My head rests against him without permission as my awareness teeters. The elevator doors open with a groan that resonates in my bones. He props my deadened form against the wall inside, steadying me until he's sure I won't fall.

The moment his hand leaves me, I push forward in a slow, graceless lurch. My legs tangle under me. My palm smears against the cool steel of the frame, leaving a faint print that fades as the gap narrows.

"Vin—" His name dies before it's fully formed. My vision blurs around the edges. Static clings to me. The air grows taut again, only this time—

Nothing flares.

He stops to pick up the book that must have escaped my grip, slipping it into his jacket without so much as looking at me.

Just beyond him, Ryder is still leaning against the far wall, eyes closed, head tipped back. Holding too still to be natural. By his side, his fist is clenched tight, the only indication that he saw anything at all.

The doors close. Taking my consciousness with them.

72

WELCOME HOME

I'm drowning in a sea of cerulean. Plummeting through a sky of suffocating white. Crashing through a wall that bleeds red.

Falling

Falling

Falling

I'm in a child's bedroom.

There's no sky above, no ocean underfoot. I'm lying on a bed draped in a sweeping pink canopy that ripples with the frigid air. Stuffed animals are piled precariously in the corner, glass eyes the only witness to my unraveling. Stacks of well-kept books line white shelves. Colorful drawings are pinned to the wall on my left, held by golden stars.

Everything's pristine, as if the room's occupant tidied up just this morning.

The wall across from me bears nothing but a painted mural. A childish depiction of some surreal landscape: The sky swirls in shades of blue, blending into hazy pinks that span the horizon line. Silhouetted butterflies of all colors flitter throughout, suspended at various stages of flight, surrounded by towering trees, lush in their foliage. At the center of it all is a golden sun with a looping 'E' threaded through the lines.

It's beautiful.

It's familiar.

Where am I?

Memories surge without permission, lapping in paralyzing waves.

A golden uniform blazer, adorned with a sun.

A little boy with hazel eyes and a malicious grin.

A gilded ballroom with a swaying chandelier.

Sparks explode behind my eyes. The reel burns at the edges, growing bright and angry before collapsing, throwing me back into my skin.

Only this time, I'm not alone.

A woman blurs into focus. Golden brown hair falls around her shoulders in waves, framing the lines of her angular face. She's seated on the edge of the low-set bed, soft hand laid over mine. Real sunlight filters through the window, casting an outline around her frame that makes it look as if she's glowing. Her glossy lips press into a smile almost warm enough to melt my apprehensions.

Behind her, a tall man looms in the doorway, posture made rigid with pride. His hair is darker, with tendrils of gray streaking near his temples. Burnished brown eyes survey me, intoxicating in their depth.

My chest seizes, but I don't move.

I have his eyes. Her smile. Their pallor.

No—

No, no, no.

I try to sit up, but it sends my head reeling. The woman presses a hand to my shoulder with a sympathetic smile, eyes glassy. "Easy now, darling. The doctor said you should avoid overexertion for a few days."

The man steps forward. "But you're safe now. The Ashford boy made sure of that."

She nods eagerly at him, golden-brown strands catching the light the way mine do. "He's been such a blessing."

"Ah," comes a voice behind them, bright and terribly familiar. "You give me too much credit, Mrs. Ellington."

Maverick steps into view. Fitted in a crisp suit with a silk tie the color of spilled wine and a smirk sharp enough to draw blood. He crosses to the bed, hands clasped behind his back. "You can stop pretending to be afraid," he says. "It's over now."

My mouth opens, but words don't form. "Wh—"

"The program's finished, Estelle. You're living proof it works." He leans down, smoothing my hair in a motion I can't fight with my hands still held beneath hers. He laughs softly. "Isn't that what you wanted?"

Flashes pop from a camera I hadn't noticed, echoing so loud it doesn't even feel real. The room tilts violently on its axis until the world's swimming around me. With a final tug, I lose what little footing I had left on reality.

Sounds garble together, dragged through water pooling somewhere beyond my periphery. Yet when Maverick's lips part, every word rings clean.

"Smile for us, little star. You're finally home."

Vincent was wrong. There is something outside the walls of the advancement program.

And somehow, it's worse.

ACKNOWLEDGEMENTS

Sitting down to write the acknowledgements for my debut novel is one of the most surreal things I've ever experienced. To be standing at the finish line of this while knowing it's only the beginning is something truly special. I would love to start with extending an indescribable thank you to every person who chose to pick up this book and read the first part of Maysie's journey.

The idea for *Nothing Out There* began as a creative writing project my senior year of high school. And although the story that became of it is very different, I'm beyond overjoyed that this book has finally left my chaotic google docs and is going off into the world. I owe this book to more people than I can name, but I'm sure going to try.

To Marilyn, thank you for catching my mistakes, my plot holes, and my constant overuse of ellipses. Handing my work off was terrifying, but I'm so thankful to have entrusted it with you.

Stefanie, my wonderful cover designer. I had so much trouble envisioning what this cover should look like, and yet you still somehow captured it perfectly. To say I'm obsessed would be a grave understatement.

My beta readers: Amelia, Kelsey, Millie, and Allie. Thank you for enjoying this book at every stage…and for putting up with my endless follow-up questions. This story is so much stronger because of you.

To Jenn Mitchell, my high school English teacher, who saw something in me I couldn't see in myself. Thank you for fostering my love for writing. For instilling the belief in me that I could do anything.

Mom and dad, there will never be enough words in the universe to describe how much I love you. Mom, thank you for never using baby words with me so you could take credit for my big vocabulary. Thank you for every musical you've taken me to see, and every improv musical we've created together on the car rides back home. Dad, thank you for reading Junie B. Jones to me with all of your silly voices. If this book wasn't narrated by a teenage girl, you'd be at the top of my list for the audiobook. Thank you both for supporting me in every crazy thing I've set out to do, big or small. And always asking "what's next," even when I didn't have an answer.

Quinn. My baby sister who isn't a baby anymore, I see so much of you in these characters, so much of you in this story. (In a good way, of course.) Thank you for every coffee shop and library trip, I truly couldn't have finished this book with my sanity intact without you. Even if you called half my characters' names dumb.

To Ollie, my precious dog, who probably thinks he's just as responsible for writing this book as I am. Thank you for being my writing buddy and never judging my chaotic late night drafting sessions.

An enormous thank you to all my friends and family who have encouraged me through this journey and believed in this story. From giving feedback on my out-of-context snippets to helping me pick a cover font, this book was far from a solo venture.

And finally, to you, my dear reader: thank you for being here, thank you for making it this far. Without you, this book wouldn't exist, and I'm sure grateful it does. I hope you'll stick around for what comes next, because Maysie's story is only just beginning.

Mae Harcourt lives in sunny central Texas, where you can find her obsessing over books, pampering her dog Oliver, or hunting down new coffee shops to fuel long writing days. Fascinated by dystopian literature from a young age, Mae crafts twisted stories that explore identity and the human experience in futures not unlike our own.

Mae can be found on Instagram and TikTok @MaeHarcourt or at MaeHarcourt.com

LOOKING FOR MORE?

Bonus chapters, sneak peeks, and behind-the-scenes content can be found on Mae's Substack.